THE
SILENT CRY

THE
SILENT CRY

Kenzaburo Oe

Translated from the Japanese by John Bester

Grove Press
New York

First published as *Man'en Gannen no Futtoboru* in 1967
by Kodansha Ltd., Tokyo.

First English-language edition published in 1974
by Kodansha International Ltd.

Published simultaneously in Canada
Printed in the United States of America

ISBN 978-0-8021-2478-4
eISBN 978-0-8021-9027-7

Grove Press
an imprint of Grove Atlantic
154 West 14th Street
New York, NY 10011

Distributed by Publishers Group West

groveatlantic.com

THE
SILENT CRY

In the Wake of the Dead

Awakening in the predawn darkness, I grope among the anguished remnants of dreams that linger in my consciousness, in search of some ardent sense of expectation. Seeking in the tremulous hope of finding eager expectancy reviving in the innermost recesses of my being—unequivocally, with the impact of whisky setting one's guts afire as it goes down—still I find an endless nothing. I close fingers that have lost their power. And everywhere, in each part of my body, the several weights of flesh and bone are experienced independently, as sensations that resolve into a dull pain in my consciousness as it backs reluctantly into the light. With a sense of resignation, I take upon me once more the heavy flesh, dully aching in every part and disintegrated though it is. I've been sleeping with arms and legs askew, in the posture of a man reluctant to be reminded either of his nature or of the situation in which he finds himself.

Whenever I awaken I seek again that lost, fervid feeling of expectation, the ardent sense of expectation that is no consciousness of lack but a positive actuality in itself. Finally convinced that I'll not find it, I try to lure myself down the slope to second sleep: *sleep, sleep!—the world does not exist*; but this morning the poison tormenting my body is too virulent to permit retreat into slumber. Fear threatens to engulf me. Sunrise must be at least an hour away; till then, there's no telling what kind of day it will be. I lie in the dark, knowing nothing, a fetus in the womb. There was a time when sexual habits were useful on such occasions. But now at twenty-seven, married, with a child put away in an institution, I feel shame welling up at the idea of masturbation, stilling the buds of desire. *Sleep, sleep!—if you can't sleep then pretend you're asleep.* Suddenly, in the darkness, I see the square hole the workmen dug yesterday for our septic tank. In my aching body the desolate, bitter poison multiplies, threatening to ooze out slowly, like jelly from a tube, from ears, eyes, nose, mouth, anus, urethra. . . .

Still in the guise of a sleeper, with eyes closed, I stand up and move sluggishly through the darkness. Each time I hit some part or other of my body against the door, the wall, or the furniture I give a painful, half-delirious moan. My right eye, admittedly, has no sight even wide open and in broad daylight. I wonder if I'll ever know what lay behind the events whereby my eye got like that. It was a nasty, stupid incident: one morning, as I was walking along the street, a group of primary school children in a fit of hysterical fear and anger flung a chunk of stone at me. Struck in the eye, I lay where I fell on the sidewalk, unable to make out what had happened. My right eye, with a split extending horizontally from the white into the black, lost its vision. Even now, I've never felt I understood the true meaning of the incident. Moreover, I'm afraid of understanding it. If you try walking with one hand over your right eye, you'll realize just how many things lie in wait for you ahead on the right. You'll collide with the unexpected. You'll strike your head and face repeatedly. Thus the right half of my head and face has never been without some fresh mark or other, and I'm ugly. Even before the eye injury I was already showing more and more clearly a quality of ugliness that often reminded me how mother had prophesied that, when we grew up, my brother would be handsome and I would not. The lost eye merely emphasized the ugliness each day, throwing it into constant relief. My born ugliness would have liked to hang back, silent, in the shadows; it was the missing eye that continually dragged it out into the limelight. Not that I neglected to assign a role to this eye: I saw it, its function lost, as being forever trained on the darkness within my skull, a darkness full of blood and somewhat above body heat. The eye was a lone sentry that I'd hired to keep watch on the forest of the night within me, and in doing so I'd forced myself to practice observing my own interior.

Passing through the kitchen, I feel for the door, go out, and finally open my eye to find the faintest whiteness spreading over the distant heights of a leaden, late autumn, predawn sky. A black dog comes running up and jumps at me. But instantly it knows itself rejected; without a sound it shrinks back into stillness and stands pointing its small muzzle at me like a mushroom in the darkness. Picking it up, I tuck it under my arm and walk slowly on again. The dog stinks. It remains still under my arm, panting heavily.

My armpit gets hot. Perhaps the dog has a fever. The nails of my bare toes strike a wooden frame. I put the dog down for the moment, grope about to check the position of the ladder, then encompass with my arms the darkness at the spot where I set the dog down; it still occupies precisely the same space. I can't help smiling, but it's not a smile that lasts long. The dog is sick, for certain. Laboriously I climb down the ladder. There are puddles here and there at the bottom of the pit, enough to cover the ankles of my bare feet: just a little water, like juices pressed from flesh. Sitting down directly on the bare earth, I feel the water seeping through my pajama trousers and underwear, wetting my buttocks, but I find myself accepting it docilely, as one who cannot refuse.

Yet a dog, of course, can refuse to get dirty. The dog, silent like one that can talk but chooses not to, perches on my lap, leaning its shivering, hot body lightly against my chest. To preserve this balance, it sets hooked claws into the muscles of my chest. I feel the pain as yet another thing that cannot be rejected, and in five minutes am indifferent to it. I'm heedless, too, of the foul water that wets my buttocks and comes seeping in between my testicles and thighs. My body—all 154 pounds and five feet six inches of it—is no different from the load of soil that the laborers dug yesterday from this very spot and discarded in some distant river. My flesh is assimilated by the soil. In my body and the surrounding soil and the whole damp atmosphere, the only signs of life are the dog's heat and my nostrils. The nostrils come rapidly sensitive, and absorb the restricted smells at the bottom of the pit as though they were of unutterable richness. Functioning at full pitch, they assimilate odors too numerous to recognize individually. Almost fainting, I bang the back of my head (and feel it directly as the back of my skull) against the wall of the hole, then go on, indefinitely, absorbing the thousand and one odors and what little oxygen is available. The desolate, bitter poison still fills my body, but no longer seems to be seeping through to the outside. The ardent sense of expectancy hasn't yet returned, but my fear has been alleviated. Now I'm indifferent to everything; indifferent, even, to the very possession of a body. My only regret is that there is no one and nothing to observe me in my total indifference. The dog? The dog has no eyes. Nor have I eyes in my indifference. Since I reached the bottom, my eyes have been shut again.

Next, I meditate on the friend whose cremation I attended. At the end of summer this year he daubed his head all over with crimson paint, stripped, thrust a cucumber up his anus, and hanged himself. His wife discovered the strange suicide on her return, spent as a sick rabbit, from a party that had lasted into the early hours. Why hadn't he gone with her to the party? He was that kind of man: no one would find it odd that he should let his wife go alone to a party while he remained in his study working on a translation (something, in fact, that we were collaborating on).

From a point two yards in front of the dangling corpse she'd fled back to where the party had been held, her hair on end in her panic, her arms flailing above her head, her mouth shaping a voiceless cry, her little-girlish green shoes flapping as she trod back over the path of her own midnight shadow that no one else could see, like a film run in reverse. After informing the police, she sobbed silently till they came from her family to fetch her. Thus, when the police had finished their inquiries, it was left to me and my friend's sturdy old grandmother to perform the last offices for the naked, crimson-headed corpse with the last of its life's semen drying on its thighs, a corpse surely beyond all salvation. The deceased's mother had retreated into an imbecilic state and was useless. Just once, as we made to wash off the dead man's disguise, she showed an unexpected determination and opposed the move. The old woman and I turned away all who came to express condolences, and alone, without interruption, the three of us held a wake for the dead man in whom the myriad cells, once treasurers of his uniqueness, were already in process of swift, furtive disintegration. Like a dam, the dry, parched skin held in the sweet-sour, rosy cells that had dissolved and changed into something indescribable. This crimson-faced corpse of my friend as it lay proudly remote, decomposing on an army-style cot, was filled with a more urgent sense of reality than it had ever had in twenty-seven years of life—life lived pitifully in a diligent effort to pass through the dark tunnel, only to end abruptly before emerging on the other side. The dam of the skin was sentenced to burst. Fermenting clusters of cells were preparing, as a wine is prepared, the real, physical death of the body itself. Those left behind must drink that wine. There was a fascination for me in the close-packed moments that my friend's body marked off in its relationship with the lily-fragrant bacteria of corruption. As I watched the passage of this pure time on its once-only flight, I was made aware again of the fragility of that other kind of time, soft and warm as the top of an infant's head, that admits of repetition.

I couldn't help feeling envious. No friend's eyes would watch, no friend would understand the true meaning of what was happening when I closed my eyes for the last time and my flesh embarked on its own experience of dissolution.

"When he came home from the clinic, I should have persuaded him to go back again," I said.

"No—the boy couldn't have stayed there any longer," his grandmother replied. "The other mental patients were so impressed with the fine things he'd done there that he couldn't possibly have remained any longer. You shouldn't forget that and blame yourself. What's happened has made it quite plain—it was the best thing possible for him to leave the clinic and lead a free life. If he'd killed himself there, he could never have painted his face red and hanged himself naked, could he? The other patients wouldn't have let him, they respected him too much."

"You bear up so well, you're a great help."

"Everyone has to die. And in a hundred years nobody's going to inquire just how most people died. The best thing is to do it in the way that takes your fancy most."

At the foot of the bed my friend's mother sat rubbing the corpse's feet untiringly, her head hunched into her shoulders like a frightened tortoise, and showed no reaction to our conversation. The small features of the flat, vegetable face that so cruelly resembled her dead son were all slack, like melting candy. It seemed to me I'd never seen a face express so immediate or so utter a despair.

"Like Sarudahiko," said his grandmother inconsequently.

Sarudahiko: the word, vaguely rustic and comic in its associations, was on the verge of suggesting some meaning, albeit vague, to my mind, but my faculties were already too dulled by fatigue to produce more than the faintest tremor, which failed to expand; the thread of meaning escaped me. Even as I shook my head in vain, the word Sarudahiko sank like a sounding line, the seal of meaning unbroken, down into the depths of memory.

But now that word, Sarudahiko, came rising to my mind, a clear outcropping of a vein of familiar memories, as I sat in the water at the bottom of the pit with the dog in my arms. The tissues of the brain relating to this word, frozen ever since that day, had thawed out. Sarudahiko—Sarudahiko the divine—had gone to Amanoyachimata to meet the gods descending to earth. Amenouzume, who had engaged in negotiations with Saruda-hiko as representative of the intruders, had gathered together the fish who were the original inhabitants of the new world in an attempt to establish his dominance, and with a knife had slashed open the mouth of the sea slug, who resisted in silence. Our gentle, twentieth-century Sarudahiko had been, if anything, a fellow to the sea slug whose mouth had been slashed. At the thought, the tears gushed from my eyes and, streaming down my cheeks and along my lips, dropped onto the dog's back.

A year before his death, he'd cut short his studies at Columbia University and returned to Japan, where he entered a home for mild cases of mental disorder. Of the whereabouts of the home and his life there, I know nothing other than what he himself reported. Neither had his wife or his mother or grandmother actually visited the place, though it was said to be in the Shonan district. He forbade all those close to him to visit him there. Thinking about it now, I feel far from sure even that such a home existed. However, if one is to believe what he said, the place was called the Smile Training Center, and the inmates, who were given large doses of tranquilizers at every meal, spent all their time placidly smiling. It was a single-story building similar to the beachside hostels to be found all over the Shonan area, and half of it was taken up by a single, large sunroom. During the day most of the patients chatted amiably to each other, sitting on the swings that were installed in large numbers on the extensive lawn. Strictly speaking, the inmates weren't even patients but travelers, as it were, on a prolonged stopover. Under the influence of the tranquilizers, they became more manageable than the most docile of domestic animals, and whiled away the hours in the sunroom or on the lawn exchanging happy, untroubled smiles. They were free to go out, and since no one felt he was being kept in confinement, no one ever ran away.

Coming home about a week after entering the home to get books and a change of clothing, my friend declared that he seemed to have adjusted to this odd place more swiftly and more comfortably than any of the placidly smiling patients who had entered before him. Three weeks later, however, on his next return to Tokyo, his smiles, though still there, looked faintly forlorn. And he confided in his wife and myself. The male nurse who brought the patients their drugs and their meals was a brutal fellow who would often treat them abominably, since under sedation they were unable even to feel anger. Sometimes as be passed a patient he would deal him a hefty blow in the belly, quite without provocation. I suggested he should protest to those in charge of the center, but he said that if he did the director would only think he was inventing it out of boredom, or suffering from a simple persecution complex, or both. After all, no one, at least along the Shonan coast, could be as bored as they were, and they were all to a greater or lesser extent out of their minds. Besides, thanks to the tranquilizers, he himself hardly knew whether he was really angry or not. . . .

Nevertheless, it was only two or three days after this that he flushed down the toilet the tranquilizers doled out to him at breakfast, did the same at lunch, and again at suppertime. The next morning, having discovered that he was indeed angry, he lay in wait for the brute and—himself suffering a considerable amount of damage in the process—ended by half slaying him. As a result of this incident he won the sincere admiration of his gently smiling friends but, following a talk with the director, was obliged to leave. As he left the Smile Training Center, waving to the mental patients who saw him off with the same amiable, fatuous smiles on their faces, he experienced a profounder sadness than ever before.

"It's as Henry Miller said. I felt the same kind of sadness as his. Actually, until that moment I'd never realized the truth of what he wrote: 'I tried to smile with him, but I couldn't. It made me terribly sad, sadder than I ever felt before in my life.' It's more than just a turn of phrase. . . . And there's another phrase of Miller's too that's been haunting me ever since: 'Let's be cheerful, whatever happens.'"

From the end of his period at the Smile Training Center until his death by hanging, naked, with his head painted bright red, there's no doubt that he remained obsessed by Miller's words, "Let's be cheerful, whatever happens." His brief and premature last years were spent in unequivocal cheerfulness. He even lapsed into a particular sexual proclivity and explored its peculiar type of frenzy. I was reminded of it by a conversation with my wife when I returned home, stunned and exhausted, after the cremation. She was drinking whisky, alone, as she waited for me. That was the first day I saw her drunk.

As soon as I got home I went and looked in the room she shared with our son. The child was still at home in those days. It was barely dusk, but the child lay on the bed looking up at me placidly with absolutely empty brown eyes, the kind of placidity with which a plant, if plants had eyes, might gaze back at someone peering at it. My wife was not beside him. If I remember correctly, she was sitting quite drunk in the gloom of the library when I found her, perched precariously on a step stool between the shelves like a bird on a swaying branch. I was so taken aback that I felt, if anything, more embarrassed for myself than for her. Getting the whisky bottle out of the niche inside the stool where I'd hidden it, she'd seated herself on its steps, taken a gulp straight from the bottle, and continued to drink little by little, getting steadily drunker as she went. Seeing me, she jerked back like a mechanical doll. Her upper lip was greasy with sweat. She couldn't stand up. Her eyes, the color of plums, were feverish, but the skin of her neck and shoulders showing above her dress was rough with goose pimples. Her whole being suggested a dog driven by sickness to chew grass furiously only to vomit all the more.

"You're ill, surely?" I asked, ridiculously.

"No, I'm not ill," she replied with open scorn, swift to sense my embarrassment.

"Then you're drunk, in fact."

Squatting down facing her I watched, fascinated, a drop of sweat, quivering on the edge of her upper lip as she stared back at me suspiciously, roll down sideways as the lip curled. Her squalid breath, laden with the damp fumes of alcohol, swept over me. The exhaustion brought by the living from the deathbed of a friend seeped like a dye into every corner of my body, and I could have sobbed.

"You're dead drunk, you know."

"I'm not particularly drunk. If I'm sweating it's because I'm scared."

"What about? The kid's future?"

"Scared that there should be people who kill themselves, naked, with their heads painted red."

I had told her that much, passing over the part about the cucumber.

"That's nothing for you to be particularly scared about, is it?"

"I'm scared that *you* might paint your head red and kill yourself, naked," she said, and hung her head in a display of unconcealed fear.

With a shudder I saw for a moment, in the dark brown mass of her hair, a miniature of myself dead. The crimson head of Mitsusaburo Nedokoro in death, with lumps of partly dissolved powder paint dried behind the lobes of his ears, like drops of blood. Even as my friend's body had been, so my own had the two ears left unpainted, token of the inadequate lapse of time between the conception of this bizarre suicide and its execution.

"I won't kill myself. Why should I?"

"Was he a masochist?"

"What makes you ask me that, the very day after his death? Just curiosity?"

"Well, supposing," she went on in a tone made excessively abject by the signs of anger in my voice (though an anger that wasn't particularly clear even to myself), "supposing he did have some sexual perversion, there wouldn't be any need for me to be afraid for you, would there?"

She jerked her head back again and stared at me as though demanding my agreement. The unspeakably naked sense of helplessness in her preternaturally red eyes shocked me. But she shut them almost at once, raised the whisky bottle, and took another gulp. The curves of her eyelids were dark like dirty finger pads. She coughed till the tears came to her eyes and whisky mingled with saliva dribbled from the corners of her mouth. Instead of being concerned on her behalf over the stain it would make on her new, off-white silk dress, I took the bottle from her hand—a hand scrawny and stringy as a monkey's—and took a swig to cover my awkwardness.

It was true, as my friend had told me with a mixture of pleasure and sadness at a point midway in his sexual progress—a point, that is, on the slope of a tendency still vague yet clear enough to the person concerned, neither shallow enough to be of the kind that anyone might experience by chance nor sufficiently indulged to be absolutely past discussing with others—that he'd long been seeking masochistic experiences. He'd visited a private establishment where some ferocious female catered to masochists. There was nothing remarkable about what happened the first day. But on his second visit three weeks later, the stupid brute of a woman, remembering his tastes accurately, announced portentously that she would henceforth be indispensable to him. It wasn't until the next stage, as he lay naked on his face and a knotted hemp rope landed with a thud beside his car, that he realized that the great brutish female had indeed assumed a place in his world as an unarguable fact.

"It was as though my body was completely disassembled, all soft and limp in each part, something like a string of sausages, without any sensation at all. But my mind was floating somewhere way up above, completely cut off from my body." And he'd fixed his eyes on me with an oddly weak, pained little smile.

I took another mouthful of whisky and, like my wife, was seized with a fit of coughing which sent lukewarm whisky through my undershirt to run down the skin of my chest and belly. Then as I gazed at her, sitting with her eyes still shut, the dark lids evoking another, false pair of eyes like the protective markings on the wings of certain moths, I was seized with an impulse to talk to her roughly.

Even assuming he was a masochist—I would say—it wouldn't mean you'd have nothing to be afraid of. It wouldn't justify your making a distinction between him and me and telling yourself I would never paint my head red and kill myself, naked. Sexual peculiarities aren't very important in the long run; they're only one distortion caused by something grotesque and really frightening coiled up in the depths of the personality. There was some enormous, uncontrollable, crazy motive force lurking in the depths of his soul, and it happened to induce a particular distortion called masochism—that's all. It wasn't his involvement with masochism that gave birth to the madness leading to his suicide, but the reverse. And I too have the seeds of that same, incurable madness. . . .

But I said nothing of all this to my wife, nor did the idea itself send its fine tendrils down into the folds of my brain, blunted by exhaustion. The fancy, like bubbles rising in a glass, fizzed for a while then vanished. Such notions pass without leaving any experience behind. This is particularly true when one remains silent about them; all one needs to do is wait till the undesirable notions pass away without damaging the walls of the brain.

If I could get by in this way now, then I should be able to escape the poison until the massive counterattack when I would finally have to accept it as an experience. Curbing my tongue, I put my hands under my wife's arms from behind and hoisted her to her feet. It felt like sacrilege to support my living wife—the mystery and vulnerability of a body made to give birth in peril and in stress—with arms contaminated by lifting the body of a dead friend; yet of the two bodies, equal burdens, it was to my dead friend's that I felt closer.

We advanced at a slow pace toward the bedroom where the baby awaited us; but by the bathroom her progress was arrested like that of a ship that has lowered anchor, and cleaving her way through the dusky, lukewarm, summer-evening air of the room, she vanished into the toilet. She was there for a long while. When finally she reemerged, breasting the now deeper gloom, I took her to the bedroom and, giving up the idea of undressing her, laid her on the bed just as she was. Heaving a great sigh as though to expel her very soul, she fell fast asleep. Some yellow fibrous substance that she had vomited clung about her lips, fine as the hairs on a flower petal yet clearly shining in the twilight.

The baby gazed up at me as ever with wide-open eyes, but whether he was hungry or thirsty or felt some other discomfort I couldn't tell. He lay with eyes open and expressionless, like a marine plant in the water of the dusk, simply and placidly exist-ing. He demanded nothing, expressed absolutely no emotion. He didn't even cry. One might even wonder if he were alive at all. Supposing my wife had been drunk all day since my early morning departure and had left the baby to its own devices, what should I do? At the moment she was nothing but a drunken slut in a deep sleep. I had a strong premonition of disaster. But as with my wife, I shrank from the sacrilege of stretching out contaminated hands and touching the baby. And to the baby, too, I felt less close than to my dead friend. However long I gazed down at him, he went on staring at me with utterly expression-less eyes. Finally, a drowsiness that drew one along with the irresistible force of a tidal wave came welling from those brown eyes. Without even fetching a bottle of milk for him, I curled up to sleep. On the threshold of unconsciousness, I told myself with a fresh sense of shock that my only friend had painted his head bright red and hanged himself, that my wife had got herself suddenly and quite unexpectedly drunk, that my son was an imbecile. To crown everything, I was about to go to sleep, jammed in an inadequate space between my wife's and son's beds, without locking up, without taking my tie off, my person still defiled from contact with the dead. All judgment suspended, like an insect impaled helpless on a pin. . . . Shrinking before a sense that I was being slowly eroded by a power that was unquestionably dangerous yet hard to identify, I drifted off to sleep. And by the morning I could no longer quite recall what I'd felt with such conviction the night before. It had failed, in short, to constitute an experience.

One day the previous summer, my friend had met my younger brother in a New York drugstore and had brought back his own testimony concerning my brother's life in America. Takashi had gone to America as a member of a student theater group. Their leader was a Diet member, a woman from the right wing of one of the progressive political parties. The troupe consisted entirely of students who had taken part in the political riots of June, 1960, but had since thought better of it. Their play was a penitential piece entitled *Ours Was the Shame*, and was followed by an apology to the citizens of America, on behalf of repentant members of the student movement, for having obstructed their President's visit to Japan. When Takashi first told me that he was going to America with them, he'd said he planned to flee the troupe as soon as it arrived and go off and roam the country by himself. However, reading the semi-satirical, semi-embarrassed accounts of *Ours Was the Shame* sent by Japanese reporters from the States, I realized that he hadn't yet brought himself to leave the troupe but was still appearing in performances of the play in Washington and cities as far away as Boston and New York. I tried to work out why he should have abandoned his original plan and gone on playing the role of a repentant student activist, but the task was beyond my imagination. I wrote a letter therefore asking my friend, who was in New York with his wife studying at Columbia, to look up Takashi at the troupe's headquarters. But he'd been unable to contact them, and it was by sheer coincidence that he'd run into my brother. Going into a drugstore on Broadway, he'd come upon Takashi, his slight frame propped against the counter, drinking a lemonade with earnest concentration. Stealing up from behind, he'd silently grabbed Takashi's shoulder. My brother swung round as though released by a spring, so suddenly that it was my friend who was taken aback. Takashi was grubby, sweating, pale, and tense. His whole appearance suggested a man taken unawares while plotting a single-handed bank robbery.

"Hi, Takashi. Mitsu wrote and told me you were in the States," my friend declared. "Seems he no sooner got married than he got his new wife pregnant."

"*I* haven't got married, or got anybody pregnant," said Takashi in a voice that was still not quite steady.

My friend laughed heartily as though he'd just heard a splendid joke. "I'm off to Japan next week," he said. "Any message for Mitsu?"

"Weren't you supposed to stay at Columbia for several years?"

"Not anymore. I got myself hurt in the demonstrations. Not physically—something happened to my head. It's not bad enough to have them put me in a mental hospital, but they've decided I should shut myself up in a kind of sanitarium."

At this point my friend noticed a profound embarrassment spreading like a stain over Takashi's face, and suddenly felt he understood the significance of the abrupt start Takashi had given when taken by surprise. And being a kindly man, he couldn't help feeling secretly sorry. He had prodded the other in what must be a reformed activist's tenderest spot. Both fell silent, gazing at the tightly packed row of jars lining the shelf behind the counter—jars brimming with a pink liquid, sweetish and raw-looking as entrails. Their two images were reflected in the distorting glass of the bottles, and whenever they moved even slightly the pink freaks swayed in exaggerated fashion. One almost expected them to break into song at any moment.

Late one night in June when Takashi, still an unrepentant student activist, was outside the National Diet, my friend had gone there too—not so much from any political motive of his own as to accompany his new wife as she took part in a demonstration with a small drama group to which she belonged—and when a disturbance broke out had had his head bashed in by a police stave as he tried to protect his wife from the onslaught of the armed riot squad. The fracture wasn't particularly serious in a simple surgical sense. But from the time of that late-night assault amidst the scent of young green leaves, something had been lacking inside my friend's head, and an obscure tendency to manic depression had taken its place alongside his other attributes. There could hardly have been anyone whom a reformed student activist was more reluctant to meet.

Increasingly embarrassed by Takashi's silence, my friend stared fixedly at the pink jars with the feeling that his own eyes, melting in the heat of his embarrassment, were being transformed into the same pink, viscous fluid as in the jars and were oozing out of his skull. He envisaged his melting pink eyeballs plopping hopelessly and irretrievably, like eggs dropped into a frying pan, onto the silver counter on which Americans of all extractions—southern European, Anglo-Saxon, Jewish—had their bare, sweaty forearms firmly planted. High summer in New York, with Takashi at his side noisily sucking up the last fragments of lemon through his straw and frowning as he shook the sweat from his forehead. . . .

"If there's anything for me to tell Mitsu . . ." my friend began by way of leave-taking.

"Tell him I'm going to run away from the troupe, will you? If I don't make it, I'll probably be deported, so either way I won't be with the company any longer."

"When are you quitting?"

"Today," said Takashi with a great air of resolve.

It dawned on my friend with a sense of urgency, almost of panic, that my brother was actually waiting for something at the drugstore. The full implication of his display of surprise as he'd jumped like a suddenly released spring, the implication of his abrupt silence, the implication of the shreds of lemon so hastily sucked up, all linked up into a ring of actuality. But he felt relieved to detect in the signs of feeling welling up and disappearing again in my brother's eyes—eyes with a dull, greasy film that brought to mind a professional wrestler—not merely a sense of constraint at having bumped into someone he would rather not have met, but an attitude of arrogant pity toward him.

"Is some secret agent coming here to help you escape?" my friend asked in an attempt at a joke.

"Shall I tell you the truth?" replied Takashi in a mock-menacing tone. "Do you see that pharmacist filling a little bottle with capsules over there on the other side of the medicine shelves?" Twisting his body round like my brother, my friend discerned, beyond the shelves with their countless bottles of drugs standing out against the dark background like a film negative of New York at the height of summer, a bald-headed man who faced away from them, concentrating intently on his delicate task.

"That medicine's for *me*, for my inflamed, tortured penis. Once it's safely in my hands I can make my escape from *Ours Was the Shame* and set off on my own."

My friend sensed the Americans around them stiffen at the single English word "penis" set like a precious stone in the otherwise incomprehensible Japanese dialogue. The vast, alien exterior that lay all about them asserted its reality once more.

"Surely you can get hold of that kind of medicine easily enough?" said my friend with an earnest dignity directed against the new surveillance under which they had come from the people about them.

"Yes, if you go to hospital in line with proper procedure," said Takashi, indifferent to the trivial psychological conflict going on in my friend. "But it's a hell of a business here in America if you can't. The prescription I've given the pharmacist was forged for me by a nurse in the medical office at the hotel. If the trick came to light a young black nurse would get fired and I'd be deported, I imagine."

Why hadn't he followed the regular procedure? Because the trouble with his urethra was obviously gonorrhea, which, moreover, he'd picked up on his first night in America by having sex with a black prostitute of an age that allowed him to see her as a mother figure. Should the facts become known to the elderly Diet member who was leader of the troupe, she would obviously send Takashi back to the country from which he'd just taken so much trouble to escape. Besides, he'd fallen prey to a depressing suspicion that since his urethra had been invaded by gonorrhea he might also be infected with syphilis, a suspicion that had quenched any urge to devote his creative imagination to some new course of action.

Five weeks had passed since he'd visited that district where black and white merged in a complex range of shades, but no primary symptoms of syphilis had appeared. Moreover, he used a sore throat as a pretext for obtaining a succession of small doses of antibiotics from the medical orderly of the troupe, thanks to which the trouble in his urethra eased somewhat; only then did Takashi shake off his inertia. Having struck up an acquaintance with a nurse in the hotel medical office in the course of their long stay in New York (the base which the troupe used for its sorties into other centers), Takashi persuaded her to get hold of a form used by doctors for writing prescriptions. The nurse, a black girl with a limitless spirit of service to others, had not only entered on the form the type and amount of medicine most suited to the trouble in his urethra, but had directed him to a drugstore in a busy part of town where there was little likelihood of the irregularity being detected.

"At first," said Takashi, "I tried to talk about the unpleasant symptoms in my penis in an abstract, inorganic way—as a kind of detached description, you know. I'd no special grounds for believing so, but I felt the word gonorrhea might be too blunt and shock her, so first I said I thought it might be urethritis. But she didn't get it. So I said I was suffering from 'inflammation of the duct.' You should have seen the fresh light of understanding that came into her eyes at that. Nothing could be less abstract and inorganic—it brought home to me all over again the sticky, fleshly reality of the suffering in my cock. And she said, 'Is there a burning sensation in your penis?' God, was I shocked! The words conveyed the reality so well I felt my whole body burning—with flames of embarrassment, that is!"

He laughed out loud and my friend followed suit. The non-Japanese around them, whose ears had pricked up at the significant words in English that sprinkled Takashi's conversation, gazed at them with deepening suspicion. The pharmacist appeared from behind the shelves, his lugubrious countenance bathed in sweat. The smile on Takashi's sunburned, birdlike face was suddenly blotted out by a look sick with longing and anxiety. Watching him, my friend felt himself go tense, but the bald-headed pharmacist, who looked like an Irishman, merely said in a fatherly voice, "This number of capsules comes very expensive. Why don't you take just one-third?"

Recovering his poise instantly, Takashi gave a laugh. "It's expensive, but anything'd be better than the agony in my tubes these past few weeks," he said.

"I'll buy them for you," my friend said in a hearty voice. "To celebrate the start of your new life in America."

Completely cheerful by now, Takashi took an affectionate look at the capsules gleaming softly in their bottle, then announced that he would pick up his belongings and set off on his solitary wanderings through America that very day. He and my friend left the drugstore, eager to get away from the scene of the crime as soon as possible, and walked together to a nearby bus stop.

"Once a problem's solved, the things that have been plaguing you seem terribly stupid and trivial," said my friend with a feeling almost of envy at the encounter between Takashi's happy face and the capsules in the bottle.

"Any trouble seems trivial once it's over, surely?" said Takashi aggressively. "It's the same with you going home to a clinic, isn't it? When the knots in your head are unraveled, maybe there'll be nothing left but the feeling that it was all a lot of fuss about something silly and unimportant."

"*If* they're unraveled," said my friend with unconcealed wistfulness. "If they're not, the silliness and the unimportance will be the sum total of my life."

"Just what are they, the knots in your head?"

"It's hard to tell. If I *could* tell, I could conquer them and begin to regret having marked time for several years. On the other hand, if I gave way to them and set out on a course of self-destruction that would really make them the sum total of my life, then that too would gradually make the true nature of the knots clear. Admittedly," he complained with a sudden, sad intensity, "the understanding in that case wouldn't be any use to me personally. Nor would there be any way of letting anyone else know that someone who'd apparently gone mad had seen the light *in extremis*."

It seemed as if my friend had profoundly stimulated Takashi's interest. But at the same time, my brother's behavior showed signs of a desire to get away just as soon as possible, and it was from this that he realized that his appeal had touched some sensitive core in Takashi. At this point a bus drew up.

Takashi got on it and, handing my friend a pamphlet through the window—in return, he said, for the cost of the medicine—was swallowed up without further ado into the vastness of the American continent. Neither my friend nor I had had any clear information about him since. True to the resolution he'd confided in my friend, he'd quit the company from that moment and set out alone on his travels.

Getting into a taxi, my friend immediately opened the pamphlet Takashi had given him. It was about the civil rights movement. The frontispiece was a photograph of a black, his body so scorched and swollen that the details were blurred like those of a crudely carved wooden doll, with a number of white men in shoddy clothes standing round him. It was comic and terrible and disgusting, a representation of naked violence so direct that it gripped the beholder like some fearful fantasy. Looking at it unavoidably brought one face-to-face with the abject certainty of defeat under the relentless pressure of fear. With the inevitability of two drops of water merging into each other, the sight linked itself immediately with the ill-defined trouble in his own head. It occurred to him that Takashi had left the pamphlet with him knowing full well the significance of giving it and its photograph to him rather than to anyone else. Takashi, in his turn, had seen into something essential in my friend's mind.

"One sometimes realizes after the event," my friend said, "that one's consciousness has caught something unexpected on its very outer edge, as though two things had somehow got superimposed. Ferreting around in the dimmer corners of my memory, it came to me that when I went up behind Takashi he was staring at that photograph as he drank his lemonade.

He seemed to be wrestling with some colossal problem. I think he wasn't really worrying about that business of the antibiotic prescription that he talked about in such detail, but about some essentially much more serious matter. Do you think Takashi's the kind of guy who'd make a fuss about a slight dose of the clap? It gave me a peculiar shock when he said, 'Shall I tell you the truth?' and I suspect that what he had in mind was something quite different from what he actually told me. I wonder what it was, though?"

Seated at the bottom of the pit on that autumn dawn, the dog on my lap, I couldn't tell what it had been—that thing in my brother's mind whose existence, if nothing else, my friend had made clear. Neither could I tell what it was that, growing and growing in his own head, had finally led him to death in such a bizarre guise. Death cuts abruptly the warp of understanding. There are things which the survivors are never told. And the survivors have a steadily deepening suspicion that it is precisely because of the things incapable of communication that the deceased has chosen death. The factors that remain ill defined may sometimes lead a survivor to the very site of the disaster, but even then the only thing clear to anyone concerned is that he has been brought up against something incomprehensible. If my friend, instead of painting his head crimson and hanging himself, had bequeathed so much as a brief cry over the telephone, there might have been some clue. It may well be, of course, that the crimson head, the cucumber in the anus of the naked body, and the death by hanging were themselves a kind of silent cry; but if so, then the cry alone was not enough for those left behind. The clues were too equivocal for me to pursue any further.

Nevertheless, none of the survivors was in a better position to understand my dead friend than myself. Ever since our first year at university he and I had been together in everything. Our classmates used to say we were like identical twins. In appearance even, I was more like my friend than my brother. Takashi bore no resemblance to me .whatsoever; and indeed there were some things in my younger brother's head as he roamed about America that I sensed as less accessible to me than things that had once had a place in my dead friend's mind. One autumn evening in 1945—the evening of the day that S, the second of my elder brothers and the only one to return alive from the front, was beaten to death in the Korean settlement that had grown up like a wen just outside the valley where our village stood—mother, lying on her sickbed, turned to our sister and made this appraisal of Takashi and myself, the only men left to our family:

"They're still children, their faces aren't formed yet. But by and by Mitsusaburo will be ugly and Takashi will be handsome. People will like Takashi and he'll lead a successful life. You should get on good terms with him while you can and stick with him even after you grow up."

When mother died, our sister was adopted by an uncle along with Takashi, thus in effect following mother's advice; but she killed herself before reaching adulthood. Though her retardation wasn't as serious as that of my own child, she was backward to the extent that, as mother had said, she was incapable of surviving without attaching herself to someone else. Only to music, or rather to sounds as such, did she show any real response. . . .

The dog barked. The outside world sprang to life once more, closing in on me at the bottom of my pit from two sides at once.

My right hand, rounded into a scoop, was scraping at the wall of the pit in front of me; already I'd clawed down toward my lap five or six pieces of brick buried till now in the Kanto loam, and the dog was pressing itself against my chest to avoid them. Urgently, my hand scraped at the side of the pit once, twice more; and I realized that someone unknown was peering down into it from above. I drew the dog close with my left hand and looked up from the hole. The dog's terror infected me: I was afraid with a truly animal fear. The morning light was clouded like an eye with a cataract. The sky that at dawn had been high with a whitish tinge now hung low and leaden. If only my eyes had both had vision, the morning light might have filled the scene more amply (I'm frequently prone to this kind of misconception), but to the one remaining eye it was a dark morning of unrelieved desolation. I sat, heedless of the dirt covering me, in a position more degraded than that of any normal inhabitant of that morning city, scrabbling with bare hands at the earthen wall, assailed by an overwhelming cold from without and a burning shame from within. Like a tower about to topple and blot out the leaden sky, the squat, broad silhouette of a human being once more blocked the entrance to the pit. It brought to mind a black crab reared up against the sky on its back legs. The dog went wild, and I was paralyzed with fear and shame. A clattering of innumerable glass objects wafted down into the pit like a flurry of hail. I strained my eyes in an effort to make out the features of the giant who peered down godlike at me, and, dazed with shame, allowed myself to give a faint, fatuous smile.

"What's the dog's name?" said the giant

The question was remote from all the possible remarks against which I'd been arming myself. Hauled safe, in that instant, onto everyday shores, I felt an immense, relaxing sense of relief. No doubt the gossip would spread around the neighborhood through this man, but it would be a scandal that in no sense stepped outside the everyday: not the kind that a moment earlier I'd contemplated with such fear and embarrassment; not the kind of scandal that would bring dog's-bristles of terror and shame sprouting from every pore of one's body, the kind that would brutally and aggressively scatter everything human to the winds, but a quiet scandal, no worse than if one had been seen, say, having intercourse with an elderly housemaid. The dog on my lap, divining that his protector had somehow been delivered from the peril associated with the grotesque thing above, fell silent, docile as a rabbit.

"Fell in there while you were drunk, did you?" the man went on, totally and finally plunging my behavior into the realms of the everyday. "It was foggy this morning."

I nodded cautiously at him (his whole body stood out in such black silhouette that to him my face, however dark the morning, must have stood out light against the darkness), then got up with the dog still in my arms. Drops of water trickled like tears from the back of my thighs, wetting the skin around my knees, which had been dry so far. Vaguely apprehensive, the man took a step back so that I was able to get a view of the whole of him from a point about level with his ankles.

He was a young milkman and wore a special tunic for carrying milk that looked like a life jacket with a bottle shoved into each of its air tubes. Whenever he took a breath, a jangling of glass striking glass arose around him. His breathing seemed to be somewhat heavier than it should be. He had a flat face like a halibut, with almost no bridge to his nose, and the whites of his eyes, like the eyes of primates, were almost invisible. He stared at me with those uniformly brown eyes, breathing heavily; his breath hung about his weak chin like a white beard. I shifted my gaze to the dogwood that displayed its autumn colors behind his spherical head, reluctant to see the emergence on his face of some expression that might mean something. Seen from a point two inches above the ground, the backs of the dogwood leaves were a burning red, threatening yet at the same time familiar, a red that reminded me of the flames in the picture of hell that I'd seen in our village temple every year on the Buddha's Birthday (it had been presented to the temple by my great-grandfather following the unhappy incident of 1860). The dogwood was a sign to me, its meaning only imperfectly clear, that produced a sudden resolve. I put the dog down onto the ground where the earth had been dug over to produce a dirty-looking mixture of black mud and withered brown grass. The dog ran away with every appearance of cheerfulness, as though to emphasize how long-suffering it had been up to now. Carefully, I climbed up the ladder. The song of at least three different species of bird bore down on me, together with the squeal of a car's tires. I had to climb cautiously in case my legs, which trembled violently with the cold, made me lose my step. As the whole of me in my dirty blue-striped pajamas appeared shivering aboveground, the milkman took another apprehensive step backward. I was tempted to give him a scare, but refrained, of course, and going into the kitchen closed the door behind me without further ado.

"When I saw you in the hole, I reckoned you were dead," the milkman shouted after me disappointedly, as though my going indoors without paying him any attention had made him see the affair as an outright swindle.

I stopped for a moment in front of my wife's room to see if she was still asleep. Then I took off my pajamas and rubbed myself down. I thought of heating some water and washing off the dirt, but abandoned the idea. Without realizing it, I'd lost the urge to keep myself clean. The trembling of my body mounted steadily. Something left a dark stain on the towel. I turned the light on and found my finger was bleeding where I'd torn off a nail in scrabbling at the earthen wall of the pit. It was too much trouble to look for disinfectant; I bound the towel round it and went shivering back to my own bedroom-study. The shivering wouldn't stop, and before long I developed a fever. My whole body began to throb with a dull ache, separate from the sharp pain in my injured finger. It was a crueler version of the ache I always felt at dawn. My fingers, I realized now, had unconsciously been trying to dig out the pieces of broken brick and bring down the earthen wall to bury me alive. The shivering and the dull ache increased unbearably. And I understood a little of that daily experience on awakening, when at dawn I felt my body dismembered and aching dully in each of its several parts.

Family Reunion

On the afternoon of the day that a telegram came from my brother announcing the abrupt curtailment of his wanderings in America and his impending arrival at Haneda airport, my wife and I met my brother's teen-age friends at the airport. There was a storm over the Pacific and the plane was late. We, the welcoming party for Takashi Nedokoro, took a room in a hotel at the airport to wait for the delayed plane. My wife, with her back to the window shaded by its plastic venetian blind (not that the blind completely shut out the light from outside, for a dim haze lingered in the room like smoke with no exit)—with her face, that is, shadowed so that no one should detect her expression—seated herself in a low armchair and silently began to drink whisky. A cut-glass tumbler was clasped in her left hand, which had a darkened appearance like the wet bough of a tree, and a whisky bottle and ice bucket stood next to the shoes beside her bare feet. She'd brought the whisky from home and ordered ice at the hotel.

Takashi's friends were sitting on the bed, which still had its cover on, huddled together like the young of an animal in their lair, and with knees drawn up to chin were watching a sports program on a transistor television set that hummed like a swarm of mosquitoes. I'd met Hoshio and Momoko twice before. Shortly after my brother had disappeared, allowing my friend to pay for his antibiotic capsules, they had come to see me, hoping to learn his latest whereabouts. By their next visit, a few months later, a picture postcard or the like must have come just for them from my brother, for they knew an address where he could be contacted, but they refused to tell me, merely demanding money so that they could send him a few necessities. Their personalities had made no particular mark either on my wife or myself, though we were mildly impressed by the way my brother's absence seemed to have left them at a loss, and by the devotion that this suggested.

As I drank my beer, which looked black in the dim light of the room, I peered through the slats of the blind at the vast space in which ponderous jetliners and gallant propeller craft were landing and taking off without cease. The area between the runways and the room where we lurked behind our blind was traversed at eye level by a steel and concrete overpass. A party of schoolgirls doing the sights of the airport passed along it, all bent forward with a cautious air. As the flock of kids in their drab uniforms reached the bend in the overpass, they momentarily appeared to be rising up toward the cloudy sky like the aircraft on the runways. The effect was oddly unsettling. But what seemed at first sight to be the girls' shoes falling away from their feet were in fact pigeons. A number of them swirled up into the air, and one came and alighted, with unnatural movements as though it had been shot down, on the narrow parapet spread with dry sand immediately beyond the blind. Taking a more careful look, I saw that it was lame. It was obviously too fat, presumably through lack of exercise, and couldn't manage a smooth landing. From its swelling neck and on down its belly lay a dark shadow like the skin of my wife's hand. Then without warning the fat pigeon took off (the space beyond the soundproof window must have been full of explosive noises which would startle a pigeon, but since none of them reached this side, all occurrences outside seemed to lack continuity), stopped quite still about seven inches in front of my eyes like a black blot in a Rorschach test, and flew off briskly out of sight.

Startled, I drew my head back. I turned and saw that my sudden movement had obviously surprised both my wife, who nonetheless still grasped the tumbler in her hand, and my brother's young friends, though they were still staring at the television.

"The storm must be pretty bad for the plane to be as late as this," I said to cover my embarrassment.

"There's no telling just how big a storm it is."

"If the plane's thrown around a lot, Takashi'll be terribly scared. The idea of dying with a lot of physical pain scares him twice as much as most people."

"They say you don't suffer much in a plane crash. It's all over in a second."

"Takashi's not the type to be scared," Hoshio broke in in a tense voice as though he could keep quiet no longer. The statement interested me, being the first words, apart from perfunctory greetings, that he'd uttered that afternoon.

"He gets scared all right," I said. "If anything, he's the type that's always been prey to some fear or other. Once, when he was still a kid, he got a tiny cut in the pad of his finger and about a hundredth of a milligram of blood oozed out. He spewed his guts up and passed out."

The blood in question had welled from a wound made when I pricked the ball of my brother's right middle finger with the point of a knife. He'd boasted to me that he could slash his own palm open without turning a hair. So I gave him the fright he deserved. He'd often insisted to me that he felt fear neither of violence, nor of any form of pain, nor of death itself, and each time I contradicted him flatly. The result had been my little game. Takashi too bad been keen to be tested and prove himself.

"A drop of blood oozed gently out of a tiny wound at the tip of his middle finger," I said, rubbing in the details in order to make fun of my brother's devoted bodyguard. "It looked like the eye of a young eel. We were both looking at it when Takashi suddenly puked and fainted."

"You can't scare Taka, I saw how cool he was in the June demonstrations—he just wasn't scared."

I found myself more and more intrigued by the naive, stubborn antagonism shown by my brother's friends. My wife was listening too, her eyes on Hoshio. I took another look at the young man, who now sat upright on the bed, steadily return- ing my gaze. He had the air of someone straight off the farm, of a young migrant come to town. His roughly hewn features, though not ugly when considered individually, were out of bal- ance, as if they'd decided to ignore each other, so that the total effect was comic. The characteristic air of dim-wittedness, a compound of the sullen and the easygoing, that lay over his face like a transparent net was absolutely typical of a peasant boy. His woolen jacket striped with light and dark brown was worn with an air of reverent care, though the odds were that it would soon deteriorate into a crumpled, baggy heap more like a large dead cat.

"Admittedly, Takashi dearly wanted to become the brutal type for whom violent behavior is the norm, but even when he happened to succeed he still gave the impression of being an amateur at it. Isn't that a little different from courage?" I was still uninterested in convincing him but hoped to put an end to the argument with this final shaft at his hostility. "Won't you join us in a whisky or a beer?"

"No thank you!" the youth replied in a tone of disgust so blatant as to render it suspect, at the same time thrusting out one hand in a rather forced gesture of rejection. "Taka said people who drink are weak when attacked. He said that if a man who drinks has a fight with one who doesn't, the one who doesn't always wins, even if they're equal in strength and technique."

Somewhat daunted, I poured a beer for myself and a whisky for my wife, who seemed possessed by a curiosity livelier than any she had shown in the past few months. Clutching our glasses with the air of two alcoholics banded together in last-ditch resistance against some superior force of non-drinkers, we confronted the stubby red hand still thrust out at us. One look at it was enough to show how short a time had elapsed since he'd left his farming village.

"I'm sure your idea of Takashi is the right one," my wife said to the boy. "Today will be my first meeting with my brother-in-law, and I'm glad to hear he's such a decent young man."

The youth gestured with his hand to show he wasn't taking any sarcasm from a drunken female, and abruptly turning his face away went back to the trivial sports program on the television. As he did so, he spoke in a low voice, checking the attacking team's score with the girl, whose eyes had not once left the television during our exchange. My wife and I, silenced willy-nilly, immersed ourselves in our drinks.

The plane was further delayed. It seemed it would be delayed forever. Midnight came and still it didn't arrive. The airfield, as I peered through the slats of the blind, was a vault of pale light, of glowing blues and hot shades of orange pierced by the jagged, off-white darkness that covered the city, as though night had come down as far as the outskirts of the vault then remained hovering there indefinitely, without encroaching any further. Exhausted, we had turned off the lights in the room, whose only source of illumination now was the fine stripes of light shining pointlessly from the television set, which my brother's friends had watched until, as the last program finished, it ceased to convey any meaning. It still seemed to hum with a sound like mosquito wings, though I wondered if this wasn't a noise in my own head.

My wife doggedly sipped at her whisky, her back to the runways as though to fend off in advance any visitor who might come through some imaginary door. She was equipped with an odd sense that gauged the depth of her own drunkenness. Like a fish that keeps to its own level of habitation and activity, she sank to a certain depth but would under no circumstances go further, nor would she willingly sober up. According to her own analysis, she'd inherited this sense, this automatic safety apparatus, from her mother, who had herself been an alcoholic.

Once she reached a certain fixed limit within the safe layer of intoxication, she would make up her mind to sleep and drop off without further ado. And since she never suffered from any hangover, each tomorrow began with a renewed search for some pretext for returning as soon as possible to that well-known stratum.

I'd told her: "You're different from other alcoholics on one score at least—you can regulate how drunk you get and stay at the same level, of your own free will. In a few weeks, I imagine, your sudden taste for drink will pass. You shouldn't connect a passing craving for alcohol with memories of your mother and try to rationalize it, or establish it as something that's here to stay." I'd said this again and again, but just as often she'd dismissed my overtures.

"On the contrary, it's the very ability to regulate the intoxication voluntarily that makes me an alcoholic. Mother was just the same. The reason I stop when I've reached a certain stage isn't that I'm holding back from the temptation to get still drunker, but that I'm afraid to slip out of the pleasant state I've reached."

It was fear and disgust in various forms that drove her down into drunkenness. But like a wounded duck that dives beneath the water, she knew that to surface would mean encountering an immediate hail of anxieties, so she was never entirely free from the fear and disgust, even in her drunkenness. When she drank, her eyes became unusually bloodshot; the fact worried her, and on one occasion she'd said, obviously haunted by the analogy with the traumatic birth of our poor baby, "In Korean folk tales they say that a woman whose eyes are red like plums has eaten human flesh."

The smell of her whisky-sodden breath hung about the room. The effect of my beer had already worn off, and every time she breathed out I was aware of it with the sharp regularity of a pulse. The heating worked too well, and we'd opened the double windows of our room to let in some air. Suddenly, the fierce roar of a belated jet tore in like a whirlwind through the narrow gap. I set my single eye, lonely fighter with reactions dulled by fatigue, roving frantically in search of the plane that must have arrived. But all it found was two parallel-moving lights on the point of disappearing into the depths of the milky darkness.

It was the engines of a jet taking off that had so startled me. Realizing the truth of this, I was nonetheless taken in more than once in the same way, though takeoffs were few and far between by now and the whole airport had a half-paralyzed look. The night alone still stood there, helpless, with nowhere to flee before the mercilessly searching lights. The planes huddled still, the color of dried fish amid a chaos of glowing blues and hot oranges.

Silent in our room, we went on patiently waiting for the delayed plane. My brother's return could have little positive significance for my wife and me, whatever might be true of his bodyguards, yet all of us there waited as intently as though he were bringing back some force that would set something basic in motion in each of us.

With a small cry, Momoko shot upright on the bed. She'd been asleep, curled up like a fetus on top of the cover. Hoshio, who had been stretched out on the floor, got up slowly and went over to the bed. My wife sat with the whisky tumbler still gripped in her hand and her head held erect like a weasel. I remained standing vacantly with my back to the blind. Powerless to do anything for this girl in the grip of her own dreams, we stared at the inverted triangle of her face, pinched with tension and wet with a stream of tears that gleamed white like Vaseline in the light from the Braun tube.

"The plane's crashed," she sobbed. "It's burning! It's burning!"

"No plane's crashed, stop crying," the youth said resentfully in a rough voice, apparently ashamed on her behalf.

"Summer . . . summer!" she breathed and, sinking back onto the bed again, curled up and moved on to another, different dream.

The air in the room was indeed hot enough for summer. My palms were beginning to sweat. Why, I asked myself, should a couple of kids feel such an intense need for my brother as their guardian deity that they would wait all through the long night, overwrought even in their dreams? Was my brother the type to fulfill their expectations? With a sense of pity for his young friends, I spoke to Hoshio.

"Won't you have just a little whisky?"

"No thank you."

"Do you mean to say you've never touched liquor?"

"Me? I used to drink. After I left my part-time high school, while I was working as a laborer, I'd work for three days then on the fourth I'd drink gin nonstop from morning to night. Sometimes I had a short sleep, but one way or the other I was always drunk—drunk awake or drunk asleep. I had some pretty weird dreams." He spoke in a voice unexpectedly hoarse with feeling.

He came to stand by my side, thrusting his back against the blind with a great rattle. Suddenly, on his face appeared the first smile I'd seen there; his eyes shone with a brilliance detectable even in the gloom, and I realized that he was proud of this story.

"Why did you stop drinking, then?"

"I met Taka, and he said not to drink because you should tackle life sober. So I gave it up. I haven't had a single dream since."

So Takashi had manifested the educative instinct: I'd never thought of him as that type before. Takashi could tell a teenager, with an air of great authority, not to drink because one should live life sober. That alone, it seemed, had been enough to make a young laborer give up his self-destructive way of life. The boy himself, moreover, could recall the episode with the most relaxed and confident of smiles.

"As to whether Taka's got courage or not . . ." he began, dragging up our earlier argument now that he saw the wonder our dialogue on drink had inspired in me. All the while he'd been lying on the floor like a dog he had obviously been racking his brains to find some way of restoring the honor of his guardian deity. "In the June demonstrations he did something completely different from the others, all by himself. You wouldn't know about that."

Intent on challenging me with some new logic, he'd raised himself into a position where he could look me straight in the eye. I looked back with an obscure sense of doubt at eyes that were now no more than a pair of dark bullet holes.

"One day he joined in with a gang and helped beat up his own side—the very people he'd fought with up till then and again fought with from the next day."

He laughed aloud. The laugh, with its ring of childishly furtive delight, was the stick that finally stirred up the muddy waters of my antipathy.

"That 'great exploit' just shows that Taka's a capricious, spoiled kid with no consistency in his actions," I said. "It's nothing to do with courage."

"You've got it in for Taka because your friend got hurt when he was hit in front of the Diet, and because you've just heard that Taka was using a stick on the side that did the hitting," the youth replied with open hostility. "That's why you won't admit he's brave."

"It was the police that hit my friend. It couldn't have been Taka. There's no connection between the two things."

"Who knows—with a free-for-all in the dark like that?" the youth insinuated slyly.

"I don't believe Taka could hit anyone's head hard enough to crack the skull, hard enough for the man to go crazy and kill himself. Don't forget I've known him since he was a kid. I know just how timid he is."

Even as I spoke, I was gradually losing my enthusiasm for such a pointless argument. Fatigue and an unexplained resentment made me feel as though a rotten tooth had overflowed; my mouth seemed filled with an unpleasant taste—the taste of futility. The memory of my dead friend awoke and rebuked me, asking whether this trivial argument with a kid was all I could do for the dead man who had meant so much to me. If anything, it suggested that there was nothing whatsoever that those left behind could do for the dead. For no definite reason, I'd been prey to a vague foreboding during the past few months.

They were the months in which my friend had died, my wife had started her whisky-drinking, and we'd been forced to put our idiot child in an institution, though the foreboding might also relate to something that had been building up even before that. It had nourished in me a conviction that I would die in a way still more pointless, absurd, and ridiculous than my friend. I was convinced, too, that those who lived on afterward would fail to do the proper thing on my behalf.

"You don't understand Taka, you don't know him at all," he complained. "You're not a bit like him. You're just a *rat*. What did you come to meet Taka for today?" He spoke in a tearful voice that was touching in its unexpectedness. Then as I averted my gaze from his pitifully working face, he left me and went and lay beside his comrade on the bed. Not a further sound was heard from him.

I retrieved from near my wife's feet the whisky bottle and a paper cup that had come with a packed lunch for sightseers at the airport, and drank some of the raw, evil-smelling stuff. She bought only the cheapest whisky. It burned my throat and I sputtered briefly.

"Hey, Rat—" my wife called to me, "are you going to spend all night staring at the airfield? I've got something to say to you." She was dispassionate, comfortably submerged at her standard level of intoxication.

Carefully clutching the whisky bottle and cup, I went and sat by her knees.

"What do you think we should say if Taka asks about the baby?"

"We don't have to say anything, do we?"

"But if he asks next why I'm drinking, I won't be able to keep quiet," she said, displaying the cool objectivity that drunkenness always gave her. "Though of course if I answer either question it'll remove the necessity to answer the other, which makes things simpler."

"Not so simple. If you understood the causal relationship between the two things as well as you think you do, you would already have got the better of both the matter of the baby and your drinking problem. You would be sober and pregnant with a new baby."

"I wonder whether Takashi'll lecture me too? 'Quit drinking! Life should be lived sober!' The trouble is," she added flatly, "I've no desire to be reeducated." I poured some more whisky into her glass. "Don't you think he may be expecting us to bring the baby here to meet him?"

"He's not of an age to go imagining anything so definite about any baby. He's hardly grown up himself yet."

She seemed to be gazing at a vision of the baby somewhere between her own left knee and my right. Balancing her tumbler precariously on the arm of the chair, she stretched out her now empty hand and seemed to sketch the outline of a plump or heavily swaddled baby in a single continuous motion that heightened my awkwardness and general sense of indignation.

"I've a feeling, for instance, Taka might bring a teddy bear or something for the baby, which would put us all on the spot."

"I don't imagine he's got the money to buy teddy bears," I said, realizing as I spoke that although I didn't want her to talk about the baby to my brother on the first occasion she met him, I was equally reluctant to have the task fall to me.

"Is he the sensitive or the thick-skinned type?"

"He's a mixture—very sensitive in some ways, very insensitive in others. Anyway, he's not a particularly desirable type for you to be introduced to in your present condition." On the bed the young man stirred, then curled up like a threatened wood louse and hemmed feebly. Takashi's henchman had made a mild protest.

"I don't want to be cross-questioned by anybody," she said defensively, abruptly excited and just as suddenly subdued, as though she'd spoken at the very moment when the ball of emotion, tossed into the air, had reached its point of rest.

"Nor do you have to," I said comfortingly, in case she should start on the interminable descent of some inner spiral staircase of hysterical self-loathing or self-pity. "There's no reason for you to be especially afraid of Takashi. You're just tense because you're meeting a new member of the family. There's nothing else to fear—not that I think you *are* afraid." I poured another shot of whisky into her tumbler. If she wasn't going to make up her own mind to sleep, she must be made to go one step beyond her usual level of drunkenness. Her mind, always suggestible, was threatened, was besieged by something, some evil specter worse than any physical pain.

She took a sip of whisky, plainly fighting against nausea. Straining my one eye, tired and aching from its struggle against the darkness, I watched her face: helpless, solitary, turned in on itself. Eventually she rose above it. The rigid outlines softened on the face which she held tilted slightly upward with closed eyes, and a young girl's face appeared in its place. The hand clasping the tumbler wavered in the space above her knees. I took the glass from her, and the thin, sinewy, sallow hand fell to her lap like a dying swallow. She was already asleep. Draining the whisky she had left, I yawned and, following the young man's example, stretched out on the floor and (*you're just a rat*) prepared to board the rickety chariot of sleep.

In my dreams I was standing at a crossroads where a broad avenue with streetcars was intersected by a sidestreet. Large numbers of people bumped into my sides and back incessantly as they passed me from behind. The leaves on the trees lining the street showed that it was late summer; the foliage was as dense as in the deep forest surrounding the valley where our village stood. Unlike the everyday bustle of the world that was my own background, this other world that I watched as one who has thrust his head beneath the waters of a river in order to see its bed, this other world now unfolding before my eyes, was wrapped in a profound, unearthly silence. Wondering why it should be so utterly silent, I realized that it was because all the people walking so slowly along the opposite sidewalk were old. The people driving in both directions along the road were all old too. The people at work in the liquor stores, the drugstores, the five-and-tens, and the customers as well, they were all old. There was a barber's just to the right of the entrance to the sidestreet, and the patrons, swathed to their necks in white cloth as I saw them in the wide mirror through the half-open windows, were all old men, and the barbers were old men too. And with the exception of the customers and employees in the barbershop, all the old men were dark-suited, wearing hats pulled down over their ears and what looked like rain boots that fitted closely around their ankles.

These old men wrapped in tranquillity—I felt, struggling to remember something that troubled me—had some deep significance. Then I realized that my friend who had hanged himself and the idiot baby consigned to an institution were both present among the old men who filled the street, both dressed also in black suits with hats crammed down over their ears and rain boots on their feet. They disappeared and reappeared amongst their fellows, and since they were almost identical with the other old men, it was impossible to distinguish all the time which was my friend and which the baby. But the ambiguity was in itself no obstacle to emotional experience; all the old men who filled the street were in some way relevant to me. I tried to burst into their world, met some invisible resistance, and gave a cry of despair:

"*I deserted you!*"

But my cry spent itself in countless echoes flying round my head; whether or not it even reached the old men's world I couldn't tell. They went on placidly walking, slowly driving their cars, carefully selecting books, sitting transfixed in the barbershop mirror, on and on forever. . . .

A pain gripped me as though someone were trampling on my guts: in what way had I deserted them? By never—I told myself—having hanged myself in their stead, with my head painted crimson; by never having been put in an institution and left to degenerate into something like the young of a wild beast. Why should this be so clear to me now, then? It was abundantly clear because I wasn't there with them in that late summer street, a placid old man in a black suit with my hat down over my ears and rain boots on my feet. . . .

"*I deserted you!*"

I'd already realized it was a dream, but the perception didn't alleviate the sense of oppression that those placid apparitions inspired in me. I *experienced* them in the most unequivocal way possible.

A heavy hand was placed on my shoulder. My eyelids were held shut by some force—whether by shame or sensitivity to the light wasn't clear. I opened them in spite of it and saw my brother, dressed like a hunter in Levi's and a jacket with a collar of (possibly imitation) badger, peering down at me. His face was deeply tanned, as though it had rusted.

"Hi!" he said in an encouraging voice.

Sitting up I saw the girl, all but naked, bending over to pick up a dark brown dress. She was about to put it on, in midwinter, with nothing underneath but a tiny pair of panties. My wife and Hoshio were watching her with the grave attention of guardians. Naked, she had the chilly, forlorn air of a plucked fowl, and I felt the sight as less erotic than cruelly desolate.

"It's an Indian hide dress," Takashi said. "The only thing I brought back from America. I had to sell sister's pendant to get the money."

"That's OK," I said, concealing my disappointment at losing the one remaining thing that had belonged to our dead sister.

"Glad you say so," he said happily, as though a load really had been taken off his mind. He walked over to the window, kicking aside with evident pleasure the whisky bottle, glass, and empty lunch box left from the previous evening, and finished raising the blind, which was already halfway up.

A faint white morning light filled the air beneath a uniformly cloudy sky, and the planes clinging to the ground like locusts were wrapped in a dismal haze. The sight filled me with the same cruel desolation—though on an incomparably vaster scale—as the naked teen-ager had done, thereby convincing me that the emotion had its origins within me, in lack of sleep and the lingering intoxication and fatigue of the night before.

In the faint light from the fully exposed window I could see Momoko in distress, shaking her small head which protruded from the broad oval collar of the leather dress. The hem of the dress was stuck on her hips, leaving her bottom half exposed, but her face glowed with naive pride at being the only one for whom Takashi had brought a present. Even the way she grumbled, as though blaming the leather dress itself, sounded more like a song of irrepressible good spirits.

"My skin and this leather rub each other up the wrong way. And I've no idea which thong fastens in which hole. Just look how many thongs there are, Takashi! I wonder how the Indians ever manage such a lot—their mathematics can't be very advanced!"

"That's nothing to do with it," Hoshio interposed in an equally cheerful tone, stretching out a clumsy helping hand. "Are you sure those leather strips aren't just decoration?"

"Decoration or not there's no reason for you to pull them off!"

My wife joined the happy band around the Indian dress and loyally helped Momoko on with it. I was startled by the natural manner in which she seemed to blend in with Takashi's bodyguards this morning. During my painful, humiliating slumber, my brother had alighted from his tardy plane and with swift magic had reconciled my wife with his young friends. The distress that had afflicted her all the evening before, and infected me as well, was now mine alone.

"The baby was badly handicapped mentally, you know," I said. "We had to put him in an institution in the end."

"Mm. I already heard," Takashi said with an appropriately consoling air of despondency.

"We went to fetch him after five weeks, but he'd completely changed in the interval; his state was such that even my wife and I couldn't tell he was our own son. Naturally, the child doesn't recognize us either. It looks as though something terrible has been done to him. You get the feeling that the barrier has come down more completely than if he'd actually died. So we came back without him after all." I spoke in subdued voice, not wanting it to reach my wife's ears.

As he listened in silence, my brother's expression had a somberly sincere quality that managed to insinuate itself among the folds of my emotions without provoking any antagonism, a quality that resembled something I had detected in his tanned, unfamiliar face when I first awakened, a quality that had been latent in his voice as he told me he'd heard of the baby's misfortune. I hadn't expected to find this shadow of grown-up seriousness in him, and I realized that I was observing one of the effects of his life in America.

"Did you hear about that too?" I asked.

"No. But I knew that something dreadful must have happened," my brother said, also dropping his voice and speaking almost without moving his lips.

"Did you hear that my friend had killed himself?"

"Yes. There was something rather special about him, wasn't there?"

I realized that Takashi too already knew the details of how my friend had died. It was the first time I'd heard such a tribute from the lips of someone outside my dead friend's immediate family.

"I seem to be surrounded by the odor of death," I said.

"If that's so, Mitsu, then shake yourself free and climb up into the world of the living again. Otherwise the odor will rub off on you."

"Does that mean you've picked up the superstitious mentality in America?" I said.

"That's right," my brother went on relentlessly, seeing through my attempt to obscure the echoes his words had set up in the void within me. "But all I've done in fact is take up again something that was very marked in me when I was a kid and that I happened to put aside later in life. Remember how sister and I built a thatched hut and lived there for a while? We were starting a new life, trying to get away from the smell of mortality. It was just after S was beaten to death, as you know."

I watched him silently, making none of the appropriate responses, and as I did so a smoldering suspicion rose into the eyes that met mine, threatening to build up into something dangerous and violent. Takashi had always lost his composure if one hinted at anything concerning our sister's death. Even now, I thought, it was still the same. But just as steel strained beyond the limits of its elasticity will snap without warning, whatever was beginning to take shape in Takashi's eyes quite suddenly disappeared. I experienced a renewed sense of surprise.

"The point is," he said in tones of unimpassioned persuasion, "she may have died, but the magic of the new life did its work all the same. Her death, you see, was designed to let me go on living. It was her death that aroused uncle's sympathy and persuaded him to send me to Tokyo University. If I'd gone on living in the same village where he lived, I would have died of depression. Don't you think you'd better start a new life now, before it's too late?"

"A new life? And where do you think I'll find *my* thatched hut?" I said mockingly, though if the truth were told the talk was beginning to have its effect on me.

"What kind of life are you leading at the moment?" he asked earnestly as though he perceived my uncertainty.

"As soon as my friend died I gave up my job at the university where we'd been working as lecturers. Apart from that there's no special change."

Since graduating from the literature department of the university, I'd been making a living mostly by translating accounts of people trapping wild animals and keeping them in captivity. One animal book in particular had gone into several editions, and the royalties guaranteed a basic livelihood for my wife and myself. Admittedly, we relied on her father for the house where we were living, not to mention the expense of keeping the baby in an institution. I imagined, too, that since I'd given up my lecturing job my father-in-law had been shouldering any unexpected household expenses. At first I'd felt some objection to the idea of having the house bought for me but, particularly since my friend had hanged himself, I hardly cared how much my wife relied on her father.

"What about your inner life? There's something wrong, isn't there? I got a nasty shock when I saw you sprawled asleep on that dirty floor. When you woke up, too, your face and voice were somehow different from what they used to be. To put it bluntly, you're headed downhill: you give the impression of being on the skids."

"I admit my friend's death took the stuffing out of me. There was the business of the baby as well," I said in hesitant self-justification.

"Don't you think it's going on too long, though?" pressed Takashi. "If it lasts much longer your face will get set in that downhill look. In New York I met a Japanese philosophy student living the life of a dropout, a kind of social pariah. He'd gone to America to study Dewey's successors, completely lost his faith in life, and that's how he ended up. You remind me of him, Mitsu—your face, your voice, your whole physical and mental bearing. They're exactly the same."

"Your bodyguard told me I was a rat."

"A rat? The philosopher's nickname was 'Rat,' too," Takashi said. "I don't expect you believe me, do you?" he added with an awkward smile.

"I believe you," I said, and flushed at the obvious self-pity that suffused my voice.

It was true, no doubt. I'd been getting ratlike, just like the philosopher who had lost his faith in life. Ever since the hundred minutes I spent at dawn in the pit intended for the septic tank, I'd been ruminating on the experience. I was perfectly aware that physically and mentally I was going downhill, that the slope I was on must surely lead to a place where the stench of death was even more intense. By now I'd quite clearly elucidated the significance of what had first shown itself as those unexplained aches, all apparently unconnected, in various parts of my body. Not that becoming conscious of their psychological nature had conquered them: on the contrary, the attacks had just become more frequent. Nor had I yet recovered that ardent sense of expectation.

"You've got to start a new life, Mitsu," repeated Takashi, stepping up the pressure.

"Yes, you should do as he says," said my wife, surveying us evenly through eyes narrowed against the light as we stood side by side against the window. "Even I can see that."

By now Momoko had decked herself out like a miniature Indian bride, all in leather, even down to the ornament in her hair. My wife had just finished helping her into the outfit and was walking toward us. At that moment she wasn't particularly unattractive, even in the morning light.

"Naturally, I would like to start a new life," I said seriously. "The point is, where am I to find my thatched hut?" I felt, quite literally, that I needed such a hut with its well-remembered scent of green thatch.

"Why not give up everything you're doing in Tokyo and come to Shikoku with me? That wouldn't be a bad way to start, Mitsu," said Takashi, doing his best to tempt me even as he clearly showed his fear that I would reject the idea outright. "After all, that's why I took a jet home."

"Taka—if we're going to Shikoku, let's go by car!" put in the youth. "It'll take the three of us easily even with our luggage inside, and one of us could sleep in the back on the way. I bought a beaten-up old Citroen in case we went."

"Hoshi's been living and working at an auto repair place for the last two years," volunteered Momoko. "He bought the old Citroen—it wasn't much better than scrap—and fixed it up to make it more or less drivable. All by himself too!"

The young man's cheeks and the skin round his eyes flushed to an almost indecent degree.

"I've already given in my notice at the shop," he said with an extraordinarily naive air of excitement. "I told the manager the day that Taka's letter arrived and Momoko came to tell me about it."

Takashi, despite his embarrassment as he listened to this, had a certain childlike expression of satisfaction.

"They're a useless crowd," he said. "Never use their heads."

"Give me some more practical details about this new life in Shikoku," I said. "I don't suppose you intend to set to work in the fields as our ancestors did?"

"Taka acted as interpreter for a group of Japanese tourists when they went round a supermarket in America," Momoko said. "One of them was interested when he heard Taka's surname. They got to talking and it seems he owns a chain of supermarkets in Shikoku. He's terribly rich, by now he controls all your part of the country, and it turns out he's set his heart on buying the storehouse at the place where you were born. He plans to have the whole building transported to Tokyo and make it into a restaurant serving country cooking."

"In short," my brother went on, "a local *nouveau riche* has turned up to take that dilapidated old wooden monstrosity off our hands. So if you agree to selling it, I think we ought to go and supervise the dismantling. Besides, I'd like a chance to ask around in the village about the true facts of the affair of great-grandfather and his younger brother. That's another reason why I came back from America."

I was not to be convinced in a hurry of the practicability of his plan. Even supposing he'd suddenly found in himself hidden talents as a businessman, he seemed unlikely to succeed in selling a run-down building to a man who, as proprietor of a supermarket chain, was presumably as up-to-date as anyone in his ideas. A restaurant serving country food? But the place didn't have the kind of charm required; it was a storehouse dating back a good hundred years. What impressed me more than such talk was the interest with which Takashi still pursued the truth about our great-grandfather and his younger brother. One day, at a time when the family, though still living in the village in the valley, was on the verge of breaking up, my brother had caught wind of the scandal involving our family a century or so earlier.

"Great-grandfather killed his younger brother to settle the trouble in the village," Takashi had said, repeating what he'd heard in a horrified voice. "And he ate a piece of the flesh from his brother's thigh. He did it to prove to the clan officials that he had no connection with the trouble his brother had stirred up."

I myself had no accurate information about the incident. Particularly during the war, the village adults gave the impression of shunning all mention of the affair, and our family too had tried to pretend the ugly rumor didn't in fact exist. Even so, in order to counter his horror I'd told Takashi another, different rumor that I remembered having once been told in private.

"That isn't true," I'd said. "After the trouble, great-grandfather helped his brother get away through the forest and escape to Kochi. He went by sea to Tokyo, where he changed his name and did rather well for himself. A number of letters from him came for great-grandfather around the time of the Meiji Restoration. Great-grandfather kept quiet about it to the end, so people had to make up the kind of lies you heard. The reason he kept quiet was that a lot of people from the village had been killed through his brother's fault, and he wanted to avoid arousing their families' anger. . . ."

"Anyway, let's go back to my place," I proposed, recalling with nostalgia the enormous influence I'd wielded over my younger brother for a period of several years just after the war. "We can consider the plans for a new life when we get there."

"All right. Since it means that the family storehouse will disappear from the village in the valley where it's stood for a hundred years, it won't do any harm to talk it over in a leisurely way."

"If you two go by taxi, I'll follow with Taka and Momoko in my car," said the young man in a sharp maneuver to push my wife and me outside their tight little circle.

"I'd like to have just one drink before we get in the car," said my wife, who by now had dropped any lingering wariness toward her brother-in-law. She poked regretfully with the toe of her shoe at the empty bottle where it lay on its side on the floor.

"I've got a bottle of tax-free bourbon I bought in the airport," said my brother, promptly coming to the rescue.

"Have you taken up drinking again, then?" I ventured, secretly hoping to achieve a little iconoclasm where my brother's bodyguards were concerned.

"If I'd ever been really drunk in America, I would almost certainly have got beaten to death in some dark corner. You know what I'm like when I'm drunk, don't you, Mitsu?" He pulled a bottle of whisky out of his bag. "I bought this for my new sister-in-law."

"You seem to have gotten to understand each other pretty thoroughly while I was asleep."

"We had quite a long time for it. Do you always spend so long over your unpleasant dreams?" said Takashi, heavily countering my own sarcasm.

"Did I say anything while I was asleep?" I asked, again profoundly disturbed.

"Don't worry, *I* don't think you would callously abandon people to their fate. Nobody thinks so," he said, taking pity on my distress. "You're different from great-grandfather—not the kind to do anything really terrible to other people."

Seeing my wife drink a mouthful of bourbon straight from the bottle, I took the bottle from her and had a swig myself in order to hide my embarrassment.

"OK! Off we go to Hoshi's Citroen!" Bubbling over with happiness, brave in her leather Indian outfit, Momoko gave the command and we, the reunited family, set off. Trailing along at the rear in my capacity as the eldest there, the one with the ratty, downhill appearance, I had a presentiment that in the end I would let myself be pushed into going along with Takashi's extremely shaky plan. For the moment, I'd lost the sheer toughness needed for a confrontation with him. As the thought occurred to me, the warmth from the gulp of whisky suddenly promised to link up with a sense of expectation in the inner depths of my body. But when I tried to focus on it I was hindered by the sober good sense that sees so many perils in any attempt to achieve rebirth through self-release.

Mighty Forest

In the very heart of the forest the bus halted without warning as though the engine had stalled. My wife was asleep in the back seat, wrapped in blankets from chest to toes, and as I stopped her mummylike form from rolling forward and restored her to her original position, I was suddenly afraid of the possible effects of this unnatural interruption of her slumber. The obstacle ahead of the bus was a young peasant woman with a large bundle on her back and something crouched perfectly still, like an animal, at her feet. Staring, I saw that it was a child squatting facing in the opposite direction. I could clearly distinguish the small, naked buttocks and, an unnaturally pale yellow against the dark setting of the forest, the small pile of excrement.

The forest road, hemmed in on both sides by close ranks of huge evergreens, fell gradually away from the front of the bus, and the woman and the child at her feet appeared to float about a foot above the ground. Without realizing it, I'd leaned the left half of my body out of the window as I watched. With

a vague sense of fear, I was readying myself for some nameless, terrifying thing to come leaping upon us from behind the
sunken boulders that my sightless right eye interposed darkly
in my field of vision. The child's evacuation dragged on pitifully.
I sympathized with him, was overcome by the same need to
hurry, the same fright and shame.

Above the forest road a narrow strip of wintry sky, walled
in by the dense, dark foliage of evergreens as though it lay at
the bottom of a deep ditch, stretched over our heads where we
had halted. Slowly the afternoon sky sank toward us, fading as
it came like a stream that changes color as it flows. At night, I
told myself, the sky would close in on the vast forest as tightly
as the shell of the abalone enfolds its flesh; the thought aroused
claustrophobic feelings. Born and bred in the depths of this
forest, I still couldn't escape the same stifling sensation whenever I passed through it on the way to our valley. At the core of
that sensation lay emotions inherited from those long-perished
ancestors who, driven on endlessly by the mighty Chosokabe,
had plunged deeper and deeper into the forest until, coming
upon a spindle-shaped hollow that had resisted its encroach-
ment, they settled there; it had a spring of wholesome water. My
suffocating sensation was still charged with the same feelings
that inspired the leader of those fugitives, the "first man" of our
family line, as he plunged into the menacing shadows of the
forest in search of the hollow he saw in his imagination. The
Chosokabe is a creature of terrifying size that exists everywhere
in time and space. My grandmother would use it to threaten
me whenever I questioned her authority. "The Chosokabe will
come from the forest and get you!" she would say, and the sound
of her words would bring home not only to the infant but to

herself, old woman of eighty that she was, the ever-present reality of the monstrous creature that still lived in the same age as ourselves. . . .

The bus had been traveling for five hours since leaving its base in the provincial town. At the fork where the road went over the hills, all the passengers except my wife and me transferred to another bus that descended around the edge of the forest to the sea. The road that runs from the town, plunges into the densest part of the forest, comes to our hollow, then runs on downward beside the river flowing from the valley to rejoin the bus route that branches off earlier toward the sea, is gradually falling into disrepair. The thought that this road we were traversing through the heart of the forest was slowly decaying struck home with a dull, unpleasant shock somewhere at the back of my mind. A rat obsessed with a dying road, I felt the eye of the forest staring at me from among cedars, pines, and several species of cypress, all of a green so murky that one perceived it almost as black.

I saw the peasant woman, the upper part of her body dragged backward by her load so that only her head was bent forward, moving her lips in vigorous speech. The child straightened up, slowly pulled up his trousers and, looking down as he did so at his own waste, made to touch it with the tip of his shoe. Without warning, the woman boxed his ear. Then, prodding him roughly before her while he protected his head with both hands, she made her way round to the side of the bus. Taking its new passengers on board, the bus set off once more through the menacing silence of the forest. Woman and child came determinedly to the back of the bus and took the seat directly in front of ours. The mother sat down by the window and the child sat sideways, lolling over the wooden armrest next to the aisle, so that the shaven head and the little pallid face in profile forced themselves on our gaze. With bloodshot eyes, red like plums, in which the traces of intoxication still lingered, my wife took note of the child. I too found my eyes drawn irresistibly and with loathing toward him. His head and the color of his skin were such as to bring back our worst memories. I was sure that the head and the bloodless pallor of the skin were loaded with insidious stimuli to the things that already saturated her inner being, ready to crystallize at the slightest provocation. They were a direct evocation of the day when our baby had been operated on for the thing on his head.

My wife and I had been waiting that morning in front of the patients' elevator on the same floor as the operating theater. Eventually the outer doors had opened to announce the arrival of the iron cage of the elevator, but the second set of doors on the green wire-netting cage inside resisted the nurse's efforts and refused to open.

"Baby doesn't want to be operated on," said my wife, peering through the wire even as she recoiled in horror as though tempted to run away.

Through the green wire mesh, in a dim, greenish light like sunlight filtering through summer foliage, we saw the baby's head, shaven like a criminal's, as he lay on the castered bed from the children's ward. His tight-shut eyes were slits in skin that was whitish and dead-looking as though powdered. Standing on tiptoe, I could see on the far side of the head, in total contrast to its look of debility and uneasy tension, the orange-colored excrescence bulging with blood and spinal fluid, a living thing in vigorous yet mindless association with the baby's head. The lump was awe-inspiring, a vivid witness to the presence of some grotesque power harbored within yet uncontrollable by the self. Might not we too—the pair who had given birth to this baby and to this growth filled with a power beyond his control—awaken one morning to find similar excrescences, crying out with life, protruding from our heads, while the spinal fluid metabolized rapidly and in great quantities between the lumps and all the organs associated with our souls? Might not we in our turn proceed to the operating theater, feeling with our shaven heads like brute criminals? . . . The nurse gave the wire-mesh door a determined kick. The jolt made the baby open his mouth wide, all toothless and dark red like a wound, and start to cry. At that time, he still had the ability to express himself by crying.

"I feel as though the doctor's going to come along and say, 'Well, here's your baby back,' and present us with the amputated growth," said my wife as the nurse bore off the baby's bed through countless doors to the operating theater.

Her words brought home to me that both of us, she as much as myself, had felt a more positive reality in the swollen orange excrescence than in the pale, limp-limbed baby lying there with closed eyes.

The operation went on for ten hours. As we waited exhausted for it to end, I—not my wife—was summoned three times to the operating theater to give blood transfusions. The last time, the sight of the baby's head all besmeared with his own blood and mine made me feel that he was being cooked in some bubbling mess of broth. So weakened were my mental faculties by loss of blood that an odd equation formulated itself in my mind: the removal of the baby's lump was equal to the physical amputation of some part of my own body. I actually

felt a sharp pain deep down inside me and had to struggle with
an urge to demand of the doctors, so doggedly continuing the
operation, "Are you sure you're not robbing me and my son of
something really vital?"

Eventually the baby came back to us, a creature no longer
capable of any human reaction apart from gazing back at one
with placid brown eyes, and I felt that I too had had a whole
group of nerves cut away, thereby acquiring a profound insensi-
tivity as a new characteristic. Nor was the loss apparent only in
the baby himself and me; if anything, it was still more directly
visible in my wife.

As the bus had plunged into the forest she had fallen silent,
drinking whisky steadily from a pocket flask. Her behavior, I
knew, would spread a ripple of scandal among the respectable
provincials riding the bus, but I had no desire to stop her. Before
going to sleep, however, she'd determined that she should be
sober to begin the new life in the village in the valley, and had
thrown the remainder of the whisky, flask and all, well back
among the trees. I'd hoped that the moment of intoxication then
leading her into sleep would be the last of its kind. Now, though,
feeling beside me the hot reality of her eyes, still bloodshot with
sleep, fixed rigidly on the peasant boy's head, I abandoned any
overoptimistic expectation that she would really start the new
life sober. My one wish was to prevent an acute revival, here
and now, of the dangerous emotional state associated with the
baby's tumor. But it was increasingly borne in on me that this
wish wasn't to be granted either. I keenly regretted the whisky
she'd thrown away.

The conductress advanced toward the rear of the bus with
her stomach thrust forward to preserve her balance. The young

peasant woman ignored her and scowled forbiddingly, gazing out of the window. The child made no response to the conductress either, but I could tell, having had him under constant observation, that he was getting steadily tenser and tenser. It looked as though they had come and sat in the seat by ours in order to avoid the conductress.

"Tickets," prompted the conductress. For a while the woman ignored the appeal, then suddenly broke into voluble speech. She attacked the conductress for demanding the prescribed fare for the whole run from the top of the hill down to the valley; she and the child had already walked two-thirds of the distance from the top; if the child hadn't complained of bellyache (at this point she poked at the child's shoulder as he clung to the wooden armrest), they could have walked all the way back. The conductress explained that the distance from the top down to the valley had recently been made the new minimum fare. It was a new policy of the bus company's necessitated by poor returns on this route—another sign, I told myself, of the decay of the road through the forest. The conductress's logic seemed temporarily to overwhelm the young countrywoman. But then there appeared on her ruddy plebeian face, hitherto so aflame with indignation, a reaction that struck me with mingled surprise and amusement. With a little giggle, she declared in a self-assured tone:

"Ain't got no money."

The boy was of course as pale and tense as ever. The conductress hesitated for a moment then, once more the helpless countrygirl, went to discuss the matter with the driver. It occurred to me that I might take advantage of the peasant woman's odd little giggle as a first step to releasing the tension in my wife. I looked round at her and smiled, but saw that her neck and the lower part of her face were covered with goose pimples, even though the eyes fixed on the boy's head gleamed with a feverish light. Seeing trouble in the offing, I hesitated, at a loss. Annoyance jumped about inside me with the aimless frenzy of a firecracker: why hadn't I stopped her from throwing away the whisky bottle? In desperation I took the plunge and made a choice.

"Let's get off," I said. "Taka will probably be at the bus stop to meet us, so we can ask the conductress to tell him to come and pick us up in the car."

My wife looked at me doubtfully and inclined her head slowly, a diver moving against water pressure in the depths of fear. I could sense her mind teetering between the fear within herself and fear of being deserted by the bus in the heart of the forest.

Realizing that I wanted somehow to persuade her before terror of the forest as such grew and pinned her to her seat in the bus, I had to admit that, of the two of us, it was I who was frantically trying to flee from the phantom of the baby evoked by the peasant boy's shaven head and sickly skin.

"What if the telegram hasn't arrived and Taka and the others aren't there to meet us?"

"Even if we have to walk we can get down to the valley by nightfall. The kid was going to walk, wasn't he?"

"Then I'd like to get off," she said with an air of liberation mingled with an indefinable lingering apprehension that made me feel both relief and pity.

I signaled to the conductress, who was talking busily to the driver, all the while keeping a self-consciously vigilant eye on the moneyless peasant woman and her son.

"My brother should be waiting for us at the bus stop in the valley," I said. "Would you give him our baggage and tell him to come to meet us in the car, please? We're going to walk from here." Under the stare of the conductress, in whose eyes a dull cloud of surprise had begun to form, I realized with consternation that I hadn't thought up any pretext for our action that would seem reasonable to an outsider.

"I'm suffering from motion sickness," said my wife, quickly sensing my predicament. But the conductress still looked dubious—or rather, went on chewing over what I'd just said, trying to understand.

"The bus doesn't go into the valley," she said. "The bridge was washed away in the flood."

"Flood? In winter?"

"It was washed away in the summer."

"Has it been left like that ever since?"

"The new bus stop is on this side of the bridge. The bus goes as far as that."

"Then my brother will be waiting there," I said. "The name's Nedokoro." But I wondered why they should have neglected until winter a bridge destroyed by summer floods.

"I know him, he came in a car," put in the countrywoman, who had been eagerly listening to our conversation. "If he's not at the stop, the boy can run up there. He knows the Nedokoros at Storehouse."

She obviously thought that "Storehouse" was the geographical name of the piece of high ground on which our house stood. I'd often found a similar misapprehension among the children I used to play with twenty years earlier. Anyway, I felt a sense of relief. If we'd had to go on walking through the forest until dark, the experience would almost certainly have implanted seeds of new trouble in my wife's mind. And if there were a mist at night, the pitch-black forest would inevitably have plunged her into a panic of some kind or other.

As the bus trundled away leaving us on the road, the faces of the peasant woman and conductress appeared side by side at the rear window, watching us. The boy's face was not to be seen; presumably he was still slumped pallidly over the armrest. We nodded to them, and the conductress waved happily in response, but the young peasant woman, still giggling to herself, clasped one forefinger in the palm of the other hand in a lewd gesture directed at us. I felt my own face flush with irritation and embarrassment, but to my wife the insult seemed to come as something of a relief. A great part of her mind was obsessed with the need for self-punishment, and the young mother in charge of the child with shaven head and lackluster skin, the child who sat as motionless as our baby, had satisfied a certain part of that need.

Hugging our own bodies through our overcoats in the damp, cold, heavily scented breeze that swept our flanks, we made our way through the rotting leaves covering the red clay of the forest road. Whenever the toes of our shoes kicked up the fallen leaves the bare earth beneath was revealed, a striking vermilion like the belly of a newt. Today, even the red earth seemed to hold a threat it never had in my childhood memories. It was to be expected, now that I'd become such a ratlike, vacillating, suspicious kind of creature, that the forest I had fled and was now seeking to rejoin should look on me with suspicion. So strong were the signs of surveillance that the passage of a group of birds screaming high above the trees was enough to make me feel the red earth rising up to clutch at my legs.

"I wonder why Takashi didn't tell us on the phone that the bridge had been washed away by the flood."

"He had quite enough to talk about even without that, didn't he?" said my wife, rallying to his defense. "It's hardly surprising it didn't occur to him to mention the bridge's state of repair when he had such an odd story to tell."

Takashi had set off for the valley two weeks earlier than us. He'd gone in the Citroen with his bodyguards and made a long car trip of it. All day long and all through the night he and Hoshi took turns at the wheel, driving swiftly and without a break apart from the one hour on the car ferry to Shikoku. They arrived at the village in the valley two days later. A long-distance telephone call made from the post office was our first news of a peculiar business that had made an immediate impression on him. It concerned a middle-aged farmer's wife called Jin who acted as caretaker of our house in return for permission to cultivate what little farmland was left to us. She'd come to us as a nursemaid when Takashi was born and had stayed with the family ever since. Even after her marriage, she still lived on in the house with her husband and children.

Parking the Citroen in the open space before the village office in the center of the valley, Takashi and his friends shouldered their belongings and were climbing up the steep, narrow, graveled road to our house when they were met by Jin's husband and children coming down all out of breath to meet them. Takashi and the others were taken aback by their skinniness, the unhealthy tinge of their skin, and in particular the large fishlike eyes of the children, whose expressions reminded them of refugee children from Central or South America. These same frail children, however, fell on their baggage, wrested it from them, and bore it off up the hill, whereupon Jin's melancholy-looking spouse tried to explain something to them in a brooding, angry-sounding voice. He was so overcome with shame, however, that all Takashi could gather was that he wanted to explain to them, before they actually met Jin, something extraordinary that had happened to her. Eventually, with every sign of reluctance, he produced from his pocket a cutting, folded in four, from a local newspaper and showed it to Takashi. The piece of newsprint, whose folds were frayed and grubby, bore a photograph so large that it must have badly disrupted the layout of the paper on the day it appeared.

Takashi got a shock when he saw it. The right half of the photograph meticulously took in the skinny members of Jin's family, tense as a wedding group in their light-colored summer clothes. The left half was taken up by Jin's enormous, bloated form. Swathed in a cotton print dress, she sat sideways, leaning on her left arm, looking like a pair of bellows. All, including Jin, stared at the camera dolefully, patiently, as though their ears were straining to hear some sound.

Strange Disease Afflicts Countrywoman
Insatiable Appetite—"Beyond Me" Says Spouse

It seems that this prefecture boasts the biggest woman in the country. "Japan's Fattest Woman" is Mrs. Jin Kanaki, who lives in Okubo village. A forty-five-year-old mother of four children, she is of average height—five feet—but her weight is an astounding 291 pounds. Her bust measures 47 inches, her hips the same, and her arms are 16 inches round. She hasn't always been so fat; six years ago, at 95 pounds, she was if anything on the skinny side. Her "tragedy" began without warning one day six years ago when she had spasms in her arms and legs and a failure of the blood supply to the brain, with a resulting fainting fit. She recovered consciousness several hours later and has been prey ever since to a pathological, uncontrollable appetite for food. She could no longer keep going, she found, unless she was forever feeding herself something. The slightest delay with a meal would bring shivering, crying fits, and finally stupor.

Nowadays she has meals hourly. She begins the morning by downing a whole pan of boiled vegetables, sweet potatoes, and rice mixed with barley. Next, buckwheat dough or instant noodles every hour until noon. At noon, lunch more or less like breakfast, and buckwheat dough or noodles again every hour until supper. For supper, another panful of boiled vegetables, dried radish and devil's tongue, with sweet potatoes and barley-rice. This is the daily menu. Thanks to this abnormal appetite, her weight has tripled in six years and she is still getting fatter.

Jin's husband is the hardest hit. To get enough food to keep her stomach satisfied isn't child's play. The great quantities of instant noodles are a particular burden financially. Jin herself earns a little by taking in sewing, but her earnings are a drop in the bucket compared to the awesome demands of her stomach. The village authorities, moved by the family's plight, are helping with food costs, but ends still won't meet.

"Somehow I can't get on with my sewing," Jin says. "I spend most of the day just sitting. I can't travel by bus; we have to have a truck whenever I go to the Red Cross hospital. I don't sleep properly at night and have a lot of dreams."

Takashi just stared, so Jin's husband explained that to get more money in the circumstances they'd rented the main building to a teacher from the primary school, but they'd persuaded him to sleep in the teacher's night room at the school while Takashi and his friends were there. He hoped they would understand. This, in fact, was what had been bothering him most of all.

"Jin herself was sitting in a dark corner of the wooden-floored space at the entrance of the outbuilding," Takashi said. "She didn't seem particularly weighed down by her misfortune. She just kept repeating 'It's wretched to have got so fat.' If you're going to bring a present when you come, a large case of instant noodles would be the best thing."

My wife mentioned it when she visited her parents before we left, and my father-in-law, who to an unusual degree for his age has retained the flexibility of mind needed to sympathize with such tragicomic mishaps, had half a dozen large cases of instant noodles, just as Takashi had suggested, delivered to us by a firm dealing in them. We sent the provisions for "Japan's Fattest Woman" on ahead of us.

The road along which we were walking, and the forest that pressed in on it from either side, stretched ahead indefinitely and monotonously. With the poor sense of perspective of the one-eyed, I had a feeling that we were marking time on a fixed spot.

"The sky looks sort of red to me," said my wife. "Do you think it's my eyes? It couldn't be that things have a reddish look because my eyes are bloodshot, could it, Mitsu?"

I looked up. The deepening shadow over the great trees created an illusion of blinds being drawn from both sides, but the reddish tinge spreading over the narrow gray strip between them was no illusion.

"It's the sunset. And your eyes aren't red anymore, either."

"It's from always being in the city, Mitsu—" she said, "it doesn't occur to one that that kind of color might only be the sunset. The gray tinged with red is just like a color photo of the brain in some medical dictionary, isn't it?"

She was still circling aimlessly around the same set of images associated with our painful memory: from the shaven head of the boy on the bus, to our child's head, and so to the damaged matter within the skull. All signs of intoxication had gone from her eyes; the blood had withdrawn, leaving two dark gray pits. The skin of her face was completely covered with tiny flakes as closely arrayed as the leaves of the forest cedars. An idea hovered about my mind, its approach heralded by a sour taste of fear in my mouth.

A jeep appeared hurtling toward us like an enraged beast, sending dead leaves and earth flying as it came. Its arrival restored my sense of perspective and liberated me from the feeling that time was standing still.

"It's Taka!"

"What's happened to the Citroen, then?" I quibbled, reacting against the too obvious pleasure in her voice even as I recognized in the headlong rush of the jeep the authentic mark of Takashi, self-made man of violence.

"Mitsu, it *is* Taka," she insisted confidently.

Amidst a flurry of red earth the jeep thrust its hood into a clump of withered grass beside the road, grazing a tree with its fender, came to a halt, shot backward at the same furious speed, then abruptly ceased switching directions and came to rest. My wife had recoiled sharply from the arm I'd put out to protect her from the onrushing jeep, leaving the outstretched arm to subside unwanted. I hoped it hadn't caught Takashi's eye as he twisted round in the driver's seat and stuck his head out of the jeep.

"Hi there, Natsu! Hi, Mitsu!" he hailed us cheerfully. Dressed in an oilskin with a hood hanging down over the shoulders, he looked like a fireman.

"Thanks for coming, Taka." My wife smiled at him, finally recovering the life she'd lacked ever since awakening in the bus.

"Seems the bridge is down," I said.

"Right. We managed to get the Citroen over to the valley somehow, but it was too much to drag it back here again just to come and meet you two. So I got the forest ranger to lend me his vehicle. He remembered me, you know, and threw in this oilskin with the jeep." He spoke with naive pride. "Mitsu—you get in the back. Natsu had better come in front."

"Thank you, Taka."

"Hoshi's taking the baggage," said Takashi. "If he just carries it on his back over the river where the bridge was, we can use the Citroen on the other side." He started the jeep up again with a caution utterly different from his driving before meeting up with us.

"How about Jin?" I asked.

"It was a shock when I first saw her. Even now she looks absolutely grotesque to me at times, but her face seems younger and pleasanter now that it's fat. You might even call her attractive—for a valley woman of over forty, that is." He laughed. "And in fact, you know, she got pregnant with the youngest kid after she started to get fat, so her husband must find her attractive sexually, even though she weighs about three hundred pounds!"

"Do they seem hard up?"

"Not as much as you might suppose from that newspaper article. I'm sure the reporter, like me, was fooled by that dreadfully gloomy face of her husband's. They get by all right because the valley folk bring them all kinds of things to eat. I couldn't figure out, you know, why such a miserly crowd should carry on doing it for six years. So when I met the priest at the temple, the one who was at school with S, I asked him about it. According to him, it's to do with the fact that the people in the valley are finding it hard to improve their living standards. Just at the right moment, they happened to find this strange creature among them who'd swollen to almost three hundred pounds. So they made her a kind of object of worship: by falling victim to this mysterious and hopeless malady Jin might be acting as the sacrificial lamb who would take upon herself the woes of all the other valley folk. That was the priest's interpretation, at any rate. Kind of metaphysical, isn't he? I expect you get like that after you've been looking after all the souls in the valley for a while. You should meet him, Mitsu—he has the best mind here."

Takashi's speech made a vivid impression on me. The idea of a lamb expiating the sins of the whole valley had something in it that stimulated a memory reaching down to the roots of my being.

"Remember the madman called Gii, Mitsu?" Takashi went on as I sat silent, delving into my memories.

"Gii the hermit, who used to live in the forest?"

"That's right. The crazy man who comes down to the valley when it gets dark."

"I remember. His real name was Giichiro. I knew him well. Some of the valley children only knew him as a legend. Some even thought he was a kind of goblin who slept all day in the forest and roamed the valley only by darkness. But our house," I explained to my wife, who couldn't share in our conversation, "stands between the valley and the forest, so we sometimes caught sight of him at dusk, making his way down the graveled road to the valley. He would scuttle down the hill with uncanny agility, like a wild dog. We would watch him go, and by the time he was quite out of sight the whole valley would be covered in darkness. He was extraordinarily accurate in the way he trod the narrow interval between day and night. As I remember him, he always had his head bent mournfully forward and was hurrying away into the shadows."

"I met him, you know," said Takashi, ignoring my admiring reminiscences. "I was wondering if we could get hold of something to eat late at night, and took the car out for a spin round the valley. We'd forgotten the shopping, you see. But the supermarket was shut and none of the other shops was open— naturally, since they're more or less bankrupt at any rate. The one thing I did do was meet Gii."

"Gii the hermit still alive? Well, that's news! He must be pretty decrepit, though. I would never have thought a madman who'd been in the forest so many years could live so long."

"He doesn't give any particular impression of being old. I couldn't see well in the dark, but he seemed to be in his fifties—early fifties at that. He's got extraordinarily small ears. There's nothing else about him that looks mad, but those ears somehow betray the whole accumulated effect of years of insanity. Our car interested him and he materialized suddenly out of the darkness. When Momoko said hello, he went all serious and introduced himself as 'Gii the hermit.' When I told him I was one of the Nedokoro boys, he remembered me, said he'd once talked to me. The pity is, I don't remember a thing about it."

"It was me he meant. When S came back from the army, Gii came to the house and stayed to talk with S and me. He wanted to know if the war was really over or not. It was to avoid being caught by the army that he ran off into the forest in the first place—he was the only draft dodger in the village. S told him there was no need to go on hiding, but he never managed to make it back to life in the village. In a town he would probably have been a hero for a while after the war. But it's just not possible here for a madman who's been off living in the forest to rejoin the valley community. Even in wartime, of course, everybody admitted that as a madman he had a right to live, so after the war he could carry on as long as he stayed put." A familiar, long-forgotten mood came welling up inside me, sapping the strength from my limbs.

"So Gii the hermit's still alive, is he? . . ." I said. "He must have been through some pretty hard times."

"And he's by no means decrepit," Takashi added. "The superman of the forest!" He laughed. "We left Gii, took a run round the valley, and were on our way back when we saw him go past in the headlights, bounding along like an earnest rabbit. He was fantastically agile. It looked at first as though he was skipping along in a desperate effort to get away from the lights, but if you ask me he wanted to show us how hale and hearty he is. He's really quite an amiable nut!"

When I was a child, we always had a resident madman somewhere in the valley. Although the place had its full quota of nervous breakdowns or village idiots, there was never more than one person recognized by everybody as a genuine nut. There couldn't be two legitimate madmen at the same time, nor did the one madman ever leave the valley; it was as though the valley community had a fixed complement of one lunatic, a component of society all the more indispensable for being out of the ordinary. On a number of occasions, I seem to remember, I was aware of a change in these madmen who, like kings, came one at a time. But from some time toward the end of the war, the role of the indispensable solitary had been taken over by Gii.

Once, military police had come from the town to investigate the rumors about him. The village veterans' association conducted a search in the hills, but I doubt if any of them were serious about it; quite apart from the fallen trees and creeping plants that block the way in the heart of the forest, they would eventually have come to government forest land, which was out of bounds. So Gii quite naturally was never caught. The MPs waited in a booth set up in the space before the village office (which lay just down the hill from our house, so that I watched the whole affair seated on the edge of the long stone wall), and all day long Gii's mother, almost literally crawling on her knees, wept and wailed before the red and white striped curtains of the booth. The next day, though, after the police had left the valley, she promptly became an ordinary village woman again and went about her work with a smile on her face.

Gii the hermit was what they called in the village an "educated man": he'd been to night school and had worked as a substitute teacher. On one occasion, a group of drunken louts just out of the army lay in wait for him as he roamed the valley late at night in search of food, and set up a hue and cry. A few mornings later they found that Gii the hermit had written a poem on a notice board set outside the village office for use in connection with the village democratization campaign. S insisted it was a poem by Kenji Miyazawa, though I have yet to come across it in his works: *Fine sport, I said, for you who join / In throwing stones—for me, it's death. / You saw how grim my mouth was then, / How pale and strange my look?*

As I read the poem among the cheerful crowd in front of the notice board, I wondered who it could be, if it was Gii who said it was death for him, that was watching the face "so pale and strange." I asked S, but instead of giving me an answer he compressed his lips, scowled with a pale and strange face, and chased me away, shaking his fist.

"I asked Gii," said Takashi, "if living a hermit's life in the forest wasn't awkward now that man is making such relentless advances there. But he denied it quite strongly. On the contrary, he said, the forest was steadily extending its power. He insisted that before long the village lying in the valley would be taken over by the forest. In actual fact, he said, the forest had got immensely stronger during the past few years and was beginning to engulf the valley. He claimed that one proof of this was the way the river, whose source is in the forest, had washed away the bridge for the first time in fifty years. If he's in fact mad, I suppose one could see that kind of talk as a sign of his abnormality."

"I don't find it abnormal, Taka," put in my wife, who had been silent until then. "Ever since that ride on the bus I've had a

lingering feeling that the power of this forest is growing. I found
it so oppressive I thought I was going to faint. If I'd been Gii the
hermit, I would have avoided taking refuge in such a terrifying
place and been only too glad to go into the army."

"You might come to feel the same way, Natsu," said
Takashi. "One might think that someone so sensitive to fear
of the forest was the exact opposite of the type who would
go mad and take refuge in it. But as I see it, psychologically
speaking, the two are one and the same type."

His words gave me a clue as to what could have happened
if he hadn't arrived in the jeep and the buds of fear that had
been visible on my wife's goose-fleshed, terrified face had been
allowed to flower. Starting to visualize the scene as she fled
insane into the forest, I hastily severed the chain of association. On the threshold of my thoughts had been something a
well-known folklorist had once written: "a woman, naked but
for a rag about her loins, her hair flaming, her eyes blue and
gleaming . . . An extremely important clue here may be the fact
that countrywomen who rushed off into the hills were often
suffering from postnatal insanity."

"Do you think they sell whisky at the village liquor store,
Taka?" I asked, driven by the instinct of self-preservation.

"Mitsu's trying to spoil my resolution to stay sober, Taka."

"No, I'm not. I want a drink myself. *You* can join Taka's
sober bodyguard."

"The only thing worrying me at the moment," she said,
"is whether I can sleep without a drink. It's not as if I've been
drinking every night lately just for the sake of getting drunk.
What about Hoshi—didn't he show signs of insomnia after he
gave it up?"

"It's not certain, you know, that he ever was such a great drinker," said Takashi. "All that talk of his may mean that he's never touched a drop in his life. He's at the age when one wants to boast of one's heroic past even if there's nothing yet to back it up. There's no telling how much of it may be lies. You should hear him lecturing Momoko about sex—it would make you laugh. He's the type who likes to talk big, like an expert, even though he's had absolutely no sexual experience himself." He laughed.

"Well then, I'll have to practice sobriety alone and unaided," said my wife with unconcealed disappointment. Her remark had too frankly pitiful a ring to invite any further objection.

The sky, trapped between the great trees whose upper branches the wind had trained to lean in the same direction, was steadily developing a blackish red tinge that reminded me of scorched flesh. Wisps of mist moved low over the trail. A miasma welling up from the depths of the undergrowth hemming in the road, it crept along slowly at the level of the jeep's wheels. We would have to get out of the forest before it rose to eye level. Takashi accelerated cautiously. Eventually the jeep left the trees and emerged, unexpectedly and with a sudden widening of the field of vision, onto a small plateau. We parked the jeep and gazed out over the spindle-shaped hollow encircled by dense forest that stretched as far as the eye could see in uniform, deep brown shadow beneath a somber red sky. The trail along which we had driven the jeep made a right-angled turn at the plateau, then descended in a straight line following the slope of the forest to the neck of the valley; here it encountered the junction between the graveled road that crossed the bridge and plunged into the valley, and the asphalt road that followed the river rising in the hollow as it rounded the foot of the plateau and flowed on down to the coast. Seen from our vantage point, the valley road seemed to climb up the hollow only to disappear abruptly, like a river running onto sand, on the far edge where the forest began. From the plateau, the cluster of human dwellings and the fields and paddies surrounding them looked small enough to be clutched in one hand, such was the power of the dense, deep forest to distort the perception of size. Our hollow, as the crazy hermit had rightly observed, was a feeble presence pitting itself against the eroding power of the forest. It was more natural, in fact, to see the spindle-shaped hollow not as a presence in its own right but as an absence of the massed trees that were elsewhere. As one grew used to the idea that the surrounding forest was the only unequivocal reality, one could almost see a vast lid of oblivion closing in on the hollow.

Mist was rising from the river at the bottom of the valley, cleaving the center of the hollow, and the village by now lay in its depths. Our family home stood on a small hill, but all about it was blurred and vague, so that the white of the long stone wall was all that the eye could detect. I wanted to point out to my wife where our house lay, but the dull ache in my eye was too bad to let me go on gazing at the spot for long.

"I think I'll see if I can find a bottle of whisky, Mitsu," she said in a timid, conciliating tone.

Taka looked round at us with profound interest.

"Why don't you try some water instead?" I urged her. "There's a spring here that the valley folk say gives the best water in the whole forest. That's if it hasn't dried up."

It hadn't dried up. At the foot of the slope on the forest side of the road, an unexpected outflow of water formed a pool about as big as the circle of a man's arms. The water—too copious, almost, to have sprung from such small beginnings—made a channel that ran down to the valley. Beside the pool stood a number of outdoor hearths, some new, some old, the clay and stones charred black and hideous inside. In my childhood, my friends and I had built just such a hearth by the spring, and cooked rice and made soup there. In a twice-yearly ritual, each of us chose the group he would camp out with, thereby determining the division of forces among the children of the valley. The outing lasted only two days each spring and autumn, but the influence of the groups thus formed by the children remained valid throughout the year. Nothing was so humiliating as to be expelled from the group one had joined.

As I bent down over the spring to drink from it directly, I had a sudden sense of certainty: certainty that everything—the small round pebbles, grayish blue and vermilion and white, lying at the bottom of water whose brightness seemed still to harbor the midday light; the fine sand that swirled upward, clouding it ever so slightly; and the faint shiver that ran over the surface of the water—was just as I'd seen it twenty years before; a certainty, born of longing yet to myself, at least, utterly convincing, that the water now welling up so ceaselessly was exactly the same water that had welled up and flowed away in those days. And the same certainty developed directly into a feeling that the "I" bending down there now was not the child who had once bent his bare knees there, that here was no continuity, no consistency between the two "I's," that the "I" now bending down there was a remote stranger. The present "I" had lost all true identity. Nothing, either within me or without, offered any hope of recovery.

I could hear the transparent ripples on the pool tinkling, accusing me of being no better than a rat. I shut my eyes and sucked up the cold water. My gums shrank, leaving a taste of blood on my tongue. As I stood up, my wife bent down in obedient imitation, as though I was an authority on how to drink from the spring. In fact, I was as complete a stranger to the spring by now as she, who had just come through the forest for the first time. I shuddered. The bitter cold penetrated my consciousness again. Shivering, my wife stood up too and tried to smile to show that the water had tasted good; but her teeth as her purple lips shrank back merely seemed to be bared in anger. Shoulder to shoulder, silent and shuddering with cold, we returned to the jeep. Takashi averted his eyes as though he'd seen something too pitiful to look on.

We went down into the valley through a mist that grew steadily thicker and deeper. In the hush as we carefully let the jeep coast downhill, the only noises about us were the sound of the tires sending small stones flying, the sound of the hood whistling in the wind, and the faint hiss of leaves falling in the open woods—of tall oak and beech with the merest sprinkling of red pine—which covered the ground sloping sharply down from the track to the paved road in the valley. Driven by a force that swept them horizontally, the leaves scattering from the uppermost branches seemed not so much to fall as to drift slowly sideways, setting up the constant tiny rustling as they went.

"Can you whistle, Natsu?" Takashi asked quite seriously.

"Yes, why?" she replied warily.

"If you whistle here after dark the valley folk get mad, really mad. Do you remember that old valley taboo, Mitsu?"

he asked with a subdued air not out of harmony with my own present mood.

"Yes, I remember. They believe that if you whistle after dark a supernatural creature will come out of the forest. Grandmother used to tell us the Chosokabe would come."

"Did she? Now that I'm here in the valley I realize I don't really remember anything much. Even when I seem to remember something, I can't be sure of its accuracy. In America I often heard the word 'uprooted,' but now that I've come back to the valley in an attempt to make sure of my own roots, I find they've all been pulled up. I've begun to feel uprooted myself. So now I've got to put down new roots here, and to do so I naturally feel some action is necessary. What that action is I don't know; I just have an increasingly strong premonition that action will be necessary. . . . Anyway, to come back to the place where you were born doesn't mean you're going to find your roots there, conveniently buried in the right place. You may think I'm being sentimental, Mitsu, but the thatched hut of the old days has gone." He spoke with an air of hopeless fatigue that ill suited his age. "I didn't even remember Jin really clearly. Even if she hadn't got so fat, I'm sure I wouldn't have been able to recognize the Jin I knew. When she began to cry because she detected in me some signs of the kid she once looked after, I was actually afraid in case this great stranger of a woman might put out her lumpy arms and try to hug me. I only hope my nasty little fear wasn't apparent to Jin herself."

Down in the valley it was already dark. From the other side of the temporary bridge twisting its way over the concrete supports, the teen-agers signaled to us with a cheerful tooting of the Citroen's horn, but it was impossible to make out the car in the darkness. Takashi, who had been to the forest ranger's lodge to return the jeep and the oilskin, was dressed in the hunting-type outfit he'd worn on his return from America, but looked pinched and small, as if he'd suddenly shrunk. I tried in vain to picture the same Takashi playing a repentant student activist in front of an American audience. . . . And yet, I reflected, the black forest seen from down in the valley was more overwhelming than any audience, and it was I, not my brother, who had to put up with its jeers when it called, "You're just a rat!"

Tense as I helped my wife over the dangerous temporary bridge, I felt the buds of pleasure at returning to the valley obstinately shriveled up inside me. The breeze blowing up off the dark waters directly beneath us stabbed at my eyes with its icy thorns, threatening to blind even the good one. From behind and below, the sudden cackle of some unidentifiable bird came wafting up to us.

"Chickens," Takashi said. "The village young men's association has a chicken farm where the Korean settlement used to be."

About a hundred yards from the bridge, down the paved road that went to the sea, lay a huddle of houses that had once sheltered Koreans doing forced labor as lumbermen in the forest. We'd just reached the center of the bridge, and the clucking of the chickens farther downstream reached our ears without any intervening obstacle.

"Do chickens normally cluck at this time of night?"

"People say they're nearly dead of starvation, several thousand of them. They're probably complaining of hunger."

My wife was shivering ceaselessly in my encircling arm.

"The young men of the valley can't do anything worthwhile without a leader," said Takashi with unconcealed disgust. "They're helpless until someone like great-grandfather's younger brother comes along. They're incapable of getting themselves out of a fix by their own efforts. When I got back to the valley, Mitsu, that's the first thing I realized about the strangers who have been living here all the time."

Dreams within Dreams

On the morning of our first day in the valley we ate breakfast around the open fireplace in the board-floored room next to the spacious earthen-floored kitchen of the main building, which had a stove and a well covered with heavy planks. Unnoticed at first, Jin's four children had turned up in the murky recesses of the kitchen and stood in a row gazing at us with eyes that looked unnaturally large in the inverted triangles of their thin faces. When my wife invited them to eat with us they gave a concerted groan which imperceptibly changed to explicit refusal. Only then did the oldest boy announce that Jin wanted to talk to me.

I'd already met Jin the evening before. As Takashi had said, she was enormous yet, certain moments apart, in no way ugly. Her doleful eyes, blurred in outline and brimming with whitish tears, were like fish-eye lenses in the great, pallid moon of her face. The shining of her eyes was the only trace of the Jin I'd once known. She gave off an animal odor, so that before long my wife felt faint and slumped forward, and we were obliged to

retire to the main building. Hoshio and Momoko, who wanted
to observe Jin at leisure, had remained. Pink-faced, holding
their noses, pinching each other's sides to prevent themselves
from bursting into laughter, they let their eyes run curiously over
the whole of Jin's body in a way that seemed to have aroused
her children's hostility. Probably it was the presence of the two
ill-mannered teen-agers sitting there smirking silently to themselves that had made the four skinny children refuse my wife's
invitation that morning. When the meal was over, Takashi took
my wife and the teen-agers to see the interior of the storehouse,
while I went with the children to the outbuilding where Jin and
her family lived.

"Hello, Jin, did you sleep well?"

I greeted her standing in the entrance. Her large, round,
mournful face loomed at me out of the shadows just as it had
done the previous night.

Surrounded on all sides by dirty pots and pans, like a pot-
ter with his work ranged about him, Jin lay on her back looking
uncomfortably up into the air, her chin resting on the pouch of
fat at her neck. She remained ostentatiously silent. In the morning light that passed over my shoulder and fell on her capacious
lap, I could tell that she was sitting sideways on a homemade
legless chair like a horse's saddle turned upside down. The
evening before, when I'd taken it for a part of Jin's fat body,
she'd looked like a conical stone mortar. Her husband, kneeling beside the chair as though about to get to his feet, stayed
poised there, still and silent. Last night too he'd waited in silent
attendance, his haggard face pensive, ready to spring up with
unnecessary alacrity and feed Jin grayish pellets of buckwheat
dough whenever a sluggish gesture showed she wanted to eat.

It may have been that Jin's appetite gave her no respite even in the bare five minutes that we were with her, but to me it looked more like a show put on for our benefit as practical evidence of the dire straits in which she found herself.

Eventually, Jin laboriously expelled a large volume of air from her lungs and said, gazing at me resentfully:

"No, I didn't sleep well! Nothing but wretched dreams, dreams of being left without a house!" I realized at once why Jin had wanted to meet me and why her husband was kneeling next to her, staring dolefully at my face.

"It's only the storehouse that we're taking down and shifting to Tokyo," I said. "There's no special reason to knock down the main house and outbuilding."

"You're selling the land, aren't you?" Jin pressed.

"I'll leave the land, main house, and outbuilding as they are until the question of where you're to live is settled."

Jin and her husband gave no special sign of relief, but the four children, who had come round to stand behind their parents and keep an eye on me, told me by the concerted smile they gave that the fears of Jin's family had been allayed for the time being at least. I felt gratified.

"What will you do about the family grave, Mitsusaburo?"

"We'll have to leave it as it is, I imagine."

"I suppose you know that S's ashes are at the temple?" said Jin. But this much conversation had already exhausted her; dark shadows that somehow inevitably inspired disgust had gathered round her eyes, and her voice rattled as though countless air holes had formed in her throat. There was no denying that at such times Jin was grotesque in a way that went beyond normal human ugliness. I averted my eyes, reflecting with a sense of horror that in the end Jin would probably die of a heart attack. She'd already told Takashi, in fact, about her premonitions of death and how she'd been worrying whether her bloated body would fit into the furnace at the crematorium.

"Jin's so fat she can hardly do any work," Takashi had said sympathetically. "Yet still she's obliged to eat enormous amounts every day and get fatter and fatter. She feels her whole life is quite meaningless. It's something of a revelation to hear a horribly fat woman of forty-five say that her days spent solely in eating are pointless. It's not just a passing mood of hers, either—she's quite convinced, from every point of view, that her existence is useless. And still she has to go on eating those stupid mountains of food from morning to night. Now, there's someone with *real* grounds for pessimism."

"I'll get S's ashes from the temple," I promised Jin as I went out of the kitchen. "I'll go and ask for them today—I want to see the picture of hell they have at the temple while I'm at it."

"If S was alive, he would never have sold the storehouse," she muttered at my departing back in a hoarse, reproachful voice. "But then, what can you expect with Mitsusaburo as head of the family?"

I ignored her and went to look for the others in the storehouse, which stood at the rear of the courtyard enclosed by the main house and the outbuilding. The doors were open—not just the thick outer doors with fire-resistant plaster set into them, but the inner doors of board and wire netting as well. The two downstairs rooms were full of afternoon light that threw the black of the zelkova timbers and the white of the walls that enclosed them into sharp contrast. I stepped up inside and examined the numerous sword marks that scarred the woodwork. They still exuded the same harsh message that had intimidated me in my childhood. The fan painting that hung in the alcove in the room beyond bore a Roman alphabet, crudely written in Chinese ink and barely distinguishable by now against paper browned with age. Twenty years before, when S had first taught me how to read it, the signature "John Manj" in the bottom right-hand corner had already been hard to make out. Great-grandfather had met the castaway on his return from America when he slipped out of the forest and made his way to Nakanohama in Kochi. According to S, the inscription was one great-grandfather had got Manjiro to write for him on that occasion.

A faint sound like someone marking time came from upstairs. I set off up the narrow staircase and immediately banged my right temple on the hard end of a projecting beam. I groaned with pain, and red-hot particles flew about inside the spherical darkness of my sightless eye like the tracks of fission fragments in a cloud chamber. It recalled too the sense of taboo that had always kept me out of the storehouse.

For a moment I stopped, stunned, then put up a hand to wipe my cheek; it came away with blood on it as well as tears. I was pressing a handkerchief to my head when Takashi's face peered down at me from the second floor.

"When your wife's alone with another man, do you always warn them by knocking on the wall and waiting, Mitsu?" he said teasingly. "You'd be the ideal husband for adulterers!"

"Aren't your bodyguards here, then?"

"They're seeing to the Citroen. Teen-agers in the 1960s aren't exactly interested in roof construction in traditional wooden buildings. I told them this was the only storehouse of its kind in the whole forest area, but they couldn't have cared less." His remark revealed the naive pride he took in showing off the architecture to his sister-in-law, who stood in the background.

I went upstairs and found my wife gazing up at the great beams of zelkova wood that supported the framework of the roof—too intent on them, in fact, to notice the blood flowing from the wound on my temple. Since I've always been prey to an irrational sense of shame whenever I bang my head against something, I was grateful. Eventually, she heaved an admiring sigh and turned round.

"What wonderful great timbers! They look as if they'd last another hundred years."

I noticed that both their faces were flushed. It made me feel that the faintest echo of the word "adulterer" used by Takashi was still drifting about somewhere up in the rafters of the storehouse. But the feeling, I told myself, was unfounded. My wife was so aware of what had happened to the baby that, ever since, she'd promptly nipped in the bud any hint of sex. For both of us, to touch on sexual matters meant imposing on ourselves a shared sense of disgust and misery which neither was prepared to face. So any suggestion of it was immediately dropped.

"With a limitless supply of zelkova like this in the forest, you could build a storehouse for almost nothing," she said.

"Don't you believe it!" I replied in as casual a voice as I could muster, unwilling to let her know how determinedly I was suppressing the pain from the gash on my head. "It seems that building this one put quite a strain on great-grandfather. In fact, I'd say the construction was pretty unusual. Even if there was plenty of timber, remember it was built at a time when the village's resources were utterly exhausted. I'm quite sure everyone found it very special. There was a farmers' rising, in fact, in the winter of the very year it was built."

"That's certainly strange."

"I imagine it was precisely because he foresaw the possibility of a rising that great-grandfather felt it necessary to build a fireproof building."

"Great-grandfather makes me sick, Mitsu," said Takashi. "He was so conservative, so careful, so farsighted. I'm sure his younger brother felt the same about him as I do. Otherwise he wouldn't have gone against his brother and become a leader of the farmers. He was one of those who resisted, who had an eye on the trends of the times."

"Don't you think great-grandfather had his eye on the trends just as much as his brother? He went all the way to Kochi, didn't he, just to pick up the latest knowledge from the West?"

"Surely it was the brother who went to Kochi?" Takashi objected. That was what he wanted to believe, so he was almost consciously ignoring the fact that it was wrong.

"No. It was great-grandfather who went to Kochi first, not his brother," I said, taking a malicious pleasure in sabotaging his mistaken memory. "It's just that some people say that later, after the rising, his brother fled to Kochi and never came back. If it's true that one of the two brothers left the forest, met John Manjiro, and brought back the new knowledge, then it can be proved that it was great-grandfather. John Manjiro was only in Kochi for a year after returning to Japan, from 1852 to 1853. At the time of the trouble in 1860, great-grandfather's brother was eighteen or nineteen, so if he went to Kochi in 1852 or 1853 it means he left the forest around the age of ten or so. It's not possible."

"But," said Takashi, shaken but persistent, "it was the younger brother who cleared a space deep in the forest and trained a batch of hotheaded farmers' sons for the rising. The training methods must have been based on the knowledge of things Western that he brought back from Kochi. It isn't likely, is it, that great-grandfather, who sided with those who suppressed the rebellion, would have taught his brother the necessary guerilla tactics? Or do you think the two opposing sides conspired to start the trouble?"

"Perhaps," I said with a conscious show of detachment, though I could hear my own voice sharpen with irritation. Ever since we were children I'd had to fight against my brother's tendency to attribute scenes of heroic resistance to great-grandfather's younger brother.

"Why, Mitsu—you're bleeding," my wife exclaimed, her eyes on my temple. "How can you get so wrapped up in these old legends when you're hurt and bleeding?"

"There's something to be learned even from legends," Takashi said irritably. It was his first open display of bad temper toward her.

She took the handkerchief still clasped in the hand hanging at my side, wiped my temple, and wetting her finger with saliva transferred it to the wound. My brother stared as though watching some obscure meeting of the flesh. Then the three of us went down the stairs in silence, keeping each other at a distance as if to avoid bodily contact. The storehouse wasn't at all dusty, yet after some time spent inside it my nostrils felt dry and clogged, as though a film of dust were clinging to them inside.

Late that afternoon Takashi, my wife, and I, together with the teen-age couple, went to the temple to retrieve S's ashes.

Jin's sons had run on ahead to let them know, so they could get out the picture of hell that great-grandfather had presented to the temple and display it just as they did on the Buddha's Birthday. When we reached the Citroen parked in the open space in front of the village office, the local children amused themselves by poking fun at the car's age and making snide remarks about the broad strip of tape over my right ear. We all ignored them except my wife, who with the good temper that went with a period of "recovery"—she hadn't drunk anything since the previous night—seemed rather to enjoy it all, even the insults that the children hurled after the Citroen as it started off.

As we drove into the temple grounds the priest, who had been at school with S, was standing in the garden talking to a young man. His appearance, I noticed, was no different from what I remembered. A close-cropped, gleaming head of prematurely white hair crowned a good-natured, smiling face as smooth and antiseptic as an egg. He'd married a teacher from the primary school, but she'd run off to the town with a former colleague, not before having stirred up a scandal so open that everybody in the valley had known about it. He managed to maintain a smile like a sickly child's throughout the whole episode, a fact that would have particularly impressed anyone who knows the cruel effect of such a misfortune on someone living in a valley community. Either way, he weathered the crisis without once losing that mild smile.

The grotesque features of the young man talking to him were in complete contrast to the priest's. Most faces in our valley can be classified into one or the other of two types, but the face now watching us warily as we alighted from the Citroen was in a class of its own.

"He's the leading figure in the group of young men who're keeping the chickens," Takashi explained to my wife and me. Getting out of the Citroen, he walked up to the youth and started discussing something with him in a low voice; the young man, it seemed, had been waiting to meet him at the temple. The rest of us were obliged to stay in the background, exchanging vague smiles with each other, during this exclusive dialogue. The young man had an enormous round head, the broad, helmetlike curve of his forehead giving the whole head the appearance of being a continuation of the face. The cheekbones projecting outward on each side and the blunt, square chin reminded one of nothing so much as a sea urchin in human guise. His eyes and lips, moreover, were set close about his nose in a way that suggested the face had been dragged outward by some powerful tractive force. Not only his face but the flaunted arrogance of manner awakened something in me that was not a memory, perhaps, but a premonition of disaster. Admittedly, my increasing tendency to shut myself up emotionally was making me show much the same reaction to anything unfamiliar and strongly characterized. . . .

Takashi brought the young man over to the Citroen, talking all the while in the same low voice. The two teen-agers still lurked inside the car, their favorite lair. Takashi put the young man in the back seat, gave an order to Hoshio at the wheel, and without further ado the Citroen drove off in the direction of the entrance to the valley.

"The van they use for carrying eggs has broken down, so he came to ask Hoshi to repair the engine," Takashi explained with naive pride in the fact that all contact with the young men's group took place through himself. It obviously satisfied his childlike sense of competition, which had been hurt in the argument about great-grandfather's journey to Kochi. "Weren't the chickens supposed to be starving to death?" I asked.

"That's the trouble—the young people have got their priorities all wrong," the priest replied for Takashi, with a shy smile as though, as an inhabitant of the valley, he was ashamed of himself as well as the young men. "Sales of eggs are going so badly they can't find the money to buy feed, and they ought to be working out some basic policy to deal with the situation, but all they can think about is a van for transporting the eggs. Of course, if the van went out of action too, then everything really would be over."

We stepped up into the main hall of the temple and inspected the painting of hell. For me its rivers and forests of fire recalled the flaming red I'd seen on the backs of the dogwood leaves as they caught the sun that cloudy dawn after my hundred minutes in the pit. In particular, the dark blotches splashing the scarlet waves of the river of flames linked up directly with my memory of the spots that had begun to stain the dogwood leaves now that autumn had passed its peak. I was immediately absorbed in the hell picture. The color of the river of fire and the soft lines of the waves, so painstakingly drawn, brought me a strange peace of mind. Peace in abundance poured from the river of flames into my inner being. Among the flames, the multitude of the dead cried out with arms lifted to the sky and hair on end as though fanned by some fierce wind. Some of them were invisible save for skinny, angular buttocks and legs sticking up into the air. Yet even their varied expressions of suffering contained something that brought me peace; for despite their manifest pain, the bodies that expressed this pain gave the impression of participating in some solemn sport. They seemed to be at home with suffering. The male ghosts, who stood on one bank with penises bleakly exposed as flaming rocks struck them on the head, belly, and buttocks, gave the same impression. The female ghosts being driven toward the forest of flames by demons brandishing iron clubs seemed almost intent on preserving the comfortably familiar chains—the bonds of tormentor and tormented—that tied them to the demons. I explained how I felt about it to the priest.

"The dead in hell have been suffering for such a terribly long time that they've got used to it by now," the priest agreed. "It may be they're putting on an appearance of suffering just to maintain the proper order of things. You know, the way the duration of suffering in Buddhist hells is calculated is most eccentric. For example, one day and night in this Burning Hell consists of sixteen thousand years of days and nights, each of which is equivalent to sixteen hundred years in the human world. That's quite a long time! What's more, the dead in this particular hell have to endure a full sixteen thousand years of those longest days and nights—plenty of time for even the most backward ghost to get thoroughly used to things!"

"You see this demon here who looks like a lump of rock— the one facing the other way, putting everything he's got into his work? His body's covered with black holes," my wife said. "I don't know whether it's the shadow of his muscles or scars, but he looks very dilapidated, doesn't he? That female ghost being beaten by him looks a good deal healthier. You're right, Mitsu—the dead seem so used to the demons that they're not scared anymore."

She went along with my views, but gave no sign of deriving the same sense of mental release from the picture. If anything, the radiant good temper she'd shown since that morning seemed to be fading. I noticed, too, that Takashi had turned away from everyone and stood stubbornly silent, facing the golden gloom of the temple's inner sanctuary.

"What do you think, Taka?" I said, turning to him unceremoniously. He ignored my question and, looking round, said abruptly:

"Why don't we get S's ashes and go, without bothering about pictures."

The priest told his younger brother, who had been watching us curiously from the veranda of the main hall, to take Takashi and get the urn.

"Taka always used to be scared of the hell picture, even when he was a kid," said the priest. Then, turning the conversation back to the young villager who had come to see Takashi, he launched into a critique of everyday life in the valley. "Whatever the question facing them, the valley folk refuse to take a long-term view. They immediately get into deep water and start flapping about ineffectually—the way the young man came to get Takashi's friend to mend the van is typical. They fuss for ages over trivialities, with the irresponsible notion that when things finally get quite out of hand the situation will somehow change and solve their difficulties for them. The supermarket affair is a case in point. Every single shop in the village, with the exception of the liquor-and-sundries store—and only the liquor side, at that—has gone under to the supermarket. But they do nothing to protect themselves, and most of them are in debt to the supermarket in some way or other. I've an idea

they're expecting a miracle: just when the situation's quite out
of control and there's no hope of paying off their debts, the
supermarket vanishes in a puff of smoke and nobody presses
for repayment anymore. A single supermarket has driven them
to the point where, if this were the old days, the only possibility
left would be for the whole village to pack its bags and leave."

At this point Takashi arrived back from the ossuary carrying a bundle wrapped in a white cotton cloth, his despondency
and bad temper transformed into something close to elation.

"I found the steel frames of S's glasses in the urn with his
ashes," he said to me. "They reminded me exactly of how he
looked when he wore them."

We got into the Citroen, which one of the young men had
brought back to the temple grounds for Hoshio and Momoko.

"You hold S's urn, will you, Natsumi? Mitsu's not to be
trusted with it," Takashi said barefacedly. "He can't even carry
his own head around without bumping it."

The impression he gave wasn't simply of love and respect
for S, but of wanting to keep me, the Rat, as far away from S
as possible. He put my wife, with the urn in her arms, in the
seat next to his and talked of S to her as he drove. Drawing up
my knees, I lay down on the back seat and let my mind linger
on the color of the flames in the picture of hell.

"Do you remember the cadets' winter uniform, Natsumi?
S came up the graveled road at the height of summer in his
dark blue winter uniform, carrying a military sword and wearing calf-length flying boots. Whenever he met one of the valley
folk, he'd click the heels of his boots like the Nazi military used
to do. I can still hear the valley ringing to the click of the hard

leather heels and his manly voice saying 'Nedokoro S, back from the forces!'"

For all Takashi's talk, *my* memory of S was quite remote from such bravado. When S was discharged, for example, he threw his cap, boots, and sword off the bridge into the water, removed his jacket, and climbed the graveled road with bent back, the jacket beneath his arm. That, at least, was how *I* recalled his homecoming.

"I remember the day he was beaten to death still more vividly," Takashi told my wife. "I often have dreams about it, even now. I can see the scene extraordinarily clearly."

S, he said, had been lying faceup on a surface of mud dried to fine white powder, with gravel crushed small and round by countless feet. In the limpid autumn sunlight, not only the road but the grass-covered riverbed far below were white with reflected light, and amidst all this whiteness the river was ablaze with the fiercest white of all. Even Takashi, who crouched a foot or two from S's head where it lay, check against the earth, facing the river, and the dog which was dashing round and round him whining shrilly, were whitish too. All three—the corpse, Takashi, and the dog—were wrapped in a cloud of white light. A single tear made a black spot on the white film of dust covering a pebble that lay next to Takashi's thumb. But it dried at once, leaving a chalky blister on the surface of the stone.

S's bare, smashed head was like a flat black bag with something red protruding from it. The head itself and the stuff protruding were already dry like some fibrous matter left out in the sun. The only smell was that of sunbaked earth and stone. Even S's broken head was as odorless as a sheet of new paper.

His arms were raised limply above his shoulders like those of a dancer. His legs lay in the position of a hurdler in midair. And the skin of the neck, arms, and legs sticking out from the undershirt and shorts that naval air cadets wore for physical training was a uniform darkish color, like tanned hide, that highlighted the white of the mud stuck to it. Before long Takashi noticed a train of ants entering S's head through the nostrils and emerging again from his ears, each bearing a small bead of red in its mouth. It occurred to him that it was due to these ants that the body was shriveled and thin and gave off no smell. S would probably go on drying up till he was as desiccated as a dried fish. The ants had completely eaten away the eyes behind the tightly closed lids, leaving red holes the size of walnuts from which a faint, reddish light guided the tiny feet of the ants as they marched to and fro, treading the trifurcated path of ears and nose. Through the thin film, semi-transparent like murky glass, that was the skin of his face, a single drop of blood could be seen in the process of drowning an ant. . . .

"You don't mean to say you actually saw all this?" I demanded.

"Admittedly, it's supplemented in part from my dreams. But by now I'm not sure where the boundary lies between dreams and what I actually saw there on the road, a hundred yards downstream from the bridge, on the day S was beaten to death. Memory feeds on dreams, you know."

Personally, I had no inner urge to dig up my recollections of S's death. But for the sake of Takashi's mental health I felt I should point out that by now a greater part of his memories than he himself realized was dependent on the fabrications of dreams.

"Taka," I said, "the things you believe you really saw—the memories you've been constantly raking over—were nothing more than dreams all the time. The picture of S's dried-up body must have been built up from seeing something else—a frog, say, run over by a car. Yes, the vision you conjure up of his head all smashed and blackened with stuff protruding suggests a squashed frog, a frog with its innards squeezed out and flattened." With this general criticism, I proceeded to put the detailed case against his memories. "It's just not possible that you could have seen S dead at all, much less lying in the road. The only people who saw him then were me, when I went with a cart to fetch his body, and the people from the Korean settlement who helped me lift it on. The Koreans may have beaten him to death, but once he was dead they were all consideration and gentleness; they treated the corpse so lovingly he might have been their own kith and kin. They gave me a white silk cloth, too. I covered him with it as he lay on the cart, and put a lot of small stones on it to stop it flapping about, then I pushed the heavy cart back to the valley. I pushed instead of pulling partly because with a heavy load it seemed easier to balance it that way, and partly because I wanted to keep an eye on the body in case it fell out or turned into a demon that got up and tried to sink its teeth in me.

"It was dusk by the time I got him back to the valley, but none of the adults came out of the houses lining both sides of the road. Even the children only peeped out, and hardly showed themselves. They were scared of having anything to do with the corpse and the misfortune it represented.

"I left the cart in front of the village office for a while and went home. I found you there, standing at the back of the kitchen with a big lump of candy in your mouth and dark brown dribble coming from the corners of your lips. The dribble made you look like a character in one of those old peep shows, with blood running through clenched teeth after taking poison. Mother was sick in bed, and sister lying beside her, playing at being sick too. In other words I couldn't look to anyone in the family for help. So I went for Jin, who was chopping firewood in the field behind the storehouse. She was still slim then, a strong, healthy girl. When we went down to the village office we found the white silk cloth had been stolen from the cart, leaving S's body exposed. I can still see his corpse lying curled in on itself, looking no bigger than a sleeping child. He was smeared all over with dried mud and reeked of blood. Jin and I tried to get him up to the house by lifting him by the legs and under the arms, but he was too heavy. We got blood all over us, too. So Jin asked me to go back and get out the stretcher we used for air raid practice. I was struggling to hoist it down from where it hung under the eaves of the kitchen when I heard mother rambling on about my appearance and yours. I seem to remember that you were still too happily eating candy in the dark corner of the kitchen to pay any attention to me. It was night by the time we got S's body up to the house by the path running round below the stone wall, and we took it straight to the storehouse; so right up to the end I don't see how you can have seen anything."

Takashi was staring intently at the road ahead, concentrating on driving. The only signs of emotion I could detect were a faint quiver and flush spreading up his neck and around his ears, and the muffled grunt that came periodically from deep down in his throat. He was obviously shaken by the basic reassessment that my recollections were imposing on the world of his memories. We drove on for a while in silence. Then my wife said, as though to console Takashi:

"But isn't it rather strange, if Taka was standing in the kitchen all the time, that he didn't show any interest in S's body when it was carried home on the cart?"

"Now I remember—" I said, delving down into the next layer of memory, "I'd told him not to come out of the kitchen. I gave him the candy to make him keep his promise, and the reason we went to the trouble of carrying the corpse up the path skirting the stone wall was so it shouldn't be seen by you in the kitchen, or by mother and sister as they lay in bed in the front room."

"I certainly remember about the candy," he said. "It was S who gave it to me. He used the handle of his dagger to break a piece off a big block he'd grabbed in the first raid on the Korean village. I remember the exact shape and color of the dagger; it was a naval one. It was just afterward that he went off on the second raid and got beaten to death. Anyway, he saw the candy as part of the spoils of war and he was in high spirits when he gave it to me. I believe he deliberately used the handle of the dagger to make the moment as impressive as possible for me, his kid brother, and for himself too. I still see the scene in my dreams—the naval air cadet in spotless white shirt and trousers grasping the dagger, handle down, and bringing it down on the candy. In my dreams, S is always brandishing a glittering dagger, with a dazzling smile on his face." He spoke passionately, as though he believed his words would promptly heal any wounds inflicted by my revisionist views.

I found a perverted pleasure in waiting for the fresh flaws that my corrections lured from Takashi's memory and shooting them down as they appeared. Suppressing a certain disgust with myself, I energetically set about stripping the heroic aura from the image of S that Takashi had just built up in my wife's mind.

"Taka—that's another dream memory. These inventions of your fantasy life have taken root in your mind with the intensity of real events. It's true that on the first raid S and his friends stole bootleg liquor and candy from the Korean village. But S, who'd been on bad terms with mother ever since he came back from the army and tried to put her in a mental hospital for observation, hid the candy in a bundle of straw in the barn, because he was ashamed to let mother know, after what had happened, that he'd stolen it. I stole a bit of it myself while no one was around. I ate some and gave some to you, Taka. More to the point, he couldn't possibly have been in high spirits after the first raid—for the simple reason that a man had been killed at the Korean village. The second raid was basically non-aggressive, being aimed at producing a victim among the Japanese from the valley as well, thus getting the matter over without taking it to the police. It was already decided well in advance who was to get killed in that compensatory raid. In short, S knew that *he* was the one. I've only one memory, like a blurred photograph, of S's appearance in the interval between the two raids, but that photograph isn't my own fabrication. While the rest of them were getting drunk on the stolen liquor, the S in my mental picture lay quite sober, curled up on the floor in the room at the back of the storehouse. He lay without moving, facing the shadowy part of the room. Maybe he was looking at John Manjiro's fan painting in the alcove. As I remember it, it was around then that I found the candy he'd hidden, and I felt disgraced when S himself discovered me with a piece in my mouth. But that memory may come from a dream, like yours; I may have made it up after I finally came to realize the shameful and stupid significance in S's mind of stealing in the Korean village. I had an awful lot of dreams about S too, you know. In all kinds of ways his death had a profound influence on us as we grew up. That's why we had so many different dreams about it. Now that we're discussing it, though, I realize that our dreams must have had quite different atmospheres." Feeling compunction at pressing Takashi too far, I was offering a means of compromise. "It seems his death had completely different effects on the two of us."

Lost in thought, Takashi ignored my conciliatory move. He was groping in the shadowy corners of memory and the realm of dreams for something that might overturn at a single stroke the hegemony of my memory. Unfortunately, though, the argument between us had also set off a dangerous landslide of anxiety in my wife, whom we had treated hitherto as a mere bystander.

"Why did S take part in the raid if he knew he'd be killed, and why in fact was he killed? Why should he submit to being killed as repayment? It's terrifying to think of him lying there perfectly still in the dark at the back of the storehouse. The idea of him, a young man, just waiting for the second raid to come round really horrifies me. All the more, too, because I saw the inside of the storehouse this morning. I can't help seeing it all just as it was. I can see the very curve of his back quite clearly!" She was already sliding headlong down the slope of the mental ant-hole that led to whisky. The new life of sobriety she'd started somewhere between the previous night and that morning was already a thing of the past. "Why did S have to be the one killed in compensation? Because it was he who killed the Korean in the first raid?"

"It wasn't that, was it, Mitsu?" Takashi put in earnestly. "It's just that he was the leader. I know even without Mitsu telling me that this is a dream memory, but I seem to remember a splendid scene—S in the winter uniform of a naval air cadet, standing at the head of a group from the valley doing battle with the pick of the men from the Korean village."

"Taka," I said, "ultimately, the distortions of your memory suggest a bad case of wishful thinking. That's quite clear. It's not that I can't sympathize . . . but S was never leader of the young men in the valley. If anything it was just the opposite. Even I, a kid brother of ten, could tell that quite easily. Why, they even used to make fun of him. After all, it isn't likely anybody in the valley just after the end of the war would have appreciated the inner motives for S's odd behavior on the day he came back from the army. To put it bluntly, S was a laughingstock. I don't imagine either of you can really understand the terrifying destructive power of that kind of malicious laughter in a backward village in the hills. And S was probably the only young man who came back to the valley after the war who didn't make any of the women. True, he'd found a place for himself as a man in the valley community. But he was still the most junior of the gang of veterans who had the job of raiding the Korean village foisted on them. He was small and weak, and timid too. Besides, the real reason for the raid on the Korean village was that the group of Korean black marketeers had more than once uncovered rice that the village farmers had hidden, and taken it to sell in the town. The village headman and other prominent farmers deliberately egged the young men on to a point where they were obliged to act. The farmers had been making false declarations and concealing some of their rice. Any appeal to the police would only have worked to their disadvantage, so they pinned their hopes on the group of valley thugs who had the strength to cope with the Koreans. Most members of the group were farmers' sons, so there was an 'inevitability of class' about their participation in the raid. But *our* farm was bankrupt even before the postwar land reforms. We didn't have so much as a grain of rice hidden away; in fact, Jin had even made contact with the Koreans to buy black market rice. But S joined in the raid just the same and assumed the role of sacrificial lamb when his wild friends killed a Korean. That was clear even to me as a child. Mother was sick and wouldn't come to see the body in the storehouse after Jin had made it decent; she said that S was the one who'd been mad when he tried to take her to the mental hospital. She was so angry at the crazy desperation of what he'd done that she'd really come to hate him. So we didn't have a funeral. Jin put in a request to the adults of the neighborhood association, which still survived from the war days, and they cremated him for us. That's why his ashes have been left unclaimed at the temple ever since. If we'd had a proper funeral it would have been easy enough to put the urn in the family grave, wouldn't it? Sister's ashes are in there all right."

"Was he forced to do it?" my wife said to Takashi, but he didn't reply. His lips were clamped shut, for the simple reason that I'd mentioned our sister's death.

"I don't think he was forced," I said. "If anything, he volunteered for the part. But that didn't stop them from leaving his dead body where it was, so that I had to go with the cart to get it."

"But why should he? Why?" she pressed, horrified.

"It wasn't in my power to find out once it was over," I said. "The others in the raid, who fled back to the village after making sure S was beaten to death, quite naturally wanted nothing to do with S's family afterward, so it wasn't possible to get the details from them. I don't imagine many of them are left in the valley now. One went to the city and became a full-time criminal. I saw a big spread about him in the local paper while I was in high school. I suspected he was the one who killed the Korean on the first raid, so I looked at the photograph in the paper and recognized him at once. Murder seems to be habit-forming."

I was trying to divert the conversation into more general channels, but my wife was too far gone in obsessional horror to be carried along by my maneuver. Instead, she pressed Takashi, who wanted to remain silent, still more insistently.

"Taka," she urged, "what do your dream memories say? Why? Why should he?"

"Dream memories? . . ." he began with a determined patience of manner unlike the Takashi I'd known since early childhood—not that this produced a satisfactory answer to my wife's query.

"In my dreams," he went on, "I've never had the slightest doubt why S had to play the role. My fantasy S was born to be just that kind of hero-victim. Besides, I never look at him critically in the way Mitsu does, whether in my dreams or out of them. It comes as a kind of shock to be asked 'Why?' In my dreams, I don't need to ask S such things. And in reality twenty years ago I had my mouth stuffed full of candy—so

Mitsu says—which means I couldn't have asked him why, even if I'd wanted to."

"Why? Why should he?" Her voice was no longer directed at either Takashi or me but chasing echoes in the void within herself: *Why? . . . Why? . . . Why? . . . Why? . . . Why? . . .*

"Why should he, I wonder?" she repeated. "It's too horrible to imagine him, a young man, lying there all hunched up and still in the darkness of the storehouse. I'm sure I'll dream about it tonight, and I won't be able to get it out of my mind either, like Taka. . . ."

I asked Takashi to drive the Citroen round to the liquor-and-sundries store the priest had mentioned. We'd got back to the open space in front of the village office some time before and had been talking in the parked car. After buying a bottle of cheap whisky, we drove back along the graveled road.

At home my wife began drinking. Silent, ignoring both Takashi and myself, she sat perfectly upright facing the fireplace in the center of the room, slowly but surely sinking into intoxication. Caught between the inefficient lighting of that uneconomical house in the valley and the charcoal fire in the open hearth, she looked exactly the way she'd been that day when I first saw her drunk in the library. So much was clear, if only from the fact that I could read the whole of my own emotional experience that day in Takashi's eyes now, as for the first time he watched her getting drunk in this fashion, and in the look of shock so unequivocal despite his feigned detachment. She'd been drunk in front of him many times since his return to Japan, but always within the family circle; it wasn't a drunkenness that made one see in her eyes and on the very surface of her skin the entrance to that spiral staircase leading down to the terrifying darkness within. Fine, closely arrayed beads of sweat clung to her narrow forehead, to the shadowy places about her eyes, to the flared upper lip and to her neck. The fierce red of her eyes showed that she was already outside our field of gravity. Slowly but surely she was descending the winding stairs to those anxious depths reeking of crude whisky and sticky with sweat.

Since she showed absolutely no interest in her surroundings, Momoko, who had returned by now, was preparing the meal instead. Hoshio had dismantled the engine and brought it into the kitchen, where he was repairing it under the watchful eye of the four skinny children, surrounded by a faint smell of gasoline that hung about him like a transparent mist. Hoshio, at least, had succeeded with the children in converting dislike into respect. Even I, who had never seen such an industrious teenager, was obliged to lay aside my preconceptions. He seemed full of a new confidence since arriving in the village, so that something approaching the beauty of harmony had appeared on his comical features. My wife continued to drink in silence, while Takashi and I sprawled on the other side of the fireplace, listening to an old record from our dead sister's collection on an ancient portable phonograph. Lipatti, playing a Chopin waltz in the last concert recording of his life. . . .

"The way she listened to the piano was quite unusual, you know," said Takashi quietly in a gruff voice. "She didn't miss a note. However fast Lipatti played, she caught every single sound that came from the piano. You even felt she was splitting up the harmonies and catching the individual notes. She once told me how many notes there were in this E-flat waltz. Like a fool, I wrote the figure in a small notebook, then lost it, but her car was really rather special." It occurred to me that this was the first voluntary mention of our sister I'd heard him make since her death.

"Was she able to count so high, then?" I asked.

"No. You see, she had a big sheet of paper covered all over with pencil dots, like tiny specks of dust. It was like a photograph of the Milky Way, only with all the heavenly bodies shown as black dots. The opus 18 waltz was all there. I spent ages calculating the figure from her diagram. But then I went and lost the result. It's a pity, because I feel sure the number of pencil dots she made was accurate." Then, unexpectedly making a conciliatory gesture toward me, he added, "Your wife seems rather special too."

I remembered how he'd used the same expression of my friend who had painted his head crimson and hanged himself, and, profoundly moved, I put it together with what he'd just said. S too had been "rather special": if Takashi meant it, then I had no further desire to attempt impertinent amendments of his dream memories. His words showed that he'd grasped the existence of something in the depths of all who had died—died in the grip of a fear they could communicate to no one else.

The Emperor of the Supermarkets

O ne clear, bitterly cold morning when the hand pump in the kitchen had frozen, we drew water from the outside well. With its heavy bucket on a rope, it stood in the long, narrow back garden, separated only by a small mulberry orchard from the densely shrubbed hillside that we'd once called "Sedawa." Monopolizing the first bucketful of water, my brother washed at great length—his face, his neck, behind his ears even—then stripped to the waist and scrubbed relentlessly at his chest and shoulders. As I stood aimlessly by his side waiting for my turn with the bucket, I told myself that Takashi, who had hated the cold as a child, must have remodeled his character. His back which, doubtless consciously, was exposed to my gaze, bore livid scars where the tissues of skin and flesh had been broken down by blows from some blunt instrument. As I saw them now for the first time I felt something clutch at my stomach as though the sight had revived memories of pain borne by my own body.

I was still waiting for my turn when Momoko with the Sea Urchin in tow came through the kitchen and out into the back garden. Despite the bitter morning cold, the grotesque-featured youth wore only a pair of light blue jeans and an undershirt with sleeves so long that they half covered his fingers. He stood shivering uncontrollably with his great head hunched into his shoulders and made no move to speak to Takashi as long as I was there. He was pale, not only from the cold but as though exhausted from the very depths of his being.

In the end I gave up all idea of washing and went back to the fireplace—not that failure to wash my face bothered me particularly by now; my teeth, for one thing, hadn't been brushed for several months and were as yellow as an animal's. In my case, though, I hadn't consciously remodeled my nature: my dead friend and the baby who had gone into the institution had bequeathed a new nature to me.

"Mitsu, do you think that young man doesn't feel the cold?" my wife asked in a low voice so that Takashi and the others shouldn't hear.

"He feels it all right. He's shivering terribly. But he wants to impress on everyone that he's an unusual, stoic type, so he refuses to wear an overcoat or jacket even in midwinter. That in itself mightn't be enough to win people's respect even here in the valley, but his whole appearance and the show he puts on of ignoring other people also help to set him apart."

"If that's enough to make someone the leader in a young people's group, then it's all rather primitive, isn't it?"

"Yes, but in practice the kind of person who puts on such a naive show isn't necessarily simple in his psychological makeup,"

I said. "That's what makes politics among the village kids so complex."

Before long Takashi came back into the kitchen with the young man, walking by his side with an exaggerated air of friendliness. He then shook hands with a vigor that even a bystander could tell was meant to be encouraging, and watched as the other, who remained silent, took his leave. As the youth stepped across the threshold his broad face, seen in the sunlight, was graven with a harsh melancholy that took me aback.

"Is something wrong, Taka?" my wife asked in a timid voice, just as startled as I was. He didn't reply directly, but came and stood by the fireplace with a towel round his neck like a boxer in training, the expression of his face torn between two fierce, conflicting emotions. It was as though he were struggling simultaneously with an extraordinary sense of the comic and shock at encountering something unspeakably depressing. Then, looking searchingly at my wife and me with eyes full of proud passion, he said in a loud voice:

"Either hunger or cold has killed off all the chickens, several thousand of them." He gave a short laugh.

I said nothing, overwhelmed with the same sense of absurdity and horror at the idea of those thousands of unfortunate chickens all lying dead. Then, as my imagination extended to the spectacle of the Sea Urchin and his friends shivering ceaselessly, even as they pretended indifference to the cold, the full horror of their plight aroused a sense of revulsion and distress in me.

"So they came to ask me to go and see the Emperor and discuss what to do with the dead chickens. I can't leave them to their fate. I'm going into town."

"The Emperor? Oh—you mean the owner of the supermarket chain. I don't imagine even he can turn dead chickens
to profit. Unless they make a hell of a lot of soup cubes."

"Most of the funds for keeping the chickens were provided
by the Emperor. The young people's group wanted to be independent of the supermarket, but obviously the need to buy feed
and ship the eggs made it difficult to keep out the Emperor's
influence. Now that all the chickens have been wiped out, the
loss to the young men's group is a loss for the Emperor as well.
So they're looking to me to negotiate with him and forestall any
charges of irresponsibility he might make against the group.
Of course, they're such a dumb crowd I wouldn't mind betting
that some of the more imaginative of them are still hoping he'll
think up some profitable way of disposing of the dead chickens."

"It wouldn't do for the valley folk to eat the dead chickens
and get food poisoning or something." I sighed, my sense of
depression deepening.

"If the chickens froze to death with empty stomachs, they
may well be every bit as sanitary as chemically grown frozen
vegetables. In fact, I might get them to give me two or three of
the least skinny ones in return for going to town, and use them
to give Jin some protein. What do you think?"

"She eats almost no animal protein in spite of her morbid
appetite," my wife said. "It's bad for her liver."

Throughout their hasty breakfast Takashi held a detailed
conversation with Hoshio concerning the time required for
a round trip to the town in the young men's van and the distance between places where gasoline supplies were available.
Their dialogue went at a brisk pace. Hoshio's knowledge of
automobiles was practical and detailed; Takashi had only to

put a question to get a reply that was concise and to the point. As Hoshio explained the shortcomings of the van's engine, the likelihood of mechanical failure during the several hours' drive through the forest became more and more apparent, and they finally decided that Hoshio should go into town with him.

"Hoshi's an expert at repairing old crates" said Momoko. "With him along, you can drive any car any distance without worrying. The older the car the better he knows how it's put together. He'll be a real asset." With this effort to be fair, she gave vent to a sigh full of childish envy: "Oh dear, I wonder what movies are on in the civilized world? I wonder if Brigitte Bardot's still around? . . ."

"We'll take you with us," said Takashi. "These teen-age girls get too worked up about everything," he added with a smile of frank sympathy at the joy apparent in Momoko's whole body.

"Drive carefully, Taka," my wife said. "There's ice on the road through the forest."

"OK. And I'll be particularly careful on the way back, as I'll be bringing half a dozen bottles of whisky, something a bit better than the stuff you get in the village. What about you, Mitsu? Is there anything you want done?"

"Nothing."

"Mitsu's past expecting anything," mocked Takashi in revenge for my surliness, "either from others or from himself."

Unerringly, he'd sensed the absence in me of any feeling of expectation. For all I knew, indeed, the signs that this feeling had deserted me might be apparent to anyone from my physical appearance alone.

"And some coffee, please, Taka," put in my wife.

"I'll bring a full load of supplies—I'll get an advance on the storehouse from the Emperor. You two have a right to get some pleasure from that money."

"If possible, I'd like a drip-type coffee maker and some fresh-ground coffee, Taka," said my wife. She too was obviously beginning to hanker after the trip to town.

Finishing breakfast, Takashi and his bodyguards ran down in a group to the Citroen waiting in the space before the village office. My wife and I, interrupting our meal, watched them go from the front garden, standing on ground made treacherous by mounds of ice needles.

"Taka's quickly making himself at home with the young men of the valley," she said. "Not like you—you're just the same here as you were shut up in your room in Tokyo."

"Taka's trying to put down roots again," I replied. "I don't seem to have any roots to put down." The self-pity in my voice disgusted even me.

"Hoshi seems to think Taka's getting too friendly with the young men," she said.

"But he's cooperating with Taka in working for their association, isn't he?"

"He cooperates more or less enthusiastically with anything that Taka does. All the same, he seems to be secretly dissatisfied this time. I wonder if he's jealous of Taka's new friends."

"If so, I expect he feels a kind of incestuous revulsion toward the other kids. After all, it's only a short while since he was living on a farm himself. I imagine he knows the peasant type too well to have as much simple confidence in him as Taka. Taka's completely forgotten almost everything about life here."

"Do you feel the same way?" she inquired, but I didn't reply. The roar from the exhaust of the Citroen carrying Takashi and the others rose with undue commotion to the stone wall where we stood, then faded into the rectangle of sky bounded by the lofty forest, leaving multiple echoes crisscrossing throughout the valley. Then, as the car vanished with the same swiftness as its echo, a triangular banner of a strangely bright yellow floated up into the early morning air of a valley empty once more of all movement. It flew gaily from a flagpole on the saké storehouse belonging to the brewers—a family as old-established as our own and, with the Nedokoros, one of the only two to have their houses attacked in the farmers' riot of 1860. The brewers had left the village by now; their storehouse had been bought up and one of its walls knocked out to make a supermarket.

"The flag has '3S2D' embroidered on it," I said, my interest aroused. "What the hell do you think that stands for?"

"'Self-Service Discount Dynamic Store,' of course. I saw it yesterday on an advertising leaflet that came with the local paper. I suppose the owner of the supermarket chain got hold of the idea during his tour of America. Anyway, even if it is Japanese English, I admire it, I think it's a very fine, powerful phrase," she said in a tone of voice that made me suspicious.

"I wonder how impressed you really are?" I said, carefully examining my imperfect memory of how the valley usually looked in order to determine whether the flag had been flying every day so far. "I don't think I've ever seen the banner before."

"I expect they've put it up because there's a sale today. Jin says that on sale days people come to shop there not only from the houses along the edge of the forest but from the next village too. They come by bus along the road by the river."

"Anyway, the Emperor seems to have his wits about him,"
I said, flinching at the sight of the triangular banner fluttering
in a breeze that had just sprung up.

"Yes, doesn't he? . . ." she said, but she was already preoccupied with a different idea. "Supposing," she went on, "all the
trees in this forest were damaged by the cold and rotted where
they stood—I wonder how long the people in the hollow would
be able to put up with the smell?"

I was about to respond by gazing at the forest round about
us when some premonition prompted a show of disapproval
and I remained looking at the ground, on which the ice needles
had already begun to collapse. My frozen breath sank down
toward them and hung there indeterminately, spreading out
horizontally with an increasing sense of stagnation yet never
finally disappearing. As I watched it I felt a memory reviving in
me, a memory of the suffocating stench given off by the fleshy
leaves of ornamental plants rotting from frostbite.

"Well, then," I urged her with a shudder, "let's finish breakfast in our own time."

But as she turned and took a step forward, the ice needles
gave way beneath her foot. She promptly lost her balance and
fell, soiling her hands and knees in the frozen mud. Her sense
of balance, in abeyance after a long night of inebriation, was
liable to be upset periodically by any force acting on her, whether
physical or psychological. At that particular moment, moreover,
the renewed memory of that smell in her nostrils had probably
upset her balance still further. She'd been brought down, in
short, by the ghosts of some ornamental plants that had died
at our home in Tokyo.

Ever since our marriage, she'd been cultivating rubber plants, monsteras, and various ferns and orchids in a small glass-walled conservatory that she'd made on the south side of our combined dining room and kitchen. In midwinter, whenever a cold wave was forecast, she would keep the gas fire on all night in the dining room and get up every hour to let the warm air into the conservatory. I suggested various compromises, such as leaving the partition between dining room and conservatory slightly open, or putting a charcoal burner in the conservatory, but she'd been too terrified of burglars and fires since childhood even to consider such suggestions. Thanks to this neurotic diligence, the conservatory was smothered from floor to low ceiling with a wild profusion of plants. But this winter it had been hard for her, drinking herself to sleep with whisky as she did every evening, to keep her mind on the conservatory all the time from late night until dawn. I was scared, too, at the idea of her handling the gas stove in the small hours when she was drunk. When the radio forecasts announced the imminent arrival of winter's first cold wave, we waited for it in the same frame of mind as some puny tribe awaiting the approach of a mighty army.

Early one morning, after a night of cold that made it hard to sleep, I went into the dining room and peered into the conservatory through the glass door to find that the leaves of the plants were blotched with darkish patches. My eyes, even so, detected nothing particularly ominous about them; the leaves were all damaged, but they weren't yet withered. Only when I opened the glass door and went in did I realize, with a severe shock, the true extent of the harm that had befallen our ornamental plants. I was knocked back by the overpowering, raw odor, like the reek of a dog's slobbering mouth, that filled the place. Once the smell had seized hold of my mind, the rubber plants and monsteras on either side, all mottled in differing shades of dingy green, began to look like tall giants dying where they stood, and the murky mass of broad-leaved orchids crouched at my feet like a sick animal. My spirits failed me. Doing nothing more, I returned to the bedroom and went to sleep, still haunted by the smell that seemed somehow to have seeped into every pore of my body. Getting up sometime before noon, I found my wife eating a late breakfast in silence, but the familiar doggy odor emanating from her immediately evoked the minutes I'd spent in the conservatory while she lay unconscious. Of all the portents of ruin that had shown themselves in our household since my wife had first started to drift in the lower depths of intoxication, none had impinged on us with such effrontery and such raw immediacy. Overcoming my repugnance, I took another look through the glass door and found that under the strong sunlight the blackish marks had already spread all over the foliage, and withered leaves were dangling from their stems like hands from broken wrists. It was only too obvious that the plants were dying.

Yes, I thought, if all the trees in the forest enclosing the valley were damaged by frost, a stench like the clammy mouths of a million dogs would engulf the villagers. The idea made me feel that I too might lose my balance on the crumbling ice needles. Retiring to the house together in horror-stricken silence, we finished our breakfast in a gloom utterly different from the atmosphere earlier, when Takashi had been at the center of our group.

In the afternoon, the postman brought a letter for Momoko and informed us that we had a parcel waiting at the post office. It contained an "Easy Stool" device that my wife had read about in a magazine advertisement and asked her family to buy. According to the catalog, it was rather like a chair without a seat. Placing it over a Japanese-style toilet, the user could evacuate in the same posture as on a Western one, with no strain on the knees. She'd conceived the idea of presenting Jin with one, thus relieving "Japan's Fattest Woman" of the strain that the weight of her enormous body must impose on her at such times. Admittedly, there was some doubt whether the light metal tubes of which the Easy Stool was constructed would stand up to a weight of 290 pounds or more; and whether the old-fashioned Jin could ever be persuaded even to use such a thing. But the arrival of the Easy Stool whetted our interest and, bored with morbidly waiting at home for the others, we set off at once down the stone-strewn trail.

As we passed the supermarket we stopped to look at the unusual bustle of people there. The lively atmosphere immediately reminded me of the crowds at the shrine festival during my years in the valley. A little apart from the throng at the doors of the supermarket, some children in their best kimonos were engrossed in an old-fashioned stone-kicking game; their gaiety, too, linked up with my memories of the festival. One small girl was dressed in a scarlet kimono with a woven gold and green phoenix design. The kimono, which must have passed into her parents' hands during the food shortage in return for a certain amount of rice, was tied with a silver sash, and there was a great gold-colored spherical bell the size of a man's fist at the back. She wore a crimson collar of imitation fur round her neck. Each time she kicked a stone, the bell set up a noisy jangling that startled the other children with her. A bright red banner hung from the eaves of the storehouse, whose walls had been knocked out and replaced with plastic. The banner bore in green letters the legend:

> 3S2D, *the store with everything,*
> *The store that everyone's talking about,*
> *Announces now, in gratitude for your patronage,*
> *A fabulous grand sale!*
> *Don't miss this last special sale of the year!*
> *Store heated throughout.*

"'Store heated throughout'—" I said, "that's really something, isn't it ?"

"All it means is they've got a few potbellied stoves around the place," said my wife, who had already taken Momoko there several times to buy supplies.

The women who had done their shopping made no move to leave, but hung around in front of the broad glass window that stretched between the exit and entrance (the glass was covered with the prices of various articles, written in white paint, so that we couldn't see inside from where we stood). One of the group had her forehead pressed against the pane, peering in beyond the maze of white lettering. Before long, a farmer's wife came out wearing a multicolored blanket over her shoulders and head like a South American Indian woman and carrying in her arms a bag full of purchases. An eddy of envious sighs swirled up from the women stationed outside. As the women around her stretched out monkey-paws to touch the blanket, the farmer's wife, a smallish woman, wriggled and squealed with high-pitched, excited laughter as though they were tickling her. Having been away from the valley for a long time, I had the impression that they must all be strangers to the village, but that could hardly be the case; this type of behavior must have developed spontaneously among the inhabitants of the valley.

We were moving away in silence when we saw the young priest from the temple coming out behind the women, likewise clutching a bundle of shopping to his chest. The flush on his good-natured, smiling face deepened steadily as he noticed us and came walking over. Beneath the close-cropped, prematurely gray hair carefully rinsed to a silvery sheen, the rosy blush on his cheeks and around his eyes gave his whole face the air of a newborn rabbit.

"I came to buy rice cakes for the New Year," he explained, looking greatly embarrassed.

"Rice cakes? Have the parishioners dropped the custom of bringing them to the temple?"

"None of the families in the valley pound rice to make their own cakes nowadays, you see. People either get them at the supermarket in exchange for the special rice used in them, or they buy them for cash. It's typical of the way the basic units of life in the valley are gradually breaking down, a bit at a time. It's like the way the cells of a blade of grass break up. You must have seen a blade of grass under a microscope when you were at school, Natsumi?"

"Yes."

"If you remember, each cell in the blade has a fixed shape. When it collapses and becomes soggy and formless it means the cell is either damaged or dead. As these formless cells increase, the blade of grass rots. It's the same with life in the valley, isn't it? You can hardly expect it to go on when each of the basic elements gradually loses its shape. But I can't very well tell the village people they ought to start sweating over their rice-pounding again, using the same old pestles and stone mortars that their fathers used. They would only assume I said it because I wanted the cakes!" He gave a little laugh.

The plant analogy had a dire effect on us, and all we could manage was the feeble smile my wife gave in response to the priest's laugh. Two or three more women came out of the super-market and were greeted by the others waiting outside, but one of them, a middle-aged peasant whose face was flushed a deep copper color with excitement, suddenly exclaimed, "What junk!" in a voice harsh with self-derision. Frowning and giggling at the same time, she was brandishing a blue plastic toy in the shape of a golf club.

"A golf club's no use in this valley, is it?" my wife said won-deringly, "even a toy one. I wonder why she buys such things."

"She didn't buy it," the priest said, turning his face away from us. "The things they've got that aren't in bags are gifts. The blanket, the toy—the whole lot of them, they're all gifts. There's a lottery stall just inside the exit where you can win all kinds of stupid prizes. That's why even those who've finished their shopping hang around, just to keep an eye on other people's little windfalls."

As the priest and I walked toward the post office with Nat-sumi between us, we discussed the disaster that had befallen the chickens and the young men's association. He already knew about the death of the birds, but he turned pale when he heard that Takashi had gone into town to discuss ways of handling the disaster with the Emperor.

"If they were going to ask Takashi to do that, why didn't they contact the Emperor *before* the chickens died? But then everything they do is at sixes and sevens! They only act when it's already too late."

"Perhaps they wanted to stay as independent of the Emperor as possible," I ventured in my capacity as neutral observer, "even if they had to create a situation where they were forced into total submission to him."

"Actually, the real cause of their failure in the first place was that they didn't want a contract to hand over all the eggs directly to the supermarket, and tried to hold on to their right to expand sales routes to other markets and retail stores. It was an odd idea to begin with. You see, the land and building where they kept the chickens both belong to the owner of the supermarkets. In theory, the land where the Korean settlement stood was sold after the war to the Koreans who'd been doing forced labor in the forest, but before long one of them got a monopoly on the land by buying it up from the rest. He went on developing and developing, and the result is the Emperor you see today."

I felt a deep sense of shock. Even after they'd heard that Takashi and I were selling the storehouse to the owner of the supermarkets, neither Jin's family nor our other old acquaintances in the valley had said anything about the Emperor's earlier career.

"I only hope Taka's aware of the circumstances in negotiating with the Emperor," my wife said. "I'm worried whether the young men's group has really told Takashi the whole story."

She was quite obviously suspicious of the Sea Urchin for having conferred with Takashi in a low voice, resolutely ignoring us.

I had too much to occupy me, however, to wonder idly what petty frustrations Takashi might meet in his positive attempt to cooperate with the Emperor. What oppressed my whole mind was the complete silence of the villagers concerning the real nature of the Emperor.

"Even if he's taken Japanese nationality by now, to give a man of Korean origin the title 'Emperor' suggests some deep-rooted malice," I said. "It's just the kind of thing the valley folk would do. But I wonder why nobody ever told me?"

"It's simple, Mitsu," said the priest. "The valley folk don't want to admit at this stage that they're under the economic control of a Korean who was felling timber as a forced laborer in the forest only twenty years ago. And I imagine the same feeling, shut up inside them, is what made them deliberately choose to call him Emperor. The valley's hopelessly decadent."

"You may be right," I agreed somberly. I had to admit that there were suggestions of a very pervasive decadence. Something indefinably murky and vicious seemed to lie at the heart of the relationship between the villagers and the Emperor. "But there's been nothing directly indicating decadence, at least in what I've seen and heard since I came back to the valley."

"They've got used to it," said the priest. "And they've learned the art of concealing it from outsiders." He spoke as though divulging some secret.

"Just what kind of man is this Emperor?"

"You mean, is he a villain or not? I have to admit, Mitsu, I've nothing directly against him. Where business practices are concerned, the valley folk are, if anything, worse than him. All the same, though, it's they who feel the pinch in the long run. The chickens are a case in point. Sometimes I get anxious, wondering what he might be plotting for the people in the valley, but at the moment that's as far as it goes, so I can't say anything."

"All the same, it's very unpleasant. It makes me increasingly aware there's something wrong with the valley as a whole."

"For us it's more than just unpleasant." His eyes rested on me for a moment with a sharp look, then he went on sadly, "I can't explain it, Mitsu. The one thing that's certain is that the valley's decadent."

He adjusted the bag of rice cakes in his arms and walked off briskly as though afraid of what I might ask next.

I walked on rapidly down the road. My wife, left behind, came trotting after me. We got the parcel containing the Easy Stool at the post office and went back up the graveled road again. At the supermarket my wife stopped and bought rice cakes for us and Jin's family. Though not completely untouched by the sense of outrage and resistance I felt toward the storehouse remodeled into supermarket, she at least didn't find it an insuperable obstacle. She came out bearing a green plastic frog that she'd won.

"To think I'd get *this* in the first lottery I've won since we were married!" she complained disappointedly.

Unwrapping the Easy Stool, we discovered a simple apparatus made by bending two tubes into U-shapes and connecting them with supports. The reality gave us food for thought: to persuade Jin to use such an object was going to be no easy matter. She might well dismiss it as "junk" with a venom many times more intense than the woman standing outside the store had injected into the same word; or she might assume it was a laborious attempt on my part to poke fun at her. So I left it to my wife to explain the Easy Stool. In the meantime I summoned Jin's children into the front garden and made a small bonfire of the rope and cardboard in which it had been packed. *As* I did so, I was busy pinching out disturbing sparks of speculation concerning this Emperor whom I had yet to meet.

The children had already heard that the chickens belonging to the young people's group had been wiped out. According to Jin's sons, the young men were patrolling the chicken houses in case the valley folk came to steal the dead birds. What had once been the Korean settlement was like a filthy beehive, completely buried beneath the many-tiered dwellings of the chickens and the shelves for drying out their droppings, and the whole area was enveloped in a dense effluvia. That morning the unfortunate creatures lay dead, each in its own narrow compartment. Jin's sons had been with the other children to have a look and had been driven away by the young men on patrol.

"They were so mad, you'd have thought *we'd* done it!" complained Jin's eldest boy. "Who'd want to steal a lot of dead chickens, I ask you? Unless they're so angry they did it themselves," he added with an indescribable blend of mildness and guile.

And Jin's skinny sons laughed in shrill unison. It was clear that their mocking laughter concealed the same cold indifference toward the young men's group and its failure to raise chickens as shown by all the adults in the valley. For the first time I felt pity for the group, caught between the Emperor—who by now I'd come to think of as some cunning monster—and the equally cunning grown-ups in the valley. It had been the same with the group of young veterans whose violent activities had culminated in S's death: the attitude taken toward them by the adults who had used them for their own purposes was founded in a deep-seated wariness and contempt. Not until I'd escaped to the outside world where I could look back on daily life in the village with objectivity—not until I myself had passed the age at which S had died—did I appreciate the truth of this. One difference, of course, was that in the past the children had gone against the adults and idolized the young men, whereas the kids today were as indifferent to the young men's group as to the grown-ups themselves.

The bonfire burned itself out, leaving a warm black sore in the frozen soil. The children, pointlessly, stamped it down.

"You can go indoors now," said my wife, coming back from the outbuilding. "There are some rice cakes for you."

But they ignored her well-meant information and went on stamping at the remains of the bonfire. They were too self-conscious, had too much pride concerning anything to do with food. I wondered if they might be thin because their mother, whose hatred of her own enormous appetite made her feel that all food bore the thorns of suffering, had implanted a dislike of it in them too.

"Jin was very pleased," my wife said.

"She didn't get angry ?"

"When she first saw it she said you were 'trifling' with her, but I finally got her to understand that I was the one who'd ordered it. She actually used the word 'trifle.'"

"Yes, she would. It used to be an everyday word here in the valley, at least until the time when I was a kid. Whenever I made a joke, mother would tell me off—said I was 'trifling' with my parents. How about it, though—do you think this controversial gadget will be any use to Jin?"

"I think so. She'll have to be careful not to fall over sideways and hurt herself, but the first tryout at least was successful." She refrained from further details on account of the children, who were obstinately hanging about with ears pricked, and said without warning, "Jin asked me, so I told her about the baby!"

"Ah, well. Anybody who'd taken along an appliance like that would naturally want to make some such confession of his own, if only to make the other person feel less embarrassed."

"You won't be so good-natured when you hear what Jin had to say about it. Not, of course, that I believe what she says." She seemed to be fighting against some barrier as she spoke. "Jin said she wondered if the baby's deformity was due to heredity on your side."

A wave of burning anger swept through me. For a moment it was enough to purge my mind of the ominous shadow cast by the Emperor. I struggled to set my defenses in order, flushing with ill-focused apprehension, as though under attack by an unidentifiable enemy.

"The grounds for her suspicion are really terribly trivial," she went on hastily, turning red in response to the flush that had spread over my whole face. "It's just that once, when you were still too young to go to primary school, you had a bad fit of convulsions."

"I had a fit and fainted while I was watching the school play," I said with a sense of relief that was deep in proportion to the first shock, though I could still feel the lingering heat of anger in every corner of my body.

Jin's sons shrieked with laughter. Perhaps their childish clamor with its determination to insult both my wife and me served to settle our psychological account, for when I scowled at them they retreated hastily, still laughing and quite undismayed, in search of their corpulent mother and the rice cakes. We ourselves went back to the fireplace. I felt I must tell her the precise nature of the evil spirit that had visited me without warning as a small child when I was watching the school play, that I must destroy the seeds of suspicion that otherwise would surely grow inside her tonight when she got drunk.

The play in question, which was frequently talked about as the last to be given at the primary school until school theatricals were started again after the war, must have been the one held in the autumn of the year the war began. My father was in northeast China doing work of an unspecified nature that remained a mystery not only to us children but to grandmother, who was still alive then, and to mother as well. For the sake of that work, he would sell enough fields to provide the money to cross the straits and spend more than half every year in China. Our eldest brother was at Tokyo University and S at a middle school in the nearby town, so the family in the house in the valley consisted of grandmother and mother, Jin, and the children—myself, my younger brother, and our newly born sister. So it was Jin and we three children who set out that day, bearing the invitation to the school play that had been addressed to father. Takashi and I sat on either side of Jin, who had the baby on her back, our legs dangling from wooden chairs in the middle of the very front row in the largest classroom of the primary school. I could recall the scene as clearly as though I had a third eye up in the classroom ceiling that gave me a bird's-eye view.

About a yard in front of us a stage had been made by placing two platforms together, and it was on this that the older pupils performed their play. It began with a number of them, wearing cotton towels round their heads (judging from the number of children in the advanced course, there couldn't have been more than fourteen or fifteen of them onstage, but to my childish eyes they were a small crowd), going through the motions of cultivating the fields. In short, they were farmers in olden times. Soon they laid aside their spades and began practicing fighting, using axes and sickles as weapons. Their leader appeared, a youth of extraordinary beauty even to my immature eyes, and under his leadership the armed peasants trained for the battle in which they were to take the head of the most powerful man in the clan. A black bundle represented the head, and the farmers were divided into two groups who practiced seizing the dummy from each other. In the second act, a man appeared in splendid costume and warned the farmers against taking the notable's head, but they were already too inflamed to listen to him, so he told them that he would take the head himself. A figure in a mask went past the dark place where the farmers lay in ambush, and without warning the character in the splendid costume fell upon him with his sword. The role of the man in the mask was played by a pupil wearing black cloth over his head, with a black ball fastened to the top, making him a figure of terror considerably taller than the other actors. The "real" head of the man attacked with the sword tumbled to the stage with a loud thud, whereupon his assailant cried out to the farmers in hiding:

"Lo! My brother's head!"

The farmers removed the mask, recognized the head of their young leader, and wept bitterly for shame.

Jin had already told me the plot and I'd seen the play many times in rehearsal, so I was completely familiar with the mechanics of the scene, but even so (either at the moment the "real" head made of a bamboo basket filled with stones fell to the stage, or when the cry of "Lo! My brother's head!" so startled me, or again—to relate things exactly as I remember them—at the critical moment when the two things converged) I was seized with fear, collapsed screaming on the floor, went into convulsions and lost consciousness. When I came to, I'd already been carried home and grandmother was at my bedside saying to my mother, "Heredity's a dreadful thing, even in a great-grandchild." I was so afraid that I kept my eyes shut and my body rigid, pretending still to be unconscious.

"Do you remember that when my first translation appeared I got a letter from a retired teacher at the primary school?" I said to my wife. "He was assistant principal at the time of the school play. His subject was mathematics, but he was also studying local history, and it was he who wrote the play. But the war began that winter. The following year the system changed to 'national schools.' There was a fuss about the play, he said in his letter, and he was demoted to the rank and file of teachers. I wrote back asking him if great-grandfather had really killed his younger brother, and got a reply saying he now subscribed to the view that in actual fact my great-grandfather had allowed his younger brother, ringleader in the rising, to escape to Kochi. I also asked about the exact circumstances of my father's death, but in his answer he said that my mother, who must have known something about it, was not only unwilling to understand its significance but tried her very best to forget it, so that by now there wasn't a soul who knew anything definite about it."

"I wonder if Taka isn't planning to meet that teacher," my wife said.

"It's true that Taka's interested in ferreting out various secrets and facts about the people who died in our family, but I doubt whether the historian will be able to satisfy Taka's taste for the heroic," I said, and broke off the conversation.

At the outbreak of the war, father had let us know that he was abandoning his work in China and coming home, but had then disappeared without trace until three months later, when his body was handed over to my mother by the Shimonoseki police. The circumstances of his death were suspicious and rumors abounded: he'd been struck down by a heart attack on board the ferry; had thrown himself overboard just as they were entering harbor; or had died under investigation by the police. But my mother, returning to the village after going to fetch the body, refused to say anything about his death. After the war, brother S had been so irritated by the blank refusal he met every time he tried to worm details of father's death out of her that it had provided the immediate motive, at least, for his plan to take her to the mental hospital and have her examined.

Around dusk a sudden breeze sprang up at the entrance to the valley, ruffling the spindle-shaped hollow as it came and bringing to the houses in the valley a strange stench, like mounds of burning animal matter, that induced an immediate physical distress and nausea. My wife and I went out into the front garden with handkerchiefs pressed over our noses and mouths and gazed down toward the valley and beyond, but all we could see was a little white smoke rising in the air. Even that wasn't particularly distinct, and soon lost itself in the swirling billows of new mist, leaving nothing in the reddish black depths of the twilight sky but shreds of smoke that tried to rise above the heavy layer of mist only to break and disperse. Where the black forest gave them a background, they stood out white and shining like gobs of saliva.

Jin's husband and sons had come out of the outbuilding and were standing in a group a few paces behind us, also watching the lower reaches of the sky. The boys were busily snuffing the air trying to identify the smell. Their small noses, like dark fingers, noisily and vigorously asserted their existence in the steadily deepening gloom. In front of the village office, too, a number of black figures had appeared and were looking up at the sky.

It was completely dark by the time Takashi and his bodyguards came home. They were all equally grubby and exhausted, but Hoshio was silent whereas Takashi and Momoko were in high spirits. My brother had kept his promise and brought half a dozen bottles of whisky for my wife, who winced involuntarily at the sight of them standing there in a row. He'd also bought a leather jacket for Hoshio and a skirt for Momoko. But despite their new clothes, the same strange odor that had shrouded the valley hung about them even more closely, like a protective membrane.

"What are you two looking so doubtful about?" Takashi asked, deliberately misinterpreting our reaction to the smell they gave off. "Anyone'd think we'd been killed in an accident deep in the forest and come back to haunt you. Admittedly, we came at top speed along an icy trail and in mist, driving a ramshackle old truck with a lousy clutch, but Hoshi handled it like a genius. He took that dark forest road with as little trouble as a dog clattering along an icy road on its claws. A mechanical age obviously produces a special breed of men whose sixth sense is oriented to machines."

He was clearly attempting to cheer Hoshio up, but the teen-age technician refused to show any favorable response. Either his nerves were frayed by the mad dash along that dangerous trail, or some other trying experience had sapped his immature energies.

"Taka," I said outright, "you may not be a ghost, but you stink!"

"Who wouldn't, after burning several thousand chickens?" He gave a short laugh. "We stripped all the boards off the chicken houses and burned everything—stiff chickens, soft shit and all. God, the stink! I'm sure it's soaked right into our blood."

"Didn't you get any complaints from people?"

"You bet we did! But we just let them talk. In the end a cop came—after all, it was quite a bonfire. But when he saw four or five of the group blocking the end of the bridge, he kept quiet and went home again. So the young men have discovered they've nerve enough to stand up to the police. They're quite bucked about it. Several thousand chickens may have died and gone up in smoke, but thanks to them the group's that little bit wiser. So it wasn't all a waste."

"There was no need to scare the cop away," Hoshio broke in as though he couldn't keep quiet any longer. "What's the point, anyway ? They got the better of him because he was alone, but if reinforcements had come they wouldn't have stood a chance."

I was reminded of his persistence in challenging me late that night when we were waiting for Takashi at the airport. Hoshio was obviously the sort of young man who insisted on his pet ideas not only in defense of his patron deity but even when they worked against him.

"But Hoshi—once it starts snowing and communications with the town and the village on the coast are cut, there'll only be a single cop to deal with anyway. When you were a kid, I bet they threatened they'd 'tell the policeman' if you weren't good."

"I'm not saying you shouldn't fight the cops," Hoshio countered stubbornly. "That June, I backed you up whatever you did, didn't I? But why get into trouble with the police just for a bunch of chicken farmers? That's what gets me."

Suddenly Momoko, who till then had been reading letters from her family, looked up and intervened in a mocking, singsong voice as if they'd been mere kids:

"Hoshi talks like that, you see, because he wants to monopolize you, Takashi. There's no point in arguing, Hoshi will only go on bitching like a girl. Let's have supper and go to bed. Natsumi's cooked up something good."

The young man turned pale and scowled at Momoko, but excitement had left him speechless, so the argument ended there.

"How about the negotiations with the Emperor?" I asked, though I was sure already, from Takashi's reluctance to launch into his report on the main proceedings, that the answer would be unfavorable.

"No go. It looks as though the young men will have all their work cut out to avoid getting still further into his clutches. The only practical proposal he made was that we should burn the chickens, all of them. I imagine he was afraid the valley folk would eat the dead chickens and sales of foodstuffs would go down at his supermarket. When I got back and said we were going to burn the chickens, some of the villagers gave me dirty looks, so it seems his fears were justified. If you ask me, though, the sheer futility of pouring gasoline on several thousand chickens and cremating them has done something, at least, to turn the self-indulgent greed in their soggy, half-baked brains into a sharper, tougher hatred."

"I wonder what kind of happy ending they had in mind when they sent you to town?" I asked, heavy-hearted.

"They didn't have anything in mind. They've no imagination at all. They probably expected me to use *my* imagination on their behalf. But my aim in going to town wasn't to serve up my imagination on a plate. I wanted to open their bleary eyes to the truth and make them realize the desperate hunger in their bellies!" He laughed.

"Did you know the Emperor originally came from the Korean settlement?"

"He told me so himself today. He said he was in the settlement the day S was killed. So I've got a personal reason for joining the young men in opposing him."

"But Taka—I get the impression that if, for example, you wanted to find justifications for ganging up with your group against that poor village policeman, you could find any number, both public and private," I said, drawing the conversation back to his argument with Hoshio in an attempt to prevent his remarks from setting up new waves of anxiety in me concerning the supermarket tycoon. "To me, Hoshi's approach seems fairer than yours."

"'Fair'? Do you still talk of justice?" he asked with an expression so despondent that even I felt chilled as I watched. And he suddenly fell silent, whereupon Momoko, who for some time past had been murmuring "Let's eat" in an effort to get us to the table, finally seized the chance to address him directly.

"All of them back home have read the book on gorillas that Mitsu translated," she declared. "They say they feel a lot happier now they know I'm under the same roof as such a distinguished scholar. Mitsu's a real member of the establishment, isn't he?" The show of being impressed was obviously phoney.

"Mitsu may have withdrawn from social life," commented my wife, who had already downed her first glass of whisky, "but he's still a member of the establishment all right. That should be obvious to someone like you, Taka, who're just the opposite type."

"Right," said Takashi, averting his eyes from me. "Perfectly obvious. Great-grandfather and grandfather—and their wives too—were the same type as Mitsu. Almost all the other people in our family died prematurely, but they lived on comfortably and peacefully into old age. You know, Natsumi, Mitsu will be ninety before he so much as gets cancer. And then it'll only be a mild case!"

"If you ask me, you're a lot too eager to find types in our family line," I countered, reluctant to give up. But no one apart from Hoshio paid any attention. "Unless you find you yourself are that type, all your efforts will have been directed at an imaginary world, and no real help at all."

After supper, Takashi gave my wife half of the advance he'd got from the Emperor, but she was already drunk and showed no interest. I was about to pocket it myself when he said:

"Mitsu—how about contributing fifty thousand yen to the football team I'm forming to train the young men's association?

I bought ten balls in town; they're in the Citroen. But expenses are piling up."

"Are footballs so expensive?" I asked meanly. Takashi had been on his university football team.

"I bought the balls with my own money. But some of the prospective team members go to the next town every day to work as laborers, you see. If I don't give them a daily allowance for a while, they won't so much as look at a football."

A Strange Sport

As I slept I could hear, in the blackness enveloping my dark form, the sound of bamboo splitting in the cold. The sound turned into a sharp steel claw and left a scratch on my hot sleeping head. My dream shifted scenes; a series of images dealing with the peasant rising in the valley flowed uninterrupted into memories of the day near the end of the war when one adult from every household in the valley had been mobilized to go and cut bamboo in the great bamboo grove. Then the series ran back on itself in a new sequence that led once more to that fateful year of 1860. I sank again into the depths of sleep, indulging a craven, uneasy temptation to let the familiar bad dreams drag on indefinitely rather than waken and face the Emperor, with his sturdy Korean body and inscrutable expression, and all the other new worries that had risen to trouble me. . . .

In my new dream, poised in time between 1860 and the last days of the war, the farmers—dressed in the standard khaki civilian dress with steel helmets on their backs, but with their hair done up in old-fashioned topknots—were busy cutting huge quantities of bamboo spears. In their persons, the men who brandished these spears as they carried all before them in the battle of 1860 were coeval with those who in 1945 were to have made last-ditch assaults on the armor-plated flanks of planes and landing craft. My mother was there with them, damaging the roots of the bamboo as she swung her ax about. She was so scared of any kind of sharp instrument that just to take hold of an ax was enough to make her feel faint, so she hacked blindly at the bamboo, the sweat beading her ashen face, her eyes tight shut. The bamboo grew so close that an accident was inevitable. Quite suddenly mother gave a great flourish of the ax and promptly dashed the handle and the back of her hand against the bamboo behind her. The ax glanced off and struck the crown of her head with a loud crack. Unhurriedly, she lowered the ax into the undergrowth, and in equally leisurely fashion put her hand to her head, then held it up before her eyes, gazing at the red stain—a bright red, like the colored cakes served at Buddhist memorial services—in the hollow of her palm. I stood rooted to the ground by a disgust and horror that reached down to the depths of my being. But mother on the contrary seemed to recover her vitality and said triumphantly to me: "I've hurt myself! Now I'll be excused training!" Abandoning ax and damaged bamboo, she moved off down the slope, seeming almost to glide on her knees over the undergrowth.

As my mother and I lay low in the storehouse, a squad of villagers shouldering bamboo spears came climbing up the graveled road. Their commander was Takashi, of indeterminate age. Since he was the only person in the valley who had actually seen America and the Americans, they doubtless saw him

as the most reliable man to lead them with their spears against
the American forces soon due to land on the coast and attack
the town. But the squad's first objective was the storehouse in
which mother and I were concealed.

"They can raze the main house to the ground, but the
storehouse won't burn! It didn't burn in 1860, either!" said my
mother, whose hair was thinning unpleasantly at the forehead
above her broad face. "Your great-grandfather, you know, drove
the rioters away by firing his gun through the loophole in the
storehouse."

I had an old-fashioned musket in my hands, but for all my
mother's incitements I hadn't the faintest idea how to handle
it. In no time the main house was destroyed and the outbuilding set on fire; I could see Jin's obese form rolling about in
the light of the flames, all escape cut off, the liquid streaming
from her suffering body. Takashi, who as leader of the mob was
by now completely identified with great-grandfather's younger
brother in 1860, bawled out challenges to mother, myself, and
the family spirits as we lurked in the storehouse. The followers
massed around him were members of the young men's association whom he'd trained with his football practice. Sea Urchin
and the other youths were dressed in uniforms consisting of
old-fashioned, horizontally striped pajamas, and had large, shiny
black topknots. And with one voice the mob joined in singling
me out for attack:

"You're just a rat!"

Until then, my consciousness in the dream had consisted
of a pair of healthy eyeballs that swept high over the valley, trailing beneath them a short coil of nerves rather like a microphone.
But their jeering brought the eyeballs crashing down, and with

them my physical self as I sat helpless in the storehouse with
the musket on my knees.

I awoke groaning. Even then, the emotional distress of the
dream persisted throughout my body; moreover, now that the
dream offered no corresponding actuality, the gloomy unease
remained disproportionately large, oppressing my waking self. I
longed desperately for my rectangular pit—now, alas, occupied
by a septic tank and covered with a lid of concrete. My wife lay
stiff and still in sleep by my side, hot as a small child with the
lingering effects of alcohol and the heat of slumber, but now
that I was awake my own body grew steadily colder.

Farther back up the valley, away from the central part of the
hollow, the river plunges into hidden folds of forest that press
in on either side, so that to an observer on the rising ground
at the entrance to the valley it seems as though the valley is
closed off at that point. From there on upstream, the bed of
the river turns to exposed rock, and a great grove of bamboo
closes in on both sides, forcing the graveled road to leave the
riverside and climb steeply uphill. The people who live in the
small clusters of houses dotted here and there along the road
as it climbs are called "the country folk" by the inhabitants of
the hollow. The great bamboo grove forms a broad belt that
joins at right angles the gash formed by the protrusion of the
spindle-shaped hollow into the forest, separating the hollow
and the "country." Once, when the valley folk had been drawn
up in the yard of the national school, armed with spears culled
from the great bamboo grove, the minor official who had come
from the prefectural office to take a look at them training had
infuriated the headman and other village worthies by carelessly
remarking that the people of Okubo village "were used to making

bamboo spears." As a result, the headman had gone into town to complain and the official had been relieved of his post.

To the village children, the sudden rage that had led the normally docile adults to pit themselves against the almighty prefectural office and, quite miraculously, defeat it was an inexplicable mystery. Every morning when I accompanied mother—who just as in my dream was afraid of axes and all sharp instruments—into the great bamboo grove with the other adults, and the renewed sound of splitting bamboo echoed steadily and imposingly around me, bringing to life again the memory of the grown-ups' fierce wrath, an indefinable fear would fill my childish mind. It was only after the end of the war, in a social studies class at school, that I heard about the farmers' rising in 1860 for the first time. The teacher made a special point of how the bamboo spears the farmers had used as weapons had been cut from the bamboo grove, and I understood at last what had made the headman and the others so angry. The bamboo grove was the most incontrovertible reminder of the 1860 rising, whose memory, during the war, had been viewed as a slur on all the inhabitants of the valley. The valley folk, unfortunately, had been set to work cutting bamboo in that same grove and made to fashion it into identical spears. It wasn't likely that they would let the official get away with a remark that reawakened so sharply the old sense of shame. By dutifully whittling spears in the service of the state, the headman and others of a similarly conformist bent, ashamed that their ancestors should have cut bamboo for use in a rebellion against the establishment of the day, were hoping to dispel the shadow of 1860 that still hung over them.

Mother's words in my dream had likewise reproduced, after more than two decades, words that I'd once heard in reality.

After father's death, my eldest brother left college and shortly afterward joined the army, while S had volunteered as a naval air cadet; whereupon mother, in whom too many such disappointments had produced delusions of persecution, began from time to time to predict that the villagers would attack our house, smash it up, and set fire to it. We must get ready, she said, to take flight and install ourselves in the storehouse as soon as the raiding party was sighted. When I objected, she told me of the outrage that had been perpetrated against our house in 1860, hoping thus to communicate her own fears to her infant son.

Mother attributed the 1860 rising to the farmers' greed and their helplessness. It started, she explained, when the farmers applied for a loan to the lord of the clan, who maintained a castle and territories with an income of three hundred and fifty thousand bushels of rice a year at the point where the river flowing through the valley runs into the Inland Sea. They were refused; so the Nedokoro family, squires of the village, lent them an equivalent amount. The farmers, however, complained that the rate of interest was unreasonably high. Cutting themselves spears in the great bamboo grove, they attacked the Nedokoro home and razed the main building to the ground. Then they raided the storehouse belonging to the valley brewers, got roaring drunk, and pressed on, attacking the homes of wealthy families and steadily swelling in number as they went, until they came to the castle town by the sea. If great-grandfather hadn't shut himself up in the storehouse and held out single-handed, firing the gun he'd brought from Kochi, the rioters would probably have taken possession of that as well. His younger brother, as central figure in the group of young men incited to action by the crafty older farmers of the valley, had preempted the title of "boss" of the whole valley, and had not only gone personally to negotiate the loan from the lord of the clan but had actually headed the violence when it was refused. Thus, at least in the eyes of other members of the Nedokoro family, he was a madman of the worst kind, who had broken up and set fire to his own home. Father, who had lost his life and property for the sake of some mysterious and profitless work in China, had inherited the same family streak of madness. As for my brothers, the eldest—who, however briefly, had taken a job on graduating from the Law Department—wasn't so bad, since he hadn't gone into the army voluntarily, but S, who had gone out of his way to volunteer, had inherited from his father the same blood as great-grandfather's younger brother. He was not *her* child, my mother declared.

"But your great-grandfather—" she would say, "there was a fine man!" Where the mob was armed only with bamboo spears, great-grandfather had been ready with a gun. He'd built a storehouse that refused to be knocked down or burned, and he'd fired at them from the second story. Which of us, now, would turn out like great-grandfather: Takashi or me?

If I stayed silent and refused to reply to such an obviously didactic question, mother would go on pressing indefinitely; and if I reluctantly declared that *I* would be like great-grandfather, she would respond with silence and a faint, doubting smile.

The former schoolteacher and local historian with whom I'd exchanged letters had neither denied nor positively affirmed mother's views on the origins of the rising. Favoring the academic approach, he attached great importance to the fact that around 1860 there had been all kinds of uprisings not just in our own fief but throughout the Ehime area, and that they could be seen collectively as symptoms of the coming Restoration of 1868. The only special circumstance that he detected in our clan was that a dozen years or so before 1860, when the lord of the clan had held office as Acting Minister of Shrines and Temples, he'd strained the finances of his estates and from then on had imposed a small daily tax on all town dwellers in his territories under the title of "universal savings." From the farmers he exacted first what he called "an advance on the rice tax" and later a "supplementary advance." At the very end of his letter, the local historian had appended a quotation from one of the contemporary documents he'd collected. "When the ying suffers," it said, "the yang is restored, and when the yang suffers the ying comes to life. Heaven and earth revolve perpetually; nothing is gone that does not come again. Man is the lord of creation; when government is unwise and men suffer, why should he not bring about change?" Such revolutionary, didactic sentiments, however, were more likely to prove elevating to Takashi than to me; perhaps Takashi really ought to meet the retired historian as my wife had said, provided he hadn't succumbed to cancer or a heart attack in the meantime. . . . For my part, I was incapable of joining a mob, either in my dreams or in reality. I might take refuge in the storehouse, but I could never fight with a gun. Given my nature, anything to do with the rising was utterly remote from me. Takashi, though, set out to be precisely the opposite type of man—and in my dreams, at least, had already achieved his aim.

A sound came from the direction of the outbuilding. Probably the middle-aged woman with the uncontrollable appetite, frightened by a nightmare, was getting up in the dark to feed herself more stuff calculated to fill the stomach with a minimum of nourishment. It was still the small hours. Stretching out a hand in the darkness, I groped for the bottle of whisky which I was sure my wife had left partly full. At once my hand contacted something cold, like the shell of a crab from which the flesh has been gouged. I switched on the flashlight by my bed and found an empty sardine can. Taking care not to shine the light on my sleeping wife's face, I moved the small bright circle about till I found the whisky, then drank straight from the bottle by the light of the flashlight. I tried to remember whether she'd been eating sardines as she drank the previous evening, but without success. By now her drinking had become a firmly established part of my everyday life. More often than not, I could watch her getting drunk on whisky with as little concern as if she were smoking.

I stared fixedly at the empty sardine can as I drank. In the center of the fingernail-shaped opening made in the lid by the can opener, a small fork was placed with obsessive precision. The tin plate on the outside of the can was cloudy-white with oil, but the interior gleamed gold through the thin layer of fish scraps and oil that remained. I could see her winding back the lid with the fragile key, rolling the tight scroll of tin to one side of the can, experiencing, as the neat row of delicate sardine tails came into view, the primitive joy of someone about to extract the soft flesh of an oyster from its lip-cutting shell and eat it. She ate the sardines, took a sip of whisky through lips moist with oil and flakes of fish, then licked the three fingers she'd used to pick up the fish. At one time, her fingers had been so weak that she always asked me to open sardine cans for her. It was only since she'd acquired the habit of solitary drinking that her fingers had got strong, a fact that served if anything to heighten the effect of pitiful degradation. Shutting my eyes, I took a great gulp of whisky in an effort to thrust the pity I felt for her back into its hole, along with the indefinably sentimental anger that welled up inside me, threatening to get out of control. The stuff burned my throat and burned my stomach, then burned the blackness in my head and I fell into a dreamless sleep.

The next morning, Takashi and his bodyguards set off for the primary school, which was on vacation now, to join the village youths who were to assemble in the playground for their first football practice. Left alone, my wife and I felt a frustrating sense of emptiness as though we too ought to be starting something. The mood became so strong that I got Jin's children to help me carry tatami mats and a charcoal brazier from the main house up to the second floor of the storehouse, and made a fresh start on the translation I'd been working on with my dead friend. The book, an amusing account by an English naturalist of a childhood spent by the Aegean, had been a favorite with my friend, who had first discovered it. When I got to work, my wife decided to start reading an old edition of the works of Soseki Natsume that had turned up while we were looking for the brazier in the spare room of the main house, so we managed somehow to keep ourselves occupied.

My friend's tough old grandmother had promised to collect the draft translation of the parts he'd already done, together with his notes and other papers, and entrust them to me. But relatives had objected, and after the funeral everything my friend had written was burned. They'd been afraid—afraid that another monster with crimson-painted head and a cucumber up its rear might leap naked out of the manuscripts and notes he'd left and threaten the world of those who had survived. Even I, admittedly, couldn't completely suppress the deep sense of relief that the meager flames from the burning papers and notebooks had kindled in me. But it hadn't been enough to free me entirely from the threat of the monster. As I went through the Penguin book that he'd left with all its scribblings and underlinings, thinking to retranslate the parts for which he'd been responsible, I found any number of pitfalls in wait for my unwary self. In the margin of a section describing a Greek turtle with a fondness for strawberries, my friend had done a sketch of a turtle, about one inch square, which he'd copied from an illustrated book of animals. It vividly revealed the humorous side of his sensibility at its gentlest and most childlike. And another passage that he'd marked with a line seemed to be sending me a message in my friend's own voice:

> "Let's say good-bye then," he started to say, but his voice quavered and broke, and tears forced their way out and ran down the wrinkled cheeks. "I'm damned if I'll cry!" he sobbed and threw out his great belly, "but it's like saying goodbye to one's own flesh and blood. I felt as though you were my own."

My wife, who was reading her Soseki in silence, also seemed to have found plenty of things to stir her own feelings. Before long, she came over and helped herself to the dictionary I was using. She looked up some English words quoted by Soseki, then said:

"Did you know that Soseki uses quite a lot of English words and phrases in the diary he wrote while he was at Shuzenji suffering from a stomach ulcer? They all seem to be appropriate to you nowadays, Mitsu. Listen: 'languid stillness,' 'weak state,' 'painless,' 'passivity,' 'goodness,' 'peace,' 'calmness' . . ."

"'Painless'? Do you really think that describes my condition? I may be too washed out to have the energy for anything except 'goodness,' but do you really believe I'm in a state of *peace*?"

"That's how you look to *me* at least, Mitsu," she insisted with the exaggerated composure of an alcoholic during a sober spell. "You've been more placid during these past few months than at any other time since we got married."

I struggled to evade the terrifying vision this evoked of myself attaining the ultimate placidity possible in the animal and going over finally into the utter placidity of the vegetable. I read once that in medieval times aged monks who wanted to turn themselves into mummies gradually reduced their food intake, so that by the time they were ready to go into their graves they had only to stop breathing and the flesh began to dry up. In much the same way, I'd played the non-animal during my pit-dwelling experience early that autumn morning, deliberately inviting death to come with as little fuss as possible. Eventually, with a profound sense of fear, I'd returned to the world, and convinced myself that I'd reembarked on ordinary life. But it seemed that in my wife's eyes I was still the same as when I sat motionless at the bottom of the pit dug for the septic tank, my buttocks wet, the dog held in my arms. Shame suffused every last capillary of my body, sending waves of hot wretchedness through the rat that I was. If my plight was apparent even to someone constantly drunk and withdrawn like my wife, it was going to be even harder to reestablish contact with that feeling of expectation. New life?

Thatched hut? I might as well resign myself to doing without them forever. . . .

"How about you—do you feel you've started a new life?" I said.

"Why ask? You know I'm drinking whisky just the same as ever, don't you? I could hardly keep it secret if I wanted to—the whisky you get here in the valley is such powerful stuff the smell's enough to give you away." She'd mistaken my question for sarcasm aimed solely at hurting, and her words were barbed and defiant. "Surely it was *you*, not me, that Takashi suggested should start a new life?"

"You're right. That's my own problem," I agreed, shrinking into myself. "But there's one thing I'd like to check on where your drinking's concerned."

"I suppose you want to know whether I see my alcoholism as a youthful experience that'll pass of its own accord, or as something I'll have to live with till I die—as a sign of the collapse from youth into old age. Well, the real source is hereditary—my mother. And I'm not so young anymore that one day's dissipation is cured the next. So I expect I'll have to live with it. I'm at the age where every time I find a new wrinkle I resign myself to taking it with me to the grave."

"If you're saying this out of a childish desire to shock me, you'd better think again," I said. "Because you *are* that age, and there's no stay of execution. If you're going to have another kid, you'll have to make up your mind to it before the year's out. Next year there'll be no going back."

Immediately, I intensely regretted my words. The malice in them was too strong even for me. We were silent together for a

while, then, fixing me with eyes that for once were red from tears
rather than whisky and filled with a forlorn hostility, she said:

"When the time comes and, as you say, there's no going
back, perhaps we'll be a bit kinder to each other."

"Why don't we go and watch Taka and the rest playing
football?" I replied, sidestepping her remark with a sense of
self-disgust.

"Then I'll make some packed lunches for the team, Mitsu,"
she said as she set off back to the main building. "If only I do
some work, the outlook for a new life might brighten a bit—
and the mist of scandal in the valley might clear a little, too."
She was mocking herself as well as me; what she referred to
as "scandal" was the rumor spreading through the valley that
the third Nedokoro boy's wife was a worthless alcoholic. She'd
heard it herself, at the supermarket.

The way she objected to what I said suggested that her
will to fight the landslide occurring in her wasn't yet completely
dissipated by alcohol. I should have stretched out a helping
hand, but a similar landslide was threatening to sweep me off
my feet too.

I concentrated on the translation, trying to ignore the
voices of my family ancestors that filled the storehouse with
their cries of "rat, rat!" In the distance, I seemed to hear blood-
curdling yells and the sound of a ball being kicked about, but
it might just have been a noise in my own head.

In the afternoon, Jin's youngest boy dropped in to say that
the young priest from the temple had come to see me. Going
back to the main house, I found the kitchen full of billowing
steam with a fragrance of bamboo grass. My wife was just taking an old and well-remembered steamer off a great pot on the

hearth, while two of Jin's sons and the priest watched, enveloped in steam up to head or chest, depending on their size. Coughing loudly, the boy who had come to fetch me went back to his elder brothers and disappeared into the steam.

"You'll burn yourself!" Jin's boys called in lofty warning as my wife, whose cheeks and ears were bright red, put out a hand toward the contents of the steamer. And when her fingers shot back to her lips they roared with good-natured laughter.

"What are you making?" I asked with a sense of relief as I joined the steamy circle around her.

"Rice dumplings in bamboo leaves. Jin showed me how. The children got the leaves from the woods for me." Her voice had a youthful élan that it had lacked completely during our conversation in the storehouse. "They seem to have turned out quite well. Do you remember them, Mitsu?"

"The valley folk always took them when they went to cut trees in the forest," I said. "Jin's father was originally a lumberman, so her recipe's sure to be genuine."

She gave each of us one of her "genuine" dumplings, which were twice the size of a man's fist. The priest and I broke them into pieces on plates before eating them, so for us the bamboo leaves still dripping with hot water were redundant, but Jin's children held the dumplings in their hands, rolling them about on wet palms as they skillfully chewed at them from the edges without spoiling their shape. They consisted of balls of glutinous rice flavored with soy sauce and stuffed with a paste of pork and fresh mushrooms. The leaves of bamboo grass in which they were wrapped were dry and whitish around the edges, but tattered though they were it must have cost the children quite an effort, if not actual fear, to gather them at this season.

Watching the expert way they ate their dumplings, I couldn't believe that the valley children's traditional dislike of going into the forest in winter had changed either.

"These dumplings aren't at all bad, but they taste of garlic," I said critically. "When *I* was living here, people never put garlic in any food, let alone dumplings." She was taking the remainder out of the steamer and transferring them to long, shallow boxes of a kind also familiar to me from childhood. Both steamer and boxes had been brought out of the storehouse at Jin's suggestion.

"What?" she exclaimed suspiciously. "Jin told me specially to put some garlic in, so I bought a supply when I went to the supermarket to get the pork."

"There you are, Mitsu—" said the priest, a fragment of food poised in his fingers, "that's typical of the way life's changing in the village. Before the war, garlic played no part in village life at all. I don't suppose most people even knew there was such a plant. But the villagers discovered it when the war began, all because of the settlement built by the Korean laborers who came to fell timber in the forest. It was their contempt for a people who could eat such a smelly root that first made them aware of garlic. You know the kind of thing I mean, don't you, Mitsu? Well, when the villagers took the Koreans to do forced labor in the forest, they deliberately told them some nonsense about not being allowed into the forest unless they took some dumplings with them. It was a way of asserting their own superiority. So the Koreans began to make dumplings too, and hit on the idea of putting garlic in to suit their own taste. That influenced the villagers in reverse, who started using it for flavoring dumplings they made themselves. It just shows how the locals' stupid pride and lack of principles bring about changes in the customs of the valley. The village never used to use garlic as a flavoring, but by now it's a best seller at the supermarket. So the Emperor has double or triple cause to be pleased with himself."

"I don't care, so long as the 'lack of principles' works out all right in my cooking," my wife said aggressively. "Even if I am going against tradition."

"It's worked out fine," I said. "If you'll permit the usual sentimental assessment, they're better than mother used to make."

"No doubt about it!" chimed in the priest. She gave us a suspicious glance, however, and refused to be mollified.

"But I didn't really come here for a free meal," the priest said, turning to me. His small round face, normally a model of amiability, puckered with embarrassment. "The thing is, I came across your eldest brother's diary which S left with me, so I brought it over."

"Come and have a talk upstairs in the storehouse," I said. "I'm not going to football practice, so I've nothing to do." I wasn't just trying to cheer him up; I really wanted to talk. "Do you happen to be interested in the 1860 rising?"

"Yes—I studied it a bit and made some notes on it myself," he said eagerly, with obvious pleasure at being rescued. "You see, the second most important role in it—after your ancestors, that is—was played by one of my predecessors at the temple, though there's no blood relationship."

Ignoring the self-preoccupied sensitivity of the priest's reactions, my wife was already giving energetic instructions to Jin's sons. They were to take some dumplings to their mother and to go and tell Hoshio, who was at the primary school playground, to come for the food in the Citroen. Then, just as the priest and I were leaving the main house she called out defiantly after us:

"I'm going to watch football practice this afternoon too, Mitsu. I want to hear what they think of the dumplings."

The embarrassed young priest and I set off for the storehouse, breathing garlic fumes like fire-belching monsters in a science-fiction movie. The diary he'd brought was a small book bound in dark purple cloth. My eldest brother had been a remote being who was usually away from home, either at his hostel in town or in lodgings in Tokyo, and rarely came back even on vacations. My only clear-cut memory concerning him was of the unpleasant impression created by the village grownups who, when he died less than two years after leaving the university, had moralized on the futility of investing in higher education for a son. I took the diary and placed it on top of the Penguin book left by my dead friend. I had a feeling that the priest was rather disappointed that I didn't start reading it then and there. But the truth was that my eldest brother's testament, far from inspiring my mind to a lively curiosity, chilled it with some imprecise yet ominous foreboding. I determined to behave as though entirely uninterested in the diary, and without waiting went on:

"Mother used to say that great-grandfather kept the mob at bay by firing a gun from the second-floor window of the storehouse. This window is, in fact, shaped just like a loophole; it makes the story seem so probable that I'm inclined, on the contrary, to doubt it. What do you think? She said the gun was one great-grandfather had brought back from his trip to Kochi. I wonder if it's possible that a peasant in Ehime in the year 1860 should have been armed with a gun?"

"The term 'peasant' hardly applies," said the priest. "Your great-grandfather was the richest overseer in the area, and there'd be nothing odd about his having a gun. It seems more likely, though, that he didn't bring it back from Kochi himself, but that it was supplied by someone from Kochi who infiltrated the village just before the riots. My father's theory was that a man from Kochi stayed at the temple and worked on your great-grandfather and his brother, through the priest of the time, to start the riots. The interloper may have been a samurai of the Tosa clan, but there's no conclusive proof. Either way, he was someone from the other side of the forest. Since it was the priest who put him in contact with your great-grandfather and his brother, he may have come through the forest dressed as a wandering monk. At that time, not only the valley but the whole clan was affected by unrest, which would have given scope for the activities of an agent sent by forces from beyond the forest, the kind of forces that would profit from anything likely to upset the ruling regime. I imagine that the priest and your great-grandfather shared the view that only a rising could bring any relief to the valley peasants. The priest took neither side, while the overseer was on the side of the establishment—but ruin for the masses would have meant their both going under too. So the real question plaguing them was what kind of rising to instigate and where. The easiest course, you see, would be to provide some outlet for the violent energies building up to a rising before things got so bad that the attack was concentrated on the overseer himself, and to keep violence in the valley to a minimum while diverting the rest to the castle town. Now, a rising needs a group of leaders, but whatever kind of success this particular rising achieved, its leaders were bound to be seized

and put to death. How were they, then, to select this group that
was fated eventually to be sacrificed yet, during the rising itself,
would exercise control over the farmers not only of the valley
but of the whole area as far as the castle town? This was the
point at which people began to take notice of the band of young
men that your great-grandfather's brother was training. Though
they may have included a few eldest sons due to inherit their
father's land, most of them were second or third sons—surplus
population with no prospect of ever having land of their own.
To sacrifice such a group would be no particular blow to the
valley. If anything, it would help get rid of a public nuisance."

"That suggests, doesn't it, that from the very beginning the
man from beyond the forest, and the priest and great-grandfather,
treated the younger brother as something dispensable?"

"It seems likely to me that the brother, unlike the rest,
had a secret agreement that after the rising he would escape
to Kochi and cross from there to Osaka or Edo. The outsider
would have been the one responsible for seeing that the promise was carried out. You've heard the popular theory, haven't
you, that your great-grandfather's brother left the forest, took a
different name, and became a high official in the Restoration
government?"

"That would mean, then, that he was one of the traitors
from the beginning. Either way, it seems I'm descended from
a line of traitors."

"How can you say that, Mitsu? The reason why your great-
grandfather went so far as to fire his gun during the raid was
almost certainly that he'd begun to doubt whether the agreement with his brother about the storehouse not being set on fire
would really be observed. Even agreed that the main building

had to be destroyed—since if the Nedokoro house hadn't been attacked at all your great-grandfather would have been held responsible by the clan officials—I suspect it was that doubt that made him keep the weapon supplied from outside without handing it over to the young men. And the young men did in fact occupy the storehouse themselves later. As a result of the rising, which lasted five days and nights, the 'advance tax' system was abolished just as the farmers had demanded: and the official Confucian scholar who'd recommended it to the lord of the clan was executed. Then, following that, your great-grandfather's brother and his group put up a fight in the storehouse to avoid having some of their number made into scapegoats. Fighting together in the rising, the leaders must have developed a sense of solidarity focused on the figure of your great-grandfather's brother."

Following the end of the rising, great-grandfather's brother and the group formed round him had shut themselves in the storehouse and defied the clan investigating officers. Armed and apprehensive, it was they who out of frustration at being besieged in the storehouse had slashed at the woodwork, leaving the sword marks that had so often inspired my childish mind with bloodthirsty fantasies. Since the farmers failed to give food and water to the group that had been their leaders until only the previous day, the besieged men found themselves isolated. They gave in, were enticed out of the storehouse, and beheaded on the small rise that now forms the open space in front of the village office. The man directly responsible for tricking the thirsty and starving youths out of the storehouse was great-grandfather. He got the village girls to dress up in their best and set up a temporary kitchen in front of the storehouse, then brought in investigators to seize the young men once they'd fallen into a drunken sleep. Grandmother used to relate the episode proudly as testimony to the resourcefulness of her Nedokoro forebears. I remember mother telling me, too, that when she first came to the valley as a bride one of the girls used in great-grandfather's ruse was still alive. At the time of the slaughter, great-grandfather's brother was the only one to escape execution and get away into the forest. In the end, he'd abandoned even the comradeship with his fellow rebels that the young priest spoke of—assuming he'd ever had it—so as a member of the same family line I wasn't likely to be very reassured by what the priest said. I wondered if great-grandfather's brother, as he fled into the forest, didn't perhaps turn when he reached the highest point and, looking back at the hollow, see his unhappy fellows below, their drunken sleep rudely interrupted, being beheaded on the mound in the valley. At that same moment great-grandfather, too, must have been either present at the execution or looking down on it from a vantage point on the stone wall.

"As for why the younger brother began giving the young men special training, I imagine it was because the *Kanrin-maru* had set sail for America," said the young priest, sensing my depression and delicately changing the subject. Despite the sensitivity this showed, it was the same man who had managed to live down all the different stories, including a malicious rumor that he was sexually impotent, that flew about the valley following his wife's elopement.

"Supposing, now," he went on, "that this brother heard a rumor that John Manjiro, whom your great-grandfather had met at Kochi, was setting off for America again on the *Kanrin-maru*. Almost certainly he would have chafed at the bit to be confined in a small valley at a time when the sons of fishermen beyond the forest were living lives of adventure in a place open to whole new realms of experience. A report came at the beginning of summer that year, you see, that the shogunate had given permission for men from this clan to go and study at the Naval Academy, and he promptly campaigned, through the temple priest, to have himself selected as one of the students. My father used to say he'd read a copy of the application, so I imagine it would turn up even now if one made a thorough search of the temple storehouse. It shouldn't have been impossible for the second son of a wealthy overseer to work his way into the lower ranks of the samurai. Why, it was just around that time that the sons of wealthy local landowners on the other side of the forest were active in the pro-Emperor, anti-foreign movement. Admittedly, his attempts didn't succeed. And not so much because of any lack of ability on his part as from the clan's own failure to show the spirit of adventure needed to send someone to the Naval Academy. As I see it, it was his sense of frustrated indignation that turned him into the kind of anti-establishment activist who would plan to give the village youths special training or undertake to represent the farmers in their attempt to get a loan from the clan. And the agent who came from the other side of the forest, together with the priest and your great-grandfather, took note of this dangerous young leader and set to work on him. That's the conclusion my studies have led me to, at least."

"It's certainly the most appealing view of the 1860 affair I've heard so far," I admitted. "If you consider it together with the incident just after the war when S was killed, the role played by the young village thugs is consistent, and all kinds of things make sense."

"To be honest," the young priest also admitted candidly, "you might say it was a bright idea I had while watching the incident in the Korean village that led to my interpretation of the events of 1860. There were things in S's behavior that could only suggest he had the 1860 rising in mind when he resolved on his own course of action. I don't think I'm just forcing an analogy in linking 1860 and the summer of 1945."

"Do you mean S was bothered because great-grandfather's brother was the only rebel leader who escaped execution, and deliberately decided that, in contrast, he alone would be killed in the raid on the Korean settlement? If so, at least it's the kindest interpretation now that he's dead."

"I was his friend, you see," the young priest said with evident embarrassment, the small face flushing beneath the prematurely white hair. "Not a very useful friend, you must admit. . . ."

"Takashi is like S," I said. "He seems to want his actions to be influenced by the 1860 affair. Today, for example, he's started getting the young men of the valley together for football practice, just because he's taken a fancy to the story of how great-grandfather's brother cut a clearing in the forest as a training ground to prepare the young men to fight."

"But the kind of rising that occurred in 1860 wouldn't be possible today," the priest replied, regaining his customary smile. "And the time's past when a killing match between the Korean settlement and the valley folk could have taken place without any police intervention, as happened just after the war. In a peaceful age like the present, not even Takashi could set himself up as leader of a riot, so I shouldn't really worry."

"Incidentally," I said, taking advantage of the smile to put out a feeler, "is there anything in this diary that might offend a good pacifist? If there is, I think I'd better give it to Takashi. Among the various human types found in the Nedokoro family, I'm the kind that refuses to be inspired to heroic thoughts by the 1860 business. It's the same even in my sleep: far from identifying with great-grandfather's intrepid brother, I have wretched dreams in which I'm a bystander cowering in the storehouse, incapable even of firing a gun like great-grandfather."

"You think, then, it would be better to give the diary to Takashi, do you?" said the priest, whose smile had frozen momentarily.

I took the purple diary off my dead friend's Penguin book and, putting it in the pocket of my overcoat, went down with the priest to the primary school playground where Takashi was practicing football with his new comrades.

In a strong breeze that blew aimlessly about the valley beneath a blue sky, the young men were kicking the football around in silence and with suffocating intensity of purpose. The Sea Urchin in particular was dashing about desperately, a thick towel wound round the head that sat so incongruously large on his short trunk. He took repeated tumbles but, oddly enough, no one laughed. Even the village kids standing round the edge of the playground were sunk in a grave, earnest silence just the reverse of the gay vitality of city children watching sports.

Takashi and Hoshio, who were standing in the center giving them instructions as they rushed about, made no move to interrupt practice even when the priest and I signaled to them. Momoko and my wife, though, came over in the Citroen to talk to us, making a wide detour round the football-playing group.

"Isn't it a terrifying sight?" I said. "Why are they throwing themselves into it so enthusiastically when they don't really seem to be enjoying it?"

"Throwing themselves into everything is the only way they know. Momoko and I like football practice when it's as serious as this. We're going to come and watch every day from now on," said my wife, refusing to share my scruples.

The ball came rolling out of the circle of youths in my direction. I tried to kick it back, but my foot contacted mostly air and the ball spun frantically before coming to rest only a short distance away. The women in the car watched me and the ball with complete indifference, not even smirking. The young priest wore his customary smile as though to smooth over my embarrassment, but it only served to fluster me still more.

After supper that evening, when we were all lying about near the fireplace, Takashi came up to me and, though he lowered his voice so as not to be heard by my wife, who was drunk, said in a tone that was ugly with cold emotion:

"Mitsu—there are terrible things in that diary."

I stared into the darkness, avoiding facing him directly. Even before I heard his next words a sense of disgust was welling up inside me.

"He studied German at college, you know. He uses the word *Zusammengewürfelt*, says the forces are a bunch of slobs. Some fellow who was hit for breaking ranks during company training actually committed suicide, he says, leaving a sarcastic note apologizing to the company commander. The company commander was our brother. 'Take a look at Japan today,' he writes. 'Utter chaos. Utterly unscientific, utterly unprepared. And half-baked into the bargain. Now look at Germany—the coupons for the rationing system actually in force at the moment were printed way back in 1933 when Hitler first came to power. I pray to God that the Soviet Union rains bombs on us. The Japanese have been poisoned by the dream of peace and got themselves in an unholy mess, but they're still rushing round and round in circles.' He also says that the only things he got out of the army were 'a certain increase in staying power and greater physical strength.' He thinks one should read widely and deeply in accordance with some objective, and he makes notes about some system of deep breathing. On one page he can write, 'In such and such a unit on Hainan Island, the commander himself said it was all right to violate a young woman as long as one took the proper steps afterward—the proper steps meaning, of course, to kill her.' And on the next page he can write in high moral tones, 'He who would climb Mt. Fuji must start from the first station.' Then he describes in detail the scene on Leyte when the unit commander executed a native, an alleged spy. 'The unit commander who captured him apparently said at first that he'd have a recruit bayonet him, but then he took over himself and, wielding a Japanese sword for the first time in his life, cut off the native's head.' Do you want to read it, Mitsu?"

"I couldn't care less about his diary, Taka," I said roughly. "And I don't want to read it. It was because I had a feeling it would contain that kind of stuff that I handed it on to you. But what's all the fuss about? Is it anything more than a perfectly ordinary set of war reminiscences?"

"For me at least it *is* something to make a fuss about," he said, firmly rejecting my criticisms. "It means I've found one close relative at least who maintained his ordinary approach to life even on the battlefield, yet was an effective perpetrator of evil. Why—if I'd lived through the same times as him, this might have been my own diary. The idea seems to open up a whole new perspective in my view of things."

His voice must have had the force to impose itself momentarily even on my wife's drink-befuddled brain. When I turned to look at him, she too had raised her head and was gazing intently at his face as he stood there, fiercely animated yet somber, with the air somehow of a violent criminal.

Procession from the Past

The next morning, on waking, I realized at once that I was sleeping alone as I normally did in Tokyo, that I could twist and turn in response to the pains scattered among the various parts of my body and the desolate lack deep down behind my ribs without that feeling of base panic lest my wife, sleeping by my side, should see me. It brought a definite, physical sense of release. I was, in fact, lying with all my frailties in full view, as careless of others' eyes as I always was when I slept quite alone. At first, I'd tried to avoid identifying the memory that was the original inspiration for my posture. But I admitted now that it was the memory of that grotesque, utterly abject thing existing in its wooden cot, the thing that we'd gazed down at so blankly when we went to the institution to get our baby back. The doctor had wondered if the baby might not die of shock if his environment changed again. But the real reason we'd left him there was that we ourselves might well have died of the disgust and shock inspired by that horrifying object. Our behavior of course was quite unjustifiable; if he'd died and come back a

frail, wasted ghost to savage us to death, I for one would have
made no attempt to escape.

The night before, my wife, disliking the idea of retiring
to my side of the sliding doors, had slept by the open fireplace
with Takashi and his bodyguards. In her whisky-heated brain
she'd mulled over our conversation upstairs in the storehouse
concerning the new life, disintegration, and death, carrying its
implications still further until she'd finally taken a resolute stand.

"Let's go to bed," I'd urged her. "You can go on drinking
there." But she refused, in a clearer voice than I, in view of
the nature of the subject, would have wished, even though she
was too drunk to talk loudly for the special benefit of Takashi
and the others.

"You talk about going back and having another baby as if
it had nothing directly to do with you. But it would mean starting again yourself, too. In practice, you've no intention of doing
so. Why should I have to obey your orders, then, and creep in
between the blankets like a faithful pet?"

With a private feeling of relief I'd left her and retired
alone. Takashi made no move to intervene in our petty conflict. Encouraged by the unfamiliar voice of his eldest brother
echoing from the pages of the purple diary, he was straining
to twist himself, like a sharp-edged screw, deeper still into
the murky recesses of his own peculiar problems. I myself
had no desire to be influenced by the ghost of this brother of
ours, nor had the diary disturbed me particularly. I preferred
to dismiss it as a perfectly commonplace account of wartime
experiences. It was much safer to go to sleep with a gap in my
imagination than to summon up the ill-omened figure of our
brother standing bloody on unfamiliar battlefields.

For the first time in many a month I thrust my head beneath the blankets and sniffed at the warm odor of my own body. It was like nuzzling down into one's entrails. I was a coelenterate five feet six inches long, plunging my head into my intestines to close the comfortable circle of my own flesh. It was almost as though the dull ache in the several parts of my body, and the sense of lack, had been transformed into an obscure and guilty feeling of pleasure, a pleasure arising from awareness that I was free from the eyes of others, that the pain and the sense of lack were at least my own. I felt I might even become pregnant with these sensations and, like the lowest order of creatures, achieve unicellular reproduction. Bearing with the difficulty in breathing, I kept my head buried in the warm, smelly darkness between the blankets, trying to picture myself suffocating to death there, the smell of my own body in my nostrils, my head painted crimson and a cucumber stuffed up my anus. With increasingly intense reality the outlines of the scene began to take shape. . . .

On the verge of suffocation, the skin of my face hot and puffy with blood, I thrust my head with terrific force into the cool air outside the blankets, to be greeted by the sound of Takashi and my wife talking in low tones beyond the sliding doors. Takashi's voice had the same elated quality as the previous night. I hoped my wife was listening with her face turned toward the shadows: not that I wanted to keep secret the signs of degradation that must be so apparent on her newly awakened face, but the idea of my brother's eyes intruding thus on our "family" inevitably damaged my self-respect. He was speaking of memory, the world of dreams and the like. Gradually, the fragments coalesced into a kernel of sense that reminded me of the argument in the Citroen.

". . . pointed out the distortions, to be honest I couldn't reply. Remember? It took all the fight out of me, left me in a state of doubt and self-questioning, but what the football team told me . . . recovered, Natsumi."

". . . Taka, your memory . . . than Mitsu's," my wife said in a flat, lifeless voice. Far from indicating inattention, the voice was a sign that my wife, a good listener when sober, was concentrating on what he said.

"No, I'm not saying my memories tally with the facts. But I didn't consciously distort them, either. After all, I did once have roots here, so to fall in with the communal aspirations of the valley can hardly be called a kink in my personality, can it? After I was separated from the village, memory combined with the communal dream to form a kind of pure culture in my mind. As a kid I actually saw, in the Nembutsu dance at the Bon festival, the 'spirit' of S, in the winter jacket worn by naval air cadets, fighting the men from the Korean settlement at the head of a party of young men, until he was finally beaten to death, stripped of his jacket, and left lying face down in just his white undershirt and shorts. I told you, didn't I, that his arms were raised as if he was dancing, with his legs spread like those of a hurdler in action? That's taken directly from a sudden moment of stillness in the Nembutsu dance, at the top of one of its wild leaps. The dance was performed in broad daylight at the height of summer, so even the white sunlight that illuminates my memory is part of what I experienced at an actual Bon festival. You see, it wasn't a memory of the real-life raid on the Korean settlement, but an experience in the world of the dance, in which the facts were reworked in visible form through the communal emotions of the people of the valley. The boys in the team told me that even after I left the valley they saw S's 'spirit' do the same dance as I remember at the Bon festival every year. All I did, in fact, was mix up the Nembutsu dance in the processes of my memory with the actual scene of the raid. That surely means that I've still got roots linking me to the communal sentiments of the valley. I'm certain of it. Mitsu must have watched the dance with me when I was a kid, and being older he ought to have a clearer memory of it than me, but during the argument in the car he deliberately kept quiet to suit his own logic. He's got a crafty side to him."

"What was the Nembutsu dance like, Taka?" my wife asked. "Does 'spirits' mean spirits of the dead?" But I got the impression that she'd already grasped the essential meaning of what he said, and understood perfectly well his pride at discovering, through dreams, his ties with the communal spirit of the valley.

"Why don't you ask Mitsu? He'll be jealous if I'm the one to tell you everything about the valley. I'm more interested in having you make lunch for the team again today. I'm thinking of having them here to live in while they train. It's always been a valley custom for the young fellows to get together at the New Year and stay for a few days. So I'm going to arrange the same thing. I hope you'll give us a hand, Natsumi."

I didn't catch her reply clearly, but it was plain to me that by now she belonged to Takashi's inner circle. That afternoon, she asked me to tell her about Bon festival customs in the valley. She naturally made no mention of the word "jealousy" that Takashi had used, so I too kept quiet about overhearing her conversation with him early that morning, and told her about the Nembutsu dance.

Of all the evil beings that descended on the hollow bringing trouble with them, the most typical was the Chosokabe,
an enemy with whom the valley folk would have no dealings
whatsoever. But the hollow was also visited by another, different type of evil, or rather evildoers, who, since they had
originally belonged among the valley folk themselves, could
not by their very nature be dealt with by simple rejection
and expulsion. Every year during the Bon festival, they came
back to the valley in a single-file procession that followed the
graveled road down from the upper reaches of the forest. I
learned from an article by a well-known folklorist that these
beings who came back from the forest to be greeted with such
reverence by the inhabitants were "spirits" who sometimes
exerted a harmful influence from the other world (the forest)
on the present world (the valley). Any persistent floods that
ravaged the valley, or any particularly virulent rice pest, were
attributed to these "spirits," and it was to placate them that
people devoted so much energy to the Bon festival. During
the typhus epidemic toward the end of the war, a particularly
spectacular dance was performed in honor of the "spirits."
The Bon procession that filed down from the forest that year,
with a figure got up like a huge white cuttlefish in its midst,
was an object of terror to the valley children. The figure probably represented the malevolent "spirit" of a louse—not a real
louse, of course, but the "spirit" of one of the village ancestors who had led a brutal life, or of some good man who had
died an unhappy death, manifesting himself that year in the
form of a louse in order to bring disaster to the valley. There
was one villager who was an expert in the Nembutsu dance
and always devoted great ingenuity to preparing the festival

procession. He was a tatami maker by trade, but when, for example, an epidemic filled the isolation hospital in the great bamboo grove to overflowing, he would be preoccupied right from the beginning of spring with working out the staging of the next Bon festival. Even at times when he was busy in his workshop, he would call out in a loud, excited voice to passersby on the graveled road, asking their opinion on some idea or other.

When the festival procession reached the front garden of our house, it would form a ring and dance, then step up into the storehouse and spend a while commenting politely on the interior, until everybody was given something to eat and drink. So where watching the Bon procession was concerned at least, I'd been in a privileged position compared with the other valley children.

The most striking change that I remember in the processions I witnessed was the sudden appearance, one summer during the war, of "spirits" in army uniform. They were the ghosts of men drafted from the valley who had been killed in battle. The number of them in uniform increased every year. The "spirit" of a young man who had been working in a Hiroshima factory and was killed by the atomic bomb came down from the forest with his whole body blackened like a lump of used charcoal. At the Bon festival the summer after S died, the tatami maker came to borrow a cadet uniform, so without telling mother I lent him the jacket of the winter uniform. The next day, the party that came down the graveled road from the forest included a "spirit" wearing the jacket, dancing for all it was worth. . . .

"It wasn't fair to Takashi not to mention that in the Citroen."

"But I didn't keep quiet about it deliberately. You see, I *know* S wasn't the leader of the young men in the valley, and

I've got my own powerful memory of S's body lying where he'd been beaten to death. So I just couldn't connect up such a heroic and attractive 'spirit' with S's actual death."

"All that means is you're cut off from what Taka calls the 'communal sentiments' of the valley folk."

"If I'm really cut off from the valley, then any trouble the 'spirits' bring here has nothing to do with me, thank God," I said, nipping in the bud the attack concealed in her seemingly harmless words. "As you'll soon realize if you actually see the Nembutsu dance, the dance of the 'spirit' in cadet uniform is performed in a ring and involves a lot of spectacular movement, but in the procession that came from the forest it was a low-ranking ghost tagging along somewhere near the back. The 'spirit' who led the procession, the spectacular central figure who was looked up to both by the spectators and the other performers, was that of the leader of the 1860 rising. In other words, the 'spirit' dressed up as great-grandfather's younger brother."

"Did the custom of performing the Nembutsu dance start with the 1860 rising, then?"

"No. It existed before that—and the 'spirits,' I imagine, have been in the valley ever since people first settled here. For several years, or even several decades following the rising, the 'spirit' of great-grandfather's brother was probably only a beginner who took his knocks at the very end of the procession, just like the 'spirit' of S. One folklore expert referred to new 'spirits' as 'novices' and labeled their training in the Nembutsu dance as a kind of 'testing' period. The dance involves a lot of violent movement wearing costume. It's quite hard work, so besides training the 'spirits' themselves, it must put quite a strain on the village youths who dress for the parts. Particularly when there's some trouble or other affecting life in the hollow, they perform with almost terrifying abandon."

"I'd like to see it once," my wife said wistfully.

"You're going to watch Takashi and the others at football practice every day, aren't you? If Takashi's activities are really rooted in the 'communal sentiments' of the valley, then that's a new form of Nembutsu dance in itself. Even if the 'spirits' don't actually take possession of them, it gives them plenty of training and toughens them up physically, so half the effect of the dance is achieved at least. At the very worst, it means that after all this football practice they won't get out of breath when they perform the dance in the summer. I'm only hoping that Takashi's football lessons are aimed chiefly at such peaceful purposes, and aren't the kind of training great-grandfather's brother gave his young men on the parade ground cleared in the forest. . . ."

On the day before New Year's Eve, I saw actual evidence that Takashi's training was having a beneficial effect on life in the valley. That afternoon, warm air was drifting through the window set in the solid storehouse wall, lapping round me like lukewarm water and thawing out the frozen hunks of head, shoulders, and sides till I gradually became one with dictionary, Penguin book, and pencil, and all my other selves evaporated, leaving only the one pressing ahead with the translation. It occurred to me vaguely as I went on with my task that if things always went like this I might even last till I died of old age, never experiencing the hardships of labor, never doing work of any particular importance. Suddenly, a cry struck at my warm, lethargic ear:

"Man in the river!"

Hauling up my flabby, waterlogged body on the hook of consciousness much as one might reel in a dead sea toad, I clattered wildly down the staircase. It was a miracle that I didn't fall. In the gloom at the foot of the stairs, belated fright at what I'd done caught up with me, bringing me to a halt. Simultaneously, I had second thoughts: it was unlikely that anyone would be carried away in midwinter when the river was almost dry. But then I heard, this time close at hand, the voices of Jin's children echoing each other, shouting "Man in the river!"

Going out into the front garden, I watched as the boys, baying like hounds after their quarry, went running down the graveled road then, almost instantly, disappeared from view. The skill with which they kept their balance as they ran, or bounced, down the steep, narrow trail furrowed by long use aroused vivid memories deep inside me, memories of feet running and men drowning. Every year during the period of late summer and early autumn floods, and especially after the indiscriminate wartime felling of trees in the forest, some unfortunate soul would be carried away in the swollen waters of the river. The first to discover him would cry at the top of his voice, "Man in the river!" Those who heard would take up the cry, forming a group that ran for all its worth down the road beside the river. But there was no way to rescue the victim as he drifted downstream. All the grown-ups did was race along the graveled road and its by-lanes, crossing the bridge and going on running even after they joined forces again on the paved road, in the vain hope of overtaking the flood in its furious onrush. The chase would go on with great commotion until even the stoutest of them collapsed of exhaustion, yet not a single practical attempt at rescue would be made. The following day, when the river had receded slightly, the adults, dressed in firemen's livery and moving sluggishly and reluctantly, wasting as much time as possible, would start off on their difficult and doubtful journey, prodding with bamboo poles the soft mud that covered thickets of bamboo and pussy willow, unable to go home until they'd discovered the drowned body.

I was firmly convinced already that I'd been mistaken about the cry, but the fact remained that it had awoken in me—even though my work upstairs in the storehouse had relaxed me into a soft mass of flesh—a reflex action that was almost as though I were a member of the valley community. The idea excited me. In order to slow down the rate at which the excitement faded, I decided to assume that I'd really heard the words "Man in the river!" and accept them at their face value. Either way, I had plenty of time on my hands. So, taking a cue from my days as a valley kid like Jin's sons, I ran down the graveled road, pressing the soles of my feet flat against the sloping sides of the furrow and flailing my arms about so as to keep my balance. By the time I reached the space in front of the village office I was almost blacking out, my breathing was labored, and both my knees were numb. All the while I was running I could hear the flapping of my own flabby body. Even so, I pressed on toward the bridge, chin thrust out like a man left far behind in a long-distance race, breathing frantic, my mind disturbed by the bulk of my heart pressing against my ribs. As I watched women and children outstripping me and disappearing ahead, I was reminded that it was several years since I'd last had to run.

Eventually, I caught sight of a crowd clad in bright colors standing at the end of the bridge. In the old days, a group of villagers would have worn the somber hues of a shoal of sardines, but the flow of shoddy clothing from the supermarket had changed all that. The people in the group were gazing ahead of them, enveloped as in a net by a dense, almost tangible silence. I stepped into the clumps of withered grass by the roadside as the children had done, and the operation in progress around the broken support of the bridge came into view.

The central pillar had given way under the pressure of water, so that the part where it had been attached to the body of the bridge now thrust out numerous joints in all directions like twisted fingers. Each of the broken joints, though skewered by its reinforcing rods, was a free-swinging mass of concrete; force applied to any part of it would send it into a complex and dangerous spin packing a tremendous punch. On one of these lumps of concrete, a child lay oddly silent with his hat pulled down over his eyes. He might already have been unconscious, so strong was the impression of stillness. Slipping down through a gap in the planks of the temporary bridge, the terrified child had clutched hold of the block of concrete, but even his weight was enough to set it rocking, and he had no alternative but to cling to it perfectly motionless.

The young men were trying to rescue the petrified figure. From the scaffolding supporting the temporary bridge, two logs, bound together, had been lowered by rope beside the central pillar. One of the men, standing barefoot in the shallow water, was tugging at a rope tied round the middle of the logs to prevent their touching the pillar. Two other youths were riding on the logs, moving gradually closer to the boulder that held the child captive. They edged their way along the logs, making the kind of soothing noises people make to a frightened animal.

As the young man in front arrived directly beneath the child, his companion behind him grasped him firmly round the waist with both arms, at the same time maintaining the balance of his own body by wrapping his legs round the logs. Then, as though whisking a cicada from a tree, the first man swept the child to safety. A roar went up from the onlookers. At that instant, the lump of concrete on which the child had been went into a bouncing, twisting motion and collided with the jagged corner of the main body of the broken bridge, sending up a heavy thud that rang through the valley and rose up over the forest. Takashi, who had been lying on his belly directing the young men's movements from the temporary bridge immediately above the lump of concrete, stood up and gave instructions for those supporting the rope to haul the three youths on the logs up to the level of the temporary bridge. The shock waves from the collision jarred fiercely and persistently inside me. Their effect stemmed in part from a deep, almost sickening sense of relief on realizing that a close relative had just come through a major crisis safely, but this was swallowed up in turn by a still more intense sense of despair at the brutality of life when I considered what would have happened if he hadn't succeeded. If the rescue operation had failed and the child's body had been dashed against the jagged surface along with the concrete boulder, Takashi, as the man responsible for the carnage, would inevitably have been driven down onto the lump of concrete as it swung like a weight on a line, there to smash his own head in. In fact, a still more cruel and disgusting punishment might have been meted out on the man who had murdered a community member of such tender years. However much I reassured myself that Takashi had in fact succeeded, I couldn't repress the bilious taste of fear that came rising into my throat. Why, I wondered with a sense of unfocused anger, had Takashi voluntarily put himself in such danger? The crowd, which the other members of the football team had been holding back until now so as to allow the rescue work to proceed effectively, pressed round the rescued child. As I turned away and set off toward the village, I remembered Takashi's somberly tense, somehow defiant face in the days when he'd insisted he wasn't scared of violence in any form, or of physical pain, or even of death, but would throw up at the sight of a drop of blood oozing from the ball of his finger. Supposing he'd seen the body of the child squashed before his very eyes, a foot or so below him as he lay on his belly on the temporary bridge, while fragments of concrete mixed with blood and bits of flesh sprayed him full in the face—had he thought that a quick vomit would let him escape from reality again?

A festive medley of excited laughter and war whoops arose behind me. Spurred on by them, I walked rapidly ahead, breathing heavily with an excitement quite different from theirs. "Man in the river"—but it was Takashi himself who had been caught in the most perilous flood of all. Now, though, the incident would probably give him and his team a certain power over the valley. It would give him confidence, at least, and make him feel that he'd put down firm roots there. The actuality of what was taking shape in his world would gradually impress itself more and more clearly on my wife, convincing her still more finally of the unlikelihood of anything ever happening to me. For the first time, the word "jealousy" that Takashi had used to my wife acquired a definite content. Just before I left, I caught sight of the Citroen parked at the back of the crowd. If I'd pushed my way through to it I could have joined up with my wife and the others. But I ignored the car and turned my back on the crowd. Crackling sparks from the word "jealousy," charged with a new meaning now, informed me that I hadn't wanted to join my wife in witnessing Takashi's success. . . .

A man with unnaturally long legs overtook me on a very ancient bicycle, riding as though practicing for a slow cycling competition, then put one foot to the ground in leisurely fashion and looked round.

"Your brother's quite a leader, Mitsusaburo." He didn't sound particularly impressed. It was the way all those of any consequence in the valley spoke. Being extremely wary, they always wore a mask of cool detachment from behind which they craftily tried to sound out the other man's feelings. At the time that I'd left the valley, the man had been assistant at the village office. By now he'd got fat and his complexion suggested kidney trouble, but the bike he was straddling as he watched with an ambiguous expression for my reaction was the same old village office machine.

"If he'd failed, he would probably have been lynched," I said in a voice as calm as his but filled with distaste. The man must have realized that I wasn't ignorant of the basic stratagems of conversation among the grown-ups of the valley. He gave a kind of grunt, noncommittal but with a lurking, private contempt.

"If he'd done his growing-up in the valley," I went on, "he would never have done anything rash like that. It was asking for trouble, like deliberately walking around the edge of a trap. He just doesn't know the valley folk."

"Oh, come now!" Somewhere behind the ambiguous smile lurked a suggestion of both timidity and untrustworthiness. "The valley folk aren't all as bad as that, you know!"

"Why did they leave the bridge unrepaired?" I asked, walking beside him as he pushed his bicycle.

"The bridge, eh—" he began and broke off, refusing to go on for a while. Then, in the mocking tone that was equally a habit of speech among the crafty valley adults, he added, "Early next year we're being merged with the neighboring town. Till then, there's no point in the village repairing it by itself."

"What'll happen to the village office if you're merged?"

"Well, for one thing, they won't need an assistant," he said. It was his first straightforward reaction. "Even now the office hardly does any work at all. The forestry cooperative was amalgamated into a group of five towns and villages ages ago, and the agricultural cooperative's gone broke, so the village office is practically deserted. The headman's lost interest in his work—stays indoors all day watching television."

"Television?"

"The supermarket, you know, set up a communal antenna at the highest point in the forest and started selling sets. Thirty thousand yen for use of the antenna. Even so, ten families in the hollow have got it."

It seemed that though the village as a whole might be on its last legs economically, there were at least ten prosperous families that hadn't gone under to the supermarket but were enjoying their own version of the consumer life—though those same ten families (if one was to believe the young priest's pessimistic theories) might well be in debt to the supermarket for part of the antenna fee and the cost of the television sets.

"Nobody pays any television fees. They say they can't get JBC programs with the supermarket antenna."

"What do they watch then, the commercial programs from the town?"

"Oh, no. Actually, JBC comes through best of all." He showed slight signs of pleasure.

"Do they still do the Nembutsu dance?"

"No, they haven't done it these five years," he said, handling the new subject warily. "There's nobody but the caretaker at your place, and the tatami maker skipped out one night. When people build a new house in the village nowadays they make Western-style rooms and don't use tatami."

"Why exactly did the Nembutsu procession have to do a dance in the garden of our house? They could equally well have chosen the garden of the headman's house or the owner of the forest land. Is it because our house is on the way from the forest down to the valley?"

"But surely, it's because it's the home of the Nedokoro family—because it's where the soul of the valley folk has its roots. When your father gave a talk at the primary school he said that in Okinawa, where he worked before he went to Manchuria, there was a local word *nendokoru* which meant just that—'the soul's roots.' He made a present to the school, too. Twenty tubs of molasses."

"My mother scoffed at his *nendokoru* theory and wouldn't hear of it," I replied. "As for the molasses, she said they made a laughingstock of father in the valley. I imagine the immediate reason for poking fun at him was the idea of a man whose family was on the verge of ruin making such presents."

"No, no, certainly not!" the man said, withdrawing the malicious trap that he himself had set with such apparent innocence. To the valley, the Nedokoro-*nendokoru* theory had in fact been a source of fun of the most spiteful and nasty kind. When

the villagers whiled away their time by relating the many and
varied failures in the life of my father, who had always been too
easily carried away by what others said, this anecdote regularly
served as a kind of climax to the merriment. For years afterward,
they'd made fun of father as the man who had used twenty tubs
of molasses in an attempt to establish his monopoly of the souls
in the valley. If I'd let the man from the village office tempt
me into affirming the Nedokoro-*nendokoru* theory, he and his
friends would almost certainly have fabricated a new anecdote
showing how much the Nedokoro boy took after his father.

"You've sold the storehouse and the land, haven't you, Mitsusaburo? I'll bet you made quite a bit out of it!"

"I haven't officially sold it yet. I probably won't sell the land,
anyway. Jin and her family are there, for one thing."

"You don't have to pretend, Mitsusaburo—I'm sure you got
a good price for them," he insisted. "Takashi and the manager
of the supermarket came to the village office to register the
sale of the land and buildings, so I know most of the details."

I went on walking: quietly, calmly smiling, so as to keep my
physical reactions under the control of my mind. The graveled
road beneath the soles of my shoes was suddenly heavily pitted
and dragged wearisomely at my feet. The eyes of the women
and old folk, watching us so vigilantly from the shadows behind
filthy glass doors still splashed with dried-up mud from rains of
long before, had suddenly acquired the sharpness of the eyes of
strangers. The village official walking by my side was representative of them all. The forest about us was sunk in gloom, the sky
overcast and threatening snow. But quite suddenly the whole
scene had become absolutely alien to me. Calmly I worked to
maintain my placid smile, worked with the absolute calmness

I'd seen in the eyes of our baby who had failed, in the long run, to establish any ties of understanding with the real world. I had shut myself up, had no interest in, couldn't be disturbed by, anything in the valley. I wasn't there on the graveled road, not there for any of the strangers who lived along it. . . .

"Must be going, then," said the official, straddling his bicycle. Somewhere in my attitude he'd sensed the peculiar mark of the outsider and, bringing the wisdom of his ancestors into play, sought to avoid getting embroiled. But the alien quality he detected in me wasn't the distress of a man whose younger brother had privately sold off his house and land to strangers. Such an affair would have been the greatest possible scandal in a valley community, and if he'd caught even the faintest suspicion of it, he would have ensconced himself promptly in the pithole of my distress much as ticks worm their way into the ears of hunting dogs and refuse to budge. The face I showed him was something different: the face of a stranger totally unconcerned with him and the rest of the village and all its affairs. So he mounted his bicycle and pedaled off with enough energy to set his lanky upper half swaying, doubtless wondering bad-temperedly as he went whether he hadn't been talking to an apparition after all. Quite unexpectedly, I'd turned into something as remote and meaningless to him as a rumor from a distant town.

"Well, good-bye," I replied in a voice whose tranquillity sounded pleasant even to my own ears. But he refused to be addressed by an apparition and with head bent mournfully forward pedaled on up the slope into the distance. I walked on slowly, smiling to myself, an invisible man treading an unfamiliar path. Some small children who hadn't reached the bridge in time gazed up at me, but I wasn't dismayed anymore by the resemblance of their grubby faces to my former self, nor did I feel particularly upset as I passed the brewers' storehouse that had been ravaged to make the supermarket. The store was deserted today, and the bored young woman behind the cash register watched me go by with dull, filmy eyes.

"You've got to start a new life, Mitsu," Takashi had suddenly sprung at me. "Why not give up everything you're doing in Tokyo and come to Shikoku with me? That wouldn't be a bad way to start." It was then that the village in the valley had come back to me as a reality for the first time in a dozen or more years. So I'd returned to the valley in search of my "thatched hut." But I'd merely been deceived by the unexpected veneer of sobriety that Takashi had acquired, like grime on the skin, during his wanderings around America. My "new life" in the valley was only a ruse devised by Takashi to forestall my refusal and clear the way for him to sell the house and land for the sake of whatever obscure purpose was firing him at the moment. From the very outset, the journey to the valley hadn't really existed for me. Since I no longer had any roots there, nor made any attempt to put down new ones, even the house and land were as good as nonexistent; it was no wonder that my brother should have been able to filch them from me with only a minimal exercise of cunning.

Haltingly and unsteadily, I climbed back up the furrowed road that only a while before the memory of my childhood sense of balance had allowed me to run down so easily. It made me vaguely disturbed, of course, that the whole valley including this road should have become so remote, but on the other hand I'd been released from the feeling of guilt, which had pursued me ever since I came back to the valley, at losing the identity that should have been mine since childhood.

Now, even if the whole valley should charge me with being a rat, I could retort with hostility, "And who are you, to insult a stranger whose affairs are none of yours?" Now I was just a transient in the valley, a one-eyed passerby too fat for his years, and life there had the power to summon up neither the memory nor the illusion of any other, truer self. As a passerby I had a right to insist on my identity. Even a rat has its identity as a rat. If I was a rat, then I had no need to be disturbed at being called one. I *was* a rat: a puny house rat running straight for its nest, heedless of the insults hurled after it. I smiled silently to myself.

Back in the house that my brother had already sold to the Emperor, the house that no longer belonged to me or any of my family, I packed my belongings into a suitcase. If Takashi had in fact sold not only the buildings but the land as well, he must have received many times the amount he'd reported to my wife and me as money paid in advance. What's more, he'd taken back over half my share of the spurious "advance," as a contribution to the football team. I could see him relating with naive pride to the members of his team how he'd not only grabbed the house and land from me but even got me to make a contribution from the fake advance. No doubt my contribution to the football team had served as a humorous denouement to the comedy in which Takashi, in his role as the cunning rogue, outmaneuvered the slow-witted man of virtue that I was supposed to play. I went and fetched the Penguin book and dictionaries, the notebooks and papers from the storehouse, packed them in the same suitcase, then settled down to await the return of my brother and his bodyguards, including the latest recruit, my wife. I would return to Tokyo, where every morning as I awoke I would feel again that dull, persistent ache in each part of my body. My face and my voice would deteriorate steadily until my mouth grew pointed like a real rat and I began to talk in low, squeaky whispers. I would dig a pit in the back garden, this time for the sole purpose of creeping into it at dawn. I would have my own hole for meditation much as some Americans have their own fallout shelters. But *my* personal shelter would help me approach death as calmly as possible. I wouldn't be trying to secure myself a base in which to outlive the deaths of others, so neither neighbors nor milkman would have cause to resent my unconventional habits. My decision, admittedly, would cut me off effectively from all future possibilities of a new life or of finding a "thatched hut," but it would give me a chance to get a deeper understanding of the details of my own past, and with it the words and behavior of my dead friend.

When Takashi and the others got back, I was asleep by the fireplace. The way I lay must have carried a strong hint of the regressive tranquillity in my mind, for as I awoke I heard Momoko complain:

"While Taka and the rest were doing such great work, a certain member of the establishment was lying peacefully in the warm like a superannuated cat!"

"A superannuated cat who's just a rat?" I inquired, sitting up. "You've got your metaphors a bit mixed, haven't you?"

Momoko naively flushed a tomato red. "Taka and the others . . ." she persisted defiantly to cover her embarrassment, but my wife stopped her.

"Mitsu knows perfectly well what happened," she said. "He was watching Taka and the others from the back of the crowd. Even so, he didn't congratulate the team—he ran off without saying a word. It's no wonder he went to sleep!"

I noticed that Takashi's attention kept straying to my suitcase, which stood at the edge of the raised floor next to the kitchen.

"I saw the assistant from the village office going after Mitsu on his bicycle," he said, carefully and probingly. "I noticed specially, because Mitsu and he were the only two who went off without waiting to see the child we'd rescued."

"He wanted to ask me about the deal on the house and land. How about it, Taka—did you make a pile on it?" I said, recapturing the lordly mood of childhood when I'd deliberately asked awkward questions to annoy him.

Takashi jerked his head up like some fierce bird of prey and glared at me. But when I looked back undismayed, he feebly averted his gaze and, as the blood rose frankly to the small, sallow face just as it had to Momoko's, he shook his head in the manner of a distressed child and said in a timid voice:

"Are you going back to Tokyo, then, Mitsu?"

"That's right," I said. "I've played my part, haven't I?"

"I'm staying here, Mitsu," my wife interposed determinedly. "I want to help Taka and the others while they're in training."

Takashi and I gazed at my wife, one from either side, equally struck by the unexpectedness of this. In fact, I hadn't considered the possibility of her departure when I packed my own suitcase, but neither had I expected her to show such positive determination to stay behind with Takashi and the others.

"Anyway, you won't be able to leave the valley for a while, Mitsu," said Takashi. "It'll start snowing tonight." He poked lightly at my suitcase with the toe of the gym shoes he'd been wearing for football practice. For the first time since I learned of his trick, anger, like a drop of red molten iron, ran from my head down through my body, but it soon disappeared.

"Even if we're snowbound I'll sleep in the storehouse, independent of the rest of you," I said. "You can use the main building as you like," I conceded with the feeble generosity of spent indignation, "to house your team during training."

"If you're going to be independent, I'll have to bring you your meals, Mitsu," said my wife.

"Won't it be cold in the storehouse at night and early in the morning?" asked Hoshio, the only one to show any sympathy. He'd been listening to our conversation in depressed silence, taking no part in it, as though even Takashi's success earlier that day had left him somehow doubtful.

"The Emperor told me he's got some imported oil stoves to put on display in the supermarket, though he was sure he wouldn't sell a single unit. I'll buy one," said Takashi recovering his energy. "There's no need to worry about the cost, at least," he added, his eyes on me with the fleeting shadow of a defiant smile.

For some time now I'd heard the young men at work in front of the house. Probably they refrained from coming into the kitchen in recognition of the alien element, myself, established by the fireplace. Before long, there came the sound of metal being hammered on an anvil. As I went out carrying my suitcase on my way to the storehouse, my new home, I found them squatting around the anvil. They twisted their heads lazily to look up at me, but their faces remained set and expressionless as though they were trying to prevent me from reading any meaning there. They were pounding with hammers and chisels at small iron implements of the kind known in the area as "mitsumata strippers." Already the upper side of the scissor-like arrangement had been detached from a number of them, and the lower halves were laid out on the ground, looking like fire hooks with the handle, the central blade, and the sharply pointed tip bent at right angles to the blade.

"Mitsumata stripping" consisted of fixing the pointed tip firmly into the tree to hold the instrument, gripping the bark, and peeling off its upper layer. Everything about the "fire hooks" as they lay on the ground—the handle, the blade, the pointed tip—blatantly proclaimed that they were intended as weapons. I was seized with an impulse to self-defense, but went on toward the storehouse without inquiring further into its significance. By now I was a stranger to anything that might happen in the valley.

Both the hollow in which the village lay and the "country" had always yielded high-quality mitsumata. In the old days, the bundles of bark peeled from the trees and dried after cutting and steaming were gathered and stowed away in the mitsumata storehouse belonging to our family. These would be separated up again, soaked in the river, stripped of the black surface with the strippers, and dried. For long years it had been the Nedokoro family's task to sort them, put them in a press to form rectangular blocks of raw material for paper, and supply them to the Government Printing Office. Stripping off the outer bark had been the principal source of extra income for the farmers of the hollow. The cart that I'd hauled along with me when I went to fetch S's body had been used for carrying the unstripped bark to the farms and collecting the bundles after stripping. The farms responsible for the work were entrusted with bark strippers specially made by the valley blacksmith. Chiseled on the handle of each instrument was a single character, which served

as the business mark of the family who used it. The number of
bark strippers was fixed, in order to protect the interests of the
fanning families who for generation after generation had relied
on the work to supplement their incomes. Thus, at least until
a while after the end of the war, possession of a bark stripper
with one's family mark on it had been a kind of status symbol
in the valley community. I remember seeing a farmer, whose
implement had been taken from him on account of a poor yield
of white bark, squatting in the kitchen pleading with my mother.
Just before she died, mother had handed over to the farmers'
cooperative all rights associated with producing mitsumata for
the Government Printing Office. The young men had brought
the strippers out from under the floorboards of the main building, where they'd been put after being reclaimed from the farmers. Almost every one of them could have found a stripper with
his own father's mark chiseled on it—a weapon (since no other
use for these objects seemed possible) bearing a mark that had
been his family's for generations past. Was Takashi thinking,
perhaps, of distributing one to each member of his football team
as a kind of ID card and instituting a system whereby—just as
grandfather and father had done in their day—he would take it
away from any black sheep discovered in his new community?
But all this too was irrelevant to me now. Even if a "fire hook"
turned up with the character for my own name, "Mitsu," carved
on it, I had no desire whatever to accept it.

   Peering out through the narrow window of the storehouse,
I could see the forest already sunk in a gloom that contrasted
with the pale pink wall of sunset in the lofty sky above and the
equally pale gray-blue of the more distant sky enfolding it. The
sky now seemed somehow brighter than the snow clouds that

I'd gazed up at during the day, but the feeling of snow was still strong in the air. In the front garden, Hoshio was repairing the lamp hanging from the eaves, which had long been broken, in order to provide light for the young men as they worked. The hammers rang against the iron, and the color of the forest suddenly began to fade. The whole forest, though still the same faded dark green all over, was quivering: snow had begun to fall up there in the high parts and was driving down toward the valley. I felt an indescribable depression settling over me. Now that I found myself freed from things outside me, I realized that my depression was a purely personal thing. If it progressed any further, it was quite clear what work my fingers would set about when I found myself sitting once more in a pit at dawn with a hot, smelly dog in my arms. Again I was overcome by the memory of that shivering and aching that had refused to go away even after I'd returned to my bedroom that morning. For me, the valley held in store neither new life nor thatched hut. I was alone and forlorn again, with no hope in sight, in the grip of a depression clearly deeper than before my brother's return to Japan. I experienced the full meaning of that depression.

Truth Unspeakable

As Takashi and Hoshio came into the storehouse carrying the oil stove, which was totally enclosed and remote in color from any associations of warmth, I saw powdery snow, dry and hard like sand, lying on their shoulders. My wife and Momoko, excited by the snow, were late with the evening meal. By the time I went over to the main building for dinner, the front garden was already covered. So far, however, it was no more than a fragile, impermanent-looking layer. The driving snow and darkness blocked my poor vision so impenetrably that when I looked up and took the elements full in my face I seemed to be drifting in a boat on a sea of falling snow, and it was difficult to keep my balance. Fine, powdery flakes stung my eyes to mechanical tears. I seemed to remember that in the old days snow in the valley had always come in damp flakes as big as the ball of one's thumb. I sorted through various memories associated with snow, but my recollection of it in the valley was blurred, buried beneath a host of memories from the towns I'd lived in. Either way, the powdery snow I felt against my skin at that moment was as remote as any that had fallen on those alien towns. I kicked aside the settled flakes with a fine carelessness as I walked. In my childhood, I'd always rushed eagerly to devour a handful of the first snow to fall in the valley; it seemed to taste of all the minerals in the atmosphere, from the heights of the sky overlying the valley right down to the earth that I trod. Takashi and the others had left the door open, and in the faint light of the lamp that hung from the eaves were watching the white flakes streaking the darkness. They were all beginning to get drunk on the snow; but I was sober.

"How's the oil stove?" my wife asked. "There weren't any in a color that would have looked better in the storehouse." Though she might be drunk with snow, she hadn't yet started on the whisky tonight.

"I'm not taking up permanent residence there. I'd leave tomorrow if only the snow would let up, so there won't be time to worry whether the stove matches the room or not."

"Taka," she said, turning to my brother since I showed so little interest, "don't you think it's odd that they should bring imported stoves from Scandinavia all the way to a place like this?"

"By displaying goods that no one here could ever hope to buy, the Emperor's thumbing his nose at the whole village," said Takashi.

It occurred to me that Takashi could use that kind of theory to incite the young members of his football team, but I didn't pursue the idea. I'd lost my enthusiasm for thinking about relations between Takashi and the valley. I ate in silence, as though I weren't really there by the open fireplace at all. Takashi's bodyguards seemed, in the natural course of events, to be realizing the qualitative change that had occurred in me; the conversation proceeded over my head as if straddling a void, without resistance and with no sense of awkwardness. From time to time Takashi, who alone among them seemed subtly disturbed by my silence, would try to draw me into the flow of the conversation, but I rejected the bait. There was no underlying motive for my refusal; it was simply that they failed to arouse my interest. Earlier, as we brought S's ashes home in the Citroen, Takashi's distorted memories had succeeded in provoking me out of my silence, but that was because I too had been desperately trying to connect up inside myself the concrete details of past and present in the valley, intent on finding some way to a new life there. By now I'd lost all such motivation, and for the first time clearly understood the events I hadn't grasped before. Takashi was talking as though the conversation were a triangle with me at one corner and himself and my wife linked by the side opposite. But I had no wish to be a factor in any three-sided relationship. I was utterly isolated, faced with a growing depression that dragged at my limbs as in some nightmare.

"You said, didn't you, Mitsu, that the evening of the day S was killed I was standing perfectly still in the dark kitchen, eating candy?" (I remained silent, ignoring the appeal in Takashi's eyes, so he feebly switched his gaze to Natsumi and addressed her instead. It showed me he was bothered by the trick he'd played, and considered himself guilty. In fact, though, the precise nature of his feelings was irrelevant to what I had experienced. His act hadn't hurt me; on the contrary, it was thanks to my younger brother that I now found myself able to see things other than my own inner self.) "I've just remembered,

Natsumi—remembered clearly what was going on both inside and outside me as the child in that scene. I was standing in the kitchen sucking happily on my candy. I moved my tongue about nimbly, keeping the passages between my gums and lips open to stop the saliva trickling down from the corners of my mouth. To a certain extent, Mitsu used imagination to embellish his memory too. He said that saliva brown with dissolved candy was dribbling from my mouth like blood, but it couldn't have been. I was devoting my finest candy-eating techniques to seeing that it didn't. You see, it was a kind of magic. . . .

"It was dusk, but as I looked toward the doorway from inside the dark kitchen the ground in the garden shone white— a more striking white, even, than the snow that's fallen today. Mitsu had just brought back S's body. Mother was in the front room, a lunatic who at any moment might open the sliding screens and start raving at imaginary tenants in the front garden. The front room, you see, was designed so that the master of the house could stay seated while he gave instructions to people standing outside.

"So, though I was only a kid, I found myself surrounded by terrifying violence: after all, corpses and madness represent violence in its ultimate forms. I was driven into a corner from which I couldn't escape, no matter how clever I was. By sucking my candy so carefully I was really hoping to make my consciousness burrow down inside my body, turning its back completely on the violence outside, much as a wound buries itself in swelling flesh. It was then that I thought up my piece of magic. If things went well—in other words, if I managed not to dribble a single drop—I'd escape the awful violence that hung about me. You know, it may be naive of me, but I've always wondered at the way my ancestors managed to survive the violence all around them and hand on life to me, their descendant. After all, they lived in a savage age. It's incredible to think of the massive violence that the people leading down to me had to fight against just so that I could be alive now."

"Let's hope you too can get the better of violence and do your bit in handing on life," my wife added in a tone suggesting the same emotions as underlay Takashi's own confession, and with the same air of simplicity.

"While I was lying on my belly on the temporary bridge today, watching that kid's life hanging in the balance, I was thinking about the problem of violence, and remembered exactly how things were while I was eating candy in the kitchen. It's not just another of my dreams." He fell silent and glanced at me again questioningly.

I went back through the snow to the storehouse and, squatting like a monkey in front of the oil stove—the first Scandinavian oil stove, I told myself with gloomy amusement, ever to be lit in the valley—peered into the round window set in the black cylinder. Beyond the window, flames shivered incessantly, the color of the sea on a cloudless day. An unexpected fly set its sights on my nose, collided with it, and crashed onto my left knee. The air warmed by the stove had risen to the ceiling, stirring up the insects that ought to have remained snugly ensconced behind the great beams until spring. Plump and fat, the fly was of a size you would never have found in people's homes in the old days. Others to match it might be found in a stable, perhaps, but it wasn't that type; except for its size, it was quite clearly the usual kind of fly that gathered about human beings. With a single scoop of my palm about four inches in front of the fly, I caught it. I'm an expert fly-catcher, though I say it myself. The accident in which I lost the sight of my right eye happened at the height of summer, and hordes of flies came to mock me as I lay in bed recovering. So I took my revenge by perfecting my fly-catching techniques, thereby also helping develop a sense of perspective using only one eye.

I watched the fly for a while as it twitched between my fingertips like the knot in an artery. Then, with minimal pressure, the fly was crushed and my fingers were wet with its body fluids. I felt as though the pads of my fingers would never be clean again. Terror rose up around me, penetrating inside me like the warmth from the stove. But all I did was wipe the tips of my fingers on my trousers. I went on squatting there, quite still, my whole body paralyzed as though the dead fly had been a plug holding the motor center of my nervous system in place. My consciousness had identified with the flames flickering beyond the round window in the stove, so that my body on this side was no more than an empty hull. It was pleasant to spend time like this, shunning the responsibilities of the flesh. My throat grew dry and hot and began to tickle. The thought that I ought to put a kettle of water on the flat top of the stove made me realize that, far from leaving for Tokyo the following morning, I'd unconsciously resigned myself to spending a considerable number of days upstairs in the storehouse. By now my ears told me that the snow had come to stay. Even at the dead of night, there in the valley in the forest, one's ears, as they grew used to the silence and developed an ability to respond to ever subtler noises, would detect a surprising amount of sound. Now, though, the valley gave off literally no sound at all. Over the entire hollow and the vast forest surrounding it the newly settled snow had spread a mantle of silence.

Gii the hermit, they said, was still leading his solitary life in the depths of the forest. But even he, who was presumably inured to its everyday silence, would surely find something new and incongruous in the total absence of sound of this snowy midnight. If he froze to death in the snowbound forest, would his body ever be found by the valley folk? What thoughts would pass through his mind as he lay in the silent darkness beneath the piling snow, face-to-face with such an ugly, unsociable death? Would he be silent, or would he mutter incessantly to himself? For all I knew, he might have dug himself a deep, rectangular hole just like the pit that had been mine for a day, and be sheltering in it back there in the forest. I cursed myself again for having filled in my pit with anything so obvious as a septic tank; why hadn't I appreciated it more? I pictured to myself two pits dug in the depths of the forest, with the hermit in the older of the two and myself in the newer, both of us seated in the damp hugging our knees to our chests, placidly waiting till the danger passed. At one time, I felt, I would have used the term "waiting" in its more positive sense, but now it occurred to me stripped of all but its most negative significance, and I realized on reflection that I'd reached a frame of mind that could sanction—could accept with neither fear nor disgust—death at the bottom of a pit, buried beneath earth and stones pulled down by my own fingers. The trip to the valley had been a distraction, but all the while my private downhill journey had been steadily progressing. And it struck me that, living alone upstairs in the storehouse as I did now, I could if I wished paint my head crimson, thrust a cucumber up my anus, and hang myself without anyone interfering. The place, moreover, was conveniently equipped with great zelkova beams that had already lasted a hundred years. But the pursuit of this fantasy only aroused new fear and disgust, and I abruptly checked the movement of my head as I lifted it to look up and confirm the existence of the beams.

In the middle of the night there were sounds in the front garden like a horse pawing at wet ground. The sounds as they occurred were stamped into the soil in a series of dull thuds without the slightest reverberation. Wiping an oval patch like an old-fashioned mirror in the murky, narrow glass window (such modern improvements to the storehouse, including the windows at the back, had been made toward the end of the war, along with electric lighting and the toilet facilities at the side of the storehouse, in readiness for evacuees—who had been put off, however, by rumors of my mother's madness and never actually came), I looked down and saw Takashi, stark naked, running round and round in circles in the snow that had settled in the front garden. The lamp hanging from the eaves, aided by reflection from the snow lying on the ground, roof, and various small shrubs beneath the eaves, suffused the white garden with a luminescence that recreated the vague light of dusk. It was still snowing steadily. The effect was oddly static, as though the lines traced by the snowflakes at that moment would be maintained unchanging, permitting no other move-ment, just as long as snow continued to fall through the space over the valley. The essence of that moment would be drawn out indefinitely; direction in time was swallowed up and lost amid the steadily falling flakes, just as sound was absorbed by the layer of snow. All-pervasive time: Takashi as he ran stark naked was great-grandfather's brother, and my own; every moment of those hundred years was crowded into this one instant in time.

The naked figure stopped running and walked for a while, then knelt in the snow and ran both hands over its surface. I saw his gawky buttocks and his long, bent back, flexible as an insect's with its countless joints.

Suddenly, Takashi gave a series of sharp grunts and rolled over and over in the snow. He stood up with snow clinging to his naked body and walked slowly back toward the area where the lamp shed more light, his disproportionately long arms dangling disconsolately like a gorilla's. I saw that he had an erection. His penis had the same air of power stoically controlled and the same odd pathos as the swelling muscles of an athlete's upper arms. He made no more attempt to conceal his erect organ than he would his biceps. As he entered the open doorway, a young woman who had been waiting inside the kitchen stepped out and enveloped his naked body in the bath towel she held spread out. My heart contracted with pain. It wasn't my wife, though, but Momoko. Unflinching, she held out the towel to receive him as he approached without concealing his erection, shivering from cold. Like a virgin-pure younger sister, I thought. Without speaking they went inside and the door closed on them, leaving nothing but the summation of stilled movement on the snow, one hundred years enclosed within a moment.

I felt I had penetrated the depths concealed within Takashi to a level that my eyes had never reached before—if not with understanding of their significance, then at least with confirmation of their existence. I wondered whether the marks where the snow was churned up by his naked body would be enfolded in new snow by the morning. Normally, only a dog or some such animal would expose its erect penis so frankly and to so pathetically little purpose; Takashi's experiences in a world of

darkness unfamiliar to me must have given him the utter frank-
ness of a lone mongrel. And just as a dog is unable to express its
melancholy in words, there was something heavy and knotted
at the center of Takashi's mind that no shared language could
ever unravel.

I went to sleep wondering how it would feel in practice to
be invaded by the soul of a dog. It wasn't difficult in the darkness to conjure up a specially fabricated beast, the body of a
large, fat, ginger-haired dog with my own head grafted on it. Its
tail, which was round, plump, and springy like a long whip, was
curled between its back legs to hide its genitals, and it gazed
at me inquiringly as it floated limp in the darkness—definitely
not the kind of dog to indulge its exhibitionistic tendencies in
the snow at the dead of night. "Woof!" I barked to drive it away,
and went back to sleep, taking great care not to summon up
ginger dogs from the darkness again.

It was near noon when I awoke: New Year's Eve, with the
laughter of a large group of young men coming from the main
house. It was cold, but not piercingly so; snow was still falling
and the sky was dark, but the earth gleamed with a gentle,
bright light. The dwellings in the valley, seen far below in distant miniature, were so simplified by the snow that the sight
no longer threatened to root up twisted things lurking in the
depths of memory. In the same way the snow had diminished
the dark, ferocious reality of the forest that lay all about. The
forest seemed to have retreated, and the hollow, though still
filled with driving snow, had become more spacious. I felt I
was dwelling in unfamiliar surroundings where everything had
a comfortably abstract quality. The spot where my brother had
rolled about in the snow the previous night looked like a scale

model of some archaeological site. Undisturbed by boot marks, its hollows and mounds were faithfully reproduced by the newly fallen snow that enfolded them. I gazed down at it for a while, listening to the laughter that rose from the kitchen and made the house sound like a students' hostel.

When I walked over to the main house and went inside, the young men of the football team, who were sitting round the open fireplace, abruptly fell silent. I felt self-conscious, an alien intrusion on the happy family circle about Takashi. My wife and Momoko were busy working beside the stove. I moved toward them in the vague hope of finding succor there, and found them still intoxicated with the valley's first snow.

"I got your boots, Mitsu!" said Momoko with innocent cheerfulness. "I went to buy them at the supermarket this morning. They had a big delivery of new stuff, ready for the snow. They say the van that brought it is stuck in the snow on the other side of the bridge. Poor, homesick Mitsu—everything seems against you leaving, doesn't it?"

"Haven't you been cold in the storehouse?" my wife asked. "Do you think you'll be all right living there for a while?" Her eyes were bloodshot from the snow, but betrayed somewhere a gleam of energy that was lacking when they were red from drink. In all likelihood she'd had no whisky the night before, and had slept soundly too.

"I'll be all right, I suppose," I said in a flat, depressed voice. My reply, I sensed, aroused both scorn and satisfaction in the young men round the fireplace, who had been awaiting it with dispassionate curiosity. In their eyes, probably, I was just a dull oaf, the only person in the valley to remain unexcited on the day the snow came.

"Do you think I could have some food?" I asked, assuming the air of the unhappy, hungry husband in the hope that mounting scorn would induce the young men to ignore the intruder.

"Do you know how to prepare a pheasant, Mitsu?" said Takashi, addressing me in an easy voice. "The father of the kid who got stuck on the bridge yesterday went out early this morning with his friends and shot some for us." In front of the team, his other self was to the fore, the one that wore a protective mail of self-confidence and authority, not the one that had rolled naked in the snow like a dog.

"I'll have a try after I've had something to eat."

Abandoning tolerance, the young men in unison heaved an exaggerated sigh of disgust. At one time, no self-respecting man in the valley would ever have prepared food himself. Even now, I suspected, the same tradition still survived. The young men had been treated to the spectacle of their leader twisting his elder brother round his little finger once again. The whole bunch of them, drunk with the snow, were in high spirits and ready for any bit of light relief. In the same way, the entire population of the valley would always get inebriated with the first snow. They would stay like that for ten days or so, during which they would be prey to a constant urge to go marching out into the white drifts, careless of the cold, driven by the fires of intoxication inside them. But once that period was over, the hangover would set in and everyone would long just as intensely to get away from the snow. The inhabitants of the area had none of the toughness of people living in the true "snow country." The fires within would soon spend themselves, leaving them powerless against the incursions of the cold, and people would begin to fall sick. Such was the pattern of the village's encounters with snow. Privately I hoped that my wife's infatuation with it would not affect her brain for long.

I sat down on the raised wooden floor where it projected into the kitchen, just as the tenants' families had done in the old days when they came to pay their respects at the year's end, and with my back to the open fireplace began my belated breakfast.

"The reason why the rising succeeded," said Takashi, picking up the thread where it had been severed by my entry, "was that the farmers, not only in this village but in all the villages round about, saw the youths as a terrifying rabble, a dangerous bunch of misfits who'd commit arson or start looting without a second's thought. I wouldn't be surprised if the farmers were more scared of their own lawless leaders than of the enemy inside the castle gates in the town." He was obviously trying to recreate a picture of the 1860 rising in the minds of the village youths and keep it fresh in their memories.

"Was it Takashi's description of the rising that made the team laugh so happily?" I inquired in a low voice when my wife came with food. The thing that puzzled me most was that the role of the young men in the 1860 rising—as I understood it at least—had been distinguished solely by its brutal cruelty and was hardly something to evoke hearty laughter.

"Takashi cleverly worked in some amusing episodes," she said. "There's something essentially alive about him, I feel—he refuses to have preconceived ideas about the rising, or to see it as exclusively depressing, as you do."

"Does the 1860 business have so many amusing episodes to offer, then?"

"That's not something you should be asking *me*, surely?" she retorted. But she gave an example even so. "He told them

how the overseers and local officials in the villages on the way
to the castle town were made to kneel by the roadside, so that
each of the peasants could deal them a single blow on the head
with his bare fist as he went past. That really had them laughing."

Undoubtedly the cruel idea of everybody taking a swipe at
these officials had the kind of crude humor to appeal to a bunch
of dumb peasant boys from a farming village. Unfortunately,
though, the men who had been hit by each member of a mob
running to tens of thousands had died, their brains reduced to
broken bean curd in their skulls.

"Didn't Takashi tell them about the old people left dead on
their faces after the mob had passed in procession?" I persisted,
more from curiosity than any desire to criticize Takashi and his
new friends. "Sprawled in front of their homes, all fouled up
with piss and shit—that would have made our young athletes
roar even more happily, surely?"

"Quite right, Mitsu!" she said. "As Takashi says, if the world
is full of violence, then the most healthy and human reaction
is not to stand in front of it moping, but to find something—
anything—to laugh at." And she went back to her place by the
stove.

"The young men were very brutal, I admit," Takashi was
saying, "but in a way their brutality served to give the ordinary
farmers a kind of security. You see, whenever it became necessary to injure or kill the enemy of the moment, they could
always leave it to the young men without dirtying their own
hands. The arrangement meant that the rank and file of the
farmers could take part in the rising without any fear of being
charged with arson or murder afterward. In this particular rising, their dread of getting blood on their hands was disposed

of right from the start. Apart from that one smart blow to the heads of the overseers, all direct violence and other unpleasantness was the responsibility of the young men—who were fitted by nature to carry it out with the utmost thoroughness. When the peasants on their way down to the castle town came across any village that refused to join them, the young men set fire to the first houses they encountered and cheerfully disposed of any farmers who came rushing out, or anyone who tried to prevent them from starting the fires. Those villagers who happened to escape death were so scared that they too joined the cause. You see, although both sides were peasants, in practice the young rebels, who were half crazy, used violence to force the respectable farmers to do their own wishes. The farmers were terrified of them. As a result, there wasn't one—from the valley all the way down to the castle town—who didn't fall in step. Whenever a new village was recruited, they would select youths to form a young men's organization there. There were no rules; they just had to swear loyalty to the young men's group from this valley—the original revolutionary group, as it were—and agree to perform any violence without hesitation. So the rising consisted of the young men of this valley—you might call them staff headquarters—with a substructure based in the villages and composed of groups of young fellows from each of them. Whenever a village was newly liberated, the boys from this valley would summon the local hoodlums and have them report on any crimes committed by prosperous households, which they would then raid. Conveniently enough, they were convinced that most wealthy households were dens of iniquity anyway. In places near the castle town, people had already heard rumors of the rising, so some of the overseers had hidden their valuables or their documents and ledgers in the local temples. The village boys visited the rebel leaders at their camp to tell them about such cases, indulging their new freedom from the influence of the older people of decent, conservative views. Neither the chief overseer, whom the ordinary, respectable farmers for generations past had seen as a source of authority, nor the temples, which the farmers held in awe as responsible for matters relating to birth and death, meant anything at all to them. The upshot was that the temples were raided and the things hidden there burned in the precincts. Then these poor starving kids, who only the day before had been considered scarcely human, took power themselves and formed a new leadership in the village.

"As for why groups of young delinquents like them should have been chosen, you could explain it briefly like this: first, they were people who had no proper position in the village, who had always been treated as outside normal village life. So they weren't like the older people who always went along with others of the same village and had an instinctive, unshakable suspicion of strangers. In their case, it was only with outsiders that they were capable of forming any relationship at all. On top of that, as soon as they went into action their basic instincts and newfound freedom made them do things—including arson and murder—that made it certain they wouldn't be admitted to the village community again once the rising was over. This gave them a professional interest in seeing it continue. They felt safer in league with outsiders, and the boys from our valley did, in fact, look after their interests well. Toward the end of the rising, there was an incident in which a number of youths who'd stayed behind to rape the daughters of local merchants were taken prisoner. It wasn't the powers-that-be from the castle that arrested them, though. The mob had pressed on as far as the main gate, where they held negotiations with those inside, but they weren't able to carry the assault into the interior of the castle, so the general attitude of the official police was to stand by without doing anything until the mob left town. Even after the main body of peasants had begun to go, however, a number of fellows still prowled the streets as though reluctant to leave. They'd probably never been in a castle town before, and were bursting with sexual frustration. It seems that for some reason or other they'd got themselves up in long, red, women's under-kimonos that they'd looted from somewhere." (At this his audience gave a half-excited, half-embarrassed laugh.) "It was then that they hit on the idea of raiding one of the houses that hadn't made the rioters welcome in the town, and raping the daughter. So they burst into a cotton merchant's. Unfortunately, an employee who realized that the other peasants had begun to leave got the daring idea of arresting these fellows in women's clothing. He was chief watchman, so he mobilized the workers under him and they actually succeeded in taking the boys captive. One fellow managed to get away and report what had happened, whereupon the valley group gave the order to enter the castle town again. At very great risk to themselves, the boys from our valley went back to rescue the wretched would-be rapists. In no time the prisoners were released, the cotton merchant's that had been the source of all the trouble was razed to the ground, the employees were punished, and the chief watchman's house burned down. So he got what was coming to him!"

Takashi laughed, and the other men dutifully followed suit. I finished my meal, piled up the dirty dishes, and carried them to the sink, where my wife met me with a grimly defensive expression.

"If you object to what Taka does," she said, "you'd better take it up directly with him and the young men, Mitsu."

"Not me. I've no desire to interfere in his propaganda activities," I said. "I'm only interested in getting the pheasants ready for cooking. Where are they?"

"Taka hung them on a big wooden peg at the back of the house," Momoko replied in place of my wife. "They're fine birds, fat as pigs. Six of them, too!" She and Natsumi were cutting up large quantities of vegetables into a bamboo basket, preparing a lunch rich enough in vitamins to meet the needs of a team of hearty football players.

"At first," Takashi went on, "the young men of the valley were objects of fear to the more level-headed farmers, but in the course of the rising they came to be respected, too—though it may only have been a surface respect compelled by their violent behavior. Either way, they found themselves popular heroes not only in the valley but throughout the country. So in the short period following the rising during which they were still free, they behaved more like a valley aristocracy than the village dropouts they'd been before. For a while, in fact, they could have had the peasants up in arms and out of the valley again whenever they chose. Elsewhere, too, groups of young thugs maintained their own strongholds from which they controlled their villages. When the rising dispersed, the valley group had exacted a pledge from participants in other villages that if the clan authorities began repressive measures, they would immediately reorganize their forces, and that any village hesitating to do so would be among the first to be destroyed. Such circumstances obliged the clan authorities to delay hunting down the leaders of the rising. During this happy period, the young villagers not only lived off the food and drink they'd looted but also seem to have been busy seducing the daughters and wives of the village. Of course, it may have been the daughters and wives who seduced *them!*" (The young men all laughed heartily again at this feeble quip.) "After all, the valley organization had started out as a bunch of hoods. It was virtually a period of anarchy for village society, with them swaggering about still armed and enjoying their authority. They mercilessly cut down people who got into disputes with them, and I'm sure there were some who, finding themselves none too popular with the women, made do in the meantime with rape. So when daily life returned to normal the farmers found they had a new set of tyrannical overlords. By the time the clan investigators came into the valley, the youths were already out of touch with the other inhabitants. In the end, they shut themselves up in the storehouse to resist the authorities, but were betrayed by the valley folk, who went back on all their promises of aid. . . ."

An indignant muttering rose from the circle around the open fireplace. With almost suspicious naiveté, the young men seemed to be identifying with the farm boys in the 1860 rising. Takashi's ruse in attributing leadership of the rising not to great-grandfather's brother but to the whole group of young men from the valley had succeeded.

I stood warming myself in front of the kitchen stove, then went out round the back where I found six pheasants suspended from a row of long wooden pegs planted in a clapboard, on which rabbits and pheasants had been hung in the old days. It was the coolest place on our property; at the height of summer, the cats would always lie sprawled directly below the row of pegs. In every detail of daily life, Takashi was trying to follow the routine that had prevailed in the past, when the menfolk had still acted together smoothly as a group. The way the pheasants were strung up with straw round their throats showed an obsessive deference to the way grandfather and father had done it. The birds were even stuffed with seaweed at their rear ends, where the guts had been removed. Takashi had been too young to be aware of his surroundings during the period when the Nedokoros were leading a respectable life, so he must be devoting an extraordinary amount of study and hard work to recreating the traditional valley way of life and reexperiencing it again as a whole.

I laid the plump birds out on the snow and began to pluck the feathers with their pattern of glossy black and reddish brown. Most of the feathers were promptly scattered by the wind among the falling snowflakes, leaving only the heavier tail feathers at my feet. The flesh beneath was cold and firm, yet had a satisfying resilience to the touch. The fluffy down between the feathers was full of tiny, translucent lice which looked as though they were still alive. Breathing cautiously through my nostrils for fear of drawing the lice-infested down into my lungs, I went on plucking the feathers with fingers that grew steadily more numb. Suddenly the fragile, butter-colored skin broke and my fingertips made disturbing contact with what lay beneath. Through the rapidly expanding split the blackish red, damaged flesh appeared, pocked all over with beads of blood and lead pellets. I plucked the remaining tail feathers from the now completely naked body, and twisted the neck round and round, trying forcibly to wrench the head off. But just as it seemed that the neck would give way, something inside me refused to make the little extra effort required. I released my grip on the head, which sprang back sharply, so that the beak stabbed me smartly on the back of the hand. It made me see the pheasant's head for the first time as an independent object, and I concentrated for a while on the emotions this evoked. A murmur of voices behind me was followed by a sudden burst of laughter, but the noise was absorbed at once by the layer of snow on the slope separating Sedawa from the mulberry orchard, leaving only the sound of the newly falling snow brushing the lobes of my ears, an icy grating so faint that it might have been the rustling of the snowflakes against each other.

The pheasant's head was closely covered with short brown feathers, which had a reddish, almost fiery gloss. The cockscomb-red around its eyes was dotted with black specks like the flesh of a strawberry. And the eyes themselves were dry and white—yet they were not eyes, but clumps of tiny white feathers; the real eyes, directly above them, had their black, threadlike eyelids firmly shut. I scraped an eyelid back with my nail, and something resembling the flesh of a grape slashed with a razor came oozing up and threatened to flow out like a liquid. Horror sent a momentary shock pulsing through me, but I gazed at it steadily and its power over me rapidly faded. It was, quite simply, the eye of a dead bird. The white false eyes, however, were not to be dismissed so lightly. I had felt their gaze upon me while I was plucking the remaining feathers from the all but naked body, even before I became consciously aware of the bird's head. That was why, too impatient to go and look for a knife, I had grasped the head, false eyes and all, and tried to twist it off at the neck. Though my own right eye was very like the pheasant's false eyes in its absence of sight, it achieved only a purely negative effect of sightlessness. If I were to hang myself like my friend, with my head daubed scarlet, naked, and a cucumber stuffed up my rear, I would have to paint in a glaring green eye on my upper eyelid for my death outfit to make any greater effect than my friend's. . . .

Laying out the six stark-naked pheasants on the snow, I went back to the kitchen in search of material for a fire, moving my head from side to side through an angle of one hundred and eighty degrees, as one-eyed persons will, in case there were dogs or cats in the vicinity.

". . . quite naturally, the young man who'd betrayed his fellows was expelled from the group," Takashi was saying. "If he'd fled in the direction of the castle town, he would have been arrested in no time; and if he'd stayed in the valley, isolated from the rest, his friends wouldn't have given him protection and the farmers he'd treated so roughly while he was still in a position of power would have paid him back in no uncertain terms. So his only hope was a sink-or-swim attempt to get through the forest to Kochi. As to whether his flight succeeded . . .

"Are the pheasants well covered, Mitsu?" he asked me, interrupting his lecture just as I was asking my wife for a box of matches to go with the bundle of old straw that I'd dragged out from under the floor. I doubted whether he had much confidence in the facts he was relating. I, for one, certainly couldn't command such detailed knowledge of the actions and daily lives of the young men following the 1860 rising.

I stamped a hollow in the snow, thrust in the bundle of straw bent into a circle, and set fire to it. The fine down clinging to the skin of the pheasants burned first, giving off an oppressive odor. Almost at once, the bodies of the pheasants were crisscrossed with dark brown threads of melting animal matter, and the skin itself turned a dull color in the smoke, with beads of yellow fat rising here and there. It brought directly to mind something my dead friend had said about the photograph of the black who had been set fire to: "His body was so scorched and swollen that the details were blurred, like those of a crudely carved wooden doll."

Someone was standing behind me, peering with equal intensity at the same thing as myself. I turned and saw Takashi, his face so flushed with the heat of his fireside eloquence that I expected the falling snowflakes to melt on first contact. I felt sure that the pheasants with their scorched down had evoked much the same memories in him too.

"My friend who died told me you gave him a civil rights pamphlet when you met him in New York. He said it had a photo of a black who'd been burned alive."

"That's right. A terrible picture, the sort of thing that tells you something about the essential nature of violence."

"Another thing he said was that you startled him by threatening to 'tell the truth.' He was worried because he got the impression you had some other 'truth' on your mind apart from what you actually talked about, but that you couldn't get it out. How about it—he never got his answer, but was the suspicion he died with at least well founded?"

Takashi went on peering at the pheasants, his eyes narrowed anxiously as though half blinded, not just by the light reflected by the snow onto his steadily paling cheeks, but also by something rising up within himself.

"'Shall I tell you the truth?'—" he said. I felt sure he'd used the same voice in saying the same thing to my friend in New

York. "It's a phrase from a young poet. I was forever quoting it at that period. I was thinking about the absolute truth which, if a man tells it, leaves him no alternative but to be killed by others, or kill himself, or go mad and turn into a monster. The kind of truth that once uttered leaves you clutching a bomb with the fuse irretrievably lit. What do you think, Mitsu—is the courage to tell others that kind of truth possible for ordinary flesh and blood?"

"I can imagine someone in a desperate situation resolving to tell the truth, but I don't believe that after telling it he would either be killed or kill himself, or go mad and turn into a monster—he would find some way of going on living," I objected, hoping to ferret out the purpose behind Takashi's unexpected talkativeness.

"No—that's as difficult as the perfect crime," said Takashi, dismissing my ill-considered view with the firmness of one who had obviously been pondering the theme for a long time. "If the man who was supposed to have told the truth managed to go on living without one of those fates overtaking him, it would be direct evidence that the truth he was supposed to have told wasn't in fact the sort—the bomb with the fuse lit—that I'm concerned with."

"Do you mean, then, that the man who tells your kind of truth has absolutely no way out?" I asked in dismay. But then I had an idea for a compromise. "What about a writer? Surely there are writers who have told the truth and gone on living?"

"Writers? Occasionally, I admit, they tell something near the truth and survive without either being beaten to death or going mad. They deceive other people with a framework of fiction, but what essentially undermines the work of an author is the very fact that, provided one imposes a framework of fiction, one can get away with anything, however frightening, danger-ous, or shameful it may be. However serious the truth he may be telling, the writer at least is always aware that in fiction he can say anything he wants, so he's immune from the start to any poison his words might contain. This communicates itself eventually to the reader, who develops a low opinion of fiction as something that never reaches directly into the innermost recesses of the soul. Seen in that way, the truth in the sense in which I imagine it just isn't to be found in anything written or printed. The most you can expect is the writer who goes through the motions of a leap into the dark."

The snow settled on the row of pheasants where they lay with their down scorched off, their bodies fleshy and heavy. I took them up two at a time and banged them sharply together to shake off the snow. They made a dull thud that set up nasty echoes in the pit of my stomach.

"My friend said he suspected that on the day you said you would 'tell the truth,' just before he startled you by coming up from behind, you'd been studying that photograph of the charred body. He was right, wasn't he? You were sitting at the drugstore counter imagining telling your own truth and being turned into a blackened corpse like that."

"Yes—I had a feeling that he understood to some extent. And I feel that I myself understand at least the significance of the way he chose to commit suicide." He spoke straightforwardly, reawakening in me the emotion I'd felt on hearing his tribute to my dead friend at the airport. "It may seem funny that I should be so sure about something concerning a friend of yours, but I've been thinking over the implications of what happened ever since I heard about it from Natsumi. Before he painted his head red and hanged himself, naked," (and—I thought—with a cucumber stuffed up his rear, though since my wife didn't know this, Takashi didn't either) "I'm sure he gave a last cry of 'Shall I tell the truth?' Even if he didn't actually shout the words aloud, I feel that the very act of jumping, with the cold realization that a moment later his body would be hanging there naked and redheaded for all to see, irretrievably dead, was in itself just such a desperate cry. Don't you agree, Mitsu? Don't you think it takes terrific courage to make one's final gesture with one's own naked, crimson-headed corpse? He told the truth through the act of dying. I don't know just what truth it was he told, but the one absolutely certain thing is that he told it. When I heard about it from Natsumi, something inside me gave the signal, 'OK, message received.'"

I understood what Takashi meant.

"It seems he made a sound deal when he paid for your medicine."

"If the time ever comes for *me* to tell that kind of truth, I'd like you to hear it, Mitsu. It's the sort that wouldn't have its full effect unless I told it to you." He spoke with the naive excitement of a child that knows it's doing something risky.

"You mean, me as a close relative?"

"Yes."

"You mean, your truth concerns our sister?" I asked, overcome by a stifling suspicion.

Takashi's body went momentarily rigid, then he stared so fiercely that I was afraid he would lash out at me. But he was merely focusing on me with intense wariness in order to gauge accurately just what lay behind my words, and after a while his body suddenly relaxed and he averted his gaze.

We stared in silence at the new snow settling on the corpses of the pheasants. The dank cold chilled our bodies to the marrow. Like his comrade of the grotesque features and inadequate clothing, Takashi was shivering, his lips blue. I was eager to get back into the kitchen, yet at the same time wanted to round off our conversation amicably. Takashi, however, rescued us from our awkwardness while I was still groping vaguely for something safe to say.

"The reason I persuaded you to come back to the valley," he said, "wasn't just plain cunning. It wasn't just so that, when I sold the storehouse and land, I could tell them at the village office that my elder brother up at the house had asked me to come and make arrangements. It's also because I want you to be a witness when I tell the truth. I'm hoping that moment will come while we're together."

"The land and the house don't matter now," I said. "But neither do I believe you'll ever tell anybody such a terrible truth—if, that is, you really *have* such a truth hidden inside you. In the same way, I don't suppose I'll ever find my new life, or my thatched hut. . . ."

So, side by side and chilled to the bone, we walked back into the house. It was lunchtime, and Momoko was just dishing out stew to the young men round the fireplace. For Takashi and his friends, living and training together like the young men's New Year communes of an earlier generation, this would be their first meal under the same roof. The ever-industrious Hoshio sat in a corner, apart from the happy circle formed by his new comrades, with a large number of footballs which, one by one, he was assiduously polishing with oil to preserve the leather. I handed the corpses of the six pheasants to my wife, put on my new boots, and scuffled my way back through the snow to the storehouse.

The Freedom of
the Ostracized

Time passed, but the powdery snow went on falling, betraying my private hope that it would change into larger, petal-like flakes, and I remained alien to it. I stayed shut up in the storehouse, concentrating on my translation, never going out into the snow. My meals were brought to me there; the only time I returned to the main building was when I needed to replenish the water in the kettle on the stove. Whenever I went, I found Takashi and his companions in a state of childlike innocence, drunk with the snow and showing no signs as yet of the fatigue or wear and tear that goes with a hangover. New snow wiped out all traces of deterioration in what had already settled, constantly renewing the first impression, so there was no chance for the devotees in the main house to recover from their snowy infatuation. Eventually, I discovered that I could use melted snow in my kettle, and my daily life was cut off even more definitively from the main building. I spent three days enfolded in the driving, alien snow, savoring the sense of relaxation of one free from all surveillance, a sense so strong that I could tell that my own expression and movements were slackening and slowing up.

Early on New Year's Day, even so, my hermit's existence had been disturbed by Jin and her family. The first intrusion came around dawn, when Jin's eldest son woke me to say that Jin wanted me, as present head of the Nedokoro family, to go and draw the "first water." The boy was as tense as one of the old folk, who were easily swayed by such peasant customs, and scowled as he held out toward me an advertising leaflet on the back of which, in a half-illegible scrawl done with a hard pencil, a map had been drawn. By the dim light of the bulb at the bottom of the staircase, and beneath the watchful gaze of the boy's small, shadowy eyes, I tried to take in this year's route for fetching the "first water," which Jin had worked out herself, but gave up and going back upstairs wrapped myself in my overcoat. The unfortunate boy, who had apparently been ordered to accompany me on the expedition, stood still and silent, shivering like a dog with wet fur as he waited.

Looking in at the main house, I found Takashi and my wife asleep side by side near the open fireplace in which a few embers still gave off a red glow. Hoshio lay beyond Takashi, and Momoko under the same blanket as my wife, but Takashi's arm, which was obviously stretched out to touch my wife's side beneath the blanket, gave the impression that the two were sleeping quite alone. As I stood at the entrance to the kitchen, half embarrassed, half unable to draw my gaze away, Jin's nimble offspring unearthed a deep bucket—the bucket destined to play such a sacred if short-lived role—from beside the stove. Then together we plunged into the snow-filled darkness. The snow driving against my face told me that the skin was burning and suffused with blood, but my emotional responses were steady to the point of inertia. Sadly I recalled the fatal sense, grown like a cancer between my wife and me, of the impossibility of any sexual activity. Surely, I told myself, it was a desirable thing in the long run that we should seize any chance to escape, dragging heavy feet like exhausted warriors, from that clogging mire of impossibility? Even so, I wasn't admitting the possibility of direct sexual relations between her and Takashi; all that had happened was that my mind, empty of everything but the pressing need to hasten on through the dark snow, was seized from time to time by a mysterious fantasy in which the powerful magnetic force I'd sensed so stoically repressed in Takashi's erect penis, as he stood naked and covered with snow, transmitted itself somehow to my sleeping wife through the fingers laid against her flank.

The snow on the road leading down to the riverbank from the main road through the valley was still soft. Jin's son must have watched intensely at his mother's side as she thumbed through her almanacs and charts of directions, working out the route for the "first water," for he plowed his way through the knee-deep snow with complete confidence. As the river came into sight, I halted in my tracks, shocked at the sight of the black water hemmed in by snow. At once, the fragments of fantasy floating about the space inside my still incompletely awakened brain condensed and fell to earth. *You're an outsider, you've no connections with the valley,* I repeated to myself like a spell to ward off the terrifying things that the black waters threatened to awaken in me. But though I might succeed in denying it all meaning, the black river imprisoned in snow was still the most threatening sight I had encountered since coming back to the valley. Assuming from my petrified air that I was stuck, afraid of losing my footing in the deepening snow, Jin's son waited for a while, but finally seized the bucket from my hand and went down to the water's edge alone, gliding knee-deep down the snowy slope. There was a furtive, almost guilty splashing, then the boy came struggling back up the slope with the water he'd drawn from the river, and I saw that besides my bucket he was carrying an old dried-milk can which he'd found somewhere and reverently filled with river water.

"You could have had some of our 'first water' if you wanted!" I said. But the boy abruptly covered the can with both palms as if to protect it from attack.

I realized what stubborn idea had just taken shape in his small head. I hadn't drawn my "first water" myself, but had let him get it for me. That made it a fraud, whereas the water that filled his own can was true "first water," since he'd drawn it for himself. Until now, Jin's family had always shared the Nedokoros' "first water," and if I had gone down to the water's edge to draw it myself he would probably have been content with a share of our "genuine" water. However, once I'd got stuck and allowed it to be drawn fraudulently in my name, he'd had the idea of drawing some of his own and taking it home. If the son of a mother so hopelessly and incurably obese could still become such a stubborn mystic, then there must be some powerful reality underlying the process. Now that my mind was completely awake, I began to feel it had been foolish and pointless to come down to the river at dawn like this, and I trudged back along the graveled road in a disgruntled mood. The task of drawing "first water" would have suited Takashi better than me. I handed the bucket to Jin's son in front of the main house so that I shouldn't have to see the people asleep in there again, told him to take it into the kitchen, and went back to the storehouse. But the ache in my half-frozen shoulders distorted the dreams of my resumed slumber, and I had a nightmare in which I struggled and cried out, my shoulders caught in the grasp of two enormous hands of terrifying prehensile power that emerged from the black waters of the river.

Shortly before noon the boy came to summon me again, announcing that Jin had come at the head of her entire skinny brood to extend her New Year's greetings. Going downstairs I found Jin, more incredibly fat than ever, seated on the edge of the raised floor in the entrance, facing the heavily falling snow outside like some enormous sphere that had rolled in from nowhere in particular. I stepped down into the entrance to save her the trouble of turning her body, and stationed myself, along with the family, in front of her and somewhat to one side. Her face, lit evenly all over by the shadowless light reflected from the snow, had an odd youthfulness. A quiver ran over the skin drawn taut and wrinkle-free across the great metal basin of her face, but she just stared at me and went on breathing heavily and painfully without speaking. The few yards' walk from the outbuilding had reduced her to something resembling a moribund porpoise. Her family refused to say anything as long as she remained silent, and having stepped down into the entrance in a mood of vague tension, I found myself strangely at a loss. Apart from Jin herself, who was enveloped in a kind of shapeless black bag with neither front nor back, top nor bottom, the family was dressed up in what was more or less the conventional New Year's outfit, but I still wore the corduroy shirt and sweater in which I'd gone to sleep, and hadn't even shaved. I began to worry in case Jin felt her effort in coming specially to offer her greetings was not receiving due recognition. However, after an interminable period spent regaining her breath, she finally cleared her throat hoarsely and feebly and began, with a generous display of goodwill:

"A Happy New Year to you, Mitsusaburo!"

"And a Happy New Year to you too, Jin!"

"Some hope!" she declared, immediately stiffening her attitude. "What's happy about it for a wretched creature like me? Suppose the whole village was to clear off again—how would I get away, I'd like to know? I'd be left to be eaten by the dogs or die of starvation."

"Why bring up that old story now?" I said. "The last time the whole village checked out was before the 1860 rising, surely?"

"Don't you believe it—I saw them go myself!" she countered in a voice full of stubborn, foolish confidence. "Just after the defeat, when the occupation forces came in jeeps. Don't you remember? All the able-bodied folk ran off into the forest, leaving the old people and disabled behind in the valley. *That's* what I'm talking about."

"But you're wrong, Jin," I said. "I know, because I was in the valley when the first jeep arrived. A GI gave me a can of asparagus, but the grown-ups didn't know whether it was something to eat or what it was, so in the end I left it in the teachers' room at the primary school."

"No—they cleared out, the whole lot of them!" Jin insisted calmly.

"Mitsusaburo," interposed her taciturn spouse, "Jin's begun to go funny in the head."

The remark upset the children, who showed signs of painful anxiety obvious even to a bystander.

I couldn't help recalling how, in my dream of the attack on the storehouse, Jin had figured as someone with no hope of escape. And yet, as I watched her sitting there—the eyes, which were small and sunken like navels in the swelling flesh of her face, still further narrowed against the dazzling snow; the small lips sucked in between her gums; the dirty, scaly-looking ears sticking out like handles on a full moon—she had an air of sturdy sanity that belied the disproportion of her flesh. The show of mental disturbance, I suspected, was a new tactic designed to stop me putting the outbuilding up for sale. Unfortunately, though, it was Takashi and not me at whom she should have directed her cunning—and Takashi had in fact already sold all the Nedokoros' land and buildings, including Jin's home. If anything really qualified Takashi for the role of effective evildoer, it was the flaw in his sensibility that allowed him so easily to betray the pitiful plans of a middle-aged woman trapped by her abnormal bulk in this godforsaken valley.

"Okubo village is going to the dogs," she announced. "People have lost their sense of decency. Take last night—it was New Year's Eve, but a crowd of complete strangers from both the village and the 'country' dumped themselves on the houses that have TV. Stopped them making their preparations for the New Year or doing anything else. Disgusting, I call it!"

"Did *you* go and watch television?" I asked the boys.

"Mm, we went and saw the New Year's Eve Show," the second son replied proudly. "Some houses were watching TV on the sly with the place all shut up, so the crowd got mad and rattled the shutters! Most of the kids went round from one place to the next and didn't go home till everybody'd put their sets away in the back room."

I went back to my lair on the second floor of the storehouse while Jin and her family made their infinitely leisurely progress through the snow toward the main house, on their way now to offer greetings to Takashi and the rest. As I peered from the window, Jin's body looked like a swaying snowman. I could see where the top of her round head was going bald in the center. I watched again a little later as several young men supported her on her way back to the outbuilding. The "evildoer" bounced around the bearers as they went, scattering the snow and directing operations in a piercing voice until it suddenly seemed too much for everybody, including Jin's children, and they burst into innocent laughter.

On the morning of January 4th, I went down to the valley for the first time to make a long-distance telephone call. Snow had been falling steadily for several days, but the narrow road that led to the open space in front of the village office wasn't difficult to negotiate, since there was a foundation of hard-packed snow beneath the thin new layer on the furrowed trail. The young members of the football team had occupied the first few dozen hours of the year—which the older men of the valley had spent dead drunk—in vigorous training, running up and down the path and treading down the snow as they went. As I passed by the supermarket I saw a vaguely disturbing sight. The store was closed temporarily behind a great shutter done in yellow and grayish green camouflage like a tank, but a number of farmers' wives from the "country" were standing perfectly still beneath the eaves, each accompanied, as if by arrangement, by a single infant. Empty baskets on their arms suggested they were waiting for the store to open in order to do some shopping or other. They must have been patiently waiting there for a considerable time already, though, for some of the children were squatting wearily in the snow. The supermarket had been closed since New Year's Day. The doors were still in fact locked, and there was no sign of any employees near them. Why should the women from the "country" be standing there with their empty shopping baskets? I walked on past them, still wondering.

The stores driven out of business by the supermarket had deep, overhanging eaves beyond which, in the darkest recesses of the interiors, the inhabitants lurked, peering out at the outside world. They were the only sign of life; there was no one on the snow-covered road, so I couldn't buttonhole a passerby and ask him the reason for the women's odd presence. Even if somebody had appeared on the road, he would probably have turned aside to urinate or found some other way of avoiding me as soon as I approached. I wondered about the people in the post office—would anyone talk to me while I waited for my long-distance call to come through? Like the shops that had gone out of business, the eaves of the post office were piled high with snow which no one had bothered to brush off. Stepping over a pile of snow in front of the main entrance, only one of whose doors was open, I entered the dim interior. No clerks were at the windows, but there were signs of people somewhere out of sight, so I called out my request for a long-distance call.

"The snow's brought the lines down. No calls can be made outside the village," came the prompt reply in an indignant, old man's voice that sounded down near the floor and unexpectedly close at hand.

"When will services be restored?" I inquired, a fragment of ancient memory stirring at the sound of the voice.

"The young fellows who work on the lines have holed up at the Nedokoro's. They won't come out and work when I go to fetch them," said the ancient in tones of obviously mounting indignation. I suddenly remembered: the voice belonged to the old postmaster, who had been just as irascible and ineffective when I was a kid. Even so, I left without discovering precisely how he'd tucked himself away down in that corner.

I was walking back in the direction of the supermarket when, ahead of me, I noticed two men standing facing each other, solemnly stretching out their hands in turn toward each other's heads. I approached with head down so as to shield my face from the snow carried by the wind, which on the way back was blowing full at me, and paid no special attention to their ritual. I was more concerned about the "country" women who stood so pointlessly in front of the firmly closed main entrance. As I drew nearer, I found that they were still there, and that in no time at all their number had swelled by more than ten. They waited just as placidly as ever, but the children, who a while ago had been walking about or squatting in the snow, were now clinging in sniveling terror to their mothers' legs. Sensing something wrong, I halted, and saw that the men immediately in front of me were in fact lunging furiously at each other. I had no alternative but to stand there and, with a deep sense of embarrassment brought close to fear by the excessively short distance between us, watch this silent exchange of blows, so measured as to suggest a predetermined ritual.

Both men, who were respectable valley folk in late middle age, wore jackets and shirts without ties—the normal form of holiday wear in the valley—and had been drinking heavily. Their faces were copper-colored and shining with heat, and their breath came in great steamy gasps amidst the falling snow. They weren't moving their lower halves at all—less, it seemed, from fear of treading in a patch of deep, soft snow and losing their footing than from sheer grim determination. They were taking turns at hitting each other with clenched fists, one blow at a time: to the ear, the chin, the neck. They went at each other with the utterly patient, silent stupidity of fighting dogs. But as I watched, the intoxication obviously began to ebb from the face of the somewhat slighter man, and he seemed almost to shrink. I felt sure that at the next blow he received, a cry would break out like sweat all over the pale, dry skin of his tense face. But at that point he frantically drew something from the back pocket of his trousers and, clasping it tightly in his hand, lunged at his opponent's mouth. There was a sound like an oyster shell being pried open with a hook, and a small fragment of something bathed in red foam came flying toward me. Covering the lower half of his face, which was still copper-colored from drinking, the injured man brushed past me with head down, and his assailant came running after him at full speed. Right next to my ear I heard the dismal, feeble groaning of the victim and the heavy breathing of the man chasing him; then I turned and watched them disappear into the distance. I squatted down and searched the snow at my feet for the thing that had fallen there. On the white surface of the snow, which was churned up but not muddied, I found a red depression about the size of an apricot stone, at the bottom of which lay something like the brownish yellow bud of a tree, a tiny lump with something a vivid pink in color and shaped like a Jew's-ear attached to its root. I stretched out my hand, picked it up in my fingers, then flung it down again, my guts gripped in a spasm of revulsion. It was a dislodged tooth and part of the gum. Still crouched there, I looked about me with the feeble despair of a vomiting dog. The women still stood in front of the supermarket gazing blankly into space. The small children, who hadn't yet recovered completely from their fear and still had fingers firmly entwined in the hems of their mothers' shoddy overcoats, stole fearful glances at me as though I presented a fresh threat. And still the people in the houses round about, who must have witnessed everything as they peered out from the gloom beyond the glass sliding doors, stayed in hiding and made no move to come out. I fled the scene precipitately, making my escape up the graveled road with the same sense of helpless urgency as when one flees some horror in a nightmare, frequently stumbling off the center into the unstable, yielding places at the side where the snow had not been trodden down.

I was so disturbed that for the first time since I'd shut myself up in the storehouse I felt an urge to tell Takashi of my experience. Arriving at the main house, I called him outside. The young men staying there were working energetically in the kitchen, and I hesitated to go inside. But though Takashi listened attentively to what I had to say, my profound distress left him quite unaffected.

"There have been lots of fights in the valley since New Year's Day, Mitsu," he said. "The adults of the village have been badly on edge these last few weeks. What makes it worse is that they've had nothing to do during the New Year's holiday except drink cheap liquor, and the wildest of the young men, who in normal years would soon have been at each other's throats, have stayed here, training for all they're worth. So the older men, who ought to know better, have been obliged to pick their own fights. The people who used to get rid of their pent-up aggression by watching or mediating in the kids' fights and quarrels are busy fighting each other this time. And did you notice that even when they do start a fight nobody tries to stop them? The older men's quarrels are more involved than the youngsters', and it's difficult for outsiders to intervene. So their fights go on indefinitely and free of interference."

"Be that as it may," I insisted, unconvinced by the way Takashi's analysis put everything within the framework of normal everyday life, "I've never seen two people from the valley hit each other so hard that one of them lost a tooth and part of his gum with it. They were punching each other in absolute silence, first one then the other, with all the force behind their fists. It's not normal, Taka, even though they were drunk."

"When I was in Boston I went to see the President's birthplace," he said. "The whole cast of *Ours Was the Shame* was taken there. On the way back, the small bus carrying us passed through the ghetto and we saw two young blacks quarreling. One of them was swinging a brick above his head, threatening the other. His shoulders were narrower and less muscular. The other man, who wasn't worried in the slightest, was jeering at him from a safe distance. But in the short time it took our bus to go by, he relaxed his guard and went just that bit too near. Immediately, the other man cracked him on the head with the brick. His head literally split wide open, so you could see the inside. And all the while the people living nearby just went on watching quite quietly, sitting on the porches of their houses in their rocking chairs or those rattan chairs with the big armrests.

In this valley, violence means a piece of gum missing at the most—you don't get any murders. Perhaps the Japanese keep some sense of proportion when they fight, or maybe they don't have the strength. Psychologically speaking, though, the valley could be becoming something of a ghetto."

"You may be right. To the best of my recollection, you would never have seen such naked violence here in the old days, especially in the morning. At one time, even, with a quarrel much less serious than that, the children would have run straight to the police station. This morning, though, everybody just stayed indoors and watched."

"The policeman's not at the station. He had a telegram summoning him to the town late at night on the day it started snowing, and he's been there ever since. No buses can get through, and the telephone wires came down along with the trees felled by the snow. So nobody here knows how the policeman's spending his New Year."

I detected a possible desire to provoke suspicion in the way Takashi spoke, but suppressed the temptation to inquire further. I badly wanted to stay detached from everything Takashi and his team did. To play Takashi's game by getting involved in the puzzling hints he doled out piecemeal was both dangerous and tedious. Besides, I had already abandoned any idea of criticizing him, whatever happened.

"Surely the supermarket's closed for the New Year's holiday?" I said, changing the subject. "The shutters were down, but there was a group of women from the 'country' in front of the entrance. I wonder what they're up to? You'd think that during New Year's week at least they could manage for food without depending on the supermarket. What was even odder was that they were standing so perfectly still in front of the closed doors."

"Oh, were they there already?" he said, perhaps trying to stir up my suspicions again. "We're putting on a bit of a show at the supermarket this afternoon. Why don't you come along and watch, Mitsu?"

"I don't feel like it," I said, all my basic wariness to the fore.

"Quite the little hermit, isn't he!" said Takashi. "Convinced from the start he doesn't want to come, without even asking what kind of show it is."

"That's right!" I said. "I've absolutely no desire to go out of my way to watch anything that happens in this valley."

"So you've no positive desire to watch anything here—let alone take part in anything, of course. In fact, you might just as well not be here at all."

"Look," I said, "I'm staying against my will, because of the snow. Whatever peculiar things happen here, all I ask is first to get out, then to forget about this hole in the forest once and for all."

Takashi smiled equivocally as though mocking me, then shook his head two or three times in silence and retired into the kitchen without more ado. I had a feeling he was anxious to keep my eyes off the work the young men were doing in the kitchen. But I had no wish to interfere either, and went back to the storehouse.

When Momoko brought my lunch, she tried to coax me into looking out of the storehouse window to see the new banners on the roof of the supermarket. Charmed by the childlike tension with which she set this obvious trap, I hadn't the heart to refuse. Two different kinds of banners, in cheerful yellow and red, fluttered on top of the storehouse that now formed the supermarket. The snow falling steadily in the valley made the whole scene resemble something out of an old and battered movie. Turning away from the window, I found Momoko watching me intently, her eyes full of undisguised expectation. Naturally, I had no idea what the two sorts of banners signified.

"Now, I wonder why you're so pleased about those banners?" I said.

"Why?" repeated Momoko and shuddered, with an almost wild look in her eyes, torn between taboo and the desire to tell all. "Aren't you happy about them, then?"

"When I get back to Tokyo, I'll send you some really nice ones, Momoko," I said to tease this junior member of Takashi's bodyguard, and set about eating my lunch.

"If you come down to the valley at four o'clock, you might find out what's going to happen, Mitsu—even a member of the establishment like you! Remember—four o'clock! I bet you'd like to know what's brewing. But I can't tell you—I can't let the team down."

I couldn't help smiling at her. She looked like some comical, out-of-date female terrorist in her leather Indian outfit which, despite the snow, she still wore proudly without any underwear as on the first day at the airport. By now it was not only a mass of wrinkles but was coming apart at the seams to reveal expanses of sallow flesh.

"I couldn't be less interested in what's going to happen, Momoko. You don't have to let anybody down."

"Oh, you establishment people are such a *bore!*" she said with mingled regret and annoyance, and set off back to her unbetrayed comrades.

At four o'clock that afternoon a great, repeated cry from countless throats rose from the bottom of the valley and came slowly twisting up in a spiral of sound. A mighty cry combining urgency with a lurking, pleasurable excitement, it titillated the most shameful part of the psyche—a fold, as it were, in its bright red, engorged mucous membrane. The sound provoked an unjustified panic in me, as though I'd been caught disgracing myself in some obscene, exhibitionistic act. At the same time, I found myself asking aloud, "What is it? What the hell is it?" Immediately, something nameless would have answered me from the corner of the storehouse, but I cried "No! No!" in fresh panic, shaking my head. The cries swelled up and swelled again, on and on, in waves. Then after a while the shouting died down and a quieter groundswell took its place, a kind of pulsating murmur like the whirring of innumerable bees' wings punctuated from time to time by brutal, throaty voices that refused to be buried beneath it and vied with the high-pitched screams of children and cries of joy. So long as the sound rose and fell in even cadences, I managed somehow to get on with my translation, but once these sharp cries, intermittent and unidentifiable, began to intervene I could concentrate no longer. Eventually I got up, went to the window and, feeling the chill radiating from the icy pane on my eyes and flushed cheeks, peered out through the clouding glass into the space over the valley, where evening was already at hand. By now only a trace of the finest snow was falling. The forest lay in deep shadow about the valley, which seemed to be filling with a murky, milky mist; even the sky with its snow clouds was like a vast, dark brown hand blotting out the valley below. As I strained my smarting eye to make out the banners of the supermarket, they gradually emerged through the mist, hanging limp and disconsolate like birds with folded wings, their color vague and pallid as fragments of china lying beneath muddy water. I had no idea what was going on at the super-market; but the memory of the women who during the silent contest between the two middle-aged men had stayed unmoving and equally silent before the shutters lingered undigested in my mind, now threatened anew by the cries from the valley. Before long I went back to my desk, troubled by an uneasy sense of inadequacy. I had succeeded in maintaining my self-imposed ban on going down to the valley, but the ban didn't prevent me from reflecting that something odd had obviously occurred there, and that almost as obviously it had some connection with Takashi and his football team. Unable to get back to my transla-tion, I took a tail joint left over from the oxtail stew I'd eaten for lunch, and occupied myself by sketching it in carefully shaded detail. The bone, the same color as the flesh of an oyster, had all kinds of protrusions and indentations running in complex directions, as well as round, jellylike flaps attached to both sides of the joint and small cavities like termites' holes whose function in the workings of the animal's tail while it was alive and active were impossible to guess at. I went on interminably with this idle sketching, but finally put down my pencil and gnawed at the flaps of jellylike substance in an attempt to recapture the remembered taste. The only taste left, though, was of cold fat and the bouillon cubes used in making the stock. My sense of impotence plumbed unfathomable depths, and I found myself floundering in a pit of depression with no hold to heave myself out by. At five o'clock, darkness fell outside the window, but I could still hear a dense clamor mingled with occasional excited cries. More and more frequently, too, I heard explosive noises of the kind that men make when they're drunk. With a sound of heavy metal objects clanking against each other, Jin's sons came home to the outbuilding, talking to each other rapidly and animatedly in voices quivering with excitement. Normally, they would have lowered their voices timidly as they went past the storehouse in deference to my work, but this time they plainly couldn't have cared less about the man sitting upstairs in solitary state. Like the grown-ups, they gave the impression of having just participated in some activity of valid consequence for the village community. Before long, Takashi and his team returned to the house, and for a while the front garden was clamorous with voices. Even late at night I sometimes heard mingled cries rising from the valley as though several groups of drunken men were fighting simultaneously.

My wife brought my dinner herself. Around her head she wore a turban of the same kind of neurotically gaudy print that I'd seen on the women in the crowd at the end of the bridge. She probably hoped to reproduce the charm of the young, dim-witted valley girls, but the turban only served to emphasize the breadth of her well-shaped forehead and give her, if anything, an air of sober maturity. Moreover, she hadn't yet started on the whisky this evening.

"A bit young for you, isn't it, that outfit?" I said. "Or are the high spirits of the football team restoring your youth?" Immediately, I could have bitten off my tongue in disgust at the vulgar overtones of the jealous husband in my remark. She gazed calmly at my face as I went red with shame and resentment, then, with the almost obsessive imperturbability that had become one of her qualities when she wasn't drunk—though definitely only since she'd taken to drinking—she launched directly into the subject that I'd hesitated to broach though it bothered me so much.

"They gave me this cloth at the supermarket, Mitsu," she said. "Did you see the banners over the roof? They were a sign that the Emperor was going to present every regular customer with one free article from the store. It was terrible at four o'clock when they opened. I imagine you heard the shouting even up here at the storehouse, didn't you? They all made a rush for the entrance—first the women from the 'country,' then the valley women, then the children, and finally even the men, so you can imagine the crush. I nearly fainted with the fight I had to put up just to get this turban."

"Very self-sacrificing of you," I said. "What do you mean though, 'one free article'? Surely you couldn't just help yourself to any item in the store, could you?"

"Takashi was in front of the supermarket taking photos of everybody as they came out with their spoils. Most of the women seemed to have got clothing or food. But after it got dark some of the men started carrying off bigger things. Apparently the ones who brought out bottles of liquor in the first struggle got drunk and went in again under cover of darkness. At first, the goods to be given away were all stacked together in a separate place from the ordinary shelves. But actually the rush was so terrific, especially the women from the 'country,' that things got out of hand almost at once."

I was about to retreat into the wry, shrinking smile of the feeble outsider so shocked by the very fact of a display of power that he loses all desire to discuss its nature and purpose, when an unsavory thought occurred to me and hauled me back unwillingly to face a more concrete suspicion. Simple surprise ebbed from my mind, and a premonition of danger with overtones of needless complications flowed in to take its place.

"But surely they didn't stock alcohol at the supermarket, did they?" I said.

"It seems that people who went into the store a while before order began to break down saw bottles lined up on the shelves along with the free gifts. Anyway, the fact is that there were any number of bottles of whisky, saké, and so on standing there."

"Was Taka responsible?" I asked. I spoke my brother's name with a feeling in which obscure nausea combined with a desire to reject the whole unpleasant world of reality and retreat into childhood.

"Yes, Mitsu, he was. Takashi bought up all the valley liquor dealer's stock and took it to the supermarket beforehand. But it seems the original plan to let every customer have one free gift really came from the Emperor himself—he does it at all his chain stores on January 4th every year. The arrangement is that you show the salesgirls your receipts for purchases during the second half of the year, and they give you some trifling article of food or clothing. The only special idea Takashi had was to slip the alcohol in among the other gifts, then increase the confusion by delaying the opening of the store, and give the customers a free hand by having the salesgirls desert their posts as soon as they began to come in. But the chaos that it actually caused made me feel Takashi has a real gift for organized troublemaking."

"But how did Taka manage to get a hold over the people in the store itself?" I asked. "Surely the truth of the matter is that the free-for-all occurred spontaneously, and Taka realized it would be a good chance to blow his own trumpet."

"The Emperor, you see, wanted to employ the young men to replace the salesgirls and warehouse guards who'd gone home for the New Year's holiday. He hoped to squeeze as much unpaid work as possible out of the people who'd been running the chicken farm, to help make up the loss on several thousand dead chickens. It was after he'd made the proposal that Takashi and the others got their idea. Anyway, it's surely not a bad thing that the women should have had a chance to get back a bit of what the supermarket's done them out of in the past."

"But I don't imagine the matter will just blow over, will it?" I said. "Especially if the men who were drunk carried off expensive items—it amounts to wholesale robbery involving the entire district." I felt a stale gust of depression sweep through my body.

"Of course, Takashi doesn't for a moment think it'll blow over. His football team kept the manager of the supermarket shut up in his house all day today. It won't be till tomorrow that Takashi's real activities begin. And the team members are really looking forward to that!"

"I wonder why they were so easily led on by Taka's talk," I complained pointlessly, with a trace of resentment.

"Ever since their failure with the chicken farm, the young men of the valley have felt trapped," she said, slowly giving rein to the excitement that till then she'd been controlling by her own private means. "They may not show it, but there's no doubt they're nursing a serious grievance. And the future here looks pretty bleak even for the most sober, industrious boy. They haven't been kicking a football around for fun—they were kicking it out of despair, because they'd absolutely nothing else to do."

Her eyes glittered feverishly and were moist right to the corners, as though with desire, but with no trace of the redness that usually afflicted them at such times. I realized that since I'd retired to the storehouse she had overcome the vague, deep-rooted fear preceding sleep without recourse to alcohol. As a result, she was no longer prey to insomnia or depression either, and had obviously planted her feet on the slope leading upward to recovery. Like Takashi's youthful bodyguard, she'd obeyed the warning to stop drinking and live life sober. Moreover, she was in the process of bridging the perilous gulf without any aid from me, her husband. Feeling like a whipped dog, I longed for the Natsumi who had got drunk while we waited for Takashi at the airport, the Natsumi who had so resolutely disavowed any desire to be reeducated.

"If you've any intention of interfering in what Takashi's doing," she said, skillfully putting her finger on what my retrogressive attempt at fraternization was hoping for and reacting immediately with a steely stare, "you'll have to approach him carefully so you don't get caught by the team." As she spoke she had an air of youth and sturdiness that reminded me of how she'd been before the unhappy childbirth. "On our way back from the supermarket I saw the priest. It looked as if he was coming to consult you about today's incident. He soon ran home, though, when the boys threatened him with those awful weapons of theirs. Do *you* still have confidence in your physical strength, Mitsu?"

Much as one hauls the flesh of a shellfish out of the depths of its shell, so she was dragging my self-respect—which I'd squashed up as small as possible and tucked away inconspicuously—out into the light for the sole purpose of inflicting damage. Anger stirred me to life.

"Everything that happens in this valley is irrelevant to me. It's due neither to antipathy toward Takashi nor the reverse, it's just that I've waived all desire to criticize the behavior of him and his team. Whatever crops up here, I intend to leave the valley just as soon as communications get back to normal, and to forget all about everything." I spoke emphatically to reassure myself that this was really how I felt. Even if those cries so strangely disturbing in their suggestion of shameful desire should come welling up from the valley again tomorrow, I intended to ignore them and get on with the translation, my inner dialogue with the friend who had killed himself. Each time I groped for a word, I would ask myself what *he* would have used at that point, and enjoy the momentary sensation of communion with the dead. At such times, my friend was physically closer to me than anyone alive.

"I'm staying behind with Takashi," said my wife. "Perhaps I'm attracted by his behavior because I myself have never once broken the law. Everything I've ever done has been within the laws of the state—right down to standing by and watching my own baby turn into little more than an animal."

"I quite agree," I said. "I've lived the same way myself. To tell the truth, I've essentially neither the desire nor the qualifications to criticize anything that anyone else does. It's just that I sometimes forget." We lapsed into an awkward silence, our eyes averted from each other. Then she said, timidly bringing her face close to my knee:

"So it was a dead fly stuck there, Mitsu. Why don't you take it off?"

Her voice had become mild and feminine, tinged with the excessive tenderness of someone who is ashamed of herself.

In a corresponding mood of infinite docility, I scraped the tiny, black, dried-up blob from my knee with an ink-stained nail. When all was said and done, I reflected, we were still man and wife, with no alternative but to go on with our joint life indefinitely in this way. We were saddled with two minds that were in too bad a state and, within that state, too entangled with each other to allow divorce.

"Schopenhauer said, didn't he, that you can squash a fly, but the 'thing in itself' doesn't die," she whispered, gazing intently at the black speck. "You've only killed the fly phenomenon. Dried up like this, it really does give the feeling of being a 'thing in itself.'" They were the first words she'd spoken that showed a letting-up of tension, that concealed no barb.

Late that night as I lay half asleep, I heard a loud cry in a girl's voice; the sound seemed almost to come from my own head, and I couldn't tell whether the cry was one of fear or of extreme rage. By relegating it skillfully to a point somewhere between daytime memories and the world of dreams, I disposed of it and prepared to go on sleeping. At the second cry, however, memories and dreams both retreated and, like an image on a screen, I saw Momoko in vivid detail, her mouth wide open, shrieking for all she was worth. From the main house came indications of a large number of people in fearsome commotion. I got up and without turning on the light shuffled toward where the window stood out faintly in the darkness. I looked down in the direction of the house.

The snow had stopped, and in the front garden where the light of the lamp in the eaves lit a vivid patch of fresh snow, Takashi in undershirt and training pants was standing with a young man in a short cotton kimono that left his chest and lower

legs bare. Beneath the eaves, the members of the football team
stood in a row with their arms folded, all wearing similar padded
jackets as though they were in uniform. The young man facing
Takashi, the only one who had been stripped of his jacket, gave
every indication of having just been ejected from the group. He
was explaining himself abjectly and at great length to Takashi. My
brother, stooping forward with his long arms hanging limp at his
sides, seemed at first to be listening intently to what the youth
said, but in fact he was making no attempt at all to understand
the weaker man's excuses. At unpredictable intervals, he started
up and dealt the young man a hefty blow on the side of the head,
as if something intensely brutal had run through the center of
his body and spent itself in a dangerous flash of purple lightning.
Unresisting, the youth allowed himself to be struck repeatedly
by Takashi, who was far shorter and narrower in the shoulders,
edging away feebly until he finally lost his footing in the snow and
toppled over backward. But even then, Takashi fell on him where
he lay and went on hitting him. A sense of real physical horror
at seeing a close relative in the act of violence thrust down hard
and massive into my stomach. With the sad taste of bile on my
tongue, I dropped my gaze and retired through the darkness to
my blankets. This brother who went on pounding an unresisting
younger man in the face had ceased to be an amateur in violence;
his spasmodic brutality and vindictive persistence were the marks
of a criminal. The aura of criminal violence that I'd detected
about Takashi grew steadily larger and shone more brightly, till it
illuminated the whole valley like a menacing aurora in the light of
which the affair at the supermarket assumed quite a new aspect.
Only retreat into the purely personal confines of sleep offered
any hope of escape from the detested light of violence; but sleep

refused to make its usual encroachments on my mind, which was like a potful of food in which heat had brought all the scum to the surface. All efforts proving in vain, I opened my eyes in the depths of the darkness and gazed at where the window loomed a milky white. At times the faint light would grow deeper, at others fade completely till it was no more than the lid on a pit of darkness. Light and darkness, moreover, succeeded each other at a bewildering pace. . . .

I wondered if something had gone wrong with my one good eye after several days in the harsh light of the snow. The fear of blindness created a moment's vacuum, serving as a relaxant for my exhausted and overheated brain; and lonely physical apprehension unexpectedly enabled me to put the poison of my brother's violence out of my mind. Staring at the alternating light and darkness of the window, I surrendered to worry pure and simple. Before long, however, the light that went past the long, narrow window was so bright that I realized it was no illusion due to failing eyesight but simply the moon shining on the other side. I got up again and went to gaze at the snow-covered forest beneath the moonlight. The surface of the forest was divided into two parts, one standing out brilliant with snow, the other a correspondingly black depression, a shadowy area where countless wet animals seemed to crouch together. Each time the moon was covered by racing clouds, the flock of animals took on a bronze tinge that deepened till they finally retreated out of sight into the darkness. Then almost at once, as the snow on the pointed part of the forest began to shine again in the moonlight, the flock of animals, recovering their wet-looking sheen, would slowly and with heads hanging come marching out once more.

Beneath the light of the moon, the lamp suspended from the eaves in the front garden barely managed to cast a small, squalidly yellowed ring of light. For that reason I hadn't noticed at first what it illuminated, but I suddenly saw the young man, utterly beaten, cringing in the trampled snow. Scattered about him were a bundle of blankets, padded kimono, cooking utensils. The team had ejected him once and for all. With his head hunched between his shoulders, which were sunk into a strange saddle-shape, he crouched completely motionless, like a threatened wood louse. I promptly lost the mild sense of elation that the moonlit forest had awoken in me. I buried myself, head and all, in the dark, intimate warmth of the blankets, but even my own breath on my chest and knees wouldn't halt the shivering of my body, and I could hear my teeth chattering. Before long I caught the sound of footsteps going round behind the storehouse and fading into the distance, moving not in the direction of the graveled road down to the valley but toward the trail rising to the forest. The faint but unmistakable creaking of the snow soon told me that this was no dog going up to the forest in search of wild hares sheltering in the snow.

The next morning, I was still asleep when my wife came with my breakfast. She told me of the incident late the night before in a voice full of loathing for this sudden eruption of naked violence. In violation of the football team's rules, the young man had drained a small bottle of cheap liquor he'd brought surreptitiously from the supermarket, then taken Momoko into a small room in a distant part of the main house and tried to seduce her. Although he was drunk and it was late at night, Momoko had gone with him quite cheerfully, clad in a nightgown which she'd personally chosen at the supermarket, but which would have been more appropriate on a harlot in the *Arabian Nights*. Casting hesitation to the winds, the young man promptly set upon this provocative young woman from the big city. When she resisted fiercely and gave a series of lusty screams, he was so startled that even while he was being hit by Takashi he still hadn't completely recovered from his uncomprehending amazement. The shock had set off hysterics in Momoko, who had gone to bed with face and body pressed up against the wall in the back room and hadn't yet put in an appearance that morning. She had thrown out the nightgown that had caused such dire misunderstanding, and putting on all her clothes was lying there as though in armor, scarcely breathing. On her way to the storehouse, my wife had seen the young outcast's weapon lying where it had fallen on the trampled snow. It was inscribed with the character "Mitsu."

"Judging from the sound of his footsteps," I said, "he seemed to go round the back of the storehouse and up the road to the forest. I wonder where he went?"

"Maybe he's planning to go through the forest to Kochi, like the farm boy at the time of the 1860 rising who was thrown out for betraying the others."

This element of fantasy in her interpretation somehow made me feel that she sympathized with the young offender rather than Momoko.

"You just don't know how overgrown and impassable the forest is," I said in an attempt to dispel her romantic notions. "To try and get through in the middle of the night in this snow would be suicidal. You've been too much influenced by Takashi's talk about the rising. Even if the boy has been expelled from the football team, I don't suppose it means it'll be impossible for him to live in the valley. Takashi hasn't got the necessary hold over the others. Last night, for example, as Taka was beating up that poor bastard for misinterpreting Momoko's unconscious invitation, the other fellows might equally well have rebelled and beaten the daylights out of Taka instead."

"But Mitsu, don't you remember what Hoshi said to you that time when he got weepy at the airport?" she countered with sturdy self-confidence. "I suspect you don't understand or even know much about Takashi as he is now. The simple, unsophisticated kid you used to know at home has survived things you couldn't even imagine, let alone comprehend."

"But even if the young man felt that being shut out of Takashi's group made it emotionally impossible for him to stay in the valley, it's more than a century since the rising, you know. Surely any fugitive would make his escape down the road to the coast? Why should he go into the forest?"

"That boy knows perfectly well that the chaos they've secretly contrived at the supermarket already constitutes a crime. If he went over the bridge and down the snow-covered road to the next town, he might get arrested by police lying in wait there, or the gang that they say the Emperor employs might set on him. At least, he could easily have convinced himself that that would happen, couldn't he? I begin to suspect that in practice you don't know much more about the group psychology of the team than you know about what really goes on inside Takashi."

"Of course," I said, retreating very slightly, "I don't persuade myself that because I was born in the valley my ties with it are still valid, or that I can fully understand the young men who live here. Just the reverse, if anything. I simply made a few objective, commonsense observations. If Takashi's pep talks have induced group madness in his team, then obviously my observations don't apply."

"You shouldn't dismiss something as madness just because you're not involved yourself, Mitsu," she persisted relentlessly. "When your own friend committed suicide, for example, you didn't dismiss it in such simple terms, did you?"

"Then tell Takashi to send a search party into the forest," I said, capitulating.

I went out to wash my face, going round the rear to avoid the entrance to the main house, and was on my way back when I encountered the young men spilling out excitedly into the front garden. A diminutive figure dressed in an old lumberman's oilskin had come into the garden dragging a rough-and-ready sledge made by tying together bamboo stems with the leaves still on them. On the sledge was the young outcast, swathed to the neck like a bagworm in a garment stitched together from old rags. Takashi had just come out to meet them. The man had half turned, with the upper part of his body twisted back, as though he was afraid the young men dashing so energetically out of the house might be about to attack him, but Takashi was restraining him. Screwing up my eyes against the dazzling morning light reflected from the trampled snow, I made out a lean and ill-favored profile, the eye a mere slit, that swiftly identified itself with Gii the hermit as I remembered him from a dozen or more years earlier. His head was small, almost like a head shrunken by savages, while the stunted ears were little bigger than the first joint of one's thumb, so there seemed to be an unnaturally large space all round them. The shallow pillbox hat on his tiny head made him look like an old-style postman.

Caught between the sunbleached hat and the yellowish goatee, his small face, covered with blemishes and something gray like carpet fluff, was paralyzed with apprehension.

Takashi was holding his team in check behind him and speaking to Gii in the kind of quiet, friendly voice one might use to calm a frightened goat. With his body still twisted back and his eyes half closed, the old man answered Takashi, his lips twitching rapidly like two fingertips trying to pick something up, then shook his head in a way that suggested he heartily regretted dragging the sledge down from the forest and was ashamed, beneath the pervasive light, of everything to do with himself. At an order from Takashi, the young man covered in rags was lifted from the sledge and taken indoors. Carrying him cheerfully, as though they were shouldering a portable shrine at some religious festival, the footballers were followed by Gii the hermit, who with Takashi's arm encircling his puny shoulders was led, protesting feebly, into the kitchen. Left alone in the front garden, I gazed down at the bundle of new bamboo, caked with hard, frozen snow, where it lay abandoned on the softer snow. Bound round and round with coarse rope, the bundle looked as though it were awaiting punishment for some iniquity.

"Natsumi's giving the hermit a meal, Mitsu."

I turned. Takashi was standing there with his sunburned checks flushed a vivid rosy hue and a wild, almost drunken light in his brown eyes, and for a moment I had the illusion that a midsummer sea lay behind us as we talked.

"Gii was down in the valley as usual during the night. He was going back at dawn when he caught sight of a young man marching steadily into the forest. So he followed him until the boy was exhausted and came to a halt, then fetched him safely back again. Would you believe it, Mitsu, he was trying to cross the forest in all this snow and get to Kochi! He was identifying with the young fellow in the 1860 rising!"

"Natsumi came to the same conclusion even before Gii brought him back," I said, and broke off.

As he struggled through the deep snow in the pitch-dark forest, driven on by shame and despair at being cast out by his comrades, he must have seen himself as the topknotted son of a peasant in 1860. And there was nothing, in fact, to convince the simpleminded youth, gripped by mounting panic as he plunged on through the darkness of the midnight forest, that a hundred years had really passed since that fateful year 1860. If he had fallen by the way and frozen to death, he would have died a death absolutely identical to that of the young man driven out in 1860. All those separate moments that coexisted in the heights of the forest would have poured into his dying head and taken possession of it.

"Now that the first signs have shown in him, I'm sure the tendency to identify with the young men of 1860 will soon take hold among the team as a whole. I'm going to spread it among all the valley people. I want to start another rising here, to reproduce the rising of our ancestors a century ago even more realistically than the Nembutsu dance. Mitsu—it's not impossible!"

"But what on earth's the point, Takashi?"

"Point?" He laughed. "When your friend hanged himself, Mitsu, did you ask yourself what the point of it was? Or do you ever ask yourself what the point of your own survival is? Even if we achieve a new version of the rising, there mightn't be any point to it at all. But at least I'll be able to experience as intensely as possible what great-grandfather's younger brother went through spiritually. That's something I've been desperately wanting to do for a long time."

Back in the storehouse, I found that the sound of dripping water, as the snow melted under the heat of the sun and began to run down through the thick layer remaining on the roof, surrounded the storehouse on all four sides like a bamboo blind. And I fancied I could use the sound to cut myself off, to defend myself from all that happened in the valley, just as great-grandfather with his gun had protected himself and his property from the modern world beyond the forest.

Imagination in Riot

The music for the Nembutsu procession, large and small hand drums with gongs, had been continuously audible since before noon. It had gone on insistently, slowly shifting its position. The same rhythm, if such it could be called—*bang,* bang, bang! *bang,* bang, bang! *bang,* bang, bang!—had continued now for four hours. I'd watched from the back window of the storehouse as hermit Gii went up the graveled road to the forest. He walked with his head cocked on one side as though deep in thought, yet climbed steadily up the steep, snowy trail, kicking strongly at the ground behind him, dragging the sledge bearing the new blanket that my wife had given him in place of his tattered old one. The music had begun shortly after that. By the time my wife came upstairs bringing rice balls and an unopened can of salmon for my lunch, the voice in which I asked her about the music was hoarse with annoyance at its inescapable persistence and sounded harsh and strange even to my surprised ears.

"Was it your leader Takashi's idea to play the Nembutsu music out of season like this?" I asked. "Does he think the music's going to remind people of the 1860 rising? If so, it's a puerile idea that'll only serve to annoy the neighbors. Takashi, you, and the rest are the only ones who're carried away. Do you really think those stolid valley types are going to get excited over a few drums and gongs?"

"Well, it's got you annoyed at least, Mitsu," she pointed out calmly, "you who're trying so hard to be indifferent to everything in the valley. The canned salmon, incidentally, is part of the spoils of war from the supermarket—the looting got going again this morning—so you'd better not eat it if you want to keep your hands clean of the affair. I can go and find you something else."

I opened the can, not as an admission of complicity with Takashi, but to show my indifference to her sarcasm. I don't even like salmon.

Where the ordinary inhabitants were concerned, the previous day's looting at the supermarket hadn't been premeditated. But according to my wife, Takashi and the others had been busy that morning spreading the idea that, since looting was illegal anyway, there was no reason for the valley folk not to go on with it once they'd started.

"Hasn't anybody objected to these attempts by Takashi and the rest to stir them up?" I asked. "This morning, after they heard what had been going on behind the scenes, didn't any of them have second thoughts and take back their looted goods?"

"There was a village get-together in front of the supermarket, but no one made any such suggestion. You don't suppose they'd go out of their way to return the goods, do you, when the girls in charge of accounts were giving juicy details of the profits the store had been making and the salesgirls were testifying to the shoddiness of the goods? Even if some oddball had wanted to, the general atmosphere wouldn't have let him go it alone."

"It's like conning a bunch of kids," I said, chewing balefully on my salmon, which was dry and full of bones and other debris. "But the reaction will soon set in."

"Anyway," she said, "feeling's running high against the supermarket. Several women who were searched in the past on suspicion of shoplifting were there, relating their experiences."

"What a dumb crowd!" I said. The looted salmon seemed to stick in my throat.

"You know, Mitsu," she said casually, "you really ought to go down to the valley yourself to see what's going on!" And she went off down the stairs. I spat the half-chewed salmon and grains of rice into my hand.

The Nembutsu music nagged at me unceasingly, torturing my nerves, sapping my mental energy. Like it or not, my can kept reminding me of the abnormal events taking place in the valley. Somewhere deep inside them, the "rising" was already an actuality. And by now the loathing the music aroused in me was irreparably tainted with the poison of curiosity, like a liver that once damaged can never recover. But I forbade myself to move from the storehouse until I found some routine reason to do so, some reason not directly related to the disorder sponsored by Takashi and his fellows. Until then, I wouldn't set foot in the valley myself, nor would I send down any scouts. The music, which in its monotony contrived to suggest nothing more than emotional poverty, might merely be Takashi's way of boasting to me that his activities were still continuing. Any action from my side would be a craven capitulation to his vulgar psychological tactics. I would hold out. Before long, the sound of a car horn from the valley added to the noise. Takashi was probably driving around down there, with chains on the Citroën's tires, putting on his own naive demonstration for the benefit of the children. Or perhaps—if the valley folk had in fact turned into a mob of rioters—he was reviewing them from the car. . . .

The stove, I noticed, was becoming less efficient. The oil in the tank was running out, and I'd already used up my reserves. The only alternatives were to send someone to the supermarket to buy some, or to go down into the valley and do so myself. At last, I was released from the agonizing bonds of endurance. Ever since the morning, for more than four hours now, I'd been tortured and ridiculed by the Nembutsu music.

In the main house I found my wife looking after Momoko, who was still in bed after her attack of hysterics. I couldn't look to them for help. The young outcast had been moved to the local clinic with frostbite, and all the other members of the team had joined Takashi and Hoshio in masterminding the high jinks in the valley. The only people who could serve my purpose were Jin's sons. I stood in front of the closed door of the outbuilding and called out, not with any idea that the children had resisted the lure of the music and were still shut up in the chilly gloom with their fat, depressing mother, but to confirm that all the conditions obliging me to go down to the valley had been fulfilled. Jin's sons made no reply. I was about to withdraw in satisfaction from the closed door when, to my surprise, Jin herself hailed me in a firm, almost cheerful voice. I opened the door and peered in, my eyes darting about like a worried bird in the unfamiliar darkness, half hoping to find her husband rather than Jin herself.

"Oh, hello Jin," I said apologetically. "I thought I'd get your boys to run down to the valley for me if they were here. I'm out of oil for my stove."

"They've been down in the valley since this morning, Mitsusaburo," she said with unusual affability as her massive body loomed slowly into view like some huge battleship appearing through mist over the sea. Her eyes directed their power straight toward me like two hot, shining magnets protruding from her round, swollen face. As her tone had already suggested, she was seated in solitary elation on the legless throne. "And the young fellows under Takashi's command came to fetch my husband, so he went down to the valley with them."

"Takashi's crowd came to fetch him?" I complained with a somewhat guarded display of sympathy for Jin's husband. "But he's such a gentle man—why do they have to drag *him* into it?"

The guardedness had been justified: Jin wasn't looking to me to commiserate with her over her husband.

"The young fellows went round getting people out of all the houses in the village," she said. "They made particularly sure to rope in families that hadn't yet taken anything from the supermarket, so in the end the whole village turned out." As she made an effort to smile, the narrow slits of her eyes flashed between the encroaching flesh, and sluggish ripples ran across the skin tightly encasing the thick layer of fat. Gone was the painful breathlessness that usually bothered her these days; she was the champion gossip again, sustained by an unquenchable curiosity. "The boys had gone off down to the valley long before, but my husband was still here, so two of the fellows came to the door and told him to go down to the supermarket. When the boys came back for a break, they were saying that with any family that hadn't taken anything from the market, no matter how rich or important, a couple of the young fellows would go and call them out to the market. Apparently both the wife of the headman's son and the postmaster's wife went to get things. And it seems the headmaster's daughter was very upset because she had to bring home a great box of detergent she didn't need at all!" Suddenly she compressed her lips as though her mouth was full of water, and snuffled noisily; then the skin of the great moon face flushed in patches, and I perceived that Jin had laughed. "So it's all fair, Mitsusaburo. Everybody's disgraced themselves equally. Isn't that nice?"

"Doesn't anybody sympathize with the Emperor, Jin?" I said, more or less sidestepping what I vaguely sensed to be a dangerous trap set by this pathologically obese middle-aged woman with her talk of "disgrace," and putting a question more remote from her bellicose chatter.

"Sympathize with that Korean?" she flashed back indignantly. Until yesterday, like most of the valley folk, she'd never so much as hinted that the all-powerful supermarket owner who had wrought such havoc in the valley was a Korean. But now she deliberately stressed the word "Korean," unhesitatingly broadcasting his nationality as though to emphasize how the looting of the supermarket had reversed the balance of power in one fell swoop.

"The valley folk have had nothing but trouble ever since the Koreans came here," she went on. "After the war ended, they climbed up in the world by grabbing the valley's land and money. We're only trying to get a bit of it back, so what's sympathy got to do with it?"

"But Jin, they didn't come here voluntarily in the first place. They were slave labor brought from their own country against their will. Besides—so far as I know at least—they've never gone out of their way to make trouble for the people here. Even with the postwar disposal of the land where the Korean settlement stood, no individual in the valley ever suffered any direct loss, surely? Why do you deliberately remember things all wrong?"

"S was killed by the Koreans!" she said suspiciously, rapidly recovering her wariness of me.

"That was in revenge for the killing of a Korean by S's friends just before. You know that perfectly well, Jin."

"Everybody feels things have gone to pieces since the Koreans came. They should kill 'em all off!" she declared with extraordinary intensity, flogging herself on in her irrationality. Her eyes had gone dark with hatred.

"But Jin, the Koreans have never willingly inflicted any harm on the people living here. The trouble just after the war was the fault of both sides. Why say such things when you know the facts as well as I do?" But she suddenly lowered her great, mournful head against my accusations. Her only visible response came from the nape of her neck, which from where I was standing looked like the neck of a seal and heaved in time with the labored breathing that had overtaken her again. I sighed in a wave of frustrated annoyance and resentment.

"It'll be the valley people who pay dearly for starting such a foolish disturbance, Jin," I said. "I don't imagine the looting of one of his chain stores will hurt the Emperor much, but most people in the valley will go on feeling wretched with guilt over the stuff they swiped. What do they think they're up to—even the older people, who ought to know better—letting themselves be put up to such things by someone like Takashi who's only just back from abroad?"

"I'm glad all the valley folk have disgraced themselves equally!" Jin repeated, talking as though it had nothing to do with her personally and stubbornly refusing to raise her head and look me in the eye. It convinced me that the word "disgrace" had some very special meaning in her vocabulary.

Now that my eyes could penetrate the recesses of the gloom, I could see various kinds of cheap canned goods piled in a ring round Jin's chair within easy reach. Steadfast and obedient, they stood there waiting, soldiers of a trusty relief force ready to do battle with a hunger that could never be cured. They were Jin's private "disgrace"—a whole army of private "disgraces" drawn up in tidy ranks for all to see, their true nature blindingly obvious even to the casual observer. I was gazing at them at a loss for words when, with a defiant display of honesty, Jin took from between the great mounds of her knees a half-opened can whose lid stuck up in a semicircle like an ear and began to wolf its unidentifiable contents. I remembered that animal protein had a bad effect on Jin's liver, but couldn't bring myself to mention it and said simply:

"Shall I draw some water for you while I'm here, Jin?"

"Don't imagine I'm going to eat so much I'll make myself thirsty!" she retorted. But her next words had an emotion more straightforward than anything I'd heard from her since the days when she and I together were keeping the Nedokoro family going. "You know, Mitsusaburo," she said, "thanks to Takashi's riot, for the first time I've got more food than I can eat. It's only canned stuff, but there's more than I can manage, really! If only I could get it all down, I wouldn't need to eat anything more. I'd go back to being thin like I used to be, then I'd weaken and die."

"Don't be silly, Jin," I said comfortingly, with the first feeling of reconciliation since my return to the valley.

"It's not silly! Wretched creatures like me have a feeling for these things. Even at the Red Cross hospital they told me it was my mind, not my body, that made me eat so much. If only I could get so I didn't want to eat anymore, I'd start losing weight the same day. I'd go back to what I used to be. And then there'd be nothing left to do but die!"

Without warning, I was seized with a childlike sadness; after mother's death, it was Jin's help alone that had seen me through the trials of boyhood in the valley. Shaking my head without speaking, I stepped out into the snow and closed the door, shutting "Japan's Fattest Woman" away in the peaceful darkness, alone with her happiness and "disgrace," amidst the great pile of food that might well fatally damage her liver. . . .

The hard-trodden snow on the graveled road had softened to a grayish color and turned slippery. I went down it cautiously. I had no intention of interfering in the looting of the supermarket; I'd simply made up my mind on no account to get involved in Takashi's actions. If the supermarket should prove to have lapsed into complete anarchy, it would be impossible to buy oil according to the normal procedure. So my plan was quite simple: I would hand Takashi or his associates the right amount of money for any can of oil that might have survived the looting, and leave at once. I, at least, wasn't going to share in the communal "disgrace." Besides, the instigators of this minor riot had deliberately omitted to haul me off to the market, which meant I was an outsider from the start and as such not required to share their "shame."

As I arrived in the open space in front of the village office, Jin's eldest son appeared out of the blue and started walking in front of me like a dog out with its master. Swiftly realizing from the look on my face that it wasn't the time for conversation, he restricted the expression of his inner excitement to a peculiarly bouncy way of walking. The houses on either side of the road, so long shut up, lay wide open today, and their inhabitants stood in the snow in front of their homes, talking animatedly or hailing each other in loud voices. The whole valley was in a state of cheerful excitement. Even the people who had come down from the "country" were standing on the road in scattered groups, joining in the conversation or drifting slowly from one spot to another. Their arms were full of spoils from the supermarket, but they still hung about, making no move to return to their homes. When a mother from the "country" asked permission for her child to use the toilet, the valley wives agreed openheartedly. Not even on festival days had I ever seen valley and "country" mingling with such freedom and tolerance, since even in my childhood the valley festivals had already lost their traditional power to shatter barriers. The children were treading down the snow on the graveled road to make slides, or mimicking the Nembutsu music, which had continued all the while. Jin's son would amuse himself by joining in the sport first at one point then at another, but soon ran back to my side again. Various adults hailed me with affable smiles as they stood talking.

It was the first time since my homecoming that they'd relaxed the barriers against me in this way. I couldn't respond immediately to their unexpected overtures and hurried past them nodding vaguely, but they were too intoxicated by their newfound sociability to be put out. My inner amazement took deeper root, put forth sturdy branches, burst into luxuriant foliage. A tall man, who had taught Japanese history as a substitute during the wartime shortage of school staff and worked since the war as secretary to the farmers' cooperative, was brandishing an open ledger above his head, explaining its contents to the people gathered about him. The young team members stood by him in silent attendance—from which I gathered that he'd been roped in as special adviser to the group sponsoring the new "rising," and in that capacity was publicly denouncing the iniquities of the supermarket management. As he caught sight of me, a warped smile, a mixture of stagy wrath and natural pride, spread over his face.

"Hey, Mitsusaburo!" he called to me in a loud voice, interrupting his lecture. "I've been exposing the way they fake the store's accounts. If the tax office gets wind of this, the Emperor'll have to kiss his throne good-bye!" Far from being dismayed by this unexpected interruption, the audience turned to look at me and made happily derisive gestures of protest against the tax-evading supermarket. There were an unusual number of old folk among them, and it struck me that the same was true of the knots of people I'd seen as I walked down the graveled road. Until only the day before, their lives had been spent huddled in darkness behind grimy windows, but today they'd achieved self-liberation with the rest and been restored to their positions as full members of the valley community.

Suddenly, Jin's son gave a shrill cry to attract my attention.

"That's him!" he shouted in a voice high-pitched with the excitement of discovery. "That's the manager of the market!"

I watched as a plumpish man jogged past on unsteady feet. He wore a leather jacket, and the head above his bull neck was completely bald even though he couldn't have been forty. Paddling the air with his arms like a landborne seal, he trotted on determinedly amidst a hail of insults from the children. He'd obviously been released from confinement in his house, but since the bridge was almost certainly under strict surveillance by the football team, he'd merely been given the run of the valley; in practice, he was as shut in as ever. So the sight of him trotting busily like a newsboy through this shower of abuse was at once comic and puzzling. Did he imagine he had some plan for getting things back to normal, alone in the valley without a single ally? Just then, one of the children discovered it was fun to throw snowballs at him, and the others immediately followed suit. A snowball struck his ankle as he ran, toppling him with the greatest of ease. He struggled to his feet and without even brushing off the snow that clung to him from head to foot bellowed an impotent threat at the half-crazed children. But they only went on throwing snowballs more gleefully than ever. In my dry mouth I tasted again the raw, spontaneous fear of that day when my eye was split open in an assault by unknown children, and felt that I'd found a clue to the long-standing riddle of why they'd thrown that stone.

Miserable and irate, the man went on shouting faintly but persistently as he fended off the volley of snowballs with both arms.

"What's he shouting?" I asked Jin's son, who had promptly joined in the attack but had now returned to my side, still bubbling with excitement.

"He says that as soon as the snow thaws the Emperor'll come with a gang and attack the village. He forgets we've got weapons to fight back with!" he added proudly. He peered into the now empty box of cookies from which he'd been eating, flung it aside, and, drawing out another of the boxes that stuffed the pockets of his short coat, crammed a fresh handful into his mouth.

"They don't think they'd get the better of a gang, do they? Violence is a gangster's specialty."

"Takashi'll teach them how to fight. He fought the rightists, so he knows how!" he declared, gulping down the contents of his mouth impatiently. "Did you fight, Mitsusaburo?" he added with indescribable acuteness.

"I wonder why they're letting the manager go about as he likes?"

"I wonder . . ." the boy began noncommittally, then gave what was, in fact, the most pertinent of answers to my vague question. "He talks such rubbish that the valley folk have stopped paying much attention to him and the Emperor. He's a Korean too, you know!"

I was disgusted at this unreasoning hostility toward Koreans in a kid born since the war, but if I tried to defend the manager, the boy would almost certainly get his gang of little ruffians together and have me running away in the same tottering, aimless fashion.

"You don't need to come with me anymore," I said simply. "Go and play with your friends."

"But Taka ordered me to come and take you to him!" he said, earnest perplexity written all over his small face. But I stoutly refused his guidance and in the end left him standing there, cheeks crammed with another handful of cookies to assuage his frustration. For the first time since Jin had developed her abnormal appetite, her skinny son too had found more food than his shrunken stomach so hesitatingly demanded. A strange sense of duty toward it, allied with an uneasiness whose nature he himself didn't understand, was making him eat and eat. He would probably spew it all up in the end.

The snow round the supermarket had been trodden into a slush, and the graveled road was an utter mess, a foretaste of the clogged days to come when the thaw set in in earnest and the whole valley turned to mud. In front of the store stood a large number of independent groups. Some were people who had carried television sets outside and were watching them there, others were looking on as various electrical appliances were taken out of their wrappings and subjected to modification.

On the TV screens, two different programs were in progress. Small children crouched in front of the sets, intent on the screens. By stationing themselves, half squatting, at points where it was possible to keep an eye on two sets at once, some of them were even managing to watch both channels. But the grown-ups standing at the rear had an unsettled air and weren't really concentrating on the television sets. Coming at the same time as the strange state of emergency in the valley, this contact with people going about their everyday lives in distant towns had had a peculiar effect on them. The blurred image of a young girl in close-up on the screen, singing with her prominent chin thrust forward and an artificial smile on her face, only emphasized the abnormality of what had happened and was still happening in the valley.

The electrical goods taken from their packages had been stood on the damp ground, and two middle-aged men were at work on them with hammers and chisels. They were the valley blacksmith and tinsmith—obviously two more special advisers taken on by the young men. The groups of onlookers were mostly women. It was clear that this was the first time the pair had undertaken such a task, and though they were probably the most skilled craftsmen in the valley the work progressed slowly and uncertainly. Its nature was mildly destructive, consisting in removing the manufacturer's nameplate and number from the appliances. At one point, the chisel with which one of the men was trying to get the nameplate off the face of an electric heater bit deeply into the bright scarlet paint on its side, and a wave of sighs from the women squatting round the workman made him shrink visibly with embarrassment. The petty task he was engaged in was far removed from the skills that were such a confident part of his being. This puerile destruction, in fact, was aimed at obliterating proof that the appliances had been looted from the supermarket, in readiness for the day when the snow thawed and the forces of the Emperor came rolling back up the paved road from the town to the hollow.

Leaving the crowd and turning toward the entrance of the supermarket, I realized that the young men of the football team were keeping an eye on my movements. They were scattered throughout the groups standing round the television sets or watching the craftsmen, lurking among them like dark blots on the festive mood of the crowd, their faces shut in and morose, their eyes glinting. Steeling myself against their unnerving stares, I gave the door a push, but it didn't open. I peered through the glass at the utter chaos inside and pushed and pulled at the handle with increasing dismay.

"Looting's over for today! There'll be another round tomorrow!"

Turning at the sound of Jin's son's voice, I found him, his cheeks still stuffed with cookies, standing grinning with his friends in a semicircle just behind me. Half expecting I would box his ears, he took a step back, and his friends with him.

"I didn't come here to loot, I came to buy some kerosene."

"Looting's over for today! Another round tomorrow!" chorused the boy's friends with the same elation, and laughed mockingly. The children had already adapted to the new style of life created by the "rising" and were now rioters to the manner born.

Hoping for some support, I called across the threatening cluster of children's heads to the team members, who still had me under their expressionless surveillance.

"I want to speak to Taka. Take me to him, will you?"

But the young men cocked their bullet heads as though perplexed and said nothing, their gawky, unprepossessing features increasingly stiff and blank. I was seized with a hysterical irritability.

"Taka *told* me to take you to him!" Jin's son said to me placatingly, his confidence restored, and without awaiting my reaction set off ahead of me along the path leading round to the back of the store. I chased after him plowing with difficulty through the deep snow that buried the path. Icicles lay in wait for me, striking me smartly beside my sightless eye before breaking off and falling.

Behind the saké storehouse that had been converted into the supermarket, there was a square yard where they'd once put the great brewing vats out to dry. The ramshackle supermarket office that had been set up there served now as headquarters for the rioters. A young man stood on guard at the door. Having brought me this far, Jin's son squatted down in the unmarked snow in one corner of the yard to wait for me. Beneath the guard's watchful gaze I opened the door in silence and entered the room, which was filled with hot air and the animal smell of young bodies.

"Hi, Mitsu! I didn't really think you'd come," Takashi greeted me cheerfully. "At the time of the Security Treaty demonstrations, you didn't even come and watch, did you?" He was swathed to the neck in a white cloth, having his hair cut.

"Aren't you getting rather big ideas to compare this with the Security Treaty disturbances?" I said scathingly.

Takashi was perched on a small wooden chair beside a potbellied stove. The valley barber, who was little more than a boy, was plying his scissors with the earnest devotion of one who had rushed to offer his services to the hero of the "rising." By Takashi's side stood a young woman with a short, cylindrical neck, whose whole appearance immediately suggested emotional instability. With her plump body pressed familiarly to his, she was collecting the falling hair in an open newspaper. A short distance away, at the back of the room, Hoshio and three of the team members were printing something on a mimeograph, presumably their ideological and factual justification for the assault on the supermarket.

Takashi ignored my sarcasm, but his fellows stopped work and watched for his response. I imagined he had educated his young, inexperienced fellow rioters by telling them about his own experiences in June, 1960, drawing a forced parallel between those events and this minor riot.

"In *Ours Was the Shame* you played a repentant student activist," I wanted to say to my brother, to whom the heat of the stove and the barber's scissors gave the look of a youthful,

simpleminded farmer. "Have you taken on the opposite role this
time?" But I managed to hold my tongue.

"How about the kerosene?" Takashi asked his companions.

"I'll go to the storehouse and see, Taka," Hoshio responded
promptly, handing the roller of the mimeographing machine to
the young man by his side. Even so, he remembered to hand
me and Takashi one copy each of the newly printed leaflet as
he went out of the room. As assistant to the leader, he was obviously a very able member of the "rising." I glanced at the leaflet.

> *Why will the Emperor of the Supermarkets have to suffer
> in silence?*
> *Because otherwise:*
>> *It would be bad business for the chain stores!*
>> *It would be awkward with the tax office!*
>> *He would never be able to do business in the valley again!*
> *Would anyone as guilty as the Emperor do anything suicidal?*

"The first thing, Mitsu," Takashi put in swiftly, obviously
hoping to forestall any criticism I might make of the wording
of the leaflet, "is to get everybody, right down to the lowest
level, thinking along these basic lines. We've got subtler and
more powerful cards up our sleeves. This sexy little piece, for
example, used to be the Emperor's liaison officer, but now she's
cooperating with us. She's bold and fearless in her attacks on
the Emperor—particularly since she hopes to get the sack soon
anyway, so she can move into town."

Her heart-shaped face flushed pink with pleasure at this
clever flattery, and she preened herself as though about to burst

into song. She was obviously the kind of girl, of whom there's one in every farming village, who from the age of twelve or thirteen becomes the object of the lustful aspirations of all the young men living round about.

"They say you stopped the priest from coming to talk to me yesterday," I said, averting my eyes from the girl, who was now directing her charm not only toward Takashi but to the non-specific plurality. "Did you?"

"Not me, Mitsu. But all yesterday, at least, the team was naturally keeping an extra-sharp eye on the intellectuals and prominent people of the valley. After all, they're an influence to be reckoned with. Supposing, for example, that just as the villagers were about to break into the supermarket again with a drunken laborer at their head, some important village figure had told the ordinary folk at the rear to stop. The looting probably wouldn't have gone any further than the first, almost accidental incident. By today, though, a majority of the valley folk have already put themselves in the wrong. If the privileged class were to get all righteous and aloof, they'd only make themselves hated. So we've switched our tactics—nobody's keeping a watch on them any longer. On the contrary, our fellows are joining them wherever they gather and giving opinions or asking their advice. Mitsu, remember the spartan hero who led the chicken farm association? He's trying to find some way for the village to take over the supermarket. His idea is to drive the Emperor out and put the supermarket under the joint management of the inhabitants of the valley. Don't you think it's an attractive plan? He's got a rather special perspective on such things, which leaves me free to concentrate on *violent* activities."

The young men laughed the dutiful laugh of officially recognized accomplices. They seemed to find Takashi's way of
talking attractive.

"But since the second round of looting, we've had to supervise the distribution of the supermarket's stock, so my own
work's quite difficult too. For example, I have to make sure
there's not too big a difference between the spoils of one group
of homes from the 'country' and another. There's method in our
looting, you see!" He laughed. "The team's keeping a strict guard
on the market and the warehouse until distribution begins again
tomorrow. The young fellows are staying here tonight. How
about it, Mitsu? What do think of our 'supervised looting'?"

"Jin referred to it as 'Taka's riot,' you know," I said. "If you're
going to keep the valley folks' interest in it alive for as long as
possible, you can't let them use up the riot's source of energy too
soon, can you? So I imagine some supervision is definitely necessary," I made no attempt to conceal my reactions to Takashi's
excited verbosity. But far from being disturbed, Takashi seemed
to find this intriguing and kept the same provocative gaze on
me as he said:

"I like that—'Taka's riot.' Though she's biased, of course.
But you know, Mitsu, it isn't just material greed or a sense of
deprivation that's got all these people, adults and children alike,
so worked up. I expect you heard the Nembutsu drums and gongs
going at it all today? Well, that's helping to keep the pot boiling—
it's the riot's emotional source of energy! The looting doesn't really
amount to a riot, Mitsu. It's a piddling little storm in a teacup, as
everyone taking part knows perfectly well. Even so, by taking part
they're going back a century in time and experiencing vicariously
the excitement of the 1860 rising. It's a riot of the *imagination*.

Though I don't suppose it ranks as a riot for you, does it? Not if you're unwilling to bring that kind of imagination into play."

"No, it doesn't."

"I see. . . ." said Takashi. Unexpectedly lapsing into a shut-in, somber mood, he fell silent and glowered, lips compressed, into the small square mirror propped up against the chair in front of him, as though he'd begun to be bored even by having his hair cut in the office now that it was under his control.

"I've found a can of kerosene, Mitsu," put in Hoshio, who had been waiting behind me for a break in our conversation. "Jin's son says he and his friends will carry it up to the house."

"Thanks, Hoshi," I said, turning round. "I'll pay for it, of course. I'm an outsider, so the market hasn't been profiteering at my expense. If there's no one to take the money, leave it on the shelf where the can of kerosene was."

Hoshio hesitated, embarrassed. He was about to take the bill I held out to him when his two friends, skipping round in front of him with startling alacrity, simultaneously thrust out hands blackened with mimeographing ink and gave his shoulders a violent shove. He fell backward, striking the crown of his head hard against the boarded wall. I stood there feeling foolish with my slender white arm still feebly holding out the money. Hoshio scrambled to his feet in a rage and, hissing like a snake through clenched teeth, glanced at Takashi for permission to counterattack. But his patron saint sat motionless, frowning at himself in the mirror as though he'd not even noticed the fearful clatter Hoshio had made in falling.

"That's against regulations, Hoshi," the girl by his side warned pertly in a high voice. To my astonishment, Hoshio suddenly went quite still and started weeping.

I walked out of the office seething with painful excitement. The Nembutsu music was still going on. It aggravated the pounding of my heart so much that I was forced to cover my ears as I walked. The young priest was waiting for me in front of the supermarket. Unwillingly, I lowered my hands from my ears.

"I went up to the house and one of Jin's children told me you'd come down here," he burst out. I realized immediately that the excitement animating him was more or less the reverse of the emotion nearly suffocating me. "I looked through the temple storehouse and found the documents the Nedokoro family left there for safekeeping!"

I took the large brown paper envelope he proffered. It was a shoddy envelope, reminiscent of the days of wartime austerity and tattered and begrimed with age. Mother must have put it in the temple's keeping just after the end of the war. However, it wasn't the contents of the envelope that were exciting the priest.

"This is most interesting, Mitsu! Most interesting," he repeated eagerly in a low voice. "Fascinating, I call it!"

His reaction was quite different from what I'd expected, and I gazed at him with deep suspicion. For a while I stayed silent and perplexed, pondering the meaning of his words.

"Let's talk as we go," he said. "All kinds of people are listening!" And he trotted off ahead of me with a briskness unbecoming in someone normally so diffident. I hurried after him, keeping one hand pressed on my overcoat in the region of my heart.

"Mitsu—" he went on, "if talk of this affair spreads, provincial supermarkets all over the country may well be attacked by the farmers. If that happens, the flaws in the economy will show up immediately. History's on the move! People often say that in another ten years the Japanese economy will come to a dead end, but it's difficult for laymen like us to see just where the collapse will begin, isn't it? But now, here are discontented farmers attacking a supermarket without warning. Supposing, next, that several hundred thousand supermarkets were raided in succession—it would undoubtedly throw a spotlight on the deterioration and vulnerability of the economy. It's all *most* interesting, Mitsu."

"But an attack on a supermarket in this valley isn't going to touch off a nationwide chain reaction," I objected. "In two or three days, all the fuss will subside and the valley folk will go back to the same drudgery as before." The unexpected excitement shown by this man who supposedly represented the decent intellectual side of the valley had depressed me to the point of real sadness. "I've no desire to interfere in the present business, but I *do* know that Takashi isn't the kind to pull off anything that could affect the course of history. I can only hope the affair won't leave him too wretchedly isolated. In practice, though, I feel that he hasn't left himself any way out this time. Now that he's made all the people in the valley share in the 'disgrace,' I don't see how he can look to them for sympathy, like a reformed student activist. I keep wondering what it is that drives him so far, but I never arrive at any definite conclusion. The one thing I feel sure of is that his inner self is hopelessly split in two. I wouldn't interfere with what he does, but I just don't understand what's made him like this. I've a feeling, at least, that the turning point came when our sister—she was retarded, you know—killed herself while she was living with him."

I fell silent, overcome by a boundless sorrow and fatigue as though I myself had been rioting all day. Although the young priest accepted what I said in silence, it was quite clear by now that just beneath the surface of his placid, impeccably decent face, there lay a protective layer of hypocritical defiance posing as good nature. After all, this same man had been tough enough to weather all the gossip in the valley after his wife ran away. His silence came from pity for my battered condition, not sympathy with my views. I realized that whereas I was concerned solely with the fate of my brother, he was preoccupied with the joint destiny of the young men of the valley. We walked together in silence, rubbing shoulders as though in deep understanding, past the men and women, old folk and children who still crowded the road and gave us friendly smiles as we went. When we reached the space in front of the village office, the priest said, by way of leave-taking:

"In the past, the young fellows were forever embarking on some foolish, shortsighted project, getting themselves into difficulties, then throwing in the towel. But this time at least they're trying to overcome some larger difficulty with their own resources. Or should I say, they've created of their own free will a situation that can't be cleared up by their own will, and have taken responsibility for it—which I find just as interesting. Really interesting! If your great-grandfather's younger brother were alive today, I'm sure he would have behaved like Taka!"

Head bowed, breathing in short gasps and worried about my heart, I climbed the graveled road, doubly dangerous now that the snow melted by the sun had begun to freeze again. Deep, reddish black forms crept up around me as I went: shadow, which had completely disappeared when snow had begun to fall, was returning to the valley. The wind had swept away the thinning clouds to reveal sunset skies. Shivering with the growing chill, I climbed between bushes weighed down with snow and anchored still more firmly to the ground by the reviving shadows. My skin, which had begun to sweat in the heat from the stove in the supermarket office, was rapidly capitulating to the cold. I could guess what kind of expression the reddish black shadows all about were engraving on the bristling skin of my face. I rubbed my cheeks with my hands, but try as I might I couldn't alter their rigid expression. I went on climbing sluggishly and mechanically like a train in the north that is forever late, overcome by such an enormous sense of fatigue that it seemed I would never reach home. Looking up, I saw the house, backed by the dark snowy slope, looking like a lump of tar surrounded by a red nimbus.

A small, dark knot of women clustered round the door of the main building. They had discarded the garish clothes with which the supermarket had filled the valley and, reverting as though by common accord to the old ways of the hollow, were dressed from head to foot in dull, indigo-striped working clothes which left no part of the skin directly exposed to the air except the face. As I entered the front garden, they turned in unison like a flock of ducks and surveyed me with faces that were expressionless and shadowed a darkish red. Then immediately they turned back to my wife, who was standing in the kitchen, and set up a clamor of complaint. They were housewives from the "country," and they were insisting that Takashi throw away the negatives of the photographs he'd taken on the first day of the looting. When they arrived home from the looting and talked about Takashi's pictures, their husbands and fathers-in-law had promptly demanded they should have the negatives destroyed. I imagined they were the first group of participants in the riot to have had second thoughts about their actions.

The setting sun flared up orange, then rapidly faded. "Taka decides everything," my wife was repeating patiently in a flat, weary-sounding voice. "I can't make Taka change his mind. I've no power to influence what he thinks. He always decides for himself."

Without warning the music of the Nembutsu dance, which like a spring had been welling up steadily from the bottom of the valley, ceased, and together with the brick-colored haze a sharp sense of absence pervaded the hollow within the pitch-black forest.

"Oh God, whatever shall we do?" wailed one young farmer's wife. The open despair in her voice made my wife falter for a moment, but it was not enough to make her change what she said.

"I go along with whatever Taka decides. Taka decides everything. He always decides for himself what he does."

The Power of the Flies

The following morning, the "rising" was still in progress, but the music of the Nembutsu dance was not to be heard, and the whole valley was wrapped in somber silence. When Momoko brought me my breakfast, I found that her experience of violence and the persistent hysterics that had followed it had left her, oddly enough, with a kind of maturity. She kept her face—pale now, and with an appropriately feminine placidity—turned downward, stubbornly refusing to meet my gaze, and spoke throughout in a small, hesitant, husky voice. That morning, Takashi's bodyguards had discovered that the manager of the supermarket had eluded the watchful eyes of the lookout at the end of the bridge and escaped from the valley. Hoping to contact the Emperor and the gang under his control, he had crossed the river, now dangerously swollen with thawing snow, and, heedless of his dripping clothes, had set off running down the snow-covered road that led to the sea. The same morning, the father whose boy had been saved from death on the broken bridge had privately brought Takashi a hunting gun and several kinds of cartridge.

"He lent it to Taka to fight back with when the Emper-or's gang comes to attack," Momoko said. "Though if you ask me, a gun makes it all the more dangerous." She spoke in the depressed, slightly fearful tone of someone who no longer takes the slightest pleasure in violence.

My own interpretation of the intended role of the gun was different from Momoko's, but I remained silent for fear of terrifying her still further. The gun, I felt sure, was not for Takashi to use, side by side with his bodyguards and the village folk, against the Emperor and his gang, but a weapon for that moment when he finally found himself utterly deserted by his fellows and obliged to defend himself alone in a hostile valley. (Admittedly, he'd made at least one ally in the valley, an ally self-sacrificing enough to lend him his precious gun.) Takashi himself, finding that none of the farmers had come down from the "country" to start looting again that morning, had put chains on the Citroen and set off to do some campaigning in the area beyond the great bamboo grove.

Having passed on these news items, Momoko suddenly asked me, with a younger sister's meekness that bore no resem-blance to the Momoko of old, whether I thought there were still any decent people left in the world. The unexpectedness of the question took me aback, and I was still hesitating when she went on.

"We'd been driving all night on the way here to Shikoku. When dawn came, we found we were going along by the sea somewhere and Takashi suddenly said to us, 'I wonder if there's really any good left in people?' But before we could answer he said yes, there was. He knew there was, he said, because people still went all the way to the plains of Africa to catch elephants, and took the trouble to send them home by sea to be kept in zoos. When he was a kid, he used to tell himself that if ever he got rich he'd keep his own private elephant. He'd have a cage built onto this house to keep it in, and would cut down all the tall trees below the stone wall, so that wherever children were playing in the valley they'd only have to glance up to see the elephant."

After all, it seemed, Momoko hadn't been hoping for an answer from me as a "member of the establishment." She'd merely used the question as a pretext for the elephant story. Ever since the unexpected brush with violence had made her shrink into herself, she'd been dwelling nostalgically on the gentleness that had existed in Takashi before he started directing his rough "rising." Momoko, I suspected, represented the first member of Takashi's personal bodyguard to drop by the wayside.

Alone again, I gave some thought to the elephant. In Hiroshima, they said, the very first group to flee to the suburbs after the nuclear attack had been a herd of cows. Supposing a vaster nuclear war destroyed the cities of the civilized countries—would the elephants in the zoos escape? Could people, perhaps, build nuclear shelters big enough to accommodate such bulky creatures? No—the holocaust would certainly leave all the elephants dead in their zoos. Supposing, then, there were some prospect of reconstructing the towns—would one's eyes be greeted by the spectacle of human beings, broken and mis-shapen by radiation, gathered on a cliff somewhere to watch as their representative set off to trap elephants on the savannas of Africa? To anyone occupied with the question of whether there was any good left in man or not, *that* would surely give a real clue. . . . I'd read no newspapers since the snows arrived, and for all I knew the world might be in still more desperate danger of nuclear war. But somehow the fear and sense of helplessness aroused in me by the idea refused to generate any more intensity than my usual solitary preoccupations.

The envelope the young priest had hunted out for me contained five letters from great-grandfather's younger brother and a pamphlet, signed with grandfather's name, entitled "An Account of the Farmers' Rising in Okubo Village." The rising recorded in the pamphlet was not that of 1860, but another provoked in the area by the edict of 1871 abolishing clans and establishing prefectures. None of the letters had addresses or signatures. Great-grandfather's brother must have wanted to keep the site of his new life secret, as well as the new surname he'd invented for use in it.

The earliest letter, though, which was dated 1863, suggested that after escaping through the forest to Kochi the former rebel leader had, as the priest surmised, been assisted in setting out for a new world by an agent from beyond the forest. It showed that less than two years following his flight, the young man had already achieved a meeting with his elusive hero, John Manjiro, and had actually obtained permission to participate in his next venture. For the man from beyond the forest to have had such a powerful influence over John Manjiro where his protégé was concerned must have meant that he was, in fact, a secret agent connected with the Tosa clan authorities. The letter told how the young man had set sail from Shinagawa in 1862 as a common seaman on John Manjiro's whaler. At the beginning of the following year, their boat arrived in Chichijima in the Bonins, then went on to the whaling grounds. There they caught two baby whales and sailed back to the Bonins, being short of fresh water. Here great-grandfather's brother gave up work on whalers, partly because of violent seasickness, but also from distress at his frequent disagreements with foreign seamen on the same vessel. Still, it was something at least that a young man brought up in a valley deep in the forest should have encountered two live whales, albeit baby ones. . . .

The second letter was dated 1867. A new sense of vigor and freedom in the style showed that several years of life in the city had awakened a youthful, humorous quality that during his period on the whaler had still been bottled up in the young deserter from the forest. The letter included an amusing article which he'd read in Yokohama in the first newspaper he'd seen in his life, and which he copied out specially for the benefit of his elder brother back home in the valley in the wilds of Shikoku:

> Today I have something that may amuse you. The newspaper in which I saw it forbids unauthorized reproduction, but I doubt that it applies to letters such as this. It seems that a man in Pennsylvania in the United States took his own life, possibly while out of his mind, as a result of unfortunate circumstances which his farewell note described as follows: "I married a widow with one daughter. My father fell in love with the daughter and married her. He thus became my son-in-law, and the daughter, being now my father's wife, became my stepmother. Next, I had a son by the widow I had married. He became my father's brother-in-law and also, being my stepmother's brother, my own uncle. My father's wife, my stepdaughter, also had a son, who was not only my stepbrother but also, being my stepchild's child, my grandson. Thus the widow I married,

as parent of my stepmother, became my grandmother. So
I found myself to be my wife's husband and grandson,
and at the same time my own grandfather and grandson."

The newspaper carries an advertisement saying:
"Wish to instruct young Japanese gentlemen desirous of
attaining proficiency in the English language." Another
says: "All aid and advice given to those visiting America
for purposes of study, commerce, travel, or tourism."

Between this letter and the next there was a gap of more
than two decades. During those twenty-odd years, the boy
whose excitement at finding himself liberated from everything
related to life in the distant valley had once made him find
that humorous article so fascinating, the boy who so obviously cherished a private ambition to go to America, may in
fact have got there. Either way, the betrayal that had enabled
him to survive the rising, leaving behind him in the valley so
many savagely executed dead, had also, it seemed, secured
him a new life of freedom.

This letter written in the spring of 1889, after so long
an interval, revealed the style of a man of ripe wisdom. It
was a soberly critical reply to a letter that great-grandfather
at home in the valley had written to express his joy over the
promulgation of the new Constitution. Wasn't it somewhat
hasty—the letter inquired rather depressingly—to become
infatuated with the word "Constitution" without even finding
out what its actual provisions were? It quoted the following
passage from a work by a member of a former samurai family
in Kochi prefecture—a possible associate, that is, of the agent
from beyond the forest:

One can naturally distinguish two varieties of civil rights. Those of England and France may be called "recovered" rights since the lower orders wrested them from those above them by their own efforts. But there is another variety that may be called "conferred," in that they are bestowed as a favor from above. Since "recovered" rights are won from below, their extent and nature may be determined at will by those receiving their benefit. "Conferred" rights, being bestowed from above, admit of no such decision; for their recipient to imagine that they may be instantly transformed into "recovered" rights is absurd.

The new Constitution, great-grandfather's brother predicted disapprovingly, would grant only a few rights conferred as a favor from above, and he urged that some organization be formed to work for more progressive civil rights. As this letter showed, he viewed the political regime following the Restoration with the eyes of a man with a "cause," in his case the cause of civil rights. It seemed likely, therefore, that the legend that he became a high official in the Restoration government was the exact reverse of the truth.

The last two letters, though written a mere five years later, suggested that his enthusiasm for the "cause" had already suffered a rapid decline. He was still the intellectual well versed in contemporary affairs that he'd been around 1889, but the desire to make assertions about the state of the nation had faded away. The overwhelming impression now was of an increasingly elderly, solitary man, anxious about the well-being of a close relative in distant parts. The Ikichiro mentioned in the letters is the name grandfather used in writing his "Account of the

Farmers' Rising in Okubo Village." Great-grandfather's younger
brother had a deep affection for his only nephew, though it is
doubtful whether they ever met in the flesh. He was very eager,
via his letters, to help his nephew evade the draft, and when
the boy unavoidably went to war he was equally concerned for
his safety. It showed perfectly clearly that the brutal leader of
the 1860 rising had also had, beneath the surface, a vein of
gentle solicitude:

> I thank you for your letter. I gather from it that you are
> thinking to request a draft deferment for Ikichiro whether
> he is accepted for the army or not. We had agreed that
> should he not be accepted there would of course be no
> need to present a deferment request. Possibly our letters
> crossed, but I had word from your wife that he had not
> been accepted, so instead of drafting the application as I
> should naturally have done, I determined to do nothing
> for the moment. Such being the case, there is no need
> for you to have anyone present the application. I hope to
> hear that you have understood and agreed.

*　　*　　*

> Your letter reassures me at least of your continued exis-
> tence, but leaves me thirsting for anything more detailed
> concerning the life you are leading in these days. Is there
> still no word of Ikichiro since his departure for China? The
> assault on Weihaiwei is still in progress, and I fear that at
> this very moment he stands in peril of his life. I am eager
> to know how he fares. I beg you, should a letter arrive, to
> let me know its purport with all haste.

This was the last of the letters. In all likelihood, great-grandfather's brother had died still peering in vain for his young warrior nephew amidst the smoke of distant battle. Nothing remained to suggest that he had survived after that.

Just before noon, the Nembutsu music started up again. Today it came from a fixed spot in front of the supermarket, without inspiring other music from the valley folk as it had yesterday, when it had sprung from several places in turn. Takashi and his team must be playing all alone. I wondered whether they would have the energy to go on indefinitely with such monotonous music if there was no sympathetic response from the ordinary inhabitants of the valley. I had a feeling that the next time the music came to an end might well mark the moment when reaction against the "rising" set in.

When Hoshio brought my lunch, he looked haggard and feverish, and his eyes followed my every movement with almost hungry intensity. It was as though abject shame at being dropped from the "rising" had swelled up inside his head until it came oozing out of his eyes. But why, I wondered, did he need to feel so ashamed toward Takashi? After deserting Hoshio when he was pushed over in the supermarket office for contravening "regulations," Takashi was hardly qualified to criticize him for falling by the way. Hoshio, after all, had taken part in the "rising" of his own free will, and had given it practical assistance as technician, even though he hadn't the slightest connection with the valley. The only possible bond tying him to the "rising" was Takashi's kindness. With such ideas in mind, I said to him out of naive sympathy:

"It looks as though Taka's 'rising' has quieted down a lot today, doesn't it?"

But Hoshio stared at me in silent rebuff, trying to indicate that, though he'd finally dropped out of the affair, he had no wish to join a bystander like me in criticism of Takashi and his football team.

"There aren't enough electrical appliances to go round," he said, confining himself to objective analysis of the situation. "When it comes to actually deciding who's going to take them, nobody has the courage to step forward."

"Anyway, Taka started it, so it's his job to carry it through," I ventured in what was supposed to be the same objective spirit. But the only effect was to heighten his irritation. The sense of shame that for some time had been wavering obscurely on his face suddenly reached explosive level, and an apoplectic rush of dark blood flooded his cheeks. When he finally raised his eyes and fixed their gaze on me, they had a steady gleam that looked as if everything they'd been concealing would spill out in a sudden burst. But he swallowed hard, like a child, and said:

"Will you put me up in the storehouse from tonight, Mitsu? I can sleep downstairs, I don't mind the cold."

"Why?" I asked, vaguely taken aback. "What's the problem?"

An almost obscene flush spread over the peasant-boy face. He pursed his heavily cracked lips, blew out strongly, then said, his whole face paling again as soon as he'd got it out:

"Taka does it with Natsumi, I don't like sleeping there."

I watched as the skin of his face, sunburned from the snow, went dry and seemed to break into a fine white powder. Until then I'd thought I was the observer, complacently attributing Hoshio's abnormal show of embarrassment to his losing his place in Takashi's "rising." In fact, it was he who had been observing my own disgrace. But witnessing the discomfiture of someone whose wife had slept with another man had affected him in turn with an unbearable sense of almost personal shame. The realization promptly volleyed the ball of shame back to me again. A surge of hot moisture seemed to suffuse the very sockets of my eyes.

"Then you'd better bring your blankets over here while it's still light, Hoshi. You can sleep upstairs with me. It's too cold downstairs." The hot defiance radiating from his eyes faded, leaving only a suspicious watchfulness. He looked at me and wondered, wavering between a naive suspicion that I hadn't understood what he'd said and cowardly apprehension in case I suddenly lashed out at him. Then, still keeping an eye on my movements, he mumbled stupidly in a voice dulled by disgust and helplessness:

"I kept telling Taka not to, that he mustn't and it was wrong, but he did it all the same." A tear so tiny it looked like a fleck of saliva ran down the whitish, finely cracked skin of his cheek.

"Hoshi," I commanded, "if this isn't just imagination or wishful thinking, you'd better tell me exactly what you saw. Either that or keep quiet!" I knew in fact that unless he described it in detail the thing would have no reality for me and I wouldn't be able to react properly. The blood had rushed to my head, where it pounded noisily, but my consciousness merely drifted about in it, unable to hitch itself either to jealousy or any other practical reaction.

Hoshi cleared his throat feebly in an effort to give more substance to his voice, then went on slowly, emphasizing the end of each phrase so as to impress on me what he was saying:

"I kept telling him not to. I said I'd hit him if he didn't lay off. I got a weapon and was going to rush into the room where they were sleeping, but when I opened the door, Taka—he had just his training shirt on, and I could see his bare ass—looked round at me and said, 'I thought you were the only member of the team that couldn't handle a weapon.' I just stood there, I couldn't hit him, I kept saying 'Don't, don't do it, you mustn't!' But Taka did it, he wouldn't take any notice of me!'"

Far from summoning up any concrete image of the sexual act between Takashi and Natsumi, Hoshio's words only succeeded in stirring the shallower, rawer layers of memory and reviving with a new reality the word "adulterer" which Takashi had used here in the storehouse and whose faint echoes had seemed to ring on indefinitely beyond the sturdy black beams. Of the two adulterers, I'd thought that my wife had completely uprooted everything sexual within herself, so that though a fleeting desire might brush her occasionally she would be unable to transplant it to sexual soil where it could grow naturally. Once, when she and I stood shoulder to shoulder trying to move a potted plant from a corner of the cramped conservatory, we found ourselves—though we'd had almost no sexual relations since the baby's conception, much less since the trauma of its birth—simultaneously overcome by desire, like a passing fever of the blood. Roughly she grasped my penis, which had risen stiff against the resisting stuff of my trousers, then frowned in distress and distaste and, walking with an odd shuffle, disappeared into the bedroom. Later, lying pale on the bed and sustained by aspirin, she'd made her excuses:

"The moment my hand touched you, I felt I'd gone back to carrying that great fetus again. I could feel my womb all big and tight, contracting and hurting with sexual excitement. I couldn't breathe for fear; I was scared I'd miscarry, lose something big. I don't suppose you can understand that, can you?"

But even as I listened to her I could feel, low in my belly, a lingering memory of the pain that a while earlier had taken a viselike grip on the buried roots of my erect penis that ran from behind the testicles toward the coccyx. . . .

"Did he rape her, then?" I pressed in horror. "Did you go in to stop him because she cried in pain?" My head was swimming with renewed anger. But Hoshio, who until now had been racked with dry sobs, unexpectedly relaxed his expression, considered my words, and with every sign of surprise hastened to deny them.

"Oh, no! He didn't rape her. When I first peeped through the sliding doors, I thought she was just too tired to stop him putting his hand on her breasts and between her legs, but by the time I opened the doors she was waiting for him to begin. I could see one of her bare soles sticking up straight and obedient-like on each side of his ass! So this time I said to her, 'I'll tell Mitsu if you don't stop!' But she just said, 'I don't mind, Hoshi,' and didn't turn a hair. Even when Taka actually started, the soles of her feet kept quite still; it didn't look to me as if she was in pain."

The adulterers were gradually becoming more real. In fact the reality was awakening a disgraceful, perverted lust in me.

"I started to shut the door because I couldn't stand watching Taka do it, but without stopping he twisted his head round to look at me and said, 'Tomorrow, go and tell Mitsu everything you saw.' His voice was so loud I was really scared in case it woke Momoko. She'd taken sleeping pills because her hysteria kept her awake, and she'd only just got to sleep."

Hoshio had awoken in the middle of the night and realized that Takashi, who had been sleeping beside him, had slipped out of his blankets. Then he heard his voice next to Natsumi, who was sleeping with Momoko beyond the sliding doors. "I felt I was being torn apart," Takashi was saying. "It was the same during my travels in America, of course. . . ." But what came next, Hoshio's still drowsy ears had been unable to follow completely. At first he heard only isolated words whose meaning would become clear sporadically without his understanding the drift of what was being said. Then gradually he became more receptive, until he could catch everything without gaps. The strange sense of urgency that replaced the sleep in his head had compelled him to do so.

". . . arrival . . . kept under supervision . . . not out of desire, just the reverse if anything . . . ghetto . . . cabdriver tried to warn me against it . . . but I felt I was being wrenched in half. Unless I gave both the forces tearing me apart some substance and assessed them . . . realize now I've been torn all along between the desire to justify myself as a creature of violence and the urge to punish myself for it. Seeing that's how I'm made, can you blame me for hoping to go on living just as I am? At the same time, though, the stronger the hope got, the more urgently I felt the need to wipe out that terrible side of myself, and the more serious the split became. The reason why I deliberately chose to get mixed up in violence during the campaign against revision of the Security Treaty—and the reason why, when I found myself associated with the violence of the weak forced into opposition against unjust violence, I chose to ally myself with unjust violence, whatever its purpose—was that I wanted to go on accepting myself as I am, to justify myself as a man of violence without having to change. . . ."

"Why do you say 'myself as I am,' Taka?" my wife put in sadly. "Why do you say 'myself as a man of violence'?"

"She wasn't drunk?" I asked, interrupting Hoshio's account. But he promptly squashed the faint hope sustaining my pitifully urgent voice.

"She never drinks nowadays," he said.

"It's tied up with the kind of experience I can never talk about so long as I intend to go on living," Takashi went on after a silence during which the eavesdropper waited with bated breath. "But you don't have to hear about it provided you believe that I really am torn between two things."

"I suppose so. . . . As long as I know you're strongly divided, there's no need to know just how it happened."

"Right. Anyway, the one certain thing is that I've had a split personality all along. Whenever life's calm for a while, I get an urge to stir myself up deliberately just to confirm the split. And it's like drug addiction—the stimulus has to be progressively stronger. Every year the stirring-up has had to be that little bit more violent."

"If you went to the black ghetto on the night you arrived in America just to 'stir yourself up,' what exactly were you expecting?" Natsumi asked.

"I didn't have any clear idea of what would happen. I just had this intense feeling that if I went there I'd probably be given a thorough shaking-up. In the end I spent that 'special' night in bed with a decrepit old black woman as fat as Jin. But don't get the idea it was sex as such that drove me to the ghetto in the first place. Even if it was a kind of desire, it was far deeper than sex. The cabdriver tried to stop me getting off there. He said it was dangerous at night, and actually offered to take me to a safe place if I wanted to sleep with a black prostitute. I refused. We had an argument, with the result that I got out in front of a saloon. Inside, the place had a fantastically long bar stretching away into the darkness, and a row of drunks sitting in solemn silence facing it—all blacks, of course. I sat down on a stool too high for a Japanese, and found there was a mirror behind the bar and that all the fifty-odd blacks reflected in it were staring at me malevolently. I had a sudden, strong desire for a double vodka—and realized for the first time that my mind was aching for self-punishment. You see, whenever I drink any hard liquor I get high and want to beat the hell out of everybody. But if some Oriental weirdo like me went into a bar in the ghetto specially to pick a fight, he'd almost certainly end up getting himself beaten to death. So when this giant of a bartender came over, I asked for a ginger ale. Along with the urge for punishment, I was scared blind. I'm always scared of death, and that kind of violent death in particular. It's a trait I've had to fight ever since the day S was beaten and killed. . . ."

"That was the first time—when he said he was afraid—that I had my doubts about Taka," said Hoshio in a voice charged with a black resentment inappropriate to his years. "So I peeped through the sliding doors. I could see because they kept the small light on for Momoko; she's still scared of going to sleep in the dark. All the time he was talking, Taka kept putting his hand on her breasts and between her legs. That was when I thought Natsumi was just letting him do it because she was too tired to push his hand away. . . ."

"I sipped my ginger ale till it was all gone," Takashi continued, "then went out and started walking down the dark street. There were only a few streetlights on here and there. It was late at night, and lots of blacks were sitting out in the cool, on fire escapes and on the stoops of big, dark, old-fashioned buildings. I could hear them talking about me as I went past, and occasionally I'd catch a few words like 'goddamn Chink . . .' I automatically walked faster, imagining the sweaty great blacks coming after me, cracking my skull open, and leaving me to die where I fell on the filthy sidewalk. But even as I oozed with fright I was turning off into some still darker and more dangerous backstreet. You should've seen how I sweated—even the black woman I slept with later said it was unusual for a Japanese to smell so much, though she herself stank to high heaven. I even barged into the courtyards of apartment blocks, my forehead burning this time with the idea that I'd be shot! And all through this forced march of mine the one thing that obsessed my brain was a ridiculous cautionary tale that the woman Diet member who headed our troupe had told us on the ship across the Pacific, hoping to ensure our good behavior in America. I expect it was in the papers at home—a Tokyo bank clerk who'd been sent to America fell to his death from the twelfth floor of a New York hotel after only one month there. An old American lady of eighty sleeping in the next room woke up in the middle of the night and found a naked Japanese on all fours on the narrow parapet outside the window, scrabbling at the windowpane with his nails. Nobody knows why he was naked and scratching at the glass—he wasn't even drunk, the Diet woman said. But I felt sure it was the act of a man using an excessive fear of death to punish himself with. And as I hurried through the dark of the ghetto late at night, I was just like that man crawling naked toward the old lady's room along that narrow ledge twelve floors up—only in my case, you see, there wasn't any stranger to wake up and give the scream that would send me to my death. After a while, I happened to come out on a wider, rather better lit street, with a cab heading in my direction. I waved at it frantically like a castaway sighting a ship. . . .

"Once one strand gives way, the whole thing collapses, you can't stop it: thirty minutes later, I was safely inside the prostitute's room, telling her my most shameful secrets in English and asking her to pretend she was giving me the punishment I deserved. I was quite shameless, begged her to act like she was a great black man raping a young Oriental girl. 'Anything, so long as you gimme the money,' she said. . . ."

"Hoshi," I put in, checking his complaint in full flood, "you're wrong if you feel guilty for not being able to stop Taka. By the time you called out 'Don't, don't, you mustn't!' it was already too late, and when you saw them having sex, it was the second time, after they'd had a rest. I'm sure they'd already finished once while you were still asleep. Otherwise Taka wouldn't have confessed to her the kind of things you've just told me. It simply wouldn't do as a prelude to seduction."

"Aren't you angry, Mitsu?" queried Hoshio, as though his own moral sensibilities found my attitude inexcusable.

"It's too late for that, too," I said. "What earthly good would it do now if *I* started saying 'Stop, stop! Don't do it, you mustn't!'?"

Hoshio stared at me with a loathing so concentrated it was like virulent poison seeping from his eyes. Then suddenly he abandoned all attempt at concern for or interest in the cuckold and, withdrawing into the solitary confines of his own mind, hugged his knees to him, hung his grubby head, and complained in a pitiful copy of the distressed wails of the farmers' wives the evening before:

"Oh hell, what a mess! What am I going to do? I've spent my savings on the Citroen and I can't go back to my job at the repair shop. What the hell am I going to do? What a goddamn mess!"

I heard, coming up toward the house, a medley of sounds: Nembutsu music, the uneasy barking of dogs poised for flight, laughter and cries from people of all ages. All the while Hoshio had been talking, I'd been aware of them as a kind of auditory hallucination, but by now they were quite obviously real and advancing on the house. The music and human clamor had just the opposite atmosphere from the subdued "rising" of that morning. As a change from commiserating with my young companion who felt himself abandoned by everything sound and healthy in the world, I got up and peered down from the window at the yard below.

Before long, two "spirits" appeared, heading a company of musicians, dogs, and spectators more numerous than at any Nembutsu dance I'd seen in my childhood. They poured into the yard, filling it completely. In the small, round clearing they left in the center, the "spirits" began a slow, circular movement. The musicians—members of the team—were playing their instruments with steady concentration, their shoulders hunched against the press of spectators behind them. Barking wildly, two ginger dogs rushed round and round inside the circle after the "spirits," leaping back each time they were struck across the head. The "spirits" themselves seemed to consider it part of the Nembutsu performance to lash the dogs to new heights of frenzy. Each time a dog was struck, a shout of cruel delight rose from the spectators.

The "spirits'" costumes were of a kind I couldn't recall seeing in any of the varied dances of the old days. The man wore a homburg with a black morning coat and a black vest to match, but with a wide expanse of naked chest showing beneath. It was grandfather's evening dress: I'd seen it before, tucked away in the storeroom along with a starched dickey. I wondered why they'd omitted the shirt from the "spirit's" formal getup. Didn't it fit the performer? Or was the fabric rotten? Or had it been rejected in accordance with the habits of the player wearing the suit, who was the grotesque young man who had so prided himself on being lightly clad? The hat had numerous slits cut in it to make it fit the crown of his head, which was fat and round like a helmet. Through the slit at the very back, which had opened into an equilateral triangle, one caught an unexpected glimpse of white neck, topped with shaggy black hair. He walked with body bent forward in an aristocratic stoop, making repeated, dignified little bows to the spectators about him as he went. He was driving the dogs frantic by suddenly flashing at them a filthy fragment of dried fish which he kept in the pocket of his morning coat. The dogs rushed about madly, tearing with sharp claws at the dark, downtrodden snow and barking furiously.

The role of the second "spirit" who walked in his wake was played by the fleshy little girl I'd seen the day before in the supermarket office, now dressed in a pure white Korean costume. The two tapes fluttering from the high, tight waist of the blouse, and the long skirt that billowed gently in the slight breeze, awakened other memories of white silk. They still looked brand-new: I wondered from what hiding place they'd unearthed them for use as a costume in the Nembutsu dance. Quite probably, the young men of the valley who raided the Korean settlement on the day S was killed not only plundered moonshine and candy but also took some Korean girl's best clothes and kept them hidden for more than twenty years. I suspected that on the first raid they'd committed not only murder but some other dreadful act that S's death alone could never atone for, and that it was knowledge of this that had driven S, even after he'd resolved to serve as sacrificial lamb on the second raid, to lie brooding in a state of despairing melancholy on the floor in the back room downstairs in the storehouse. So far as the murdered Korean was concerned, the presentation of S's corpse by the valley folk had wiped the slate clean, so it seemed likely that some other crime must have lain behind the village's sale to the Koreans of the land on which their settlement stood. Flushed pink and pretty from an almost indecently obvious excitement, the girl walked gracefully in the wake of the young man in homburg and morning coat, her small face smiling the thrilled, rapturous smile of the star of the moment, her eyes half closed in ecstasy, her body swathed in the white clothes that her elder brothers, in the summer of 1945, must have torn off the girl from the Korean settlement after they'd had their way.

The spectators too had an air of contented excitement. Shouts of joy—some innocent, some cruel—burst from their smiling faces. Among them I saw the women from the "country" who at dusk the day before had come, clothed once more in the working garb of the hollow, their whole beings exuding dark despair, to make their appeal. They were still in the same drab, indigo-striped peasant dress, but were now outdoing all the rest with their peals of cheerful laughter. The "spirits" of the Emperor and his wife in Korean dress had rekindled a new excitement in all these people from the valley and the "country" beyond.

I looked for Takashi among the throng, but the heaving of the crowd in response to the movements of the "spirits"

and dogs within the circle was so vigorous that to focus on
them was physically trying. Turning my exhausted eye away, I
caught sight of my wife standing on the threshold of the main
house and stretching up to peer over the heads of the crowd
into the circular clearing. With her right hand she supported
herself against the doorpost, and with her left she was shading her eyes against the sun as she watched the dance. Her
hand cast a shadow over her forehead, eyes, and nose so that
I couldn't judge the expression on her face. It was quite apparent, even so, that she was intensely feminine and relaxed, like
the heavily pleated white silk skirt worn by the "spirit" of the
Korean girl—a far cry from the exhausted, frustrated, unhappy
woman I'd vaguely and quite groundlessly expected. I realized
that thanks to Takashi she'd recovered from the sense of the
impossibility of sex that had eaten at the heart of our married life like a cancer. For the first time since our marriage, I
managed to see her as a truly independent being. The hand
shading her eyes moved a fraction, threatening to expose to
the sunlight the upper half of her tranquil, newly softened
features. I drew back from the window in a reflex movement,
as though scared that the direct sight of them might turn me
to stone. Hoshio, who by now was more interested in the
clamor outside the storehouse than his own anguish at being
deserted, came up swiftly behind me and pressed his nose
to the window in my place. I went and sprawled face up by
the table, gazing at the black zelkova beams. Now that my
companion, his back turned to me, was completely absorbed
in the new dance, I found myself for the first time since the
news of my wife's adultery completely free from the gaze of
others. I lay there breathing peacefully, sending the blood out

from my heart seventy times each minute and drawing it back again, dimly aware of the 98° F of warmth within my body. At the very center of my head I seemed to feel the blood, heated rather above body temperature, rushing round and round murmuring in a tiny whirlpool. Then two unrelated images appeared, and sending the eye of consciousness down where the darkness in my head was faintly illuminated by their light, I closed my other, seeing eye. One image was a scene that took place at dawn on the day father left for China on the last journey of his life. Mother was standing on the threshold of the house as she directed the workmen who were to carry his luggage to the town on the coast. When father discovered where she was standing, he knocked her down in a fit of rage, then set off, leaving her senseless and covered with blood from her nose, while grandmother explained to us children that whenever a woman stood on the threshold some disaster invariably befell the head of the family. Mother always refused to accept this piece of folklore. Quite simply, she hated father for leaving on such a violent note, and despised grandmother for trying to defend her son's action. Even so, when father died as an outcome of that journey, I couldn't help feeling a mysterious sense of awe toward mother. I wondered if in fact she believed in the taboo even more firmly than grandmother and had deliberately stood on the threshold. I wondered, too, whether awareness of her intention had made father behave so brutally and stopped grandmother and the workmen from making any move to restrain him.

The other image was a vague, futile groping for the shape and color of my wife's naked body. I tried to picture something beautiful and erotic, but the only clear visions I achieved—both calculated to inspire a deeply instinctive distaste—were of the soles of her feet, given reality thanks to the testimony of the witness to her adultery, and of her anus, where a split caused by a passing fancy on our part to try some deviant sex had left a ridge of flesh. Jealousy, moreover, was gradually becoming a positive fact, sticking hot and rough in my bronchial tubes as though I'd inhaled poison gas. The same irritating vapor attacked the eye of my consciousness, so that the details of her naked body were lost in a reddish obscurity. I had a sudden, startling feeling that I'd never really possessed her. . . .

"Mitsu!" called a hearty voice full of animal good spirits and confidence from downstairs. It was Takashi.

I opened my eyes to see Hoshio's back stir and draw into itself where he stood glued to the window. By now the Nembutsu music, the barking of the dogs, and the cheerful clamor of people were on their way down to the valley.

"Mitsu!" called Takashi in a voice still more heartily extrovert than before. Ignoring Hoshio, who made a reflex movement to stop me, I went halfway down the stairs and sat down. Standing in the entrance with the outside light behind him, Takashi was fringed with a halo like rainbow-hued wool. Not only his face and body, which were turned toward me, but his outspread arms as well were completely shadowed. If I was to deal with him on equal terms, I would have to keep my own face strategically buried in the darkness too.

"Mitsu, did Hoshi tell you what I did?" the black figure asked me, glittering all around with tiny bubbles of light like sunshine refracted on a rippling sea. It made the silhouette look like a salamander rising from water.

"Yes, he told me," I said calmly. I wanted to show how unemotional I was compared with him, this younger brother of mine now preparing to flaunt his adultery before the cuckold with much the same eagerness as the child who once begged me to watch while he let a silly little centipede attack his own finger.

"I didn't do it just for the sex. It was a way of getting at the meaning of something very important to me."

I shook my head in silence to indicate my doubts about what he'd said. Takashi, just like the dogs barking at the "spirits," was wavering between excitement and tense apprehension, and this dart of ill will struck straight home.

"It's true, it wasn't for the sex!" he protested indignantly. "Actually, I didn't feel any desire at all. I had to do all kinds of things by myself to get properly worked up."

For a moment I felt my face flush hot with a mixture of rage and a desire to laugh. It freed me from all feelings of jealousy. So he'd had to do all kinds of things "by himself," had he? The anger made me tremble, and at the same time I had to clench my teeth to keep back the laughter. How hard he must have worked at it, all "by himself"! Why, the vulgar kid—little did he realize that, if anybody, it was my wife who as a sexually mature human being (if she had in fact shaken off that sense of sexual impossibility) had achieved something "by herself." How desperately he must have worked on his first act of adultery, scared in case failure to ejaculate in the proper way should afflict him with a stifling sense of shame not only toward his fellow in adultery but toward me as well! The whole thing had the effect of some dreary memory from adolescence.

"Mitsu, I'm going to marry Natsumi. I hope you won't interfere with us," he said, shaking the black silhouette of his head exasperatedly.

"Are you going to try all kinds of things 'by yourself' even after you're married?" I asked mockingly. "Without even wanting it?"

"That's up to me!" he shouted, covering his humiliation in a show of anger.

"Right. It's up to you and Natsumi. But that assumes you can somehow survive the collapse of your 'rising' and get out of the valley safely, taking her with you."

"Look, the rising is thoroughly back in its stride. You saw how wild both the valley and 'country' folk were about the 'spirits,' didn't you? We've given the rising a transfusion. We've restored its strength with a stiff shot of the blood of imagination!" His voice had recovered the excitement it had had when he first called upstairs to me. "They were afraid our violence mightn't carry the same authority as the Emperor's gang. But having a good laugh at the two 'spirits' has given them the emotional strength to despise him! They've got the guts again to see that the man they call the 'Emperor of the Supermarkets' is only an ex-lumberjack, a Korean who happened to amass a certain amount of wealth. So they promptly showed their bullying contempt and twisted self-interest by stripping the store of its electrical appliances and everything else in sight. Once they decide the enemy's a helpless weakling, they feel they can trample all over him. And the crucial fact here is that the Emperor's a Korean. They've always been thoroughly aware how wretched their lives were. And they've always kept low, feeling they were the most insignificant species in the forest. But now they remember the delicious superiority they felt toward the Koreans before and during the war. They're intoxicated at rediscovering the existence of outcasts even worse off than themselves, and they've begun to see themselves as almighty. They're like a lot of flies—I only need to organize them and I'll be able to carry on resisting the Emperor indefinitely. They may be small and nasty like flies, but that's just what gives a lot of them together a special power of their own."

"But do you imagine your 'flies' are never going to realize how much you despise the people here? Wait and see—you'll find the power of the flies directed against yourself one day! In fact, maybe your 'rising' won't be complete until that happens."

"That's just the false perspective of a pessimist looking down on the valley from his house on high," declared Takashi, who had acquired a certain ease of manner by now. "The rising of the past three days, you see, has revolutionized the outlook of the fly elite, who are a cut above the rank-and-file flies. By 'elite,' I mean the owners of forest land. They always used to believe that even if life in the valley came to a dead end and all the inhabitants of the hollow moved out or died off, they at least would only need to wait till the trees had grown big enough to make lumbering possible again. But this rising has given them practical proof that flies driven by despair are something to be feared. It's been a practical lesson in the history of the 1860 affair. Moreover, the moment they realized as a concrete fact— admittedly, the concreteness was a fraud, but anyhow—when they realized that the 'spirit' of the Emperor was only a pathetic Korean, they all became patriots overnight. Psychologically, it was just the same kind of patriotism, in a rigid, strictly local sense, as shown by their lousy ancestors who took seats in the prefectural assembly—once cutting down part of the forest had given them the funds—even though they had no practical politi- cal program to offer. They're getting ideas of wresting economic

control of the valley back into the hands of the Japanese. And
fortunately for them, the enemy is that stupid old Emperor who
walks in procession in an old-fashioned morning coat without
even a shirt, much less a tie and gloves. . . . So the idea, which
has turned into a definite plan, is to have several of them put up
the funds to take over the supermarket, including its losses from
the looting, and to have it run jointly by the valley storekeepers
who've gone out of business. The young priest has been rushing
all over the place preparing the ground. You know, Mitsu, that
priest is more than a mere philosopher—he's got the enthusiasm
of a revolutionary who's keen to put his cherished fantasies into
practice. What's more, he's the only person in the hollow who
hasn't the slightest trace of egotism. He's our surest ally!"

"I agree that he's quite selfless in taking the side of the
ordinary people of the valley," I said, "because, Taka, that's been
the priest's job at the temple for generations past. But don't
assume he's on the side of people like you, who thoroughly
despise the valley folk."

"I don't care. I'm leading a rising, a successful one too. I'm
an 'effective evildoer,' like our eldest brother on the battlefield."
He laughed. "I don't need real allies. All I need is the appearance of cooperation."

"You know best, Taka, so you'd better get back to your
battlefield," I said, getting up. "I can't share your sense of humor
about it, I'm afraid."

"How's Hoshi now?" he asked. "Try to be nice to him. After
he watched us making love I saw him quietly being sick. He's
only a kid!" And he hurried off.

At that moment I was suddenly seized with the notion,
which soon became a conviction, that Takashi's project might

succeed. Even if the "rising" as such failed, I felt sure he would soar above the decadence and muddle, and escape to start a new, ordinary, and eminently uneventful married life with a Natsumi similarly freed from the toils of her own personal crisis. The placid life, moreover, would be the life of someone who had once been a creature of violence, backed up by the proud memory of having lived through a major upheaval. By then, his completely uneventful routine would have closed once and for all the rift between the desire for self-punishment created by some nameless thing inside him and his awareness of his own love of violence. The letter from great-grandfather's brother that I'd read that same day served to heighten my conviction. Even though he'd led a rising that ended in disaster and despair, hadn't he got away and lived on to enjoy a peaceful old age?

I went back upstairs and found the young man—abandoned, not to say ridiculed, by his guardian deity—still glued to the window. Without turning round, he complained:

"The snow in the garden's all wet and sticky from those people trampling over it. I hate it—it messes up the car and you can't do a thing about it."

Late that night, as Hoshio and I lay side by side in our blankets, each hugging his chilled body to himself, passing the time in a wakeful effort to stave off the cold of the thaw that had set in in earnest, my wife suddenly came silently up the stairs; and in an exhausted and unpleasantly hoarse voice, without even wondering apparently whether we mightn't be fast asleep in the darkness, she said:

"Come over to the main house. Taka's tried to rape a girl from the valley and killed her. The team's deserted him and gone home, and in the morning the men of the valley will come and get him."

Both Hoshi and I sat up in the darkness. For a while we stayed rigid and silent, listening to my wife's breath rasping as she began feebly to sob.

"We'd better go," I forced myself to say. But my body, suddenly heavy like a skin full of water, was being drawn irresistibly down by a honeyed drowsiness just the reverse of the insomnia of a moment before. If only I closed my eyes, let myself fall backward, and curled up like a fetus, I could deny the whole of reality; and if reality ceased to exist, then my criminal brother and the crime itself would vanish too. But in the end I shook my head in resignation and repeating, "We'd better go, we'd better go," hauled myself slowly to my feet.

A Way beyond Despair

In silence my wife, the young man, and I plowed our way across the front garden, our heels crunching unsteadily into the half-frozen slush. I peered down at the dark, silent void of the valley, now a bottomless pit from whose depths rose a cold, dank wind. The door of the main house stood open. We halted in a hesitant group as though held back by the faint light that seeped from inside, then finally stepped across the threshold together. Sitting with head bent beside the open fireplace, Takashi was holding the shotgun, which was broken open, polishing it skillfully with one hand as though he'd been doing the same thing for years. The small man who stood quite still in the dark kitchen facing him stirred at the sound of our entrance, but he had difficulty even in turning his head to look at us, being so rigid with tension that he threatened to topple over at any moment. It was Gii the hermit.

Takashi stopped work with an air of reluctance and looked up at us. His dark-skinned face was oddly twisted, and at the same time somehow shrunken. His hair and his face from his left ear down to the corner of his mouth were soiled with something black and sticky. Moving as in a dream, he slowly spread out his two hands toward me. The little finger and ring finger of his left hand were hidden beneath a broad cloth bandage, but the rest of both hands was entirely covered with dark blotches. He hadn't bothered to wipe his hands before polishing the gun. The stuff there and on his head was blood. He fluttered his outstretched fingers, watching with eyes like a mournful monkey's as I shrank back, then gave a feeble giggle that went on and on as though he were blowing bubbles from between his compressed lips. The beastliness of it made me recoil again. Suddenly my wife, who had stepped up alone to stand by the fireplace, struck with her fist at the frozen grin on Takashi's mouth. Then she sank to her knees, and one round breast slipped out through the front of her night kimono like an undamaged part protruding from a broken machine. Repeatedly, she rubbed her fist on the front of her nightdress; and only when the blood was gone did she cover the breast.

Takashi's smile vanished instantly. He gazed inquiringly at me, but didn't even glance at the woman who had hit him. His upper lip was stained with fresh blood, this time from his own nose. He pursed his lips and noisily drew in a great breath, sucking the blood from his nostrils in with it. I was sure he had swallowed his own blood. His face turned darker and darker till his head looked like some somber-plumaged bird. The fact that he'd slept with my wife was brought home to me with a new and convincing reality. She shifted her gaze from Takashi to the hermit, who retreated clumsily into the shadows by the stove, afraid she might hit him next.

"I tried to rape that sexy little piece you met yesterday, Mitsu, and the little bitch actually put up a fight. Kicked me in the guts and tried to scratch my eyes out. I went crazy. I held her down on the Whale Rock with my knees and pinned her arms with one hand, then grabbed a stone with my free hand and smashed her head with it. She hollered 'No! No!' at the top of her voice and twisted her head from side to side to show she meant it, but I hit her again and didn't stop till I'd battered her skull in." The feeble, blurred voice seemed to come from somewhere far away. The blood-smeared hands were held out still as if to make sure I'd seen them properly. But somewhere down in the voice was a note of defiant exhibitionism, as though he wanted to strip off and flaunt his shame before the world. The way he spoke lacked all intonation and direction; his voice might have rambled on forever. I found it acutely disgusting.

"While I was beating her to death," he continued, "Gii the hermit was hiding behind the Whale Rock. He saw everything, so he's a witness. Gii can see in the dark!"

He called trustingly toward the dark shadows by the stove where the witness to his crime lurked—"Gii, Gii," as though summoning some weak but cherished protégé to his side—but the hermit, far from coming forward, neither stirred nor replied.

"Why did you try to rape her—were you drunk?" I asked solely to check this unnerving flood of talk. I hadn't the slightest interest in the origins of his urge to rape the girl, the girl with the pink face whom Korean dress had suited so well.

"I wasn't drunk. I practice what I preach about facing reality sober. I always have, Mitsu. I was sober—but I couldn't help myself. I *had* to rape her!" A faint, ravaged smile stirred beneath the tense skin of his face.

"But didn't you say you felt no desire in bed with Natsumi?" I asked, lobbing a mortar shell of malice at him and my wife, who was still sitting on her heels beside him, staring at him again in stupefaction. With deepening disgust, I observed the almost shameful consternation this aroused in Takashi; but my wife's eyes remained fixed on him, the white mask of her features still showing no expression other than stunned amazement. The face smeared with dead blood was dark and swollen now with the live blood flooding up beneath the skin, and it was he who was longing to cry "No! No!" in panic-stricken discomfort and shame. His reaction at being given away in front of my wife showed an oversensitivity and immaturity incongruous in a "man of violence." I wondered if his purpose in sitting there without even washing off the blood of his victim was not just to flaunt the bloodstains before me, but also to ensure his continuity as a criminal. He struggled by sheer force to replace the dismay written all over his face with a more brutal excitement. He gave me a cunning look, then said coyly, as though unsated desire was still smoldering in his guts:

"She was a nice piece of ass. Young, too—the kind of kid to get you worked up!"

Humiliated, my wife shuffled on her knees into the background. She was no longer watching Takashi or anyone else, and I seemed to detect a gleam of anger in the forlorn despair of her downcast, shadowy eyes. She'd ceased to be Takashi's mistress: that much was certain. But it didn't mean that she had come back to me. In tales of adultery, this was always the fate of the husband who took it out on his wife's lover. Not, in fact, that I had really punished him: I'd simply and contemptuously confirmed that he was still the child who had figured in the centipede episode. The feeling of contempt restored my free powers of observation. For the first time since I heard the news of this deadly trap into which Takashi had so abruptly fallen, I was released from my straitjacket of bewilderment and frustration. I stepped up to occupy the space vacated by my wife, motioning Hoshio to follow. With a swiftness that belied his sluggish air Takashi pulled the gun closer to him and put a space between us so that we faced each other at a suitable distance for debate.

"Taka," I said, beginning my critique of his account, "you say you tried to rape the girl and battered her to death with a stone because she resisted. But that's a lie, isn't it?"

"Ask Gii—get him to tell you what he saw!" he retorted in a voice suddenly stiff with distrust.

"He's just a nut, he'd churn out anything you put into his head. I don't believe you committed murder, Taka."

"How can you be so sure, Mitsu? Look at the blood I've got on me. Go to her home, where the football team took her body, and see for yourself! Her head's smashed to a pulp. How can you stand there sneering at me, so sure of all these wild theories you're cooking up?"

"I've no doubt she's dead. Her head may be smashed in too, poor kid. But I doubt whether you did it as a deliberate crime. You couldn't do it. Even as a boy, when you let the centipede bite your finger, you carefully chose the kind that doesn't sting. You're a cowardly bastard, aren't you? I bet she died in an accident!"

"Tomorrow morning," he said, "when the flies come in a raging swarm from the valley to get me, Gii will tell them what happened. Why not listen then, rather than dream it all up for yourself? He'll tell you, all right. He'll tell how I hit her with the rock—that dumb, sexy little bitch who thought she could lead me on—while she fought back like a crazy cat. It'll show you how dangerous it is to fool around with the leader of a full-blown rebellion."

"Who's going to believe the testimony of a madman?" I said, feeling the first pang of pity for this aspiring murderer so stubbornly clinging to his infantile fictions. "Particularly the valley folk, who've known how crazy he is for dozens of years now."

At the mention of his name, Gii had poked his upper half up from behind the stove and turned a stunted ear, like a clump of speckled brown and gray hair, to catch our conversation. We might have been judges sitting to determine his fate, deliberating whether or not his demented hermit's existence constituted a crime. But though he listened in attentive silence, he gave no more sign of understanding than if our conversation had been in some foreign tongue. As though deep in thought, he heaved an audible sigh.

"Take it easy, Gii!" Takashi called encouragingly to the old man. "There's nothing for you to do until tomorrow. Till then, why don't you go and sleep in the storeroom out of people's way?"

Gii promptly scuttled off into the dark, making no more sound as he went than some nocturnal animal. I imagined Takashi didn't want him to hear my criticisms of his own confession. My theory that the girl had died in an accident and that Takashi was using her body for his own devices became a conviction. Doubt still remained, though, as to just why he should use a madman's testimony in order to proclaim himself a murderer: was he thinking of taking on the whole valley? If I wanted to, I could testify that what Takashi claimed as murder was, if not entirely unconnected with him, at least an accident. But it would be for Takashi himself to decide whether to accept my aid and abandon his plan to team up with the hermit.

"Why exactly did you take her all the way to the Whale Rock?" I queried, rather like a defense counsel going against his client's wishes. The Whale Rock was a huge boulder that rose out of the ground at the point where the graveled road through the valley dipped sharply down toward the bridge. It made a bottleneck in the road and shut off the view of the bridge. The fifty yards' descent from there to the bridge was not only steep but winding. It was the most frequent site of automobile accidents in the valley, but hardly the place for a lovers' tryst late on a winter night.

"I wanted to rape her on the seat of the Citroen, and I was looking for the best place to stop," Takashi replied with the same air of stubborn caution. "If you park the car beside the rock, nobody—apart from Gii, that is—is going to come all the way from the valley to spy on you. Besides, the rock screens you from the team member who's on guard all night at the end of the bridge."

"Since you say you held her down against the rock and hit her with a stone, I assume she resisted and escaped from the car, and that you caught her again?"

"That's right."

"If she really resisted in the cart I don't imagine she struggled in silence, did she? And I don't suppose she ran in silence after she got out, either. She was an active member of the 'rising' and presumably knew that one of her friends was on guard by the bridge, so surely she would have shouted for help? You

say, too, that after you'd caught her, while you were knocking
her skull in, she kept shrieking 'Don't, don't!' Why, then, didn't
the guard standing only fifty yards below come and stop you
killing her?"

"After I finished her off, I discovered Gii had been spying
on us. I was just speaking to him when the lookout came running up. He was shocked at what I'd done, and ran off to get
someone to help carry the girl's body. So I fetched Gii out from
behind the rock, put him in the car, and came away."

"Only the young lookout's evidence could give us an objective picture of what happened," I said. "If it was light enough
for you to catch the girl as soon as she ran away, he should at
least have got a glimpse of you beating her brains out with that
lump of rock. The whole business only took a few minutes. So
though the lookout might have missed her scream from inside
the car, he ought to have been right behind you by the time you
dealt the last blow. He would have heard her groan at least."

"When he ran up, it's just possible I was back in the driver's
seat, turning the car round ready to make my getaway," Takashi
amended after a moment's thought. "He *might* testify I was in
the car when he first saw me."

"I'm perfectly sure that's what he'd say," I pressed, elated
by this new and promising lead. "The snow was thawing, and
you'd taken her for a drive in the Citroen along the graveled
road. Then something happened between you, so that she
jumped out of the car and staved her head in on the Whale
Rock. The reason you've got blood on you is that you picked her
up after the accident. Or you may have deliberately smeared
yourself with the blood pouring from her head. Besides, you
were driving the car in a place where the view was poor and

with a bridge only fifty yards ahead, at a speed fast enough for the girl's head to be smashed to a pulp if she jumped out. Say what you like, I'm sure you were too busy steering to have time to mess around with her sexually, let alone rape her—though *something* must have happened to make her jump out. I suspect the reason you were in the car when the lookout came was simply that you'd slammed on the brakes and were going back to the site of the accident. It was probably the squeal of the brakes that brought the lookout running. In fact, I'm sure you hadn't got out of the car at all. You may not even have found her until after the lookout went to fetch his friends. As for Gii, I doubt whether he actually witnessed anything. I bet you picked him up on the way home and primed him with details of your fictional murder."

Takashi sat in silence, head bowed, as though chewing over what I'd said. Once more he had retired warily into his shell of solitude, and it was impossible to tell from looking at him whether my conjectures had succeeded in tearing the fabric of his vaunted crime.

"Taka !" Hoshio, who till then had stayed silent, spoke in a childish, high-pitched voice that trembled violently from something more than the cold. "You know perfectly well she always wanted to do it with you. Even in the daytime, she used to try to get you into a dark corner of the house. You didn't need to rape her—you could've had her just by taking her pants down. I bet she pestered you so much in the car that you drove fast to give her a fright. I remember you saying you used to play around like that in the States. Then I bet she was so scared she lost her head and jumped out to save her own skin, because she was sure you'd never make it round the bend by the rock!"

"If that's really so, Taka, then you can't call it murder, can you?" I went on, encouraged by these remarks from the car expert. "It's either an accident or negligence. Even if it's negligence, it's not entirely your fault but partly the girl's too, poor kid."

Still silent, Takashi was loading a cartridge into the gun. He worked carefully, concentrating on the task for fear of an accident; but I could tell that the face, downturned and entirely in shadow beneath the ridge of his eyebrows, and the slight body stiff with tension, were dominated from within by some brute force that precluded all attempts by others to understand. I had a strange fancy that our baby who had lain with brown eyes open and expressionless, simply and quietly existing, had grown up without ever reestablishing communication with the outside world and was here now, the blood on his body proclaiming the crime that he'd committed. And I suddenly felt my own security—whose only guarantee as I waxed so eloquent had been the distress and lack of confidence Takashi showed—falling apart at the seams. Though I was sure of my ability to demonstrate the unreality of Takashi's professed crime, his stubborn silence as he sat with his face in the shadow, handling the gun like a small child absorbed in a new toy, gradually fostered the grotesque fear that I was looking at an animal.

"Do *you* believe he committed such a crime?" I was driven by his silence to ask my equally silent wife.

She sat thinking, and made no immediate response. Then, without looking up, she said in a dry voice that withered incipient emotion:

"Since he says he killed her, I can only believe him. He's not the type, at least, to whom murder would be absolutely impossible."

She was an unfamiliar, unapproachable stranger who had heard none of my speech as counsel for the defense. Ears closed and eyes downturned, she'd been letting herself respond directly to the unmistakable aura of criminality surrounding Takashi. He too raised frankly wondering, almost innocent eyes to look at her, and something, the fleeting shadow of a cloud, passed by deep beneath his skin. Then as he began carefully inspecting his gun again he said:

"She's right. I killed the girl by hitting her repeatedly on the head with a rock. Why won't you believe it, Mitsu?"

"There's no why or wherefore. It's not a question of believing or not believing. I'm just saying that it seems possible you didn't commit murder."

"Oh, I see. The scientific treatment." He laid the loaded gun cautiously across his knees, and with his dirty right hand began to unwind the broad cloth band from the little and ring fingers of his other, equally filthy hand. "I'm not opposed to the scientific approach either, Mitsu."

Blood-soaked gauze appeared beneath the cloth. It was bound round so thoroughly that it seemed to go on unwinding forever. But finally a pair of oddly shrunken, orange stalks emerged and blood spurted suddenly from the two level, rounded tips. With blood dripping onto his knees, he held the open wounds up for me to see, then the next moment clamped his right hand over the base of the two fingers and, thrusting them between his knees, bent forward and began moaning and twisting in pain.

"Shit!" he groaned. "God, it hurts!" He raised himself with an effort and began to wind the dirty gauze and cloth round his fingers again, but it was so obvious that this would do nothing to lessen his pain that Natsumi and I could only look on in horror.

Like an old and moribund dog, Hoshio crawled unsteadily to the edge of the raised floor and stretching out his neck disgorged the contents of his stomach.

"Hell, it hurts. Oh God!" Then, recovering slightly from the worst of the pain, he glanced up at me from under half-closed lids and explained in unnecessary detail, "I was pressing down on her face with my left hand . . . bashing her head with the lump of rock in my right. At first she kept shouting, 'No! No!' But suddenly her mouth closed over my left hand with a great crunching sound. I pulled it away in a hurry, but her teeth were clamped onto the first joint of the little finger and the second joint of the next. All I could do was hit her jaw with the rock to make her open her mouth. But her teeth were too sharp—it only made her mouth shut once and for all, biting off the tips of my fingers. I tried later to force her mouth open with a stick and get them back, but it was hopeless. The smashed head still has a couple of pieces of my finger in its mouth."

Backed up by the obvious reality of pain, his words struck home, despite my justifiable incredulity, with a shocking conviction that transcended logic. I felt the reality of the "criminal" Takashi, and with equal certainty the actuality of the crime. Like Hoshio, I was seized with a fear and loathing for Takashi's person that amounted to physical nausea. Not that I'd begun to believe he really battered the girl to death with a rock: I could still only think that she'd taken fright at the fierce speed with which the car negotiated the dark curves in the road and had jumped out. But his monomanic eagerness to attain criminal status and claim his fictional crime had then driven him to another grotesque and unbearably horrible act. He'd used a stick to force her mouth open as she lay dead with her skull staved in, deliberately inserted two fingers of his left hand between her teeth, and shut the mouth. I could almost hear it snap shut. Then, grasping a lump of rock in his right hand, he must have struck at her jaw till the dead teeth bit through his fingers. At each blow to the dead girl's chin, he would have been sprayed all over with blood and brains from the smashed skull and broken mouth, and with his own blood too. . . .

"Taka, you're a crazy murderer!" I said hoarsely, but lacked the will for anything further.

"*Now* I feel you've got me right at last!" Takashi declared, drawing himself up defiantly. Suddenly Hoshio, who was still on all fours, cried in a tone of utter despair:

"Stop it! Stop it! Why don't you do something to save Taka? It was an accident, I tell you!"

"Natsumi, give Hoshi some of those sleeping pills that Momoko took—twice the regular dose," said Takashi, reverting for the first time in a long while to the gentle, avuncular tone he customarily used toward his young bodyguard. "Hoshi, you'd better get some sleep. Hoshi's like a frog, only better," he added. "Whenever he gets wind of something that his mind—not just his body—can't swallow, he promptly flips his stomach and throws up."

"I won't take them," Hoshio objected petulantly. "I don't *want* to go to sleep." But Takashi ignored this and watched with a kind of silent authority as my wife handed Hoshio a glass of water and the sleeping pills, which Hoshio after a feeble show of resistance finally gulped down. We all heard the slight, familiar sound as the water slid down his throat.

"They'll soon take effect," said Takashi. "Hoshi's a barbarian—he's almost never taken drugs before. Natsumi, you stay with him till he goes to sleep."

"I don't want to go to sleep, Taka! I feel I might never wake up again," said Hoshio, making a final, limp protest in a voice obviously tinged with fear even as he began to succumb to the effect of the pills.

"No—go to sleep, and tomorrow morning you'll wake up with a healthy appetite," Takashi said, and callously dismissing the young man turned to me. "Mitsu, I've a feeling the valley people will be coming to lynch me. If I'm going to defend myself with the shotgun, I suppose I should shut myself up in the storehouse as great-grandfather's brother did. So change places with me tonight, will you?"

"They'd never lynch you, Taka," said my wife with an obvious uneasiness that belied her words. "I just can't imagine you holding off a lynch mob with a shotgun. It's all in your mind."

"I know the valley better than you, Natsumi. They're just beginning to get fed up with the rising, and with themselves for taking part in it. So some of them, I'm sure, will get the idea that they can atone for everything by shoving all the blame on me, then beating me to death. And in fact they're right. It would make quite a lot of things simpler if I played the sacrificial lamb in the same way as S."

"A lynching's just not possible," she insisted, and shot an imploring look at me, as the nearest object to hand, her eyes already swamped with a helpless need for alcohol. "Mitsu, you don't think there could be a lynching, do you?"

"Either way," I replied, "as the brains behind a 'rising of the imagination,' Taka naturally wants to keep the sparks of fancy flying right to the very end. The deciding factor will be how well the valley folk themselves play their imaginative part. I wouldn't care to make a prediction yet." I watched her gaze turn away disappointedly.

"He's right," said Takashi with a similar air of disappointment, and clutching the shotgun and a box of cartridges in his undamaged hand he slowly got to his feet. I could tell he was completely done in, so much so that if the weight of the gun had pulled him down he would probably have passed out on the spot.

"Give me the gun," I said, "I'll carry it for you." He darted a fierce glance at me and refused with open hostility, as though I'd tried to trick him out of his only weapon. A passing suspicion that he might be mad awoke real fear in me. But almost immediately his eyes regained their look of numb exhaustion.

"Come back to the storehouse with me, will you?" he begged simply. "And stay with me till I go to sleep."

We were going out of the kitchen into the front garden when my wife called to him as though in last farewell:

"Taka, why don't you save yourself? You seem to be *trying* to get yourself either lynched or condemned to death."

Takashi made no reply; his abnormally pallid, goose-pimpled, grubby face stayed sullenly shut in on itself. Already he was behaving as though he'd lost all interest in her. For no definite reason, I suddenly felt that both my wife and I were hopeless losers. Looking round, I saw her sitting motionless, her head sunk on her chest. The young man beside her was frozen into an unnatural half-sitting, half-lying position, like a wild animal paralyzed by a poisoned dart. Thanks to Takashi's powers of suggestion, he was already completely under the influence of the sleeping pills. Hoping at least that my wife had some whisky concealed somewhere to help her face the cold and tedium of this longest night, I walked shivering in my brother's wake beneath the faint light from the lantern in the eaves. He too was shaking violently, and staggered more than once. In the storeroom, Gii the hermit was making a sound like a dog sneezing. Nothing stirred in the darkness of Jin's outbuilding; "Japan's Fattest Woman," freed from all frustration where food was concerned, was sleeping her first untroubled sleep in six or seven years. The mud in the front garden had frozen hard and no longer gave way under our heels.

Still wearing his bloodstained jacket and trousers Takashi crawled in between my blankets and curled up beneath them to take his socks off, looking like a snake caught in a bag. Then he drew the gun to his side again and, squinting up at me as I stood watching him settle down for the night, asked me to turn off the light. The request suited me very well. As he lay staring up into space, my brother's blackened, grimy face was sunken like an old man's at the cheeks and around the eyes, more unprepossessing and shifty-looking than at any time of trouble I remembered in the past. His body too, which scarcely made a bulge beneath the blankets and quilt, was pitifully slight. As I waited for the image of Takashi lying on his back to fade from my retina into the newfound darkness, I wound Hoshio's blanket round my waist and sat down with my knees drawn up to my chest. We were silent for a while.

"You know, Mitsu, your wife sometimes hits the nail on the head," Takashi began in an ingratiatingly compromising tone. "It's true—I don't want to save myself. I *want* to be lynched or condemned to death."

"I know. You haven't the courage to set up a violent crime on your own, but given an accident that could be mistaken for one, you thrust yourself into the picture and do your level best to make sure you'll be either lynched or executed. That's how I see it."

Takashi lay silent, breathing deeply, as though to encourage me to supplement my remarks. But I had nothing more to say. I was extremely cold and unutterably depressed. Eventually, he spoke again.

"Do you intend to stop them tomorrow?"

"Naturally. But I don't know whether I can effectively interfere with your plan for self-destruction now that you've got so deeply entangled in it."

"Mitsu, there's something I want to tell you. I want to tell you the truth." He spoke diffidently and shyly, half as though he doubted he would be taken seriously and half as though his attention were elsewhere. But the words came across strongly, setting up immediate echoes inside me.

"I don't want to hear it, so don't try to tell me," I hastily protested, with a sudden urge to flee my memories of an earlier conversation with Takashi about "the truth."

"I'm going to tell you, Mitsu!" he declared in an unpleasantly insistent tone that only intensified my desire to flee. I was shaken anew by his air of abject capitulation.

"If only you'd listen, I think you might cooperate, at least to the extent of standing by without interfering while I'm lynched."

I abandoned any further attempt to keep him silent. Then with a preliminary sigh of exhaustion and despair, as though he had already told what he was about to tell and, deeply regretting it, sought frantically and in vain to take back his words, he began. At each word he seemed to be overcoming some resistance in himself.

"Mitsu . . . I've always said that I had no idea why our sister killed herself. Uncle's family backed me up too, they said it was suicide without any apparent motive. So I've always been able to keep the real reason to myself. Nobody ever attempted, in fact, to ask me about it seriously. I've kept quiet all along. Just once, in America, I told someone—a black prostitute, the merest stranger—but that was in my inadequate English. For me, talking to someone in English is like wearing a mask. So for all practical purposes I've never told anyone. It was a fake confession; it left me just as I was. Thanks to which, the only punishment I received was a mild dose of VD. Never once have I talked about it in the language I share with you and shared with our sister. It goes without saying that even to you I've never said a word about it. The only thing is, you may have dimly suspected there was something odd about her death from the way I always lost my cool if I felt you were dropping hints about it. That day you prepared the pheasants, for instance, you asked if 'the truth' had something to do with her. At that moment I was convinced you knew everything and were playing with me. I was so angry and ashamed I could have killed you. But then I told myself that you couldn't know about it, and got myself under control. The morning she killed herself, before I went to tell uncle and the rest, I searched every corner of the outbuilding where she and I lived in case she'd left some message that would arouse suspicion. Then I began laughing and crying, torn between a new sense of guilt and relief at being released at last from the pressure of fear. I didn't go to report her suicide at the main house till I was sure I'd got myself in hand and wouldn't burst out in another fit of laughing. I found her that morning squatting in the toilet, dead from a dose of agricultural chemical. If you wonder why I felt such a deep sense of release once I was sure she'd left no last note, it was because I'd always been afraid that, being half-witted, she would give our secret away. I felt her death had somehow erased the secret, almost as though it had never existed at all. But reality, of course, refused to work out like that. On the contrary—her suicide implanted the secret deep down inside my body and mind, where it began steadily poisoning my daily life and the outlook for the future. All this happened when I was a junior in high school. Ever since, I've been torn in two by the memory." He paused and began to sob: an indescribably gloomy, wretched sound, the memory of which, I foresaw, would plague me for the rest of my life with spells of depression that made survival itself a burden.

"Although she was half-witted, she was really a rather special kind of person. The one thing she cared for was beautiful sounds; she was happiest when she was listening to music. Sounds like an airplane's engines or a car starting up would make her complain of a burning pain in her ears. And I'm sure they really did hurt her. You know that you can break glass by making the air vibrate? Well, it seems it was like that—a pain as though something delicate was breaking inside her ears. Anyway, there was no one else in the village where uncle lived who understood music and had an absolute need for it as she did. She wasn't ugly, and kept herself spotless. She was almost unnaturally clean in her person; together with this abnormal fondness for music, it was one of the features of her idiocy. Some of the young fellows in uncle's village would make a point of coming to gawk at her while she was listening. Once the music

started, she was reduced to a pair of ears. Everything else was
shut out, nothing else could penetrate her consciousness. So
the peeping toms were quite safe—but if ever I found them at
it I'd throw myself at them in a blind fury. For me, she was the
one feminine thing in my life, and I felt I had to keep her safe. I
didn't, in fact, have anything to do with the other girls in uncle's
village; when I went to high school in the town, I never even
talked to the girls in the same class. I made up a tale about us
being a couple of aristocrats whose family had come down in
the world, and took an exaggerated pride in our descent from
great-grandfather and his brother. If you took the sympathetic
view, you might say I was doing it to shake off my inferiority
feelings at being taken care of by uncle and his family. I told
her we were a special elite of two, and we wouldn't and mustn't
get interested in anybody apart from each other. The way we
behaved made some nasty-minded adults start a rumor that we
were sleeping together. I got my own back by throwing stones
at the houses of people who said such things. But all the while,
the rumors were exerting a power of suggestion over me. I was
only a high school kid of seventeen with an unformed mind full
of fanatical ideas and lonely enough to be susceptible to such
persuasion. Late one afternoon in early summer, I suddenly
got drunk. It was the day the last rice-planting was finished in
uncle's field, and a crowd from the village who'd been called in
to help were drinking over in the main house. She and I, being
'aristocrats,' naturally hadn't helped with the planting, but the
young fellows hauled me in and gave me my first drink, which
went straight to my head. Uncle found me drunk, told me off,
and sent me back to the outbuilding. At first, sister was amused
and laughed at my drunkenness. But when the farmers got

foully drunk and started singing and playing music in the main house, she suddenly got scared. She pressed her hands over her ears and hunched up into herself like a shellfish. Even so, it was more than she could take, and soon she was sobbing like a little kid. They went on and on singing their vulgar songs in their thick peasant voices until late at night. I got really mad; I hated society and anything to do with it. I held her to me, trying to calm her down, and as I did so I felt a queer kind of excitement. Before long, I'd had sex with her."

We were silent, acutely embarrassed by each other's presence as brothers. We lay still and withdrawn in the darkness, scarcely breathing, trying to hide from the huge and terrifying thing that was coming to denounce us. I wanted to cry out, "No! No!"—the same cry that, if Takashi was to be believed, the unfortunate girl had uttered at the point of death as the rock battered her head—but even that simple cry refused to emerge from a body in which the flesh and bones were independent and unrelated, aching with the dull pain of those evil awakenings.

"It's absolutely no excuse to say I was drunk the first time we had sex," Takashi went on slowly in a voice faint to the point of vanishing, "because the next day I repeated the same thing when I was sober. At first she didn't like the sex for its own sake, and was scared too. But the idea of refusing me in anything was quite foreign to her. I wasn't unaware that she was suffering pain, but I was too far gone in desire and anxiety to consider things from her side. In order to calm her fears about sex, I fetched some old erotic prints from uncle's storehouse and persuaded her that all married people did the same thing. What worried me most was that she'd tell our secret to uncle's family in the daytime, while I was at school and she was alone in the house. So I told her that if anybody else got to know what we were doing, they'd do frightful things to us. I hunted out some illustrations in the dictionary to show her, pictures of people being burned at the stake during the Middle Ages. And I told her that if we were careful not to let other people know, we could live together as brother and sister all our lives, doing the same thing without ever marrying anybody else. That was what we both really wanted, I said, so what did it matter as long as we managed not to get caught?

"I really believed what I said. I believed that if only she and I resolved to go on living in joint defiance of society, we'd be free to do everything we most desired. Until then, it seemed she'd been worried at the idea that sooner or later I'd get married and leave her to live alone. I reminded her, too, how mother before she died had told her to stick close to me always. She was vaguely convinced that she'd never get along apart from me. So when I persuaded her, in terms she could understand, that we should turn our backs on everyone else and go on living together, brother and sister, in league against the world, she was genuinely delighted. Before long, she stopped being reluctant about sex and started initiating it herself. At one period we were leading a more or less completely self-sufficient life, like a pair of lovers, just happy to be together. I at least have never been so happy as I was in those days. Once she'd made up her mind, she was strong and unwavering. She was proud of the idea that she'd do everything with me until we died. And then . . . she got pregnant. Our aunt realized it first. When aunt warned me about it, I was half crazy with anxiety. I felt sure that if my sexual dealings with her came to light, I'd die of shame on the spot. But aunt didn't suspect me in the slightest, so in the end I committed an unforgivable act of treachery. I was a vile schemer without an ounce of courage in me. I didn't deserve such a straightforward sister.

"I ordered her to say she'd been raped by some unknown young man from the village. She did as I said. So uncle took her into town and not only made her have an abortion but had her sterilized, too. When she came back she was completely prostrate, not just from the experience of the operation but from the menacing roar of car engines in the town. But she'd courageously obeyed my instructions and hadn't breathed a word about me to anyone, even at the inn when uncle apparently pressed her—she, who'd never told a lie!—to recall any distinguishing features of the man who'd raped her."

He stopped and sobbed for a while. Then, still not completely free of his fit of weeping and interspersing his account with little moans, he related the cruelest experience of his life. I lay listening to him with utter passivity, wretched and shrunken like a dried fish, overpowered by the cold and the aching in my head.

"It happened that night. Too frightened to be able to pull herself together, she was looking to me to rescue her. How could you blame her? And since sex was already a habit between us, she took it into her head to find comfort there. But even someone with as little accurate sexual knowledge as I had in those days knew that sex was impossible immediately after that kind of operation. I felt fear at the idea of her sexual organs all wounded deep down inside, and a sense of physiological disgust too. You could hardly blame me either, could you? But she couldn't grasp what would seem obvious to ordinary people. When I refused her—the first time ever—she suddenly turned stubborn. She crawled in beside me and tried to touch my prick. So I hit her—the first time she'd ever been hit in her life. I've never seen a human being look so startled, or so sad and forlorn. . . . Then after a while she said: 'It wasn't true what you said, Taka. It was wrong, even though we kept it secret.' And the next morning she killed herself. *It wasn't true what you said, Taka. It was wrong, even though we kept it secret. . . .*"

Not the faintest sound arose from the valley. Any noise would have been smothered at once by the blanket of snow that lay, still undisturbed, over the forest. Even the snow that had begun to thaw had frozen again in the cold. Yet all the while a shrill voice, its frequency too high to be caught by the human ear, seemed to skirl between the high, black walls of the surrounding forest. It was the cry of the huge creature whose coiled body filled the void that lay above the hollow. One midwinter in my childhood, after a night of that voice whose presence was so intensely experienced though never heard, I discovered the trail of some huge snake on the shallow bed of the clear stream flowing along the bottom of the valley, and shuddered to think it was the mark of the monster I'd heard crying all night long. Now once again I felt the overpowering presence of that soundless howling.

Growing used to the dark, my eye detected in the faint light from the window all kinds of vague black shapes looming about me. The whole interior of the storehouse was crowded with apparitions like serried ranks of dark, dwarfish Buddhist images, all whispering to each other: *We heard, we heard!*

I was seized with a sudden, uncontrollable fit of coughing. It felt as though the membranes of my throat, my bronchial tubes, even my lungs had suddenly erupted in a crimson rash.

I had a fever; that was why I'd felt the flesh and bones of my whole body dismembered and plagued with sharp pains. I had barely recovered from the fit of coughing when Takashi, who showed signs of recovering at least slightly from the profound prostration of his spirit, spoke to me in a tone of utterly defenseless self-commiseration.

"Mitsu, as long as you don't interfere, I'm sure I'll be executed even if I survive tomorrow. Either way, whether I'm killed in the lynching or executed, I want to give you my eyes so you can use the retinas for an operation on your own. Then my eyes at least will survive and see lots of things after my death. It would be a consolation just to serve as a kind of lens. You'll do it, won't you, Mitsu?"

An overpowering urge to refuse shot through my body like a shaft of lightning. The crying of the forest ceased and the small black apparitions filling the storehouse vanished.

"No! Nothing would persuade me to take your eyes," I declared in a voice shaking with indignation.

"Why? Why not? Why won't you accept them?" Takashi shouted in a forlorn voice in which the note of self-pity dried up and was replaced by a growing, desperate suspicion. "Is it because you're so angry with me about our sister? But you only knew her when she was a small kid! While I was living with her in someone else's house, you were here in the valley with Jin to do your bidding. And you used the money left to us to go to high school in the town and to university in Tokyo as well, didn't you? If you hadn't hogged the money for yourself, the three of us could have lived together in the valley. You're not in a position to criticize me where she's concerned. I didn't tell the truth just to have you pass judgment on me about her!"

"And that's not what I mean either!" I shouted back, cutting short his protest as a new and ferocious excitement started to grip him. "To begin with, I'm not prepared, emotionally, to accept your eyes. But on a more practical level what I mean is this: you won't be lynched tomorrow morning, nor is any court going to sentence you to death. It's just your sense of guilt—you're hoping to punish yourself for the incest and the death of an innocent person that it brought about; and you're hoping that the people here will install you among the valley 'spirits,' so that you're remembered as a man of violence. I admit that if that fantasy *should* become a reality, the two sides of your personality would come together again in death. And in a hundred years you might even be looked on as a reincarnation of great-grandfather's brother, your idol. But Taka—though you're always playing at putting yourself in peril, you're the type who invariably has a way out at the last moment. You acquired the habit on the day that sister's suicide allowed you to go on living without either being punished or put to shame. I'm sure this time, too, you'll work some nasty little dodge to go on living. Then, having so shamefully survived, you'll make your excuses to her ghost: 'In fact,' you'll say, 'I deliberately put myself in a tight corner where I had no choice but to be lynched or executed, but a lot of interfering bastards forced me to go on living.' It was the same with your experiences of violence in America—you weren't really committed at all. You merely hoped to find a pretext for carrying on for a while, free of your painful memories. All you did in practice was catch a touch of VD, thereby providing an excuse for not taking any further risks during your stay in the States. It's the same with the grubby little confession you've just made: if I were to guarantee that even *that* wasn't the absolute truth either, that one mention of it wouldn't mean your being killed, or committing suicide, or going mad and turning into a monster, don't you think you'd immediately feel saved? It may have been unconscious, but didn't you ramble on so long in the expectation that I'd accept you as you are, along with all your past experiences, thus releasing you at one stroke from your divided state? For example, do you think you'd have the guts to confess again in front of the valley folk tomorrow morning? That would *really* be taking a risk. But I don't imagine you've got what it takes. You may not admit it consciously, but you're expecting somehow to survive their kangaroo court. If you're sent for trial, you'll implore them to execute you with an air of sincerity convincing enough to deceive even yourself. But in fact you'll be sitting pretty in your cell until investigation confirms that your only crime was mutilation of a body following accidental death. Don't lie to me about giving me your eyes after you're killed, as though you believed you only had a while to live! You know I'd be glad even of a dead man's eyes; you're just playing around with someone else's disability!"

Takashi raised himself with obvious difficulty in the dark. He set the gun on his knees and, placing his finger on the trigger, turned to face me. I thought he might shoot me, but didn't flinch; I felt too contemptuous, contemptuous of the way he always left himself some escape from any trap he allowed himself to fall into, to be impressed by this sudden vault into threatened violence. Even the sight of the gun and his small black head swaying in time with his heavy breathing left me untouched by fear.

"Mitsu, why do you hate me so much?" he demanded in a voice tearful with impotent grief, peering impatiently through the darkness to ascertain the expression on my face. "Why have you always loathed me? You hated me, didn't you, even before you knew what I did to our sister and Natsumi."

"Hated? It's not a question of what I feel, Taka. I'm simply giving my objective opinion that even someone like you who chooses to live in pursuit of a dramatic illusion can't keep up the critical tension indefinitely unless, say, he actually goes insane. Take our eldest brother—he may have enjoyed violence on the battlefield, but if he'd come home alive I'm sure he would have discarded the memory and settled down again with the greatest of ease to a placid daily routine. If it weren't so, the whole world would be swamped with violent criminals after every big war. As leader of the rising, great-grandfather's brother, on whom you pin so much faith, was responsible for mass murder, and in the end he even abandoned his comrades to their fate so that he could get away through the forest. Do you think that after that he deliberately plunged into new perils and went on leading a brutal life simply to justify his pose as a man of violence? Well, he didn't. I read the letters he wrote. They show that he stopped being a man of violence. What's more, even in his own mind he lost the enthusiasm he'd had as a rebel leader. Nor was it a case of self-punishment. He simply forgot his experiences in the rising and spent his last years as a perfectly ordinary citizen. He tried all kinds of feminine wiles to help his beloved nephew dodge the draft, but he failed. And the one-time revolutionary seems to have died peacefully in his bed, brooding mournfully over the fate of that same nephew—no news had come from him since he was sent to fight at Weihaiwei. In practice he died a mere sheep of a man, absolutely unqualified to become any kind of 'spirit.' You too, Taka—you won't be lynched tomorrow morning; you'll go down to the valley to have your damaged fingers treated, you'll be arrested, and after being put on probation or serving three years or so, you'll take your place again as a perfectly well-behaved, ordinary member of society. All fantasies that ignore those facts are meaningless in the long run. You don't have sufficient confidence in the facts. But you're too old, Taka, to get burned up about heroic fantasies of this kind. You're not a kid anymore."

I stood up alone in the darkness and, feeling for the top of the steps with my foot, went downstairs. Behind me, I heard Takashi's unspeakably dismal voice again (and felt that this time I might really be shot, though fear of threatened violence refused to become a reality, and I could only feel the discomfort of the fever within me and the nagging ache in each part of my body):

"Mitsu, why do you resent me so much? Why have you always disliked me? We two brothers are all that's left of the Nedokoros, aren't we?"

In the main house my wife was still drinking whisky, staring vacantly in front of her with eyes already bloodshot like the man-eating woman of Korean folklore. Beyond the open sliding doors, Hoshio lay next to Momoko, fast asleep on his face like a dog that has collapsed of exhaustion. I sat down within my wife's field of vision, took the whisky bottle from between her knees, drank a mouthful straight from the bottle and had another fit of coughing; but she continued to drift on the stormy seas of drunkenness as though I didn't exist. I watched as tears sprang into her dark, bloodshot eyes and ran down the dry skin of her checks. After a while, a shot rang out from the storehouse, its echoes reverberating interminably around the night-shrouded forest. As I ran barefoot across the yard, there was a second shot.

Just then, Gii the hermit came rushing out of the storeroom in panic-stricken flight. We all but collided, and started back from each other in fright. At the foot of the steps, I called up to the room above. The light was on now.

"It's me, Mitsu," came Takashi's voice, calm and psychologically armed once more. "I'm testing the power and spread of the different cartridges, ready to do battle tomorrow morning with my imaginary mob." On my way back to the main house, I found Jin's children standing still and silent in the yard and assured them that nothing had happened. My wife was staring fixedly at her glass in which whisky and water shone with a dark luster, equally indifferent to the shots and my sudden exit, her downturned face seemingly turned to bronze. Hoshio and Momoko stirred uncomfortably and went on sleeping. Thirty minutes later, there was another shot. I waited ten minutes for a fourth shot. Then I pulled boots onto my dirty feet and went over to the storehouse. Takashi didn't reply when I hailed him from the foot of the stairs.

I ran up the steps, banging my head here, there, and everywhere as I went. A man sprawled half-propped against the wall directly ahead. The skin of his face and bare chest was torn and bloody as though studded with split pomegranates. He looked like a bright red, life-size plaster dummy dressed only in trousers. Starting automatically toward the figure, I grunted as a hunting gun tied to the great zelkova beam struck me heavily over the ear. A piece of gut connected the trigger to one of the red dummy's fingers where they drooped on the tatami floor. And on the plaster and timber of the wall, at just the height where the dead man would have stood staring at the muzzle of the gun, the outline of a human head and shoulders was drawn in red pencil, with two great eyes carefully marked in on the head. I took another step forward and, with the feel of pellets and slippery blood beneath the soles of my feet, saw that the penciled eyes had been blasted full of shot, so that two leaden orbs seemed to stare out at me from the hollows. On the wall beside the head was written, in the same red pencil:

I told the truth

The dead man gave a deep groan. Kneeling in the blood, I touched Takashi's crimson, shredded face, but he was definitely dead. I had a feeling, a spurious memory, of having encountered just such a dead man, and in this very storehouse, on countless occasions before.

Retrial

The damp, heavy wind that all night long had circled the hollow in the forest came blowing in, forming constant small eddies of air in the cellar where I crouched. I awoke from a short, anguished sleep to find my throat painfully swollen and constricted but my drunkenness gone and my brain, which had been enlarged and feverish before my sleep, shrunken to its normal size, leaving a gap into which gloomy depression had wormed its way; my head was hopelessly, wretchedly clear. With one hand still clutching at the blanket which the instinct of self-defense had kept wrapped round my shoulders and waist even during my dreams, I stretched out the other into the darkness beyond my knees and, groping for the whisky bottle containing water, took a mouthful. The cold of the water seemed to soak right through to my lungs and my sadly oppressed liver. In my dreams, Takashi had stood in a mist about five yards in front of me, still looking like a crumbling red plaster dummy with his upper half split open like ripe pomegranates. Countless glittering pellets studded the sockets of his eyes, transforming him into an iron-eyed monster. He stood at one corner of a tall triangle of which I was the apex; at the remaining corner a bent-backed, sallow-faced man stood watching us in silence. Seen from my present position, hunched so close to the floor that my head was actually lower than my knees, they seemed to be standing on a high platform. I was sitting in the center of the front row of a theater whose ceiling was disproportionately high for its size, and the two ghosts were side by side up on the stage. High above their heads, as though the gallery were reflected in a mirror at the back of the stage, I could see a host of old men in dark suits with hats pulled down over their ears, looking like mushrooms clustering in some dark, damp spot. One of them had obviously once been the friend who painted his head crimson and hanged himself, another the baby who showed no more response than a vegetable. Up on the stage, Takashi opened wide the mouth that with lips shot away was no more than a gaping, reddish black hole and cried in triumphant hatred: *Our retrial is your trial!* And the old men in the gallery, whom I suspected in fact of being a jury organized by Takashi himself, removed their hats and waved them with menacing significance at the great zelkova beam directly above their heads. I awoke in exhaustion and despair.

The place where I now sat motionless—hugging my knees, just as I'd sat that autumn dawn the previous year in the pit for the septic tank in our back garden—was a stone cellar that the Emperor and his men had discovered and begun to rescue from its long oblivion when they came to make preliminary surveys for dismantling the storehouse. The inner space where I sat had an anteroom with a privy and even a well. It would have been possible for someone to live there in self-imposed confinement, though the well by now was blocked and gave off no smell of water, and the privy was unusable, caved in long ago. From both the square holes came the odor of millions of mold spores; there might even be some penicillin among them. I had eaten a smoked-meat sandwich, drunk some whisky, and dozed off where I sat. If I had tipped over sideways as I slept, I would have hurt my head against the wooden posts, countless as the trees of the forest, that supported the storehouse floor. Their corners were as hard and sharp as ever.

It was still the middle of the night. Since early morning, when word had come that the Emperor was making his first personal visit to the valley since the "rising," the southerly winds heralding the end of winter had swept the forest and the hollow, and they had raged on unabated into the small hours. If I peered through the crack in the floor above my head, toward the gap made in the first-floor wall of the storehouse facing the valley, my line of vision was blocked by pitch-black forest. During the morning the sky had been free of clouds, but dust from the continent had hung a deep, yellowish brown shadow about it, weakening the sun's rays. The same darkness had persisted even after the wind grew stronger, and had finally sunk unrelieved into night. As the gale mounted, the forest gave off a deep-throated roar like a stormy sea, the sound swelling till the very soil seemed to cry out. Here and there, I could distinguish isolated voices rising like flecks of foam to the surface: the great trees towering over the belt of land between the forest and the valley were moaning in the wind, calling to me in individual tones that awoke vivid early memories. Like recollections of old folk in the valley to whom I'd spoken once or twice in childhood and remembered ever after, the giants of the forest were still alive in me: not in any complex or profound way yet with individual characters of their own. One day when I was small, an old worker from the soy sauce store, who lived at a different stratum of valley society from myself and with whom I'd never before exchanged a single word, had taken me unawares on the path leading down to the river past the storehouse where they brewed the sauce. Twisting my arm while I raged and struggled helplessly, he'd poured into my ears a torrent of coarse abuse about my mother's insanity. And just as I clearly remembered the old man's great doggy face, so I could see now the aged horse chestnut that grew on the hillside behind the house. As I listened to its sound, the whole tree surged into sight in vivid detail on the screen of my memory, bending and shouting in the gale.

Even during the morning, when the wind hadn't been so fierce, I'd lain in the gloom by the open fireplace, listening to the great trees sounding in the wind. Brooding vaguely I'd wondered, among other things, whether to visit the trees for one last look before I left the hollow. It occurred to me that once I left I should never see them again, a thought which made me extremely doubtful about the reliability of my sight on that last occasion, and made me directly and vividly aware in turn of the death that awaited me someday. My main preoccupations, though, were two letters offering me jobs. One was from the professor of my old department in Tokyo, the other from the office of an expedition going to Africa to catch animals for an open zoo to be set up somewhere in the country. The professor offered me both lectureships in English literature that had been held ready at private universities for myself and the friend who had hanged himself. The offer carried the promise of a stable

future. The letter from the expedition office was a hasty sum-
mons, reeking unmistakably of danger, from a scholar, a man
of about the same age as S would have been, who had given
up a post as assistant professor of zoology in order to organize
the zoo. It was he who had praised my translation of the book
on trapping in the book-review section of a leading newspaper.
I'd met him several times; he was the kind of man who would
board a sinking ship as its new captain after even the rats had
left. Now he wanted me to join the expedition as its official
interpreter.

The first of the two letters probably represented my only
remaining chance to return to that kind of post; when my friend
died, I'd thrown over the lectureship my old university had given
me, without even consulting the professor of my department.
Moreover, since Takashi hadn't left me any of the money he'd
got from the sale of the house and land, I would have to decide
on some occupation sooner or later. The lectureship was ideal,
but still I hesitated. My wife, with whom I hadn't yet discussed
the question of my next job and who only learned of the two
offers because of the telegrams that came pressing for answers,
had said quite coolly:

"If you're interested in the work in Africa, why don't you
go, Mitsu?" I immediately had a crushing premonition of all the
difficulties and discomforts such unfamiliar work would entail.

"I'm sure that 'official interpreter' means not only paper
work but giving orders to native porters and camp workers," I
said. "I can just see myself shouting 'Forward march!' and the
like in abominable Swahili!" I spoke in tones of utter depression,
but in my mind's eye I saw a still more dismal vision: of myself
all bloody from banging my temple, my cheekbone, even my

sightless eye on African trees with iron bark and African rocks hard enough to contain diamonds. I saw myself finally falling victim to acute malaria, groaning under a high fever that made me resent even the indomitable zoologist's scoldings and exhortations, and stretched out exhausted on the marshy ground, crying in Swahili to the bitter end, "Tomorrow we leave!"

"But surely it would at least give you more chance of a new life than lecturing in English at a university?"

"Taka, of course, would have gone and carved out a new life for himself immediately. According to Momoko, the kind of people who'd go all the way to Africa to catch elephants were humanity's only hope in his eyes. He had a vision of the first man going into the wilds of Africa to catch elephants after all the zoos had been destroyed in a nuclear war. His elusive 'Mr. Humanity.'"

"Yes, Taka would have leaped at the offer. But I realize now that you're the type who'd never, deliberately at least, choose any work that might involve constant risks. You leave those jobs to other people. Then, when they've survived the dangers, got over their exhaustion, and written a book about their experiences, you step in and translate it."

She might have been making an objective appraisal of some complete stranger. But dismayed though I was to find such dispassionate powers of observation in her, I reflected that she was probably right. I was the type who, rather than discover a new life for himself, rather than build a thatched hut of his own, would choose to live as a lecturer in English literature, without a single student who pinned any serious hopes on his classes, fated to be disliked by them all unless he missed at least one lecture every week or so, living in seedy bachelorhood (for there was point in going on with this marriage) and labeled "Rat" by his students, like that philosopher whom Takashi had met in New York. Set, in short, on a course in which the only changes remaining were old age and death.

At the time of his suicide, Takashi had transferred all the notes and coins left in his pockets to an envelope addressed to Hoshio and Momoko and put it away in a desk drawer where his blood wouldn't get on it. Immediately after his funeral (we buried him in the only vacant lot left in the family graveyard, and S's ashes with him), Hoshio got the Citroen unaided over the temporary bridge, refusing all offers of help from the young men, and with Momoko by his side moved off down the paved road, driving carefully over the half-thawed slush still covering it. Before his departure, he delivered the following speech to my wife and myself while Momoko, standing docile and extremely feminine at his side, kept up a succession of small nods in support of his remarks:

"Now that we don't have Taka, Momo and me will have to manage by ourselves. So I'm marrying her. After all, we're both past the legal age of consent. We can make a living together—I can find a garage somewhere and Momo can get a job as waitress in a coffee shop. I'm hoping to have my own gas station someday. Taka used to say I should try the kind of station he saw in America, the sort that can handle quite serious repairs and serve snacks as well. Now that he's dead, Momo and me have to go it alone, there's no one else we can look to."

My wife and I would have left the hollow with them, begging a lift in the back of the Citroen at least as far as the small town by the sea, but I had a feverish cold. Even after that, my hands had a hot, prickly feeling that lasted for three weeks, as though they'd developed a spongy layer that prevented me lifting anything. Then, when I got better, my wife started saying she wasn't up to a long journey. She was, in fact, suffering frequent spells of nausea and faintness. I had no trouble in deducing what she was preparing herself for psychologically, what she was hoping for with her whole body, but I had no desire to discuss it. For us, it fell into the category of things already settled.

With a vague sense of resignation, I brooded over this question of my new job, while Natsumi sat in the gloom on the other side of the fireplace looking like a doll firmly weighted at its base. There was no one left in the main house to interrupt our dialogue. But nowadays she would lapse almost at once into a profound silence, fleeing beyond the sphere of conversation. For a while after Takashi's death, she'd been in a state of constantly renewed drunkenness. Before long, however, she voluntarily disposed of all the remaining bottles of whisky and took to spending her time, except when she was asleep and at mealtimes, sitting silent and correct on her heels, with her hands folded over her belly and her eyes half closed. I suspected that for her the suggestion about Africa had been no more than a disinterested comment on the choices facing some complete stranger. I no longer cast any deep shadow across the world of her awareness, nor she on mine.

In the afternoon, Jin's eldest son crept into the kitchen, moving quietly in deference to my wife's silence.

"The Emperor's crossing the bridge," he reported. "He's got five young guys with him."

By now, none of the valley folk believed the Emperor would bring a gang with him. As soon as the thaw set in, he'd sent a representative who settled all the complex questions created by the "rising" in as simple a fashion as possible. Specifically, he'd piled goods onto the first heavy truck to enter the valley, and reopened the supermarket. He demanded no compensation for the looting, nor did he report the matter to the police. The plan put forward by the young priest and the Sea Urchin for getting the more prosperous inhabitants to put up the funds to take over the supermarket, losses and all, was dismissed out of hand. There was a rumor, in fact, that no formal proposal had ever been made to the Emperor at all. Within a short time after Takashi's death, the forces behind the "rising" had collapsed at the center. They'd lost all power to influence the Emperor by threatening to rekindle the riot. The housewives of the valley and the "country," filled with abject gratitude and satisfaction at not being questioned about the looting, were quite happily buying foodstuffs and household goods costing an average twenty or thirty percent more than before the trouble. As for the electrical appliances and other larger articles that had been looted, people came, one by one and in secret, to return them to the supermarket, where they were put on sale again as damaged goods and sold out at special discounts in no time at all. The women from the "country" who had taken part in the "rising" and fought with each other over cheap articles of clothing now proved to have appreciable sums of cash hidden away, and were among the most eager customers at the sale. And the owners of forest land shut themselves up again in their snug shells with audible sighs of relief.

I walked down to the valley behind Jin's son, my eyes stung by the thick dust whipped off bare fields by the boisterous wind. Everything around me—the dark brown stretches of withered grassland where the snow had completely vanished, leaving the soil parched and powerless as yet to put forth new

life, even the somber evergreen heights of the forest beyond
the groves of great deciduous trees—had an air of indefinable loss, like the dead ruin of a human being, that awoke an
obscure uneasiness in me as my gaze roved across the hollow.
I dropped my eyes and saw the back of the boy's neck, where
grime had made a splotchy pattern. For hours on end he had
crouched on top of the great boulder where the wretched
little sexpot had met her end, braving the buffets of the dust-
laden wind in order to catch sight of the Emperor making his
entry into the valley. The boy walked hurriedly with drooping
head, his rear view exuding an air of fatigue that was strange
in a child. It was the fatigue of a member of a family that had
finally surrendered. I felt sure that the whole valley awaited
the arrival of the Emperor and his subordinates with the same
weary air. The hollow had capitulated.

The boy wouldn't have played the part of sentinel so enthusiastically if my purpose in going down to meet the Emperor
hadn't been relevant to his mother, who ate almost nothing now
and was rapidly growing thinner. I doubted, otherwise, whether
he would have worked for me that day at all, since Takashi's
death had divorced me once more from the daily lives of the
inhabitants of the hollow. By now, even the children made no
attempt to poke fun at me. When we arrived in the open space
before the village office, I immediately recognized the Emperor
and his followers, who seemed to have bypassed the supermarket and were marching straight up the graveled road. The large
man who came striding along with military precision, kicking up
the bottom of a long black overcoat reaching almost to his heels,
was the Emperor. Even at a distance, the round face beneath
the deerstalker was obviously plump and fresh-complexioned.

The young men surrounding him, who came walking with the same long, vigorous strides, all had similar sturdy physiques. They were dressed in shoddy overcoats and were bareheaded but, following their leader's example, they walked proudly with shoulders back and heads held upright. I was vividly reminded of the day when the occupation forces' jeeps first came into the valley; the Emperor and his party were like the calmly triumphant aliens of that midsummer morning. The grown-ups of the valley had found it difficult to get used to the feeling of being occupied even after they'd witnessed practical confirmation of the nation's defeat, and had gone on with their daily tasks, ignoring the foreign troops. But all the while their souls were suffused with shame. The children were different: promptly adapting to the new situation, they ran after the jeeps shouting "hello, hello!"—a piece of emergency education imparted at school—and were given canned foods and candy.

Today, too, any grown-ups unfortunate enough to encounter the Emperor's procession averted their faces or hung their heads like shy crabs longing to scuttle away into some convenient hole. On the day of the "rising," they'd acquired a destructive impetus through their frank, head-on acceptance of the shame involved. It had brought them all together. But the shame tormenting them now that they'd capitulated wasn't the right kind to provide fuel for hatred, but a squalid, impotent variety. Their individual "disgraces" were a series of stepping-stones across which the Emperor and his subordinates paraded ostentatiously. The discrepancy between the "spirit" of the Emperor in morning coat with no shirt, and the reality of the Emperor himself, made me speculate with a spasm of almost personal shame how it would have been if the young man dressed as the "spirit" had had to wait at the side of the road as the Emperor came by. The group of valley children who brought up the rear of the procession were silent, as though preoccupied with the howling of the fierce wind that came spiraling down from the upper reaches of the forest. They were the first to adapt to the new situation in the valley, just as I and my fellows had done in our childhood. But they too had been participants in the "rising," and as such had lost their voices, troubled by as much shame as their childish heads could accommodate.

Before long, the Emperor became aware of my existence. After all, I was the only human being in the valley who waited for him with head erect, unafraid to meet his gaze. He halted in front of me, backed by the group of young men whose facial features showed so clearly they were of the same race as himself, and stood there in silence, the skin between his eyebrows contracted in vertical wrinkles that indicated no more than careful concentration, gazing calmly at me with his large eyes. His followers likewise watched me in silence, and their heavy breathing formed white clouds in the cold air.

"My name's Nedokoro," I ventured in a voice that went husky against my will. "I'm the elder brother of Takashi, who made the deal with you."

"I'm Paek Sun-gi," said the Emperor of the Supermarkets. "I'm really sorry about your brother. Such a tragedy—he was a rather special young man."

I surveyed him with a mixture of unexpected emotion and suspicion: the wide-open eyes watching me levelly with an expression of welling, unconcealed sorrow, the well-fleshed cheeks and jowls, the whole of the cheerful face. Takashi hadn't told us the Emperor was like this. He'd taken us in, and the valley folk as well, by deliberately presenting the Emperor as a particularly contemptible "spirit." In fact, I suspected he himself had been deeply impressed by the Korean, and had told him he was a "rather special" kind of person. So the Emperor had probably used the same expression as a private means of returning the compliment to the dead. His eyebrows were thick and broad and he had a strong nose, but the small lips were red and moist like a girl's and the ears had an almost dewy look, which lent the whole face a youthful vitality. With a flash of white teeth, he gave a straightforward, decent-looking smile to encourage me as I stared at him in silence.

"I was coming down to make a request," I said.

"And I was just on my way up to have a look at the storehouse," Paek replied, still smiling and with the same wrinkles between his brows. "And to offer my condolences at the same time."

"It's about this kid's family," I went on. "They live in the outbuilding. The mother's sick at the moment, so if possible I'd like you to leave the place for a while without knocking it down."

"The patient's getting so thin she says she'll be dead by summer!" Jin's son put in to supplement my account. "The canned stuff she ate affected her liver. She's already gone down to about half her old size, and now she's stopped eating. She won't last long!"

Paek's smile disappeared and he scrutinized Jin's son carefully. Unlike me, the boy was not an outsider staying temporarily in the valley. He treated him accordingly with a sober interest that contrasted with the easy, sociable tone of his conversation with me. Almost immediately, however, he recovered the affable smile with the small, almost self-reproachful frown and said:

"I don't see why the people in the outbuilding shouldn't stay there so long as it doesn't interfere with the dismantling and removal of the storehouse. But they may have to put up with some inconvenience while the work's in progress." Then, with pauses between each phrase as though to impress what he said on the boy's memory, he added, "However, if you stay on after the work on the storehouse is finished, I won't pay you compensation for getting out."

Jin's son stalked away with his neck arched like a cockerel's, a sign of his displeasure. Antagonism toward the Emperor had rekindled in his mind. At the same time, his rear view seemed to emphasize that my failure to object to Paek's statement had lost me the last vestige of his friendship.

"We're going to knock down part of the storehouse wall as a preliminary to dismantling it," said Paek as we watched the boy disappearing into the distance. "I brought along some young men who're studying architecture."

We walked in a body up the road toward the storehouse. The students, who were all freckled and had wrestlers' bodies topped with heads like cannonballs, were extremely uncommunicative and didn't even whisper among themselves.

"If there's anything valuable left in the storehouse, would you mind bringing it out?" said Paek when we arrived in the front garden.

For form's sake I retrieved the fan painting, on which the letters written by John Manjiro were totally illegible by now. One of the young men got implements out of a sack he'd been carrying over his shoulder and spread them on the ground in front of the building. The watching children shrank back as though they'd been weapons. At first, the youths removed the doors of the storehouse and carried out the tatami and other movables with almost reverent care. But after a while Paek gave an order in Korean, and they suddenly began to look much more like demolition workers. As they knocked down the wall of the first floor facing the valley, the plaster and bamboo laths, crumbling to a powder after standing there for more than a century, rose into the air and rained down on the heads of myself and the valley children who had come to watch.

The youths taking turns at wielding the sledgehammer seemed almost totally indifferent to the structure of the storehouse and its equilibrium once the wall had been knocked down. The same was true of Paek, who stood directing operations quite unconcerned by the dust. Somehow it felt like a deliberate gesture of violence toward the people of the valley. In hammering down the wall of this oldest surviving symbol of the valley's traditional way of life, Paek and his followers were demonstrating that if they cared to they could destroy the valley folk's whole livelihood. That much was clear to the children as they watched the operation with bated breath, and the adults must have sensed it too, for no one came up from the valley to protest about the waves of dust threatening to engulf it. Though the walls were crumbling with age, they still supported rooftiles as heavy as they'd been a century before, and I worried in case removing even part of them mightn't bring the whole storehouse crashing down in the strong wind. A suspicion seized me that Paek had never had any intention of carrying away the framework of the storehouse with its great beams and setting it up again in the town, but had bought it simply for the pleasure of destroying it in front of the valley people.

Before long, almost a third of the wall facing the valley had been knocked open from ceiling to floor, and the pile of plaster left by the wind was removed with shovels. Standing behind Paek, the children and I peered into the interior of the storehouse, cruelly illuminated now by the naked light of day. It lay open to the valley with the air of a stage set—an impression that before long was to be reproduced in my dreams. It looked strangely cramped, and all the irregularities of its interior stood revealed. The memories of a century's gloom had fled forever, and, as I looked, the memory of S lying there motionless, facing the rear of the room, became unreal and vanished too. The space where the wall had been knocked down afforded a view of the valley from an unexpected angle—the football ground where Takashi had put the young men through their paces, and the bed of the river, deep brown now that winter's drought had taken over from the snow again.

"Do you have a crowbar anywhere?"

Paek had been talking in Korean to the architectural students, whose immediate task was finished. But now he came over, causing the watching children to shrink back as he passed through their midst, and spoke to me with a smile, though the vertical furrow still remained between his dust-caked eyebrows. "I'd like to take up some of the floorboards to have a look at the cellar. Cellars in this kind of place have stone walls and floors, so we'll need more laborers if we're going to take it as well."

"But there isn't any cellar."

"There must be," one of the students, his face chalk-white with dust, said with a calmness that shook my confidence. "You can tell from the way the floor's raised."

I took him to the storeroom to fetch the iron bars the valley folk used whenever they turned out together to repair the graveled road. At the entrance to the storeroom lay a neat pile of bark strippers. The team had abandoned the weapons in the front garden when they defected, and I'd gathered them together and left them there the morning after Takashi's death. We dragged out a rust-covered bar from under the storeroom floor. Then, still not convinced of the possible existence of a cellar, I stood beside Paek in the doorway of the storehouse, watching as the young men pried up the floorboards. Rotten with age, the boards soon gave way, and the onlookers frequently had to turn aside to avoid fresh clouds of dust. Then suddenly a black mist of fine, damp dust, like the cloud of ink I'd seen ejected by an octopus in some movie of underwater life, arose from the back of the storehouse and slowly advanced toward us. We shrank before it, but could hear the young men levering the floorboards wider open still. When the dust finally settled and Paek and I went inside, we found a long gap running continuously from the alcove at the back of the room to the edge of the raised floor in the entrance. A young man's innocently smiling face emerged from the opening. Calling to Paek in cheerful-sounding Korean, he handed him the worm-eaten front cover of a book.

"He says there's a well-made stone cellar under the floor," said Paek happily. "Did you really not know about it? There are a lot of wooden posts that make it difficult to move about, but it has two rooms, and the front one even has its own toilet and well. He says it's full of books and old papers like this one. I wouldn't be surprised if they once kept a lunatic or deserter down there."

On the dirty cover he held in his hand I could read the title, *A Catechism of Government by the Three Inebriates,* and the words "published by Shuseisha, Tokyo." Caught thoroughly off guard, I drifted away on waves of amazement. The shock forced up something inside me which rapidly expanded and finally assumed the form of a revelation. And it was the same revelation that lay behind my preoccupations as I sat now in the cellar by night.

"There are lots of holes to let light in on the side where the stone wall is," Paek went on, translating a report from another young man down in the cellar. "I suppose they're undetectable from outside. Do you want to go in and have a look?"

I shook my head in silence, still drunk with my revelation, which was taking increasingly well-defined shape. The central core of it, the realization that after the 1860 rising great-grandfather's brother had not in fact abandoned his fellows to their fate and set off through the forest in search of a new world, was already unshakable. Though he'd been unable to prevent the tragedy of their decapitation, he himself had carried-out his own punishment. On the day of the final annihilation, he'd shut himself up in the cellar and there maintained his integrity as leader of the rising, albeit in a negative way, without ever going back on his beliefs. The various letters that had survived him must have been written in his hideout and handed to those who passed his meals down to him. He must have penned them in the intervals of reading, as he imagined to himself the kind of letters he would have sent if he could have spent his life in some other place, and progressed slowly from youthful dreams of high adventure to the sadder, more realistic visions of maturity. The absence of any sender's address on the letters confirmed that the writer had never left his cellar. From great-grandfather's side, too, contact had presumably been exclusively through letters. For a man living this life of voluntary imprisonment, for a man who pored for hours on end over printed matter thrust down to him in his cellar and whiled away his days in such flights of imagination as the invitation to study in America or the whaling episode off the Bonin Islands, more realistic questions would have been correspondingly remote. It must have been difficult for him to be sure, even, what perfectly ordinary, trivial events were taking place right next to his hideout. Down in his cellar he would have strained his ears to catch what was going on. And anxious about the safety of the soldier nephew whom he would probably never meet though they lived so close, he had written his message to those who lived in the world above: "I beg you, should a letter arrive, to let me know its purport with all haste."

My head feverish with these new revelations, I was about to retire to the main house when quite unexpectedly Paek began to talk about the incident of the summer of 1945. The impulse must have overtaken him as he tried to fathom the real reason for my tense silence, which was too marked to be accounted for by simple surprise at the discovery of the cellar.

"About the death of your brother in the Korean village after he came home from the army—no one can say for sure, you know, whether it was we or the Japanese who killed him. There was a great mix-up, both sides hitting each other with sticks; he came unarmed into the thick of it and stood stock-still with his arms at his sides till he was killed. In a sense, we and the Japanese killed him together. He was another rather special young man, you know!"

Paek stopped and watched for my reaction. I said nothing, but nodded as though to say, "Yes, I suppose you're right. S was that kind of man," and went into the main house, closing the door to shut out the dust that came after me. In a strained voice, I heard myself call "Taka!" into the gloom surrounding the open fireplace, but realized at once that Takashi was dead, and regretted his absence more keenly than at any time since he killed himself. It was he, more than anyone else, who deserved to hear the new facts about the storehouse. As my eyes grew accustomed to the darkness, my wife's puffy face, an almost perfect circle, gradually floated into view. She was watching me doubtfully.

"There's a cellar under the storehouse," I announced. "It seems great-grandfather's brother was holed up there all the time, doing penance as leader of the rising that failed. . . . Taka died feeling ashamed for both great-grandfather's brother and himself, but great-grandfather's brother led a very different life from what we imagined. I only just found out. There was nothing for Taka to be particularly ashamed about, at least where his ancestor was concerned." I spoke urgently, more and more convinced of the truth of what I said.

"But it was *you* who let Taka feel ashamed as he stood at the brink of death!" she shouted. *"You* who left him prey to his sense of disgrace. What's the use of that kind of talk now?"

Bemused by my new discovery, I'd been hoping for some wifely words of consolation; it hadn't occurred to me that she would choose that moment to turn on me instead. I found myself paralyzed, trapped between the effects of the discovery and her undisguised hostility.

"I don't believe you actually drove him to suicide, but I do think you imposed on him the most beastly and shameful kind of death," she went on with mounting intensity. "You kept shoving him down into his shame, till finally that wretched kind of death was the only possibility left. Once he'd decided to die, I'm sure it was on you that he pinned his last hope of conquering his fear. But you refused the offer of his eyes, didn't you? Even when he all but went on his knees and begged you to tell him why you hated him, you wouldn't say, 'I don't hate you.' No, you had to sneer at him and make him feel twice as ashamed as before. You deserted him, so that he had no choice but to shoot his face to shreds in that ghastly, pitiful way. And now that he's dead and it can't be undone, you start saying he needn't have been 'particularly ashamed' about great-grandfather's brother! Just to have known about the man, even if it didn't show Taka a way to go on living, might at least have given him spiritual strength on that last day, in the moments before he killed himself. If you had told him then what you're trying so smugly to get through to him now that he's dead, his suicide needn't have been so horrible!"

"The facts I've just told you weren't discovered until the Emperor started his survey of the storehouse. That night, such a thing would have seemed impossible. But it's quite clear now—great-grandfather's brother shut himself up under the storehouse and lived there in isolation until his death."

"Mitsu—now that Taka's dead, what difference does it make to him what you didn't know, or what you know now? You thrust people aside and leave them to die without hope, but all you can do to make up for it is cry out 'I deserted you!' in your dreams or weep tears of self-consolation. Now, just as in the past, and in future, and forever! New discoveries may renew your own tears, but they won't console *them* for dying so horribly and in such despair!"

I gave up, and contented myself with watching her eyes, which were so rigid with hatred that the wrinkles about them looked like folds of stiff glue. I hadn't told her about Takashi's confession of incest. Even if I had, she would only have pointed out quite justifiably that if, after hearing his confession, I'd told him he had already made adequate amends by living so many years in the painful shadow of "the truth," it would have alleviated to some extent the horror of his suicide.

Her eyes remained fixed on me, but the wrathful aura faded and, without losing the glint of hatred, they acquired a new shadow of sadness.

"But now," she said, "anything new that shows he needn't have killed himself in such a ghastly way only makes it all the more horrible." And she burst into a flood of tears, as though the hard shell of hatred had broken to release the yolk of grief within. After a while she recovered and unhesitatingly, with the obvious assumption that I'd already inferred the truth, said, "I've been debating for the past two weeks whether or not to have an abortion, but now I've decided to have Taka's child. I can't bring myself to permit yet another cruelty where he's concerned."

She turned away to face the still deeper gloom at the back of the room and drew a shutter down on herself, obviously determined to reject any response that went against her decision. I gazed at her broad-based back as she sat—the newly expectant mother—with the weight of her body resting firmly on her heels; something about it had the same air of absolute physical and mental equilibrium as when she was pregnant with my own child. And I understood her resolve to give birth to the child in her womb, to Takashi's child: understood it with the same physical immediacy as one might a lump of rock lying before one's eyes. The understanding settled firmly in my mind without creating the slightest emotional disturbance.

Going out into the garden again, I found the Emperor standing, legs braced apart, in the doorway of the storehouse, giving loud directions in Korean to those inside, while the watching children formed a tight, intent circle behind his back. None of them paid any attention to me. I decided to visit the temple and tell the young priest of the discovery of the cellar and the revelation it had inspired in me, so I set off alone down toward the valley, walking rapidly in the teeth of a gusty, dust-laden breeze. While reading the "Account of the Farmers' Rising in Okubo Village" given me by the priest, I'd come across a rather peculiar passage. The discovery of the cellar had abruptly thrown that passage into vivid relief, and it lay now at the very heart of my revelation, convincing me that great-grandfather's brother had, in fact, lived in voluntary confinement in the storehouse.

Grandfather's booklet was a collection, with commentary and notes, of various accounts of the 1871 disturbances as seen by the authorities and the ordinary citizen.

The incident—the booklet said—is usually referred to as the "Okubo Disturbances."

The inhabitants of Okubo cut down a large bamboo grove and made spears for everybody.

The cause of the disturbances lay in dislike of the new government, more particularly its compulsory small-pox vaccination and the word "blood tax" used in the official notification to refer to military service, which led to a rumor that blood was to be taken from the public for

sale to foreigners. This rumor caused public alarm resulting in the rising.

No investigation was made of the ringleaders and
others concerned in the rising, and no one was punished.

The passage giving the authorities' account of the disturbances
was as follows:

The order promulgated in July, 1871, abolishing the clans
and establishing prefectures aroused opposition among the
conservative-minded inhabitants of Okubo village, and in
early August reports came that a conspiracy was afoot to
resist the measures. An official was promptly dispatched
to explain the measure, but they refused to be convinced.
Inciting other villages to join them, the inhabitants as-
sembled on the dry riverbed north of Ohama castle (one
mile from the prefectural office) on the evening of the
same day. Disaffection spread steadily until more than
seventy villages were involved. By the 12th of the same
month, the mob had reached nearly forty thousand. They
occupied themselves firing their guns into the air, raising
battle cries, and fabricating baseless rumors. Very soon
they poured into Ohama, armed with bamboo spears and
pistols, and took over the streets. The rumors they spread
claimed that the former governor's return to Tokyo was
entirely engineered by the Chief Councillor, that the
census was aimed at getting blood from the public and
vaccination a ruse to poison the government's opponents,
and other fabrications too numerous to mention. Their
behavior grew steadily wilder. The crowd stayed where it

was, without presenting any demands, until the prefectural office was virtually under siege. The officials sent out to calm them eventually met the chief representative of the troublemakers, who insisted that the former governor should not go back to Tokyo, that the pre-Restoration form of government should be restored, that the present officials should be dismissed, and that the former administration should be reinstated in their place. On the 13th, when it seemed they were about to launch an assault on the prefectural office, it was decided to use troops to keep them in check; this made them hesitate, and the assault never took place. The prefectural assembly, however, was thrown into disorder. Its previous decision was reversed, many now opposing suppression by force, and it was decided to summon a number of pre-Restoration officials to take charge of the situation. On the 15th, the former governor appeared personally to reason with the mob, but still they refused to disband. At dusk that day the Chief Councillor suddenly left the prefectural office, and shortly afterward word came that he had taken his own life at his home.

The rioters were much moved on hearing this report. The crowd began gradually to disperse. By the afternoon of the 16th the situation was in hand, and the officials sent to deal with the affair were able without exception to return to the prefectural office.

The other account, written from the common man's point of view, treated the disturbances less as history than as a rather romantic tale. The leader who figured in it—the man who negotiated with the authorities as "chief representative"—was described as "a large man of unknown origins, easily six feet tall and with bushy hair." Another passage said: "The strange man with long hair often mentioned in this account was a quite extraordinary creature: large in build, standing over six feet tall, with bent back and deathly pale countenance. Yet despite the oddity of his appearance he astonished all with the eloquence of his tongue and his outstanding ability in everything he did." As for the unlikelihood of participants in a rising within such a small provincial community having no idea who their leader was, grandfather contented himself with adding the following, extremely implausible footnote: "Most of the participants had blackened their faces with soot, so that it was impossible to tell one man from the other. *Ed.*" He thus failed completely to elucidate the question, which he himself had raised, of exactly who the "extraordinary creature" was. The final passage relating to the stranger read: "Following the report of the disbanding of the dissidents at the entrance to Okubo village on the 16th, their ringleader disappeared as though wiped off the face of the earth." After this came silence.

The outstanding qualities of leadership in the big man with bent back and pale face were already apparent in the skill with which he had the prefectural office surrounded—thereby putting pressure on the foe without ever provoking the army into action—and maintained a delicate balance of power between people and authorities until the course of debate in the assembly finally changed. But grandfather also had this to say in his praise: "What is most remarkable, looking back on the disturbances, is that not a man should have suffered a scratch. It argues extraordinary powers of leadership that he should have staged such a mighty upheaval without getting a single man injured."

So my "revelation" became in turn a conviction that the tall man with stooping shoulders and ashen face was great-grandfather's younger brother, suddenly reappearing above-ground after ten years spent in solitary meditation on the rising of 1860. He'd invested everything won during more than ten long years of self-criticism in a second and successful rising utterly different from the first. The first rising had been bloody and doubtful in its achievement. In the second, no one was killed or injured either among the rioters or the bystanders. In effect it drove the Chief Councillor, the target of attack, to suicide. And all the rioters, moreover, got away scot-free.

In the main hall of the temple, where the picture of hell that I'd come to see with Takashi and my wife still hung on the wall, I told the young priest what I felt, and in the process convinced myself still more strongly of its truth.

"Is it likely that the farmers at that period of change, when the wounds of the 1860 rising had made them so sus-picious, would entrust the leadership of their new cause to some stranger of unknown origin? I doubt it. The thing that moved them to act was undoubtedly the reappearance of a 'specialist' in risings—in other words, the legendary leader of the 1860 affair. Judging from the actual outcome, the central aim of the 1871 rising was the political one of removing the Chief Councillor from office. That almost certainly means that someone had concluded this was absolutely necessary if living conditions were to be improved for the farmers. But such an abstract idea wouldn't have been enough in itself to stir up the peasants. So the recluse in the cellar, who'd been reading the latest publications, took advantage of the vaccinations and the ambiguity of the term 'blood tax'—though he himself was quite free of any misconceptions—to incite the local inhabitants and organize the disturbances that ended in the defeat of the Chief Councillor sent by the new government. That done, he went back to his cellar and disappeared for good, spending his last twenty years or so in deliberate isolation. That's what I believe. Takashi and I were always trying to find out what kind of man great-grandfather's brother became after the 1860 rising, but we never discovered anything substantial, the reason being that we were chasing a phantom—the man who got away through the forest."

The priest, who had maintained his smile throughout my long discourse, his small, eminently decent face flushed a bright red, made no immediate move either to affirm or to deny what I'd said. His own undisguised elation during the days of the "rising" still bothered him when he was with me, and he contrived an almost exaggerated composure toward my own excitement now. After a while, however, he came up with an idea that corroborated my theory.

"Come to think of it, Mitsu, the legend of the man with the stoop in the 1871 disturbances is so well known in the valley that you'd expect him to be included among the 'spirits' of the Nembutsu dance, wouldn't you? Perhaps they deliberately left him out because he would have duplicated the 'spirit' of your great-grandfather's brother. Of course, that would only be negative proof, but . . ."

"Speaking of the Nembutsu dance," I said, "the performers go into the storehouse, make a few formal comments in praise of the interior, then have something to eat and drink there, don't they? Mightn't that be connected with the fact that one of the most important 'spirits' once spent years of confinement beneath it? If so, it would be a piece of positive proof. As I see it, when grandfather annotated this booklet, he knew perfectly well that the strange figure with the stoop was his own uncle, and was secretly expressing his affection for him."

The priest made no direct reply, almost as though he were reluctant to see his own hypothesis enlarged by my imagination, and turned instead to the picture of hell.

"If your theory is correct," he said, "I suppose it means that your great-grandfather had this picture painted for his brother while he was still living in the cellar."

The painting brought me the same profound sense of peace as when Takashi, my wife, and I had seen it together, but the peace this time wasn't something passively evoked in my own mind, but was essential to the picture itself. It was there on the paper, independent of me. In a word, the thing that radiated so positively from it was *tenderness*. In all probability, it was this—the ultimate essence of tenderness—that the man who commissioned the painting had asked the artist to portray. Since the picture was aimed at giving peace to his brother's soul as he grappled in his self-imposed confinement with his own private inferno, it must of course portray hell. But the red of the river of fire was to be the red of dogwood leaves catching the morning sun in autumn, and the waves of fire were to be done in lines soft and gentle as the folds of a woman's skirt. In practice, the effect of the river of flames was to be one of absolute gentleness. In his own person great-grandfather's brother had comprised both the dead man shrieking in agony and the devil who tortured him, and since the picture was designed to bring repose to this soul run wild, it must depict the sufferings of the dead and the cruelty of the demons with equal accuracy. Yet dead and demons, however intent on the expression of agony or the infliction of torture, were at the same time to be bound spiritually by a serene tenderness. Quite probably, one of the men with disheveled hair who lay spread-eagled on the red-hot boulders, or thrust the withered triangles of his buttocks out of the river of flames toward the fire raining out of space, was a portrait of great-grandfather's brother himself. Indeed, once the idea had occurred to me I began to feel that all the faces of the dead had the same characteristic air, and a nostalgic glow of recognition stirred somewhere in the depths of my conscious-ness as though they were my own kin.

"The sight of this picture always put Taka in a bad temper, didn't it?" the priest said reminiscently. "He'd been frightened of it ever since he was a kid."

"I tend to think he wasn't so much afraid of the picture as opposed to the gentleness of the hell it shows," I said. "That's how it seems to me now, at least. He had such an urge to self-punishment, such a feeling that he ought to be living in a crueler hell than he was, that I suspect he wanted to reject this mild, comforting kind of torment as false. He worked hard in his own way to preserve the harshness of his personal hell."

The meaningless smile on the young priest's small face gradually disappeared, to be replaced by a definite air of wari-ness. I knew from experience that if his views were challenged his face, which never on any account showed doubt, would assume a shut-in, half-defiant look. But I had no desire to give him any further account of my inner problems, since ultimately he wasn't really interested in anything apart from the lives of the people in the valley. For me, at least, the hell painting was further, positive proof, and with my other evidence would amply justify a review of the verdicts I'd hitherto pronounced on great-grandfather's brother and Takashi.

As he walked with me as far as the main gate of the temple, the priest updated me on the activities of the young men of the valley since the "rising."

"You remember the spartan young man who worked with Taka? They say he'll get a seat on the council when the first elections since the amalgamation of the villages are held. Taka's rising might seem to have been a complete failure, but at least it served to shake the valley out of its rut. The young men who formed what was, at first, essentially Taka's group have extended their own influence relative to the older, conservative-minded bosses, to the point of getting one of their members onto the local council. So where the future of the valley as a whole is concerned, the rising was effective after all. It did something to reestablish vertical communication within the valley community, and to firm up horizontal communication among the younger people. You know, Mitsu, I feel that a definite prospect for future development in the valley has opened up at last. I feel sorry for S and Taka, but they both played their part."

When I got back, the Emperor was no longer at the storehouse, and the children I'd left gazing at the hole in the wall and the gap in the floor were scampering off down the graveled road like birds alarmed by the first signs of dusk. Even when I was a kid the children of the valley—unlike the "country" children who went on with their play even after it was dark—would rush home breathlessly the moment dusk began to fall, unless it were a festival or some other special occasion. Today's children might not be scared of the Chosokabe who lived in the forest, but their habits at least hadn't changed.

For my evening meal my wife had left by the fireplace a plate of sandwiches made with smoked meat, of which she'd bought a stock at the supermarket, and had gone to lie down in the back room, presumably to devote herself to the welfare of the baby in her womb. Wrapping the sandwiches in wax paper, I thrust them into the pocket of my overcoat and went round the back to hunt out two whisky bottles, one full and one empty. I washed the empty bottle and filled it with hot water, though I knew it would soon be cold enough to sting the gums like iced water. Guessing that it would be chilly during the night, I crept past where my wife lay, intending to get some extra blankets out of the closet. But she hadn't been asleep, and said suddenly:

"I was doing a bit of quiet thinking." She spoke sharply, almost as though I'd been looking for an opportunity to creep in under the blankets with her.

"I've been going over various details of our married life in my mind, and I've come to the conclusion that under your influence I've let you share responsibility for a whole lot of my own decisions. It's meant that when you deserted somebody, I was party to the desertion too. But now it really disturbs me, Mitsu. I'm going to start thinking again—about the baby in the institution, and about the baby that's not born yet. Thinking for myself, independently of you."

"Go ahead—my judgment isn't to be relied on anyway," I said dispiritedly, and added silently to myself: "and *I'm* going to shut myself up in the storehouse cellar to do some thinking too. With new evidence to consider, I have to get rid of my preconceived ideas about great-grandfather's brother and Takashi and review their cases from scratch. To understand them correctly may be meaningless to them now that they're dead, but for me it's essential."

I got down into the cellar and, squatting with my back against the white wall at the far end of the back room, just as the voluntary captive must have done a century earlier, wrapped three blankets tightly round me on top of my overcoat. Then, as I ate my sandwiches and took alternate mouthfuls of the whisky and the contents of the other bottle—warm water at first, soon turning to cold, though it wouldn't freeze as long as the strong south wind continued to bluster about the hollow—I started thinking again. From a corner of this cellar where no human being had set foot for so many years, a dank smell arose where the wind had formed a pile of fragments from books and old papers eaten away by silverfish, a low writing desk long since disintegrated, and the remains of tatami mats that had rotted to pieces then dried out again. A similar smell arose from the stones of the floor, which were faintly damp like cold, sweaty skin and worn to a soft texture. A fine dust clung moist and heavy around my nostrils, lips, and even the rims of my eyes, alarming me in case it fatally blocked the pores. I suddenly recalled painful memories of childhood asthma, twenty-five years earlier. I smelled my fingertips; already they were stained with a pungent dust that wouldn't come off when I rubbed them on my knees. For all I knew, a spider grown to the size of a small crab after long days spent in that claustrophobic darkness might come rustling out from behind the pile of debris and bite me behind the ear. Down inside me, the idea aroused a physical revulsion which instantly filled the blackness before my eyes with giant silverfish peering at me, sow bugs half the size of real sows, and unseasonable crickets every bit as large as dogs.

A "retrial"? Yet here was the cellar, and if great-grandfather's brother had indeed shut himself up here and maintained his identity as leader of the rising to the end of his days, that alone was enough to upset the verdict in which I'd always placed my faith. It was the same with Takashi, who had lived in an attempt to copy great-grandfather's brother's life: in the light of his ancestor's newly demonstrated integrity, his own suicide began to look like a final, heroic attempt to put the whole of his "truth" on show for the benefit of me, the survivor. I looked on helplessly as the verdict I'd passed on Takashi fell irremediably to pieces in turn. Since the image of great-grandfather's brother that I'd ridiculed every time Takashi thrust it at me had not been an illusion after all, Takashi's position now looked considerably more favorable.

In the depths of the cellar where the darkness stirred with fierce eddies of wind, I saw the eyes of a dying cat, a tabby tom that I'd kept from my student days until I married and my wife was about to get pregnant. I remembered the eyes from that unhappy day when I found him run over with something like a red, skinned hand protruding from between his legs: the eyes of an old cat, perfectly calm and clear, their yellow irises like tiny, shining chrysanthemums; the eyes of a cat that, despite the sharp flashes of pain darting about the seat of sensation in its tiny brain, kept suffering firmly locked away and, at least to one peering in from outside, remained calm and expressionless; the eyes of a cat that treated its agony as something exclusively its own and, as such, nonexistent to others. I'd shown no imagination toward the human beings whose eyes concealed a similar private hell. I'd been consistently critical of Takashi's attempts, as one such human being, to discover some way to a new life.

I'd even refused aid in the face of his pitiful request made when death was already upon him. So Takashi had dealt with his hell alone and unaided. *As* I contemplated them in the darkness, the eyes of my cat, companion of many years, became Takashi's eyes, and the eyes of great-grandfather's brother whom I'd never known, and my wife's eyes, red like plums; and they all linked up into a shining ring that was rapidly becoming an undeniable part of my being. They would go on multiplying, I felt throughout the time remaining to me, till a hundred pairs of eyes would glitter like a chain of stars in the night of my experience. And I would live on, suffering agonies of shame under the light of those stars, peering out timidly like a rat, with my single eye, at a dim and equivocal outer world. . . .

Our retrial is your trial! And the old men waved their hats at the great beam.

I sat hunched up, scarcely breathing, as though I were indeed crouched alone before the judges and jurors of my dream, my eyes shut against the darkness to avoid the other eyes fixed on me, my head a strangely alien sphere cradled in the overcoat and blankets that wrapped my arms. Must I then live out my days to no positive purpose—vague, indeterminate, depressing days, remote from the sure sense of existence of those who had risen above their private hells? Or was there perhaps some way of letting go and retreating into a more comfortable darkness? As in a sequence of photographic stills, I saw another me slip free from my drooping shoulders as I sat hunched like a body in a burial urn, and, rising, crawl through the gap in the floorboards, then go climbing up the steep staircase, the clothes bundling its body fluttering in the gusts of wind that blew straight up from the valley. As my ghostly self reached the point on the

stairs where it could see the valley stretching out below the
hole knocked in the wall, I could suddenly feel, still crouched
at the bottom of the cellar though I was, the sickening ver-
tigo that seized the figure standing there halfway up the stairs,
defenseless and paralyzed before the deep, black, wind-filled
space; and I pressed my fingers to my temples to soothe the dull
ache in the core of my head. But when the apparition arrived
directly below the great wooden beam, I suddenly realized in
terror that I still hadn't grasped the "truth" which, as I hanged
myself, I would cry aloud to those who went on living; and the
apparition promptly vanished from sight.

I couldn't even share that "something" inside my friend
that had made him paint his head crimson and kill himself,
naked, with a cucumber stuck up his anus. Even the eye that
I'd believed to be watching the blood-filled darkness inside
my head had in fact fulfilled no function at all. If I hadn't yet
grasped the "truth," I was unlikely to find the strength of purpose to take that final plunge into death. It hadn't been like
that with great-grandfather's brother and Takashi just before
they died: they had been sure of their own hell, and in crying
out the "truth" had risen above it.

So real was the sense of defeat that surged up in my chest
like boiling water and spread with stinging pain throughout my
body that I made a further discovery: just as Takashi from childhood had been fired with a sense of opposition to me, so I had
been hostile to Takashi and his idol, great-grandfather's brother,
and had sought meaning in a placid way of life quite different
from theirs. When, despite everything, I had the accident that
blinded me in one eye as surely as if I'd been leading a life of
danger, I was doubly indignant, and spent my hospital days

miserably killing off flies. But Takashi, despite my objections, had persisted in a series of highly doubtful, rather disreputable ventures. And in that final moment when he stood facing the muzzle that was to split the naked upper half of his body into a mass of ripe pomegranates, he'd succeeded in achieving self-integration, in securing for himself an identity given consistency by his desire to be like great-grandfather's brother. The fact that I'd refused his last appeal hardly mattered in practice. Almost certainly, he'd heard the voices of great-grandfather's brother and all the other family spirits that filled the storehouse, heard them calling to him, recognizing him, and accepting him into their midst. With their aid, he'd been able to face up to his own agonizing fear of death for the sake of rising above his private hell.

"Yes, you told the truth," I admitted meekly beneath the gaze of the same family spirits who earlier had gazed on Takashi at his death, keenly aware as I did so of my own utter wretchedness. I felt an extraordinary sense of inadequacy, a sense that like the cold seemed to grow steadily deeper. In a half-masochistic, half-despairing frame of mind, I ventured a pathetic little whistle summoning the Chosokabe to come and destroy the storehouse and bury me alive beneath it. But of course nothing happened. I spent several hours in utter prostration, shivering like a wet dog. Eventually, the gap in the floorboards above me and the half-blocked secret windows at the side grew white. The wind had dropped by now. Oppressed by a desire to urinate, I struggled up on frozen legs and thrust my head up through the floor. The forest that occupied almost all the space where the wall had been knocked down was still dark and mist-shrouded, with only the narrowest halo of purple reflecting the dawn, but up in the top right-hand corner of the hole the flame-red sky itself was visible. I'd seen the same flaming red on the backs of the dogwood leaves that daybreak as I lurked in my pit in the garden. It had summoned up memories of the painting of hell back here in the hollow, and impressed me as a kind of signal. The meaning of that signal, uncertain then, was readily understandable now. The "tender" red of the painting was essentially the color of self-consolation, the color of people who strove to go on quietly living their murkier, less stable, and vaguer everyday lives rather than face the threat of those terrifying souls who tackled their own hell head-on. Ultimately, I felt sure great-grandfather had commissioned the hell picture for the repose of his own soul. And the only people who had drawn consolation from it were those of his descendants who, like grandfather and myself, lived out their lives in vague apprehension, unwilling to allow the urgent inner demand for sudden, unscheduled leaps forward to grow to the point where action was necessary.

In the pale darkness just outside the entrance where several layers of doors had been, a dim figure stood gazing down at my head, which from there must have looked like a melon lying on the floor. The figure stirred. It was my wife. How does one offer casual greetings, how does one behave in a normal, everyday manner when discovered with one's head poking out of a crack in the floor, staring at a patch of red in the morning sky? Petrified with embarrassment as though my head had literally become a melon, I could only gaze up at her.

"Hello, Mitsu," she said, addressing me in a voice hard-edged with tension yet controlled so as to moderate my alarm at being taken unawares.

"Hello," I said. "Don't worry—I may have startled you, but I'm not mad."

"I've known for some time that it's your habit to go underground to think. You did it once in Tokyo, didn't you?"

"I always thought you were asleep that morning," I said, mortification adding to the burden of fatigue.

"I kept an eye on you from the kitchen window," she said, "until the milkman came and I was sure you'd be restored to life aboveground. I was afraid something nasty might happen," she added reminiscently. Then, as I stayed silent, she went on in a more energetic voice as though to encourage us both:

"Mitsu—wouldn't it be possible for us to have another try together? Couldn't we make a new start, bringing up the two babies together, the one in the institution and the one that's not yet born? I've thought about it for a long time, and decided on my own that that's what I want. I came to ask you whether it was totally impossible or not. And seeing you were down there thinking, I thought I'd better put it off till you came out of your own accord. So I've been waiting here. For me, it was more frightening than that time in the pit in the back garden. I was afraid the wind might bring the storehouse down—it's so unsteady with the wall knocked out—and I was terrified when I heard whistling coming out of the depths! But I went on waiting, because I didn't feel I had any right to fetch you out."

She spoke slowly. Already she was pressing her hands to the sides of her belly in the cautious way of pregnant women; it gave the black silhouette of her body, even standing, a spindle-shaped stability, but I could see it trembling with suppressed tension. She stopped speaking and wept silently for a while.

"Let's try. I'll take on the English teaching job," I said, breathing out heavily and using what little air remained in my lungs in an attempt to sound offhand. Nevertheless, the regret in my voice was obvious enough to set my own ears burning.

"No, Mitsu. I'm going to take the two children to stay with my family while you're working in Africa. Why don't you cable the expedition office? I think the need to oppose Taka has always made you deliberately reject the things that resembled him in you. But Taka's dead, Mitsu, so you should be fairer to yourself. Now you've seen that the ties between your great-grandfather's brother and Taka weren't just an illusion created by Taka, why don't you try to find out what you share with them yourself? It's even more important to do so now, isn't it, if you want to keep your memory of Taka straight?"

It occurred to me with wry self-derision that working as an interpreter in Africa wasn't going to solve everything, but the feeling wasn't strong enough to make me argue. My voice betrayed my inner uneasiness, but all I said was:

"If we fetch the baby back from the institution, do you think we can get him to adapt to life with us?"

"I was thinking about that for ages last night, Mitsu, and I began to feel that if only we have the courage we can make a start on it at least," she said in a voice pathetic in its obvious physical and spiritual exhaustion. Afraid she might faint and fall, I wriggled and kicked down with my feet, struggling to haul myself up onto the floor as quickly as possible. But I got stuck, and it was a long time before I finally scrambled up to ground level. Then, as I walked toward her, I heard a voice inside me reciting quite simply what Takashi's bodyguards had said when they announced their plan to get married: "Now that we don't have Taka, we'll have to manage by ourselves." And I had no mind to squash the voice into silence.

"I made a kind of bet with myself—that if only you came out of there safely you'd accept my suggestion. I was on tenter-hooks all night long," she said in a tearful, naively apprehensive voice, and trembled more violently than ever.

One day soon after, my wife, who was wary of traveling in case it affected the unborn baby, made up her mind to cross the bridge, on which repair work had already started, and leave the hollow. That morning, a man came from the valley to say good-bye to us, bringing with him a newly made wooden mask. It represented a human face like a split pomegranate, and the closed eyes were studded with countless nails. The man was the tatami maker who had once absconded from the valley and had been summoned back from the town to help revive the Nembutsu dance that summer. Now he was working again, making mats for the valley assembly hall, which was due to be restored with funds specially allotted at the time of the merger, and for various other places where jobs had been found for him. And at the same time he was planning different costumes for each of the "spirits" in the dance. We presented him with the jacket and trousers that Takashi had had on when he came back from America, for use by the performer who wore the mask of Takashi's "spirit."

"Lots of young fellows have said they want to come down from the forest in this mask," the tatami maker said proudly. "They're already arguing about it among themselves."

We passed through the forest, my wife and the unborn baby and I, as we left the hollow in which, in all probability, we would never set foot again. As a "spirit," Takashi's memory was the common property of the valley; there was no need for us to tend his grave. The work awaiting me away from the hollow, in the days while Natsumi tried to bring our newly reclaimed son back into our world and simultaneously prepared for the birth of the other child, would mean a life of sweat and grime in Africa. Shouting commands in Swahili from beneath my sun helmet, typing English day and night, I would be too busy to consider what was going on inside me. As chief interpreter for the expedition, I could hardly persuade myself that an elephant with "Expectation" painted on its huge gray belly would come lumbering out before my eyes as we lay in wait among the grass of the plains, but now that I'd accepted the job there were moments when I felt that, at any rate, it was the beginning of a new life. It would be easy there, at least, to build myself that thatched hut.

CPSIA information can be obtained
at www.ICGtesting.com
Printed in the USA
JSHW021341310323
39748JS00001B/6